Praise for *All Change*

'Let joy be unconfined, this blissful wodge of a book is the fifth volume of Howard's magnificent, addictive Cazalet Chronicles . . . deeply enjoyable, beautifully written'
The Times

'Love and relationships are the abiding themes of Howard's novels, but in this latest instalment in the sprawling Cazalet saga it is familial love that dominates: now, in its waning phase, increasingly mingled with forgiveness, sacrifice and regret. Howard's stepson Martin Amis has praised her "penetrating sanity"; in an irony surely not lost on its author, *All Change* is ultimately a novel about constants – loyalty, kindness, compassion – and like the best of its characters, is never less than heart-warming and wise'
Observer

'This is a good old-fashioned family saga . . . Howard is such an astute observer of human behaviour. She conveys volumes with tiny, brilliant touches . . . I found myself at one in the morning, weeping over a deathbed scene, unable to put the book down. This is Howard's true magic: her humanity transcends the individual. *All Change* really is the gold standard of comfort reads'
Sunday Times

'Reviewing *All Change* was the ultimate luxury . . . Howard has lost none of her creative imagination, none of her insight, none of her comedy and none of that rare and miraculous ability to magic us into a room with the characters. Also, since *All Change* is the final shout in this series, I would like to praise another of her gifts: the perfect evocation of the past'
Spectator

'A lyrical read, full of period detail, pricked with the sharp emotional intelligence for which Howard is rightly feted'

Literary Review

'Howard's brilliance lies in her forensic depiction of sexual and emotional loneliness'

Times Literary Supplement

'Since her first novel, *The Beautiful Visit*, was published in 1950, winning the John Llewellyn Rhys Prize, Elizabeth Jane Howard has continued to publish impressive fiction to this day'

Daily Telegraph

'It was almost enough of a joy to have had four volumes of Elizabeth Jane Howard's great saga about the Cazalet family . . . to have a fifth volume is a huge treat'

Daily Express

'There remains something deeply and comfortingly old-fashioned about what we are told will be the last slice of Cazalet life . . . What the Cazalets had on their side was the strength of Howard's characterisation and her canny blend of sympathy and curiosity. Despite her finale's title, that has not changed'

Guardian

'Beautifully written and utterly engrossing'

Woman and Home

'If you haven't come across Elizabeth Jane Howard until now, you are in for a treat. The twentieth-century saga that follows the vast Cazalet family from their London houses to Home Place, their country pile in East Sussex, is pure escapism, and completely addictive'

Stylist

ALL CHANGE

Elizabeth Jane Howard was the author of fifteen highly acclaimed novels. The Cazalet Chronicles – *The Light Years*, *Marking Time*, *Confusion* and *Casting Off* – have become established as modern classics and have been adapted for a major BBC television series and most recently for BBC Radio 4. In 2002 Macmillan published Elizabeth Jane Howard's autobiography, *Slipstream*. In that same year she was awarded a CBE in the Queen's Birthday Honours list. She died in January 2014, following the publication of the fifth Cazalet novel, *All Change*.

ALSO BY ELIZABETH JANE HOWARD

Love All
The Beautiful Visit
The Long View
The Sea Change
After Julius
Odd Girl Out
Something in Disguise
Getting It Right
Mr Wrong
Falling

The Cazalet Chronicles

The Light Years
Marking Time
Confusion
Casting Off

Non-Fiction

The Lover's Companion
Green Shades
Slipstream

ALL CHANGE

The fifth and final volume in
The Cazalet Chronicles

ELIZABETH
JANE HOWARD

PAN BOOKS

First published 2013 by Mantle

This paperback edition published 2014 by Pan Books
an imprint of Pan Macmillan
The Smithson, 6 Briset Street, London EC1M 5NR
EU representative: Macmillan Publishers Ireland Ltd, 1st Floor,
The Liffey Trust Centre, 117–126 Sheriff Street Upper,
Dublin 1, D01 YC43
Associated companies throughout the world
www.panmacmillan.com

ISBN 978-0-330-50898-8

14

A CIP catalogue record for this book is available from the British Library.

Typeset by SetSystems Ltd, Cambridge, CB22 3GN
Printed and bound by CPI Group (UK) Ltd, Croydon, CR0 4YY

CONTENTS

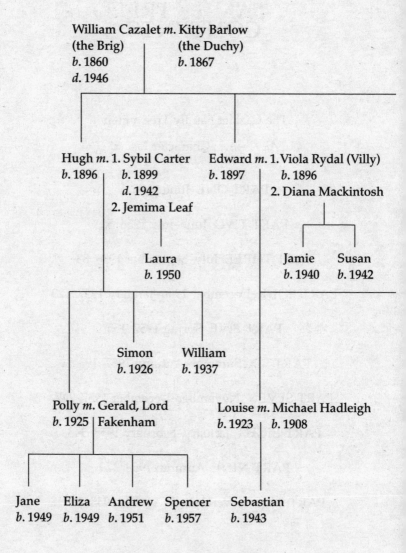

THE CAZALET FAMILY TREE

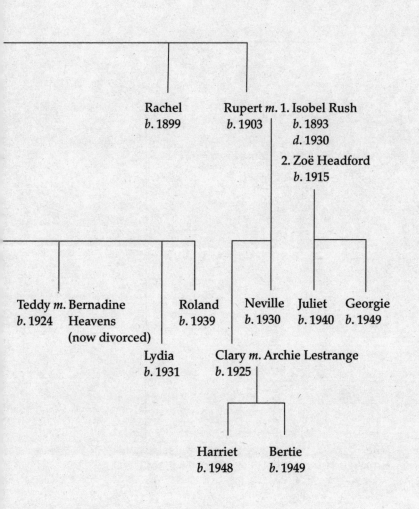

Rachel
b. 1899

Rupert *m.* 1. Isobel Rush
b. 1903   *b.* 1893
          d. 1930

2. Zoë Headford
b. 1915

Teddy *m.* Bernadine
b. 1924   Heavens
         (now divorced)

Roland
b. 1939

Neville
b. 1930

Juliet
b. 1940

Georgie
b. 1949

Lydia
b. 1931

Clary *m.* Archie Lestrange
b. 1925

Harriet
b. 1948

Bertie
b. 1949

THE CAZALET CHRONICLES: ALL CHANGE

Character List

WILLIAM CAZALET, known as the Brig (now deceased)
  Kitty Barlow, known as the Duchy (his wife)

HUGH CAZALET, eldest son
  Jemima Leaf (second wife)
    Laura
  Sybil Carter (first wife; died in 1942)
    Polly (married Gerald, Lord Fakenham;
      their children: Jane, Eliza, Andrew, Spencer)
    Simon
    William, known as Wills

EDWARD CAZALET, second son
  Diana Mackintosh (second wife)
    Jamie
    Susan
  Viola Rydal, known as Villy (first wife)
    Louise (married Michael Hadleigh, now divorced;
      their son: Sebastian)
    Teddy (married Bernadine Heavens, now divorced)
    Lydia
    Roland, known as Roly

Rupert Cazalet, third son
    Zoë Headford (second wife)
        Juliet
        Georgie
    Isobel Rush (first wife; died having Neville)
        Clarissa, known as Clary, (married Archie
            Lestrange; their children: Harriet and Bertie)
        Neville

Rachel Cazalet, only daughter
    Margot Sidney, known as Sid (her partner)

Jessica Castle (Villy's sister)
    Raymond (her husband)
        Angela
        Christopher
        Nora
        Judy

Mrs Cripps (cook)
Ellen (nurse)
Eileen (maid)
Tonbridge (chauffeur)
McAlpine (gardener)
Miss Milliment (Louise and Lydia's old governess, now
    Villy's companion)

FOREWORD

The following background is intended for those readers who are unfamiliar with the Cazalet Chronicles, a series of novels whose first four volumes are *The Light Years*, *Marking Time*, *Confusion* and *Casting Off*.

Since the summer of 1945 William and Kitty Cazalet, known to their family as the Brig and the Duchy, have lived quietly in the family house, Home Place, in Sussex. The Brig died in 1946, of bronchial pneumonia, but the Duchy lives there still. She is not alone: she and her husband had four children – an unmarried daughter, Rachel, and three sons. Hugh is a widower, but is no longer mourning his first wife, Sybil, with whom he had three children, Polly, Simon and Wills; he has recently married Jemima Leaf, who had been working at Cazalets', the family timber company. Edward has separated from Villy, his wife, and is contemplating marriage to his mistress, Diana, with whom he has two children. Rupert, missing in France during the Second World War, has returned to his wife, Zoë, Clary and Neville, the children of his first marriage, and Juliet, the daughter who was born to him and Zoë in 1940, after his disappearance. The couple have succeeded in rebuilding their marriage after a difficult start.

Edward has bought a house for Villy. She lives there, unhappily, with Roland, her younger son. She has also taken in the old family governess, Miss Milliment. Villy's sister, Jessica, and her husband have come into money, an inheritance from an aged aunt. Their son, Christopher, a pacifist and vegetarian, has become a monk.

Edward's daughter, Louise, hoped to become an actress, but married at nineteen. She has left her husband, the portrait painter Michael Hadleigh, abandoning also her small son, Sebastian. Her brother, Teddy, married an American woman while he was training with the RAF in Arizona. He brought Bernadine home to England, but she was unable to settle and left him to return to America.

Polly and Clary have been living together in London. Polly has been working for an interior decorator and Clary for a literary agent. Through her work, Polly has met Gerald Lisle, Earl of Fakenham, and visited his ancestral home, which needs restoration. Shortage of money had prevented work starting, but Polly has recognised a large number of paintings in the house by J. M. W. Turner, some of which may fund it. She and Gerald are now married.

Clary has had an unhappy love affair with the literary agent but has always been drawn towards writing. Encouraged by Archie Lestrange, a long-standing friend of her father, she has completed her first novel. Throughout her girlhood, Archie had an avuncular relationship with Clary, but they have grown closer, so much so that they have fallen in love and it seems they will marry.

Rachel lives for others, which her friend, now lover, Margot Sidney, known as Sid, a violin teacher, finds difficult. So difficult, in fact, that she had an affair with another woman. When Rachel discovered the truth, a period of estrangement followed but they are now happily reconciled.

All Change begins nine years later, in 1956.

PART ONE

JUNE 1956

RACHEL

'Not long now.'

'Duchy, darling!'

'I feel quite peaceful.' The Duchy shut her eyes for a moment: talking – as did everything else – tired her. She paused and then said, 'After all, I *have* exceeded the time allotted to us by Mr Housman. By twenty years! "Loveliest of trees" – I could never agree with him about that.' She looked up at her daughter's anguished face – so pale with smudges of violet under her eyes from not sleeping, her mouth pinched with the effort of not weeping – and, with enormous difficulty, the Duchy lifted her hand from the sheet. 'Now, Rachel, my dear, you must not be so distressed. It upsets me.'

Rachel took the trembling, bony hand and cupped it in both of hers. No, she must not upset her: it would indeed be selfish to do that. Her mother's hand, mottled with liver spots, was so wasted that the gold band of her wristwatch hung loosely, the dial out of sight; her wedding ring was tilted to halfway over her knuckle. 'What tree would you choose?'

'A good question. Let me see.'

She watched her mother's face, animated by the luxury of choice – a serious matter . . .

'Mimosa,' the Duchy said suddenly. 'That heavenly scent! Never been able to grow it.' She moved her hand

and began fretfully fumbling with her bedclothes. 'No one left now to call me Kitty. You cannot imagine—' She seemed to choke suddenly, trying to cough.

'I'll get you some water, darling.' But the carafe was empty. Rachel found a bottle of Malvern water in the bathroom, but when she returned with it, her mother was dead.

The Duchy had not moved from her position, propped up by the square pillows she had always favoured; one hand lay on the sheet, the other clasping the plait of her hair that Rachel did for her every morning. Her eyes were open, but the direct, engaging sincerity that had always been there was gone. She stared, sightless, at nothing.

Shocked, mindless, Rachel took the raised hand and placed it carefully beside the other. With one finger she gently closed her mother's eyes, and bent down to kiss the cool white forehead, then stood transfixed as she was assailed by streams of unconnected thoughts – it was as though a trapdoor had suddenly opened. Childhood memories. 'There is no such thing as a white lie, Rachel. A lie is a lie and you are never to tell them.' When Edward had spat at her standing in his cot: 'I don't listen to people who tell tales.' But her brother was reprimanded and never did it again. The serenity that rarely seemed disturbed – only once, after seeing Hugh and Edward off to France, aged eighteen and seventeen respectively, calm, smiling, while the train slowly left Victoria station. Then she had turned away, and had pulled out the tiny lace handkerchief that was always tucked into her wristwatch. 'They are only boys!' There was a small but distinct strawberry mark on the inside of that wrist, and Rachel remembered wondering if she kept the handkerchief there to conceal it, and how she could have had such a frivolous thought. But the Duchy did cry: she cried with laughter – at the antics of Rupert who, from his earliest years, had made everyone laugh; at Rupert's children – notably Neville; at people she regarded as pompous; tears would stream down her face. Then, too, at ruthless Victorian rhymes: 'Boy gun, joy fun, gun bust, boy dust', and 'Papa, Papa, what is that mess that looks like strawberry jam? Hush, hush, my dear, it is Mama, run over by a tram'. And music made her cry. She was a surprisingly good pianist, used to play duets with Myra Hess, and had loved Toscanini and his records of the Beethoven symphonies. Alongside her rule of plain living (you did not put butter *and* marmalade on breakfast toast; meals consisted of roast meat, eaten hot, then cold and finally minced with boiled vegetables, and poached fish once a week, followed by stewed fruit and blancmange, which the Duchy called 'shape', or rice pudding), she lived a private life that, apart from music, consisted of gardening, which she adored. She grew large, fragrant violets in a special frame, clove carnations, dark red roses, lavender, everything that smelt sweet, and then fruit of every description: yellow and red raspberries, and tomatoes, nectarines, peaches, grapes, melons, strawberries, huge red dessert gooseberries, currants for making jam, figs, greengages and other plums. The grandchildren loved coming to Home Place for the dishes piled with the Duchy's fruit.

Her relationship with her husband, the Brig, had always been shrouded in Victorian mystery. When Rachel was a child, she had seen her parents simply in relation to herself – her mother, her father. But living at home with them all of her life, and while continuing to love them unconditionally, she had nevertheless grown to perceive them as two very different people. Indeed, they were utterly unalike. The Brig was gregarious to the point of eccentricity – he would bring anyone he met in his club or on the train back to either of his houses for dinner and sometimes the weekend, without the slightest warning, presenting them rather as a fisherman or hunter might display the most recent salmon or stag or wild goose. Whereupon – with only the mildest rebuke – the Duchy would tranquilly serve them with boiled mutton and blancmange.

She was not reclusive, but was perfectly content with her growing family, her children and grandchildren, accepting her three daughters-in-law graciously. But her own world she kept very private: the japes of her youth (of an apple-pie-bed nature) or Sardines, played daringly in some remote Scottish castle, surfaced only fleetingly when she told stories to some grandchild who had fallen out of a tree or been thrown by the pony. Her father, Grandpapa Barlow, had been a distinguished scientist, a member of the Royal Society. One of four sisters, she was the beauty (although she had always seemed unaware of that). A looking glass, she had taught Rachel, was for making sure that one's hair was neat and one's brooch pinned straight.

In her old age, when gardening became difficult, she had taken to regular cinema outings, largely to see Gregory Peck, with whom she had quite fallen in love . . .

I didn't ask her enough. I knew hardly anything about her. This, considering fifty-six years of intimacy, seemed dreadful to Rachel now. All those mornings of making toast, while the Duchy boiled water on the spirit lamp to make tea, all those afternoons out of doors in summer, cosy in the breakfast room when it was too cold to be out, in the holidays with grandchildren, who had to eat one plain piece of bread and butter before they were allowed either jam or cake, but most of the time alone together: the Duchy machining curtains for Home Place; making Rachel beautiful frocks, tussore silk smocked in blue or cherry red, and then for the grandchildren – for Louise and Polly, Clary and Juliet; even for the boys, Teddy and Neville, Wills and Roland, until they were three or four and objected to wearing girls' clothes, while Rachel struggled with beginners' knitting, mufflers and mittens. These had been made during the interminable years of war – the awful months and months when letters were longed for and telegrams so dreaded . . .

She had grown up, the daughter of the house, and, except for enduring three dreadful homesick years at a boarding school, she had never left home. She had begged every holiday to be allowed to remain at home – 'If they see a single hair in my hairbrush they give me an order mark' she remembered sobbing, and the Duchy saying, 'Then do not leave a single hair, my duck.'

Her role in life was to look after other people, never to consider her appearance, to understand that men were more important than women, to attend to her parents, to organise meals and deal with the servants who, to a man or woman, loved Rachel for her care and interest in their lives.

But now, with both parents gone, it seemed as though her life's work had finished. She could be with Sid as much as either of them pleased; an alarming freedom had come upon her; something heard in one of the free-thinking schools, a young pupil saying, 'Must we do what we like all the time?' now applied to her.

She was conscious that she had been standing beside her mother's deathbed as all these disjointed thoughts overwhelmed her – realised that she had been crying, that her back ached intolerably, that there were many, many things to be done: ring the doctor, contact Hugh – he would surely ring the others for her, Edward, Rupert and Villy – and, of course, Sid. She would have to tell the servants – here she was brought up short: since the war the servants had consisted of Mr and Mrs Tonbridge, the ancient gardener who was now too arthritic to do much more than mow the lawns, a girl who came three mornings a week to do the cleaning, and Eileen, now returned after her mother's illness. Rachel turned again to her dear mother. She looked peaceful, and strikingly young. She picked a white rose out of the little jug and put it between her hands. The small strawberry mark on her wrist stood out more clearly; the watch had slipped down to her palm. She took it off and laid it beside the bed.

When she opened the large sash window, the warm air scented with the roses growing beneath came softly into the room, wafted by little zephyr breezes that fanned the muslin curtains.

She mopped her face, blew her nose and (in order that she would be able to speak without crying) said aloud, 'Goodbye, my darling.'

Then she left the room and set about the day.

THE FAMILY

'Well, one of us should go. We can't leave poor Rachel to cope on her own.'

'Of course we can't.'

Edward, who had been about to explain that he couldn't easily cancel his lunch with the blokes who were in charge of the nationalised railways, noticed that Hugh had begun to rub his forehead in a way that announced one of his fiendish headaches and decided that he should be spared the initial painful rites. 'What about Rupe?' he said.

Rupert, the youngest brother and technically a director of the firm, charmed everyone; he was the obvious candidate but his inability to make up his mind and his intense sympathy for the point of view of anyone he met, client or staff, made him of questionable use. Edward said he would talk to him at once. 'He needs to be told anyway. Don't you worry, old boy. We can all go down at the weekend.'

'Rachel said it was completely peaceful.' He had said this before, but the repetition clearly comforted him. 'Rather the end of an era. Puts us in the front line, doesn't it?'

This both made of them think of the Great War, but neither of them said so.

When Edward had gone, Hugh reached for his pills

and sent Miss Corley out for a sandwich for his lunch. He probably wouldn't eat more than a bite, but it would stop her fussing about him.

Lying on the leather sofa in his dark glasses he wept. The Duchy's tranquillity, her frankness, the way in which she had welcomed Jemima and her two boys ... Jemima. If he was now in the front line, he had Jemima beside him – a stroke of unbelievable luck, an everyday joy. After Sybil's death he had thought his affections would ever after be directed only to Polly, who would naturally marry, as she had, have her own children, which she most certainly had done, and that for the rest of his life he would be first for nobody. How lucky I have been, he thought, as he took off his glasses to wipe them dry.

∞ ∞ ∞

'Darling, of course I'm coming. If I'm quick, I can catch the four twenty – could Tonbridge meet me, do you think? Rachel, just don't fuss about me. I'm perfectly all right – it was just a touch of bronchitis, and I got up yesterday. Is there anything I can bring you? Right. See you soon after six. 'Bye, dearest.'

And she rang off before Rachel could try any more to dissuade her.

As she walked shakily upstairs, the enormity of the changes that now lay ahead struck her. She was still weak, although the marvellous penicillin had more or less knocked the bug on the head. She decided to skip lunch and pack a few things in a bag that would not be too heavy to carry. Rachel would be anguished by her mother's death, but now she – Sid – would be able to look after her. They would really be able to live together at last.

She had loved and admired the Duchy, but for so long and so often her times with Rachel had had to be cut short because Rachel had felt that her mother needed her. And it had got worse after the Brig had died, in spite of the affectionate attentions of the three sons and their wives. This last illness had been an enormous strain upon Rachel, who had not left her mother's side since Easter. Well, it was over, and now at the age of fifty-six, Rachel would at last be able to call her life her own, but Sid also realised that this would be – initially, at least – alarming for her, rather like letting a bird out of its familiar cage into vast open country. She would need both encouragement and protection.

She was so early for her train that there was time (and need) to eat a sandwich and sit down. After some patient queuing, Sid procured two slices of grey spongy bread, scraped with bright yellow margarine and encasing an extremely thin slice of soapy Cheddar. There were very few places to sit, and she tried perching on her suitcase, which showed signs of collapsing. After a few moments a very old man got up from a crowded bench leaving a copy of the *Evening Standard* – 'Burgess and Maclean Taking Long Holiday Abroad' was the headline. They sounded like a couple of biscuit manufacturers, Sid thought.

It was a great relief to get onto the train, after she had struggled against the tide of people who got off it. The carriage was dirty, the upholstery of the seats threadbare and dusty, the floor spattered with extinguished cigarette ends. The windows were so smoke-ridden that she could hardly see out of them. But when the guard blew his whistle and with a lurch the train began to puff its way across the bridge, Sid began to feel less tired. How many times had she made this journey to be with Rachel? All those weekends when to go for a walk together had been the height of bliss; when discretion and secrecy had governed everything they did. Even when Rachel met the train, Tonbridge had been driving; he could hear every word they said. In those days simply to be with her was so wonderful that for a long time she had needed nothing more. And then she did want more – wanted Rachel in bed with her – and a new kind of secrecy had begun. Lust, or anything approaching it, had had to be concealed – not only from everyone else but from Rachel herself for whom it was terrifying and incomprehensible. Then she had been ill, and Rachel had come immediately to nurse her. And then ... Remembering Rachel offering herself still brought tears to her eyes. Perhaps, she thought now, her greatest achievement had been getting Rachel to enjoy physical love. And even then, she thought, with wry amusement, they had had to battle through Rachel's guilt, her sense that she did not deserve so much pleasure, that she must never allow it to come before her duty.

Sid spent the rest of the journey making wildly delightful plans for the future.

∞ ∞ ∞

'Oh, Rupe, I'm sorry. I could join you tomorrow because the children won't be at school. But you'd better ring and see if that is what Rachel would like. Would you like me to tell Villy? . . . OK. See you tomorrow, darling – I hope.'

Since Rupert had joined the firm they were much better off – had been able to buy a rather dilapidated house in Mortlake, on the river. It had not cost too much – six thousand pounds – but it was in a poor state, and when the river was high, the ground floor was often flooded in spite of the wall in the front garden and the mounting block where a gate had once stood. But Rupert didn't mind any of that: he was in love with the beautiful sash windows, the splendid doors, and the amazing room on the first floor that ran the whole width of the house, with a pretty fireplace at each end; the egg-and-dart ceiling friezes; the bedrooms that rambled on the top floor, all leading into each other, culminating in one very small bathroom and lavatory that had been modernised in the forties with a salmon-coloured bath and shiny black tiles.

'I love it,' Rupert had said. 'It's the house for us, darling. Of course we'll have to do a certain amount to it. They said the boiler wasn't working. But that's just a detail. You do like it, don't you?'

And, of course, she'd said yes.

Rupert and Zoë had moved in in 1953, the year of the Coronation, and some of the 'details' had been dealt with: the kitchen had been extended by adding the scullery to it, with a new boiler, new cooker and sink. But they could not afford central heating, so the house was always cold. In winter it was freezing. Rupert pointed out to the children that they would be able to see the Boat Race, but Juliet had been unmoved by the prospect: 'One of them's got to win, haven't they? It's a foregone conclusion.' And Georgie had simply remarked that it would only be interesting if they fell in. Georgie was now seven, and since the age of three had been obsessed with animals.

13

He had what he described as a zoo, comprising a white rat called Rivers, two tortoises that constantly got lost in the back garden, silk worms, when the season allowed, a garter snake that was also a virtuoso at escaping, a pair of guinea pigs and a budgerigar. He longed for a dog, a rabbit and a parrot, but so far his pocket money had not run to the expense. He was writing a book about his zoo, and had got into serious trouble for taking Rivers to school concealed in his satchel. Although Rivers was now confined to his cage during school hours, Zoë knew that he would be accompanying them to Home Place but, as Rupert pointed out, he was a very tactful rat and people often didn't know he was there.

As she prepared their tea – sardine sandwiches and flapjacks she had made that morning – Zoë wondered what would happen to Home Place. Rachel surely would not want to live there alone, but the brothers might share ownership of it, although this almost certainly meant that they would never go anywhere else on holiday and she longed to go abroad – to France or Italy. St Tropez! Venice! Rome!

The front door slammed, followed by the thud of a satchel being dropped on the flagstones in the hall and then Georgie appeared. He wore his school's summer uniform: a white shirt, grey shorts, tennis shoes and white socks. Everything that was supposed to be white was of a greyish pallor.

'Where's your blazer?'

He looked down at himself, surprised. 'I don't know. Somewhere. We had games. We don't have to wear blazers for games.' His grubby little face was wet with sweat. He returned Zoë's kiss with a casual hug. 'Did you give Rivers his carrot?'

14

'Oh dear, I'm afraid I forgot.'

'Oh, Mum!'

'Darling, he'll be all right. He gets lots of food.'

'That's not the point. The carrot is to stop him being bored.' He rushed to the scullery, knocking over a chair in his haste. He returned a moment later with Rivers on his shoulder. He still looked reproachful, but Rivers was clearly delighted, nibbling his ear and burrowing under his shirt collar. 'A mere blazer is nothing compared to a rat's life.'

'Blazers are not mere, and Rivers wasn't starving to death. Don't be silly.'

'All right.' He smiled so engagingly that, as usual, she felt a shock of love for him. 'Could we start tea now? I'm really hungry. We had poison meat and frog spawn for lunch. And Forrester was sick everywhere so I couldn't eat it.'

They were both sitting at a corner of the table. She smoothed his damp hair back from his forehead. 'We must wait for Jules. Meanwhile, I have to tell you something. The Duchy died this morning. Quite peacefully, Aunt Rachel said. Daddy's going down to Home Place today, and we may be joining him tomorrow.'

'How did she die?'

'Well, she was very old, you know. She was nearly ninety.'

'That's nothing for a tortoise. Poor Duchy. I feel very sorry for her not being there.' He sniffed and brought an unspeakably filthy handkerchief out of his shorts pocket. 'I had to clean my knees a bit with it but it's only earth dirt.'

A second bang of the front door and Juliet came into the kitchen. 'Sorry I'm late,' she said, not sounding it at all, wrenching off her crimson tie and school blazer, which fell to the floor with her satchel.

'Where's your hat, darling?'

'In my satchel. There are limits and that hat is definitely one of them.'

'You'll have scrunched it all up,' Georgie said, his tone a subtle mixture of admiration and cheek. At fifteen, Juliet was eight years older and Georgie desperately wanted her to love and be interested in him. Most of the time she alternated between being carelessly kind and sternly judgemental. 'Guess what?' he said.

Juliet had cast herself into a chair. 'God! What?'

'The Duchy's dead. She died this morning. Mum told me so I knew before you.'

'The Duchy? How tragic! She wasn't murdered or anything?'

'Of course not. She died very peacefully with Aunt Rachel.'

'Is she dead too?'

'No. I meant Aunt Rachel was with her. You'll have to be far older before you know a murdered person,' she added.

Georgie was eating sandwiches rather fast, and Rivers was getting fed bits of them.

'Mummy, must we have tea with that rat?' And then, feeling that it was rather a heartless remark, Juliet said in her school-drama voice, 'I feel so upset, I don't think I can eat a thing.'

Zoë, who knew a good deal about her stunningly beautiful daughter's ways (had they not been her own when she was that age?), spoke soothingly: 'Of course you're upset, darling. We're all sad because we all loved her, but she was quite old, and it's just good that she didn't suffer any pain. Eat something, darling, and you'll feel better.'

'And,' Georgie continued, 'Dad's gone down to Home Place, and we'll all go first thing tomorrow morning if Aunt Rachel wants us to. Which she will.'

'Oh, Mummy! You were going to take me shopping, to get my jeans! You promised!' And at the thought of this betrayal, Juliet burst into real tears. 'We can't buy them on a weekday because of horrible school and that means I'll have to wait a-whole-nother week. And all my friends have got them. It's not fair! Couldn't we go shopping in the morning and then go on an afternoon train?'

And Zoë, not at all feeling like a continuing scene, said weakly, 'We'll have to wait and see.'

Georgie said, 'And we all know what that means. It means we aren't going to do what you want, but we're not going to tell you that now.'

POLLY

'I would start all this at half-term.'

She had been kneeling in front of the lavatory having been wrenchingly sick, as she had been every morning for the last week. It was a very old-fashioned lavatory and she had to pull the chain twice. She bathed her face in cold water and washed her hands just as it was reluctantly turning tepid. There wasn't time for a bath. There was the children's breakfast to make – the nauseating smell of eggs frying came immediately to her, but the children could make do with boiled ones.

There was one of those biscuit tins upholstered in padded chintz by her bed, a relic from her mother-in-law, now filled with Carr's water biscuits. She sat on the bed eating them. Two previous pregnancies had taught her some tricks of the trade. In another eight to ten weeks the sickness would disappear and she would start the fat, backache stage. 'It isn't that I don't love them once they're here,' she had said to Gerald. 'It's all the trouble of having them. If I was a blackbird, for instance, it would simply be a matter of sitting on lovely tidy eggs for a week or two.'

'Think of elephants,' he had replied soothingly, as he stroked her hair. 'It takes them two years.' On another occasion he had said, 'I wish I could have them for you.' Gerald often said he wished he could do whatever was required for her, but he never could. He was neither good at making up his mind nor at acting upon whatever uneasy conclusion he drew about anything. The only thing that Polly could completely, utterly, unfailingly rely upon was his love for her and their children. At the beginning this had astonished her: she had read about marriage in novels, had thought she knew it progressed from the rapturous being-in-love stage to a quiet settlement of whatever would turn out to be the status quo, but it was not at all like that. Gerald's love for her had brought out qualities in him that she had neither known nor imagined any man to possess. His even, steady gentleness, his perspicacity, his continuous interest in knowing what she thought and felt. Then there was his secret sense of humour – he was shy and unforthcoming with most people, his jokes reserved for her, and he could be very funny – but perhaps above all his great talent was for being a father. He had stayed with her throughout her first long labour, had wept when the twins were born and had been a hands-on parent, both with them and subsequently with Andrew, two years later. 'We have to populate this house somehow.' He would be calm about this fourth baby, she knew that – he had probably sensed it already and was waiting for her to tell him.

By now she had struggled into her shirt, pinafore dress and sandals, and brushed her copper-coloured hair into a ponytail. She no longer felt sick, but a bit shaky about cooking. Thanks to the amazing cache of Turners she and Gerald had discovered during that first tour of the house about ten years ago, they had been able to mend the acres of roof, then convert one wing into a comfortable house, with a large kitchen in which they could all eat, a second bathroom and a large playroom (it

19

had begun as a day nursery). Nan had been offered a warm room on the ground floor, but she had insisted on sleeping next to the children: 'Oh, no, m'lady. I couldn't have my babies sleeping on a different floor. It wouldn't be right.' Her age, which was considerable, was unknown, and she clearly suffered from what she called her rheumatics, but she hobbled about, her eyes and hearing hardly impaired. A good many adjustments had had to be made over the years. Nan's notion of the part that parents played in the upbringing of their children (teatime with Mummy in their best clothes and then a goodnight kiss from her and Daddy) had perforce undergone significant change. Gerald had effected this. In Nan's eyes he could do no wrong, so if he wished to bath his children, read to them, even, in the early stages, to change their nappies, she put it all down to his eccentricity, which she knew the upper classes went in for. 'People have their little ways,' was one of her sayings when anything happened that she disapproved of or did not understand.

In spite of all they had done, the very large remaining parts of the enormous Edwardian house still defeated Polly. It required a lot of attention. Rooms had to be aired regularly in an attempt to fight the damp that crept through the building, leaving swags of weary wallpaper, infesting attics and passages with a minute speckled black fungus that Gerald had remarked looked like Napoleon's disposition of troops before battle. The children, or at least the twins and their friends, played endless games of hide-and-seek, Sardines and a game devised by them called Torchlight Ogres. Andrew minded very much about being left out, and several times Eliza allowed him to join them, but he always got lost and cried. 'I told you,

Mummy, he wouldn't enjoy it,' Jane would say. These were everyday arguments and Gerald usually stepped in with a plan that restored goodwill.

He met Polly at the bottom of the stairs to tell her that the Duchy had died. Rupert had gone down to Home Place, and would tell them, once it had been arranged, the date of the funeral.

RACHEL

'I poached her an egg. She's usually partial to an egg.'

'I can't help it, Mrs Tonbridge. I put the tray by her in the morning room, and she just thanked me and said she didn't want nothing.'

The poached egg lay on its bed of butter-soaked toast. Eileen eyed it hopefully. If Mrs Tonbridge turned out not to fancy it out of respect, she wasn't going to throw it to the birds. 'I've drawn all the blinds on the first floor,' she offered. 'And Miss Rachel said Mr Rupert is coming down tonight. She asked to see you.'

'Why didn't you say so before? Whatever will she think – me dawdling with Mrs Senior lying upstairs?' She gave one of her kirby-grips a vicious shove, took off her apron, smoothed her dress over her bust and made off.

The doctor had been and the district nurse would be coming later on. Tonbridge had better go to Battle to do some shopping – more family would be arriving for the weekend. Oh, and Miss Sidney would be coming down on the four thirty so would he please meet her? 'I'll leave the housekeeping to you, Mrs Tonbridge – something light and simple.' She really couldn't bear to think of food . . .

This produced conflict for Mrs Tonbridge. On the one hand it seemed only right that Miss Rachel should show respect for her mother in this manner, but on the other she was seriously worried by her evident exhaustion and the knowledge that the poor lady had been eating very little for some weeks. This was not right. As cook to the family for nearly twenty years – she had been with them long before she married Tonbridge and had had the courtesy title, enjoyed by all cooks then, of Mrs Cripps – there was nothing she did not know about their eating habits. Miss Rachel, like her mother, preferred plain food and not much of it, but since Mrs Senior's illness she had only picked at her food.

'If I was to send you up a nice hot cup of consommé before you have a rest, to be ready for when Mr Rupert comes?'

And Rachel, realising that it was much easier to consent than refuse, thanked her and agreed.

When Eileen arrived with the consommé she was lying on the stiff little buttoned day-bed that the Duchy had decreed would be right for her back. It had been a considerable concession as the Duchy, who had sat on hard and upright chairs all of her life, had never, in any context, thought much of comfort. The day-bed was, in fact, uncomfortable in an entirely different way, but by tucking a cushion in the small of her back, Rachel had managed to use it.

Eileen, speaking in what the family called her church voice, asked whether she would like the blinds drawn and her crocheted blanket if she wished to put her feet up. Sipping the consommé, Rachel agreed to all of this, and watched while Eileen knelt creakily to undo the laces on her sensible shoes (the maid's rheumatism clearly hurt her), lifted her legs onto the sofa and tucked the blanket very thoroughly round them. Then, as though Rachel was already asleep, she tiptoed to the window to pull down the blinds, and practically glided out of the room. Affection, Rachel thought. It is all affection for the Duchy. So long as it was an oblique gesture, she was able to accept it. She put down the cup and lay back on the hard buttoned velvet. My darling mother, she began to think, and as a few weary tears slipped from her eyes, she fell into a merciful sleep.

CLARY

'You really mustn't get so worked up, sweetheart. It's only a week, after all. A week in a caravan. It will be a marvellous change – and a rest.'

Clary didn't answer. If Archie thought that a week in a caravan with the children was going to be remotely restful from her point of view he was either mad or didn't care what it would be like for her because he had stopped loving her.

'It will be much cheaper as well. Last time we had to spend a fortune taking the little dears on outings all over London and for endless meals out. And they never wanted to do the same things. In my day you got one treat on your birthday and one at Christmas.'

'You can't think that four of us going on the ferry with the car and then hiring a caravan is actually going to be cheaper! You just want to go to France.'

'Of course I want to go to France.' His voice was loud with anger. He put down the brush he had been cleaning and looked at her, bent over the sink, trying to clean the porridge saucepan, her hair hanging round her face. 'Clary! Darling girl. I'm sorry!'

'What are you sorry about?' Her voice was muffled. By now he had turned her round to face him.

'You do have the most outsize tears, my darling. And

you are my darling, as I have been telling you for at least the last ten years. Is it starting to sink in?'

She flung her arms round his neck; he was far taller than she. 'You wouldn't rather have married Polly?'

He pretended to consider. 'No – I think not.'

After he had kissed her, she said, 'Or Louise?'

'You seem to forget that she got snapped up before I could even think about it. No – I just had to make do with you. I was looking for a writer, a rotten cook, a kind of untidy genius. And here we are. Except that you've got much better at cooking. No, darling, I've got to go. Some pompous old Master of the Worshipful Company of Sardines will be sitting at the studio waiting for me to paint his ghastly old face. I can't wait any longer to debase my art.'

'I suppose,' she said, watching him pack up his brushes, 'you could just make a good picture of him? Just paint what you see.'

'Out of the question. If I did that, they wouldn't take it. It would be a thousand pounds down the drain. Then we'd be lucky to spend our holiday in a caravan somewhere off the Great West Road.'

We've had both those conversations a hundred times, he thought, as he walked to the bus in Edgware Road. Me reassuring her, she always wanting me to paint only what I want to paint. He did not mind this. Clary was worth anything. It had taken him time to recognise that the desperate insecurities of her childhood – mother dying, father missing in France for most of the war, very possibly dead – could safely manifest themselves only in retrospect. Ten years of marriage and their two children had naturally wrought a sea change: from their first months together, comparatively carefree, the years when they had travelled or lived in a studio with their bed in a gallery, when money was tight but had been of no consequence, when he was seeking commissions and painting landscapes – which were occasionally included in mixed exhibitions at the Redfern, and once a Summer Exhibition at the Academy – when she had written her second novel and John Davenport had praised it – it had been a wonderful start. But with the arrival of Harriet, closely followed by Bertie – 'I might just be a rabbit!' she had sobbed into the kitchen sink – they had had to find somewhere larger to live, and with two babies, Clary had had neither the time nor the energy to write at all. He had resorted to part-time teaching.

For summer holidays they had gone to Home Place, and to Polly for several Christmases, but Clary was a haphazard housekeeper and they had become chronically short of cash and behind with bills. Since the children had started primary school, Clary had taken a job as a part-time proofreader, work that she could do mostly at home, and Mrs Tonbridge had kindly taught her to make a corned-beef hash that used only one tin of corned beef, cauliflower cheese, and a bacon roly-poly that used very little bacon. She had bought a book by Elizabeth David on French cooking, and garlic (unknown until after the war) had certainly cheered things up. Garlic, and the return of bananas, which Harriet and Bertie regarded as the equal of ice cream, had widened the range; the real trouble was how much things cost. A shoulder of lamb was thirteen shillings and only lasted for two meals with a few scraps left over to mince. And she earned three pounds a week for her proofreading, while Archie's work was always uncertain – for weeks he might be paid nothing and then a lump would come in. Then they would pay for a babysitter and have a night out at the cinema and the Blue Windmill, a very cheap Cypriot restaurant where you could have lamb cutlets and dolmades and delicious coffee. They would come back on the 59 bus, her head on his shoulder. She often fell asleep then – he could tell because her head and his shoulder became perceptibly heavier. We should have splashed out on a taxi, he often thought on the longish walk down the street to their home. They would get back to find Mrs Sturgis asleep over her knitting and he would pay her while Clary went to see the children, who shared a small bedroom. Bertie slept wedged between fourteen woolly animals lining each side of his bed, and one – his favourite monkey – with its paw in his mouth. Harriet lay flat on her back. She would have undone her pigtails and pushed all her hair to the top of her head, which she usually did 'for coolth', she had once explained. When Clary kissed her, a small secret smile would flit across her face before it was again abandoned to the stern tranquillity of sleep. Her darling, beautiful children . . . But those were rare days and usually ended in the often temperamental flurry of children's supper and bathtime.

Sometimes Archie cooked supper while Clary read proofs. Occasionally her father, Rupert, and Zoë came to supper, bringing treats like smoked salmon and Bendicks Bittermints. Rupert and Archie had been friends since the Slade – well before the war – and Clary's marked hostility towards her pretty stepmother had mellowed into friendship. Their boys, Georgie and Bertie, were both seven and despite their different interests – Georgie's menagerie and Bertie's museum – they had good times together at Home Place in the holidays. What a blessing that house had been, with the Duchy and Rachel always pleased to see them! So, on the morning that Archie had gone off to paint his City worthy, while she was sorting out the children's clothes for the coming week in France, it was a shock to be rung by Zoë and be told of the Duchy's death. Everyone in the family had known that she had been ill, but telephone calls to Rachel had always elicited a stalwart response, 'She's doing well', 'I think she's on the mend', that kind of thing. She hadn't wanted to worry them, Zoë said Rupert had said.

No, Clary thought, Aunt Rachel would say those things. It was odd how, when people didn't want to worry each other, they worried them more than ever. Poor Aunt Rachel! She felt sadder for her than for the Duchy, who had had a long, serene life and had died at home with her daughter beside her. But I feel sad for the old lady as well. Or perhaps I just feel sad for myself because she was there all my life, and I shall miss her. Clary sat at the kitchen table and had a small weep. Then she rang Polly.

'I know. Uncle Rupert told Gerald.'

'Do you know when the funeral will be?'

'I should think they'll arrange all that at the weekend.' Polly seemed faintly shocked.

'I know it sounds awful, but we're supposed to be going to France, and of course we won't go if it means missing the funeral. I just wondered . . .' Clary tailed off to silence.

'Well, you'll be able to go later, won't you? Sorry, Clary, but I've got to go. Andrew's on the loose. It's one of his days for not wearing clothes. Gerald has taken the girls to school and then Nan to the dentist to have a tooth out. See you soon.' And she rang off.

Clary sat looking at the telephone. She wanted to tell

Archie, but he hated being interrupted when he had a sitter. She felt besieged by guilt. Someone she loved had died and all she was doing was worrying about the holiday and the financial implications. Archie would have had to pay for the caravan and probably their tickets on the ferry. They almost certainly wouldn't be able to pay for all that a second time. And going to Home Place would stop: she couldn't imagine Aunt Rachel living there alone . . . It seemed both frivolous and greedy to be thinking of money at a time like this. She never used to think about money at all, and now she seemed to think about it all the time. Her eyes filled again, and she had another weep, this time about her rotten character.

Going to task with the children's clothes, she discovered that Bertie had a hole where his big toe came through his sand shoes and this meant he probably needed a larger size in his other – more expensive – ones. There it was again. Shoes cost money. Everything cost money. She blew her nose and decided to make some fishcakes for the children's tea. The recipe said tinned salmon, but she only had a tin of sardines. If she put quite a lot of mashed potato with them, and a splash of tomato ketchup and an egg to bind the mixture, it ought to make four quite large and unusual fishcakes; and then she would ring Archie just after one, when his fat sitter had gone off for lunch. The thought of talking to him suddenly cheered her.

VILLY

And of course I shan't be able to go to the funeral because That Woman will be there.

Such thoughts – bitter and repetitive – buzzed in her head like a disturbed wasps' nest.

It was nine years now since Edward had left her, and she had carved out some sort of life for herself. The dancing school she had started with Zoë had faltered and finally shut down. Zoë's pregnancy, the fact that she and Rupert had moved so far away and that Villy was then unable to find a new business partner who came up to her standards, had finished it off.

For a while after that, she had had to content herself with the house Edward had bought for her. Roland now went to a public school where he had been disconcertingly happy. At the beginning, she had expected (had she even wanted?) a desperate little boy already deprived of his father (she would not dream of letting him meet That Woman, so he saw his father once a term when Edward took him out to lunch) and then deprived of her, his loving mother. She had envisaged sobbing telephone calls, mournful letters, but the nearest she had got to these was when he had written, 'Darling Mother, I am board, board, board. There is nothing whatever to do here.' After that the letters were full of a boy called Simpson Major and the amazing crimes he committed without ever being

31

found out. However, Miss Milliment, the girls' governess, was still with her; on discovering that she had no living relatives, Villy had offered her a home for life. In return she received a steady affection that touched her blighted heart. Miss Milliment's attempts in the kitchen were disastrous, as her sight was very poor and she had not cooked anything since her father had died a few years after the First World War, so her help was confined to feeding the birds and sometimes the three tortoises, and going to the local shops if Villy had forgotten anything. She was largely employed in editing a work of philosophy written by one of her former pupils. In the evenings they were taking turns to read *War and Peace* aloud. So when Villy took an ill-paid and dull clerical job with a charity that a rich cousin of her mother persuaded her into, it was comforting to come back to a home that was not empty.

The family had been good to her, too. Hugh and his nice young wife Jemima had her to dinner sometimes, Rachel always visited when she was in London, and the Duchy usually invited her to Home Place during term time. Teddy turned up about once a month. He was working in the firm, but found conversation about it tricky as he kept nearly mentioning his father, which he had discovered early was a no-go area. The trouble about nearly all of this was that she felt they only made the effort because they were sorry for her. Like most people who are sorry for themselves, she felt she had to have the monopoly of it. She called it pride.

No. The people she loved were Roland (how could she ever have contemplated not having him?) and dear Miss Milliment – who wished to be called Eleanor, but Villy had only managed that once just after they had discussed the matter.

She must write to Rachel, who had been a wonderful daughter to both of her parents – unlike mine, she thought. Louise made duty visits if Villy was ill – prepared supper, if necessary, and made small-talk, but was utterly unforthcoming about herself, varying evasion with spasmodic efforts to shock. And her mother *was* shocked. When Louise had suddenly announced, 'But I have a rich lover now, so you really don't have to worry about me,' there was a frozen pause before Villy had asked, as calmly as she could manage, 'Is this wise?' Louise had retorted that of course it wasn't but she wasn't to worry, she was not allowing him to keep her. All of this was in her bedroom, out of earshot of Miss Milliment. 'Well, please don't talk about this in front of Miss M,' she had begged, and Louise had said she wouldn't dream of it.

Her theatrical career had come to nothing but she was tall and thin, with abundant reddish blonde hair and an undeniably beautiful face – high cheekbones, wide-apart hazel eyes and a mouth that reminded Villy uncomfortably of the sensual depictions so loved of the Pre-Raphaelites. She was long divorced from Michael Hadleigh, who had instantly got married again, to his former mistress. Louise had refused any alimony, and scraped along in a small maisonette over a grocer's shop with her blue-stocking friend Stella. Villy had been there only once when she had paid a surprise visit. The place smelt of dead birds (the grocers were also poulterers) and damp. The flatmates had two small rooms each, and the third floor had been turned into a kitchen and dining room, with a very cramped bathroom and lavatory built out onto a flimsy extension. On the day that she visited, there was a plate of distinctly high mackerel

lying on the dining table. 'You're not going to eat those –
surely?'

'Good Lord, no! Somebody we know is painting a
still-life, and he wants us to keep them till he has
finished.'

'There, you've seen it all now.' So why don't you go?
It was not said, but she'd felt it.

'What about your rent?'

'We share it. It's quite cheap – only a hundred and
fifty pounds a year.'

Villy realised then that she had no idea what her
daughter did to earn her living. But she felt miserably
that she had clearly been inquisitive enough for one day.
Going home on the bus she was struck afresh by her
awful loneliness. If only Edward was there to discuss the
matter! Perhaps he was paying her rent; it would at least
be respectable. She couldn't talk to Miss Milliment about
it – with all the business of lovers and sex, it was out of
the question.

But, as it happened, it was Miss Milliment who elicited
the facts.

'And what are you doing these days, dear Louise?'
she had enquired when, later that month, Louise had
dropped in for tea.

'I'm modelling, Miss Milliment.'

'How very interesting! Are you using clay? Or are you
perhaps cutting stone? I always imagined the latter
would be very hard work for a woman.'

'No, Miss Milliment. I'm doing photographic model-
ling – for magazines. You know – like *Vogue*.' And Miss
Milliment, who thought that magazines (excepting the
Royal Geographic Society's) were generally for people

who found reading difficult, murmured that it must be most interesting.

'Do they pay you?' Villy had asked then, and Louise had answered – had almost retorted – 'Of course. Three guineas a day. But when you're freelance you never know how much work you're going to get. I must go, I'm afraid. Dad has asked me to go to France with them. Two weeks, and he's paying for everything. He's taken a villa not far from Ventimiglia and there's a beach.'

It was a careless parting shot. She can have no idea of how that makes me feel, Villy thought, as she lay sleepless, far into the night, struggling with bitterness and rage. Their honeymoon had been in Cassis, west along the coast, in those far-off post-war pre-war days.

Except for the difficulty of so much sex that she had neither wanted nor understood, it had been a golden time. Then there had been those skiing and sailing holidays with a mixture of family and friends. She had excelled at skiing, and was a good sailor. By then, she had learned to pretend about sex – always said it was lovely – and, incurious, he had seemed easily to believe her. Her pregnancies had also provided welcome relief, then the drab, anxious, interminable years of war when she had been incarcerated in Sussex, and he had been seeing to the defence of Hendon Aerodrome until the urgent need for timber had put him back in the firm. It was he who had made clear that their London house, which she had loved so much, had to be sold. It was he who, after the war, when she had thought that a good ordinary life together would at last return, had urged her to find a smaller house, and she had chosen this odd little place with only one upper floor that faced north

35

and south so that only three of the rooms got sun ... and then abandoned her in it. And for months, years, he had been carrying on with That Woman. Divorce had followed, which her mother would have considered unthinkable. And Louise had known about it and had never told her. Darling Roly, when she had told him, had promised, with tears streaming down his face, that he would never leave her. Teddy and Lydia had been shocked too; they had not been part of the conspiracy. But she saw little of Teddy and virtually nothing of Lydia, who had gone through an acting school and now had a job with a repertory company in the Midlands. It was a weekly rep, which meant, as Lydia explained in one of her rare, sprawling letters, that you performed one play while rehearsing play number two in the mornings, and learning your lines for play number three in bed at night. She said that it was very hard work, but she loved it and, no, she hadn't the faintest idea when, if ever, she would get a holiday. Villy sent this daughter ten pounds each birthday and Christmas; she was grateful that she could feel natural, untainted love for her.

After Zoë's telephone call about the Duchy, she went to tell Miss Milliment, who was in the sunny sitting room seated in her usual chair by the open French windows that looked out onto the garden. Here she read *The Times* every morning, and did the crossword, which she completed in less than half an hour. Usually she also spoiled *The Times* for Villy by telling her the stories that had struck her most. This morning, though, she had reverted to the unfortunate Ruth Ellis, arraigned last year for the murder of her lover. 'I really do think, Viola, that whatever a person has done they should not be executed for it. It is one of our most uncivilised laws, don't you agree?'

And Villy, not replying to this (people who murdered other people should surely not be allowed to get away with it), instead told her about the Duchy, ending with a bitter tirade about not being able to go to the funeral because of That Woman.

'But you do not know that she will be there. Might it be possible to find out before you distress yourself so much?'

'Well, Edward will certainly go.'

'Yes, but she may not. Perhaps you could ask Louise or Teddy.'

'I could ask Teddy, I suppose. Rupert has gone down to Home Place, and I don't suppose anyone will know when the funeral is to be until after the weekend.'

'Viola! My dear, I'm afraid I have a confession to make. I knocked over the cup of tea you so kindly brought me. I was asleep, and I have no idea why, but I thought it was the afternoon, and I was feeling for the switch of my bedside lamp and, of course, if it had been the afternoon, the tea would not have been there. I'm afraid I have not made a very good job of clearing it up, but in any case, it will dry during the day and I shall not mind it at all. But I felt I should tell you.'

A light rattling of the newspaper in her hands showed Villy that poor Miss Milliment was nervous. Her compassion for her companion, for the years of nasty landladies that she must have endured, filled her heart now with real feeling, and she put her arm round the bulky shoulders. 'You mustn't worry. Anybody can spill a cup of tea.'

In the bus later, on her way to the dreary office in Queen Anne Street, she realised that this was already the third episode of tea-spilling in a month.

DIANA AND EDWARD

'Oh, darling! How awful for you! Poor Duchy!'

'She had a very good life.'

'Of course she did.'

'Although people always say that, as though it makes everything all right.'

'She didn't suffer any pain, though, did she?'

'Rachel said not, according to Hugh. Let's have the other half, shall we?'

She walked across the room to pick up the cocktail shaker that stood, with a large array of drinks, on the ebony table. She was wearing a crêpe dress of an electric blue that careless people might have said matched her eyes.

'But it doesn't alter the fact that she's gone – no longer there.'

'Of course it doesn't, my poor darling.'

As she bent down to refill his glass he could see the immensely comforting size of her breasts. 'I'll have to go down tomorrow.'

She was silent while he lit a cigarette. 'Want to come with me?'

Diana seemed to consider. 'No,' she said at last. 'Of course I'd love to, but I think Rachel should have you to herself.'

'That's what I love about you. You're such an unselfish person. Well – one of the things.'

'Also, we had promised to take Jamie out to lunch on Sunday. I don't want to let him down.'

Jamie was in his last year at Eton, which Diana had persuaded Edward to pay for on the grounds that her other two sons had been there, and Jamie was actually his. He was now eighteen, very like his brothers in appearance, and showed no signs of being a Cazalet. What with him, Roly at Radley and Villy's allowance (he had made the St John's Wood house over to her and had set up a trust to pay her maintenance), he was pretty pushed, and had used up most of the money the Brig had left him. Diana had set her heart on renting a villa in the south of France, had invited her brother and his wife, so he had had to splash out on that, his only stipulation being that Louise should come with them – 'My two favourite women,' he had maddeningly said – and, although she knew that Louise disliked her as much as she disliked Louise, Diana had had to comply.

She had been married to Edward for just over five years, and they now lived in a large, neo-Georgian house in West Hampstead with a housekeeper, Mrs Atkinson, who occupied a flat on the top floor. There was also a cleaner, who came three times a week to do the housework, and so, for the first time in her life, Diana had no money worries and was free to do as she pleased. There had been one setback soon after they moved in and before they were married when Edward had been quite seriously ill after a minor operation; she had been afraid he might die before they were married, and that she would be back to widowhood with three boys, hostile in-laws, living on the pittance that an army pension provided (Angus's parents had never forgiven her for living with a man she was not married to, a married man who had left his wife for her with the ensuing disgrace of a divorce).

All those thoughts made it sound as though she didn't love Edward when of course she did. At the beginning she had thought of him with agony and intermittent delight, but as the affair settled to a rut of romantic assignations with no sign that the situation would ever change, she had recognised that excitement and uncertainty no longer satisfied her. She longed for security – a home rather than rented flats or cottages, a husband who earned enough to keep her and the boys in the manner to which her mother had taught her she should be accustomed. And there was Edward. Although, before she met him, she had heard that he had a reputation with women, she was pretty sure that once their affair had begun he'd remained faithful to her. 'I've fallen for you,' he had said. 'Hook, line and sinker.' And the less she felt about him, the more she encouraged the notion that theirs was a great romantic attachment which nothing could destroy.

Much of this was concealed, even from herself – dishonesty of this kind needs to begin at home, as it were – and once he had taken the step of leaving Villy for her, she had done everything in her power to make him feel she had been worth it. Strong Martinis were on hand the moment he came home from work; she encouraged him to talk about what sort of day he had had; Mrs Atkinson learned how to cook the game that he shot exactly as he liked it; she sympathised tactfully with him over the differences he was beginning to have with Hugh about how the firm should be run, and did what she could to ingratiate herself with his family. When he worried and complained about Villy refusing to allow Roland to meet her, she had explained that she entirely understood Villy's attitude: that it was unwise to split Roland's affections, and how, had she been in that situation, she would probably have done the same. She expertly skimmed this particular guilt off him with an ease that increased his need for her.

'Darling! Of course you mustn't let Jamie down.' Did she detect some relief in his voice? Possibly, but it didn't really matter.

LOUISE

'What I can't stand is when she looks me in the eye and starts a sentence "Quite frankly . . ." There's absolutely nothing frank about her at all!'

Joseph Waring regarded her with amusement. Indignation became her, and he told her so. They were dining, as they often did, at L'Étoile in Charlotte Street, where the food was good and, by English standards, unusual and delicious. Louise, her blonde hair scraped back from her forehead and secured by a black velvet bow, wore a black dress that had a low round neck and short sleeves, both finished with scallops made of the same material. In it, she looked very young and ethereal but she had an appetite that never ceased to amaze him, and which was much approved of by the *patron*, who had one day suggested she might like to lunch there every day on the house – provided she was prepared to do it at the window table. 'But I would feel like those women in Holland – you know, the tarts,' she told Joseph, and blushed faintly at the very idea.

They had met at a party that Stella had taken her to. Stella had become a political journalist: she was an ardent Labour supporter and had been devastated when 'stuffed-shirt Eden' had won the election, ousting her beloved Attlee. She wrote regularly for the *Observer* and the *Manchester Guardian* and occasionally reviewed books for the *New Statesman*. She was popular and got asked, or got herself asked, to a great many parties and sometimes took Louise with her 'to broaden her mind'. Louise privately thought Stella a bit of a fanatic, and Stella had derided Louise's Torydom. 'Of course you'll vote for them: most Tories don't have any political convictions at all – they simply vote the way their class always has.' This silenced her because in her case it was true. Louise wasn't interested in politics and her family – excepting Uncle Rupert – had always voted Conservative.

The party, which was large, seemed to have every kind of person in it. The room was thick with smoke and the steady oceanic sound of a great many people trying to make themselves heard. She had felt completely at sea, paralysed by a shyness that she now recognised always overcame her when she had to enter a room full of unknown people. Stella had been swept away by the current that always embraces those who know their way around, greeting friends, waving to colleagues, having her cigarette lit, laughing at something somebody said to her, managing to grab a glass of fruit juice (she did not drink), only turning back to Louise when she was practically out of sight . . .

'I have the impression that you're not enjoying yourself.'

'No – I, well – no. I mean yes. I'm not enjoying this party.'

The man who had addressed her had nearly black hair and was wearing a dinner jacket.

'Shall we go and have a much smaller party somewhere else? Give me your hand.' And she found herself being led away, out of the hot, noisy room to the hall where the coat-racks were.

'I haven't got a coat.'

'Neither have I.'

'Where are we going?'

'I've got a house in Regent's Park that has some sandwiches in it. And a nice cold bottle of Krug. You can see that I'm not abducting you really.'

She hesitated. Regent's Park was very near her flat. Stella might – indeed often did – bring friends from a party back to it. She was hungry. She was also intrigued. He was looking at her with frank admiration, but he was also waiting for her to choose. This last decided her.

'Just for a bit.'

'Hop in.'

They had been standing in the street beside a sleek dark grey car.

∞ ∞ ∞

'You're not married, are you?'

Brief scenes from her marriage slipped across her mind like a succession of dull and faded photographs. 'Have been. Not now. What about you?'

She felt, rather than saw, a blind come down.

'Oh, yes,' he said. 'Married. A wife and three boys. I keep them in the country. Go down for weekends. But this is my London pad.'

They had entered the slip-road to one of the terraces and he parked. The terrace had been painted since the war and now looked pearly and festive in the dusky spring evening light – like the iced sides of a yet to be decorated wedding cake, she thought.

There were steps up to the house, and inside it a grand staircase richly dressed with a dark red carpet.

Up two flights and they were in his drawing room. It was lit by a pair of lamps on low tables, which gave the impression of a mysterious twilight, in which sofas loomed, rugs glowed, and mirrors reflected themselves, making corridors of anonymous repetition; only the white marble chimneypiece shone stark and intricately beautiful. He lit another lamp, and she saw that the walls were lined with a tobacco-coloured silk. And there, on the low table in front of the deeply dark brown sofa he indicated she should sit in, was a silver platter covered with a napkin, and a bucket containing a bottle.

'I keep my sandwiches, as Peter Sellers would say, "covered by a dazzling white clawth".' He wrapped the napkin round the neck of the bottle and gently eased out the cork. He was pretty used to opening champagne, she thought, as, after the magic little drift of smoke, he poured it neatly into two glasses without either of them overflowing.

'Now: I am Joseph Waring, and you are?'

She told him. She had gone back to being called Cazalet.

'Well. Let's drink to us.' He leaned towards her to bring his glass to hers, and as their hands touched, she was conscious of being very much attracted to him.

'To Louise Cazalet – and me.' He waited a moment. 'Your turn.'

She felt herself blushing, which annoyed her. 'All right. To you, then.'

'Joseph,' he prompted.

'Joseph Waring.'

'Now we can both have a swig. I must say, you sounded rather cross. Never mind. Have a sandwich.'

She took one. Smoked salmon – delicious.

45

But all the while they were eating them a confusion of thoughts kept her silent. He was married. No good falling in love with him. What would it be like if he kissed her? Why were the champagne and, worse, the sandwiches arranged here as if he had planned for her to join him? But he couldn't have because they hadn't known one another. This meant that he had planned to seduce someone – anyone – when he went to the party . . .

'I'm not a tart.' She said it with her mouth full so it came out rather muffled.

He made a kind of snorting noise – like the beginning of a laugh – but then she saw that he was regarding her with something like affection. 'I never, for one instant, thought that you were.' His eyes were brown and friendly.

She felt better, but determined to pursue this vexed subject to its end. 'Then, how come you have all this laid out?'

'Oh, well, you know, I like to live on the dangerous side. I was hoping I might meet someone worthy of the sandwiches, and then I found you. Finish your drink, and then I shall drive you home.'

In the car, she felt infinitely relieved, light-hearted, carefree. It was a short drive to her flat off Baker Street, and after she had told him where it was, they were both silent.

'I'll pick you up at eight, then,' he said, as he saw her to her door. 'To take you out to dinner.' He had said it as though it was an arrangement already made.

That had been the start of it. For five nights practically every week he took her out to dinner; the remaining two he spent in the country. On the first evening, he asked if he might come back to her flat, and once there he'd kissed her. And then they'd gone to bed. It had all seemed so simple, so marvellous – and right.

'You'll never be able to marry him,' Stella had said, the next morning.

'I don't want to marry him. I don't want to marry anyone.'

She was in love, and she was a mistress. All that seemed fine to Louise. But her romantic situation required some strict rules, which she firmly enforced. One evening, just before his summer holiday, he took her to see a flat that he said he thought would be better for her. It was indeed desirable: a first-floor conversion in a crescent near the park. When she asked how much it would cost, he had named a sum, which, though modest for its state, was well beyond her, and she said so. If he would allow him to help her? Of course not. She was not going to be a kept woman – certainly not. He had shrugged and said it had been worth a try.

In the summer, he rented a villa on Cap Ferrat for a six-week holiday with family and friends. This was a hard time. She imagined his glamorous life going on without her, it seemed for ever, while she sat in the baking little flat from which not even a single tree could be seen. There was not even the comfort of letters. So when this year, her third with Joseph, her father had invited her to go to the south of France with him, she had accepted. But, knowing Diana's dislike of her, Louise had had an uncomfortable meeting with her stepmother at which she had said that she didn't think Diana would actually want her there. The result had been one of those 'quite frankly' times that she was protesting about to Joseph in the Étoile.

'Well, your father clearly wants you. So go and enjoy it. Enjoy it, darling.'

He sometimes calls me 'darling', but he never actually says that he loves me, she later thought. Lying alone in the bed that was still warm from their lovemaking, Louise had had to accept that he would never stay the night. He always smoked one cigarette with her, dressed in an instant, and was gone.

JEMIMA, LAURA
AND HUGH

'When you're dead, can you fly?'

Jemima had just finished explaining to Laura about the Duchy (Hugh had telephoned to tell her and said he would like it if all three of them went to Sussex, so she had thought it necessary to tell her before they went), and Laura had listened intently. She was six and Jemima thought that she was the most intelligent as well as the most beautiful child in the world – which she wrongly thought she concealed from everyone.

'I don't know, darling – I expect so.'

'Cos I don't see how she could get up there if she couldn't.'

Laura's only experience of death had been when they had had to put Hugh's old spaniel down. Heaven had seemed the most comforting option and had therefore been carefully explained to her. 'I suppose he grew wings,' she had said, as the final tears made their way. She had cross-examined Hugh about Heaven, and he had elaborated – a place full of delicious bones, walks whenever Piper wanted them and endless rabbits to chase. All this was rather backfiring now.

'I don't think Duchy would like bones everywhere, or rabbits cos they ate her garden. Poor Duchy!'

Jemima battled weakly with her. Heaven was different for each person. For the Duchy there would be lovely gardens with flowers everywhere and, yes, of course, if she needed wings to get there, she would have them.

'I would like wings now. Then I could fly up and see them both.'

'It's so difficult,' she said to Hugh, over supper. 'When we go down people are bound to be talking about the funeral and being buried and the poor little thing will be utterly confused.'

'Well, we'll just have to do a lot more explaining.'

'I don't know how to do that without telling her a pack of lies.'

'You don't believe in Heaven?'

She shook her head. 'I just believe in now.'

'Sweetheart. You don't have to come with me.'

'I want to.'

'And I want you to.'

His relief washed over her: he needed her and she loved him.

In bed they reassured one another; it was comforting to him that Jemima had also loved the Duchy, who had received her into the family so kindly when she was still Jemima Leaf, had been good to her twins – the Leaflets – who wrote thank-you letters that were filled with lists of what they had most enjoyed during their visits: castle puddings, making a dam at the stream in the wood, having real cider with ginger ale, hardly ever having baths, driving the Brig's old car, now relegated to a corner of the field where it was gracefully subsiding in a bed of nettles. These had been young letters; now they were thirteen the letters had become more stilted. The Duchy had made it plain that she approved of Jemima, though the same could not be said of Edward's new wife, Diana. And Hugh, fiercely loyal to Villy, could not bring himself to be ever more than courteous to her.

'Do you think he'll bring her?' he said.

'Darling, I don't know, but I guess not.'

'Why do you guess that?' He was sifting her straight silky hair between his fingers.

'Because she won't want to go. And I think she usually gets what she wants.'

'So? I want you to get what you want.'

'I want the same things as you.'

'But you'd tell me if you didn't, wouldn't you? I don't want you saying anything simply because you think I'd like to hear it. We made a pact, don't you remember, the day we married?'

'Oh dear! I was just going to say that you're a lovely husband, an excellent father, a wonderful stepfather and a very good lover. What a pity!'

He put his arms round her bony shoulders. 'I bask in your good opinion, you know I do. Couldn't do without it. I hope you do a bit of basking yourself.'

'From morning till night. And it's night time now.'

She could tell from his face when he'd got back that evening that he'd had one of his awful headaches, but had learned long ago not to mention them. He simply needed a good long sleep.

'I just need a good long sleep,' she said.

PART TWO

JUNE–JULY 1956

THE FAMILY

'I'm not saying that we shouldn't explore all the possibilities. I just don't think we should do it behind Rachel's back.'

'Archie, you sound as though you think I don't mind about her.'

They were sitting on the bench by the tennis court where they had gone for some privacy – difficult to find in the overcrowded house.

'Of course I don't think that. You love her. We all do. What I meant was that it would be a good idea to iron out any of the disagreements before we talk to her. She's exhausted – she doesn't want to have to deal with a lot of bickering relations.'

'What on earth do you mean by that?'

'Come off it, Rupe. You know Hugh thinks that at all costs we should keep the house, and Edward thinks we should get rid of it. And, by the way, I'm not clear what you think.'

'That's because I haven't made up my mind.' He pulled out a battered packet of Gauloises and offered it before taking one himself. 'I mean,' he said, after a short silence while he tried to think what he did actually want, 'it all depends on what Rachel wants. She won't want the Regent's Park house, that's for sure. The Duchy hated it – said it was far too grand for her. This was her home, and Rachel may feel that as well. I really think it's for her to decide. And the children all love it here.'

'I know they do. My lot look forward to it every holiday. But who is to pay for it?'

'I suppose we could split the costs of upkeep between us.'

He had been dreading this. 'Rupe, I have to tell you now that I'm afraid you'd have to count me out on that. I simply don't have the dough to promise anything on a regular basis. Money has been rather tight lately.' His voice tailed off to an apologetic smile. It was Rupert's beloved daughter he had married, and he was hardly keeping her in a state to which she had been accustomed.

'My dear old boy, I wasn't expecting you to chip in. It ought to be Hugh and Edward and me and Rachel – if she wants to live here.' Even this kindness was humiliating. 'And we would always want you and Clary and the family to come – just as you always have done. The Duchy would have wanted that.' Mentioning his mother made Rupert's eyes fill with tears. 'She always regarded you as family,' he said, rubbing his face furiously.

'Why do you think Edward is so keen to get rid of Home Place?' Archie asked, to distract him.

'Because Diana doesn't like it?'

'Well, I don't think she takes much to the family as a whole.'

'Mm. She has ugly hands,' Rupert said absently. 'The kind that rings only make worse. Don't laugh, Archie – you must have noticed them. Time we got back to the fray,' he said, as they finished their cigarettes.

'Is there going to be a fray?' Archie asked, as they strolled back across the tennis court to the house.

'If marked differences of opinion surface, I think it's likely.'

∞ ∞ ∞

There were marked differences of opinion among the children. Laura wanted to sleep with her cousins, Harriet and Bertie, who had already determined that they would share with Georgie: 'She's hardly six, Mummy, we can't possibly have her with us. She's far too young – she'll spoil everything.'

'I'm more than six. It's not fair!'

'There you are, you see. Crying about the least little thing. Anyway, there isn't a fourth bed.'

Jemima and Clary, who had battled with the children's baths, looked at one another in despair.

'And Rivers,' Georgie now said. 'That's a fourth person anyway. He doesn't like girls,' he added triumphantly, to Laura. 'He'll probably bite you in the night.'

'Couldn't you stop him?'

'Not if *I* was asleep. He only likes people who are at least . . .' he paused, he was seven himself '. . . at least seven.'

'If you sleep with Daddy and me, you can wear your pirate's hat. How would that be?' Jemima wiped the tears from Laura's face. She could see that that was doing the trick: Laura adored her hat.

Meanwhile Clary had been enjoining her two to be nicer to their young cousin. 'When you were six, you wouldn't have liked being left out.'

'That was ages ago,' Bertie said uneasily, and Harriet echoed him: 'Ages.'

'Well,' Clary said, loudly enough for everyone to hear, 'I can remember being let down by my cousins and it felt awful. They didn't want me to share a room with them.'

'What did you do?' Georgie had a soft heart and was beginning to feel guilty.

'I went and slept in Aunt Rachel's room.'

This impressed them. 'Of course, I was older than Laura, but the feeling is the same. Don't gargle with your milk, Bertie, drink it.'

Bertie made the double effort of swallowing his milk and twisting in his chair to hug his mother. Milk went everywhere.

'You can't help your age,' Georgie said to Laura, when things were cleared up. 'You can stroke Rivers, if you like. He won't mind at all.'

But Rivers felt differently. He endured Laura's nervous stroke, but when Harriet and Bertie joined in, he fled to the safety of Georgie's dressing-gown pocket.

∞ ∞ ∞

Archie, having persuaded Clary to have a bath with a promise to 'settle the monsters', found them all in one bed arguing about which book they wanted to have read to them, but the moment he appeared Harriet rushed to him. 'Be a dinosaur, Dad. Just for a bit, please, be one.'

'If I do, it means no reading. Anyway, you can all read.'

'We can, if we want to. But we prefer you to read to us.'

'Shut up, Bertie. Let him be a dinosaur – he's awfully good at it.'

'My father is often a monkey or a sea lion,' Georgie said. Archie admired his loyalty.

'Go on, Dad!'

Archie straightened himself up, then made his arms long, arched his back and took enormous strides towards his daughter, uttering huge cries that began as an unearthly croak and ended with a trumpet-like squeal. He scooped her up with his claws and dropped her – shrieking with pleasurable fear – onto her bed. Then he turned his – surely by now – bloodshot eyes on Bertie and repeated the manoeuvre. Fear made Bertie giggle with relief after he was dropped onto the bed.

That left Georgie, whom he could see was really frightened. He became Archie again and sat on Georgie's bed. 'Don't want to frighten Rivers,' he said.

Georgie stopped trembling and gave Archie a look of gratitude: his face had been saved.

He kissed all three of them, ignoring the routine protests: 'It's perfectly good daylight outside, so why can't we be in it?' 'Why should I go to bed at the same time as much younger people of six?' Injustice stalked the room, and he escaped, leaving them to Zoë, who had come to see that Rivers was safely in his cage.

When Archie got back to their bedroom, he found Clary, wrapped in a bath towel, asleep on their bed. She lay on her side, her knees drawn up, one hand cupping her cheek; she looked, he thought, like an exhausted thirteen-year-old. He sat beside her and gently stroked her hair until she stirred, opened her eyes and smiled at him. 'It was the gorgeous hot bath. I just passed out.'

'We must dry your hair, my darling.'

'Are the children all right?'

'They're fine. I left them with Zoë. I did my dinosaur – they're bottled.'

'I heard your dinosaur. You never do him for me.' Her voice was muffled because he was towelling her hair.

'You're over age. I don't ever do him for people of thirty. Have you brought a dress?'

'Of course I've brought a dress. The Duchy didn't like us to wear trousers in the evening. It's my blue linen one. It probably got a bit crumpled in my case and, oh, gosh, I forgot to sew up that bit of hem. Never mind. I've got lots of safety pins – it won't show. I think I left my bra and knickers on the floor somewhere.'

'Here. You look so nice, so lovely without clothes.' Her skin was pearly, translucent, almost white, very difficult to paint, he had discovered over the years, but lovely in every other way, as he told her now. She still found it difficult to accept compliments, unless he made a joke of it. 'I'm so vulgar and depraved that I like people with skin that looks as though they have been kept under a paving stone.'

Clary now seized her comb and wrenched it through her hair, which she fastened with an elastic band that snapped at the last moment. 'Oh, bother! Oh, damn! I didn't bring a spare.'

'You'll have to make do with a girly ribbon. Bunch your hair and I'll do it for you.'

'Have you talked to Rachel?'

'Haven't had a chance. She's being rather guarded by Sid. I think she feels she's the only person to look after Rachel just now.'

'At least they won't have the strain of concealing anything from the Duchy.'

'At least that.'

∞ ∞ ∞

But several times during that evening Archie wondered whether there might be other, less definable strains.

After remarkably stiff drinks made by Edward, they assembled in the dining room for poached chicken with vegetables followed by strawberry shortcake and cream.

Neither Rachel nor Sid ate much in spite of urging each other to eat more.

After some abortive efforts, the safest subjects turned out to be politics (the men) and the children (their mothers). The unrest at the local docks was embarking on its sixth week, which was beginning to affect the family firm as it depended largely upon imports of hardwoods. Hugh, as chairman, was very exercised by this and irritated when Rupert said that their men had a point. Edward said he doubted whether Eden had the right cabinet to deal effectively with a national strike of any kind. It was uncomfortably agreed that he had not been in office very long, and he had been good in the Foreign Office. Rachel sat through all this, gaunt with grief but smiling if anyone caught her eye. Stories about the children were a relief. Georgie and Rivers and the rest of his menagerie, Laura sleeping in her pirate's hat, Harriet and Bertie trying to divide a lone banana with a ruler . . .

Archie became aware that something was terribly wrong with Sid, who was sitting next to him. He had thought she wasn't looking well – she'd had some bug, she'd told him at the beginning of dinner, but she was fine now. She didn't look it, her usually rather sunburned face sallow with mauve smudges under her eyes. She had picked at her chicken but, except for urging Rachel to eat more, she had remained silent. Now, when Eileen put the strawberry shortbread before her, he heard her being suddenly horribly sick into her napkin. She got unsteadily to her feet, and as he rose to help her there was Jemima, quick as a flash putting an arm round her, adding her napkin to the soiled one, and making soothing noises as she took her out of the room. Rachel made to follow, but Sid called – almost shouted – 'No. Please leave me alone.'

And Rachel stayed. 'She isn't at all well. She should never have come.' Then she pressed her knuckles to her eyes to stop any more tears.

Hugh, who was sitting next to her, leaned across to take her hand with his good one. 'Rach, darling, she came because she loves you, as we all do so much.'

And Zoë, who had been swallowing hard – the one thing that made her want to be sick was being present when other people were – said, 'The more I loved someone, the less I'd want them round me if I was sick. I'd just want to be on my own.'

'Jemima will look after her,' Hugh said.

Edward looked at his brother. He couldn't help remembering that Villy had always been the one who had looked after everyone when they were ill, fell off a pony or got their fingers slammed in a car door. Of course, she knew about first aid because she'd gone in for it before the war, but she also had a most practical compassion for anyone in trouble. The thought that Diana was not like that crossed his mind: she certainly had not liked him being ill, but on the other hand she was good with her sons. She would certainly look after *them*.

Lately Diana had been suggesting that they should sell the house in West Hampstead and buy one in the country.

A nice Georgian house within commuting distance of London. He had the feeling that she was pretty determined on this, in which case there would be absolutely no point in his taking a share in Home Place, where Diana, in spite of protestations to the contrary, had never felt comfortable. He would have to talk to Hugh about it. The trouble with the family was not property but lack of cash. Too much of the firm's capital was tied up in property. They not only owned Home Place and his parents' house in Regent's Park, on a long and expensive lease, but two valuable wharves in London, one in Southampton and very expensive offices in Westminster. The overheads on all this were not being earned by the sale of enough timber. He had tried several times to discuss this with Hugh, but he had refused to consider selling off anything and, as head of the firm, he had the ultimate say. And Rupe, bless his heart, would always agree with the last person he'd talked to.

These thoughts now made him feel queasy. He was prone to indigestion these days, and the condition was not helped by the faint but unmistakable stench of vomit. He remembered a trick he had learned in the trenches in the first war, and picked up a box of matches lying on the table for lighting the candles, struck one and let it burn itself out. Hugh noticed this at once, and a small but infinitely comforting look passed between them. He handed the box to his brother who repeated the action. The air cleared, and some of those round the table set about the strawberry shortcake, and soon Zoë was explaining Juliet's absence, staying with a best friend and shopping for jeans.

Clary said, 'It's funny, isn't it? When I was Juliet's age, I never minded what I wore.'

'It's a good thing you didn't. Apart from clothes coupons, there weren't any clothes.'

'I remember you made me two frocks. You made them even after I was so horrible to you. It must have been awful being a stepmother.'

These remarks engendered a good deal of affection – from Rupert and Zoë and Archie, who said, 'She still doesn't mind much. So I choose her clothes.'

Rachel, making a valiant effort, said, 'When I was young, the Duchy always made me wear pinafores. And if I was going to a party, and was dressed in lots of white petticoats under my party dress, she made me sit on a table until it was time to go.'

'I remember you doing that,' Hugh said. 'But at least you weren't dolled up in sailor suits, like Edward and me. Rupert escaped all that.'

Rupert, who immediately thought of what else he had escaped – the nightmare of trench warfare that his older brothers had endured – spoke quietly: 'It's a pity, really, because I simply loved dressing up. You remember that old black tin trunk we had full of dressing-up clothes? Well, once, when our parents were giving a garden party, I dressed up as a girl in a heavily beaded pink dress – you know, one of those tubes that flappers used to wear – with a silver lamé turban and an ostrich fan. I went out onto the lawn and the Brig was furious, but the Duchy simply laughed and told me to go back into the house, change, then come back and help hand round the cucumber sandwiches.'

There was a short silence before Rachel said that, if they would forgive her, she would see how Sid was, and then she would go to bed. The men all rose and

64

Archie, who was nearest, opened the door for her, then closed it.

'Ring for Eileen to fetch the plates, Rupe.'

'Hugh, it's nearest to you.'

Hugh fumbled under the table where Rachel had been sitting. Edward went to the sideboard to get the port. Clary said, 'If the ladies are meant to withdraw at this point, I think I'll withdraw to bed. Goodnight, all.'

Zoë said, 'I'll wait in the drawing room until Jemima returns and then I'll be off as well.'

Eileen, having removed the pudding plates, asked if the gentlemen would like their coffee in the dining room.

'Anyone for coffee?' Hugh asked, but nobody seemed to want it. Eileen was told to take the tray to the drawing room and, yes, that would be all. There was a faint, but unmistakable feeling of tension in the air.

The port went round and all four men filled their glasses.

Hugh said: 'Before we start on things that have to be done, I suggest we all drink a toast to our dear mother and,' looking at Archie, 'friend.'

So they all stood and did that.

This seemed to lighten things a little. When they sat down, cigarettes were lit, in Edward's case a cigar.

'With Rachel's agreement,' Hugh began, 'I went to see the vicar to organise a date for the funeral, and we agreed on Monday week. I asked for next Saturday, but it was not convenient, so it will be at eleven thirty on the twenty-fifth. I have also drafted announcements for *The Times* and the *Telegraph* to appear this Monday. I have included the time and place of the funeral for people who may want to attend it. That's as far as I got.'

Rupert said, 'Did Rachel say anything about where she wants to live?'

'Nothing. Only that she didn't want to keep the London house.'

'It belongs to the firm anyway,' Edward said. 'That's something we can sell, at least.'

'I can't understand why you're so keen on selling anything. The Brig always said that property was the best investment of capital and, as chairman of the firm, I have every intention of following his advice.'

'Well, perhaps you've forgotten that the firm also owns Home Place. Rachel surely won't want to live here on her own, and it's worth a hell of a lot more than when the Brig bought it. If we sold that, we could buy Rachel a nice little house or flat in London.'

'You surely don't want to get rid of the place where we've all spent so much of our lives, where our children grew up, which was our home during the last war? You cannot want to do that!'

Oh dear, Archie thought, as he looked helplessly at Rupert. I feel just like Hugh, only I can't do anything about it.

But Rupert came to the rescue. 'I agree with Hugh,' he said. 'I feel that even if Rachel doesn't want to live here we could all chip in and keep the house, for her, for the children and, speaking for myself, for me.'

At this point they all looked at Edward.

He stirred uncomfortably in his chair. 'For goodness' sake, don't think that I don't care about the house. The fact is that Diana wants to live in the country, and that will mean my selling the lease on Ranulf Road, for which I shan't get much as it has only ten years to run, and buying somewhere. I'm fairly strapped for cash as it is, really not in a position to pay for a second property.'

Hugh began to say that that left three of them, and almost at the same time Archie, very tentatively, suggested that perhaps they should wait until Rachel had been consulted. And also, was it possible that the Duchy had expressed some wishes about it in her will?

This seemed to lower the temperature a bit. Rupert agreed that there was not much point in pursuing the subject any further, and they fell back on reminiscing about the early days of Home Place, the Brig facing the Duchy with all manner of stray and unknown guests, and how the Duchy had comforted the young Jewish nurses from the Babies' Hotel when it was evacuated to Home Place during the war by inviting them in the evening for tea and biscuits and Beethoven on the gramophone. Affection slowly replaced sibling differences.

Then Jemima came down to tell them that Sid had settled for the night, and had been asleep when Rachel came to see her, and they all decided to call it a day.

∞ ∞ ∞

Zoë undressed in the familiar room with its wallpaper of peacocks and chrysanthemums, then sat in front of her dressing-table mirror, cleansing her face and remembering the first time she had come here, how nervous she had felt. Her clothes had seemed all wrong, and though she had been welcomed as Rupert's wife, she had felt that she would never fit in, would never withstand Clary's hostility, could never be a stepmother. Well, to be honest, she had never wanted to be a mother at all, and was both bored and defeated at the prospect of Clary and Neville watching and criticising her. And then that awful incident in London, when she had played – had overplayed – the flirt and paid the price of the disastrous sad child that had mercifully, from her point of view, died. What a heartless little bitch I was, she thought, thinking of nothing but my appearance and wanting Rupert to admire me from morning till night. But I did love him in the end.

She remembered now how incredibly tactful and kind the Duchy had been when she had fallen in love with Jack Greenfeldt, leaving them alone for what proved to be their last meeting. The anguish she had felt about him had changed her life entirely. She had believed that Rupert was dead, and when Jack, unable to bear what he had seen in the German camps, had shot himself, there seemed nothing to live for – excepting Juliet. She had been going to the small temporary hospital that had been set up for badly wounded men who were nursed between operations to repair what could be saved of their ravaged bodies. Most of them had faced a life of dependence, and most of them were under twenty-five, but it was only after Jack's death that she had begun to imagine what it would be like to be another person, a person infinitely less fortunate than herself, and to take a great deal less for granted.

It had been a shaky start, as most beginnings are, but here she was now, with Rupert, whom she had come to recognise she loved, Juliet, who was as wilful and pretty and self-absorbed as she herself had been when she was that age, and the newest treasure, her zoophilic son, who had wept when, on his fourth birthday, they had given him a beautiful stuffed monkey, 'He's not real! I wanted a real monkey!' and had had to make do with a guinea pig.

When Rupert came up he found her in tears. 'Oh, sweetheart, what is it?'

'Nothing really – everything. I'm so lucky – to be here with you. I love you so much.' She was sitting up in bed and held out her bare arms.

'How lucky that I feel just the same. Lovely creamy skin you've got.' He wiped her eyes on a corner of the sheet. Years ago that sort of remark would have made her sulk (her awful sulks, how had he borne them?). Now the years, with the affection of intimacy, had overlaid such nonsense. They had grown into each other.

∞ ∞ ∞

'She shouldn't really have come, you know. She'd been in bed, on penicillin, and I'm pretty sure she has a temperature. Poor Sid!'

'And poor Rachel! It really is rather the last straw for her. Nursing the Duchy for weeks and now this.'

'I don't know. It may help her. Your sister always wants to be needed. She wanted to see Sid, but she was asleep and we both thought it best not to disturb her.'

They were talking quietly, as Laura, encased in her pirate's tricorn hat, lay spread across their bed. Hugh picked her up very carefully to transfer her to her bed, but even so the hat fell off. Jemima retrieved it, and managed to put it on again. Laura simply gave a deep, rather irritable sigh, as one interrupted in something very important, turned onto her side and continued to sleep.

'Well done.' He looked at his wife, standing barefoot in her white cotton nightdress, with her golden bobbed hair, and felt an absolute joyous longing for her. 'Help me out of my shirt, darling.'

She pulled the second sleeve over his black silk stump and he put his arms round her. 'I cannot,' he said, after he had kissed her, 'imagine life without you.' And with no more words they went to bed.

∞ ∞ ∞

What a day! Edward thought, as he got out of his clothes. He didn't feel too good – the usual touch of indigestion that he had suffered from for some time now, plus a general feeling of malaise. He was used to being popular, charming, and liked by people; being in a minority about anything didn't suit him at all. If only Diana had taken more to Home Place, they could have had it and, of course, the family could have stayed whenever they liked.

But she was determined on her own house, and he couldn't see her wanting much of the family in it. Though Louise and Teddy, and Lydia if she was ever available, must be able to come there – he would insist on that – but vaguely, in the back of his mind, it occurred to him that surely he shouldn't be put into the position of having to insist. He had done a lot for her boys, after all, particularly the youngest, who he was now pretty sure was not his.

He shook a couple of Alka Seltzer into his tooth glass, filled it with water and knocked it back. It usually did the trick or, at any rate, half the trick. This bloody dock problem. Time was that when their men had wanted to come out on strike, he had gone down to the wharf and talked to them, and resolved it. No chance of that now.

The firm had grown since those days. Before the war, if he'd felt like a day off shooting or playing golf or being with Diana, he'd simply taken it. Hugh could always be relied upon to hold the fort or, when the Old Man had been in control, to cover for him. And he and Hugh had been so close: regular games of squash, chess on winter evenings, sharing out the work. He had been the best at selling, and the Brig had taught him to buy the timber, both here and in the Far East. Hugh was meticulous about dispatches, and ran their fleet of blue lorries (an uneconomic colour since it faded so fast but which distinguished them from all other heavy transport on the road). It was simply that while he could clearly see they were over-extended in terms of property, and that eventually the bank would not wear their steadily increasing over-draft, Hugh seemed utterly oblivious to the financial dangers, and since his elevation to chairman, his obstinacy – always a key factor – had worsened.

He went to the window overlooking the front garden and opened it; immediately, the night air, gentle and warm, assailed him. It was heavily scented with all the flowers the Duchy had planted for that purpose. Moths flew at random from the dark into the light of his room. As he got into bed and turned off his bedside lamp, the Duchy filled his mind. He had gone with Hugh to her room to say goodbye. She was lying there, with white roses in her hands, her face as smooth and pale as alabaster. She looked as young as when he had been her child. 'You were always my naughtiest son,' he remembered her saying, when he had become engaged to Villy and had taken her to meet his parents. When Villy had pressed the Duchy to elaborate, she had looked directly at him: 'You tried once to bite your sister. And whenever

71

you were naughty and punished, you simply did whatever it was again. You used to spit,' she finished, and smiled at him with frank serenity. That tranquil, direct gaze! He knew no one who was as simply direct as she. Even Rachel, who was certainly frank, was not tranquil. 'And I shall never see her again.' His eyes filled with unbearably hot tears. Without anyone – without Diana – he was able to mourn her.

∞ ∞ ∞

Archie was the last to go upstairs. This was because, after that odd and difficult evening, he felt a great need to be alone. He slipped out of the front door and into the garden. The air was like warm velvet, the sky trembling with many stars. In beds at this side of the house there were white tobacco and night-scented stocks; a jasmine, whose delicate starry flowers were belied by its extravagant vigour, hung onto a climbing rose.

To the left of the lawn, in the corner, the monkey puzzle stood dark and stark against the softer sky. It was a kind of Victorian joke, but the Duchy was immune to the family's teasing about it. 'It was here when we came,' was all she would say in its defence, but she had once confided in him that she loved it. 'It reminds me of home at Stanmore,' she'd said. 'My father loved strange trees. We had a Ginkgo as well.'

He turned right to walk slowly round the house, past the sunken tennis court that lay on a lower piece of ground. Bats were flittering about in dizzy confusion, but inaudible to him. The path became cinder as it approached the greenhouses, and Archie could smell the ripening tomatoes. At the far end were the courtyard, the old stables and the garage. The Tonbridges had a cottage above the stable but their light was out. Turning right again, there was the drive and a steep bank leading to the wood.

An owl gave a fractious little yelp, and he remembered how this had upset Bertie the first time he had heard it. 'It's hurt, Daddy. It made a hurting sound. We should rescue it.' Archie had had to impersonate a donkey, a cow and an elephant to show what different languages animals had. At the end Bertie had simply said, 'Well, how do you know when any of them are hurt?' Couldn't answer that one, but there was nothing, he had discovered, that worried children so much as ignorance. 'You do know, really – he does, doesn't he, Mummy? He knows everything.' And when Clary had asked who had told him, he had answered, 'The Queen, of course, in telegrams.'

Right again, through the white-painted gate, and he was back to the tobacco and stocks.

He would be sad indeed if Home Place came to an end. Perhaps, he thought, I should have done what Rupert did, given up art and got some sort of regular job. But he was the only person who knew what it had cost Rupert to become a Sunday painter. 'Which we both know, Archie, is as good as giving up.' And when he had tried to be soothing about it – the main thing was to keep doing it anyhow – Rupert had retorted, 'Pointless. If you want to be an artist of any kind, you bloody well have to practise it.'

If the family did give up the house, it would be the end of the wonderful holidays that the Duchy had given Clary and the children. An ignoble thought, perhaps, but inescapable.

He let himself in, walked softly across the hall and climbed the stairs. At the top, he stood for a moment because, at the end of the corridor on his right, he could hear what he knew to be the faint sound of Rachel weeping. It crossed his mind to go to her, but he dismissed the thought. Grief must sometimes (perhaps always) be allowed to be private.

Now he must go to rescue Clary, who, he bet, would be sleeping on her sopping pillow.

∞ ∞ ∞

'They'll never do that!'

She had all her curlers in, which meant she didn't want him to do you-know-what.

They were having a last cup of tea and, in his case, some strawberry tarts, and were sitting in the downstairs room of their cottage. She was still upset that they hadn't eaten all the pudding, but they were In Mourning, after all, and the thought of Madam lying upstairs in the house had upset her greatly.

'They took her away this afternoon. Eileen saw.'

'Why didn't you call me?'

'I was fetching Miss Sidney from the station.'

'I was only in the kitchen. She could've called me.'

'I presume she didn't think.' He was glad it wasn't his fault. 'But mark me,' he continued, 'Madam passing away like that may well cast a different hue on the situation. It's a big house for Miss Rachel all on her own. So I say they may give it up.' He was sitting opposite her in his shirt and braces; he'd taken off his tie as soon as they'd got back to the cottage.

The practical implication of this struck them both at

the same moment, but they stayed silent. He, because he just didn't have the energy to discuss alternatives (the cottage would, of course, go with the house), and she because she felt it would show a lack of respect.

'You've had a long day,' he said at last. 'Best go up now.'

She heaved herself out of her chair. She had got rid of her shoes before sitting and now wore slippers that were much the shape of very old broad beans. By the end of each day her terrible bunions came into their own, and she dreaded having to walk anywhere, least of all the steep, narrow little staircase that led to their bedroom.

But he went ahead, held out his hand to help her. 'Whatever comes to pass, you've always got me,' he said, looking down on her with his mournful bloodhound's eyes.

A threat? A promise? As always, when he presented himself thus a wave of irritation followed by a protective feeling overcame her. He was the one who needed looking after, she knew that, but he meant well.

'I know,' she said. 'I know I have.'

THE YOUNG MEN

'I appreciate that it has become something of a cliché, but my grandmother has actually died and I do want to go to her funeral.'

His editor looked at him with some distrust.

'Neville, I seem to remember that your grandmothers have died a number of times during the last year.'

'I know, but this is for real.' He smiled charmingly. He was wearing a black velvet jacket – much the worse for wear – a white shirt open at the neck, corduroy trousers that had once been black, and tennis shoes. 'Every now and then, real life catches up with one. Or death, I suppose,' he added. He looked at the floor when he said that, then raised his eyes to hers. He looked, she thought, exactly the way you would imagine a poet to look, if you'd never met one, but he was surprisingly practical, demanding and good at his job.

She looked through her diary. 'You have a big shoot coming up next week.'

'I know. On Friday. Outside the Albert Hall.'

'Friday and Saturday.'

'Sue, I really don't need two days for that. If you agree, I can get Simon to ring all the clothes places and the agency for the models. I've said which ones I want. It's all organised – honestly.'

'OK. You win. But don't you dare let me down. '

'Rest assured, my darling.' And he looked at her with bland blue eyes in a manner she had learned to distrust, but also found hard to resist. He was, after all, only twenty-five, and she had discovered him, and as he was not yet well enough known to go freelance, she wanted to keep him. He had worked as an assistant to both Norman Parkinson and Clifford Coffin – a good grounding – and only a few months ago, when they were not available, he had come to her and suggested that he stand in. He had done a surprisingly professional job, was brilliant at using a model's best points and concealing any bad ones.

'Off you go, then,' she said dismissively. She was his boss, after all.

Back at the ranch, as he sometimes called the grotty little basement flat in Camden Town that he shared with Simon, whom he found washing up coffee cups, he said, 'All clear. Get me a cup of coffee, then ring Pansy and tell her to arrange all the clothes for Friday.'

Simon wiped his hands on a dripping teacloth and looked about for the kettle. 'She won't be pleased at that. She likes to be consulted, not told.'

'Tell her it's our grandmother's funeral. That usually shuts people up. And, Simon, do stop behaving as though you're under water. You're my assistant. That means you have to work twice as hard as I do.'

Yes, and for a measly three pounds a week, Simon thought, as he filled the kettle and set it on its wheezing way. He was four years older than his cousin, and look at the situation!

A lock of his blond hair fell over his high forehead as he bent over the tin of Nescafé to scrape out its remains. This was proving to be yet another job that was not for

77

him, and goodness knows there'd been a good many of them in the last six years. University had been fine, national service had been awful – he'd never wanted to be an officer – and he had then learned half-heartedly to be an electrician. His father had wanted him to go into the firm, but he didn't want that either. So he had drifted from one pointless job to another, while Teddy, roughly the same age as him, now had a salary, a flat of his own and a car (admittedly given him by the firm but, still, his to drive). And Neville was so sure of himself. When he'd persuaded Simon to work for him – 'Three pounds a week and rent free' – it had seemed an exciting opportunity. But all the job consisted of was lugging heavy and fragile pieces of equipment in and out of Neville's beaten-up MG, and doing all the housework in the flat where he had only a cupboard under the stairs to sleep in. Neville had the only room and that had to be used for everything else – parties, desk work, eating, the lot. There was another cupboard that had been converted into a kitchenette, and a very small bathroom that smelt of mushrooms and made you feel almost dirtier after you'd had a bath in it. In spite of all this, Neville contrived a kind of battered glamour, while Simon looked, well, like somebody who was very nearly down and out. He seemed to be the only person he knew who hadn't the slightest idea of what he should do – or, indeed, what he was for.

He reviewed the older cousins. Christopher was a monk, and he must have wanted to be one pretty badly to go for it. Teddy, well, Teddy was fast becoming like Dad and the uncles – a businessman. Simon had never wanted to be one of them, a fact confirmed by the awful three months he'd worked there. The girls were all right: they got married, like Polly and Clary, or had a vocation, like Lydia. The younger ones didn't count: they just had daft notions of being engine drivers, or spacemen, or, in the case of Juliet, a film star. He didn't even have a girlfriend. He'd had one for a short time, but she had wanted to go dancing practically every evening he saw her; he was rotten at dancing and in any case couldn't afford the whole business of supper, paying to get into the dance hall and drinks while they were there, plus Peggy had wanted him to see her home in a taxi and had clearly expected him to kiss her in it. Her hot face with runny make-up had put him off, and trying to divert her from any clinch had made him stammer. Not a success. 'I don't want to go out with you again,' she had said. 'You're mean and you can't dance.' If she had loved him, she would never have said that. But, then, he hadn't loved her, there hadn't been a crumb of romance – except he'd liked her hair. After that, any girls he encountered had always been when he was in a humiliating situation: clearing things up, making tea or coffee for people, being shouted at and told to get a move on, do things faster. He slept a lot – found it increasingly difficult to get up in the mornings. In a funny way, he was quite looking forward to the funeral because Polly would almost certainly be there. And he loved Polly – more than anyone.

Nothing had been the same since Mum died. Sybil, she had been called. It seemed funny to him that he could love someone so much and had never called her by her name. When he talked to her now – which he did sometimes – he called her Sybil, her grown-up name. He could talk to Polly about her, but not to his father, and Wills, who was soon to start national service, in spite of looking everywhere for her when he was a baby, did not remember her at all.

∞ ∞ ∞

'I've got to go. Sorry, darling, but they'll have my guts for garters if I'm late.'

'Oh, Teddy! You're always saying that. I thought we had the whole afternoon. You said.' She propped herself up on her elbow and made a provocative face. 'You really are the limit!'

'I didn't say that. I said I'd got a long lunch and it's nearly four o'clock. I'm late already.' He sprang out of bed and began dressing.

She watched him. 'Well, at least the weekend is coming up. You said you'd take me to that posh restaurant in Bray.'

'I'm afraid we haven't.'

'Haven't what?'

'Got the weekend. I've got to go down to the country with my family.' And before she could start to wail, he added, 'My grandmother has died. It's her funeral on Monday.'

'Oh. I'm sorry. Couldn't you at least come back on Monday evening?'

''Fraid not.' He was knotting his tie now. 'Get up, sweetie, I've got to lock up the flat.' He looked at her, charmingly dishevelled, her blue-black hair falling over her amazingly white shoulders. She had wonderful skin, like silk. When he'd put on his jacket, he pulled the sheet off her. Her breasts were small but well rounded, her nipples a deep rosy colour; he had only to touch them to excite her. Bed was her element, but one couldn't spend one's life there. They'd had no lunch, and he realised he was desperately hungry. He'd only had coffee in his flat for breakfast – wasn't much of a hand at cooking – and Annie seemed to have no interest in food, unless it was served up in a restaurant.

She got dressed in the end and he put her in a taxi. Miss

Corley – the secretary he shared with Hugh – would probably get him a sandwich if he asked her nicely.

He did not know how he felt about the Duchy's death, he reflected, as he drove through London. Death seemed to him so unreal, so mysterious and awful that it left him speechless. It was the going-on-ness of it that defeated him. Finality – that was the word. Even Dad leaving Mum, awful though it had been for Mum, and embarrassing for everybody, didn't mean that they didn't go on being there. And now he would never see the Duchy again. He realised that tears had come to his eyes because the traffic was blurred. He quickly rubbed his face. One shouldn't blub. He hadn't cried when Bernadine had left him; actually, it hadn't made him sad but rather relieved in the end. Although, looking back on it, he had to admit that she'd taught him a thing or two about sex. When they had begun, sex had seemed not only the most marvellous thing in the world but something that would only be marvellous with her. And when she'd wanted to marry him, he had been thrilled, and had married her at once without telling the family. He had been so sure that he was in love that it had all seemed glorious – until she'd come to England.

She'd hated everything – mostly discovering that he was not in the least rich, as it became clear she'd imagined. Well, he'd been divorced for some years now, and there had been several girls since then, but he hadn't wanted to marry any of them. He'd concentrated on work, playing squash, tennis in summer, and collecting records of jazz pianists. About once a month Dad and Diana invited him to dinner where he got a really square meal and an awful lot to drink, and also about once a month he spent a rather difficult evening with Mum. She was so bitter; she always asked after Dad, and he never knew what to say. She also asked about Diana, apparently innocuous questions, but uttered with a venom no less poisonous for being suppressed. The awful thing was that, though of course he loved and was sorry for her, he could not imagine anyone wanting to go to bed with her, whereas with Diana – whom he did not very much like – he could see she was just the ticket for Dad. He felt sorry for Roland too: he hardly ever saw their father. He was seventeen now, and just about to finish his public school. Boarding might, for him, have been better than living with Mum.

It was hot in the car, and as he wiped his face with his hand, he could smell Annie on his fingers.

PART THREE
JULY–SEPTEMBER 1956

ARCHIE AND CLARY

They had had to postpone the holiday because of the funeral. They had lost the ticket money for the car ferry, but the French firm had been able to let them have a caravan for a week without forfeiting their deposit. But that seemed to be the end of their good luck. The crossing was very rough and both children were helplessly sick; Clary had had to sponge them down in the insalubrious cabin, which contained a basin and a lavatory, unpack to get them fresh clothes, and beg a bag from the steward in which to put the soiled ones. Nobody got any sleep, the cabin smelt of vomit, and both children were miserable. He had done everything he could to help Clary, fetching the suitcases from the car, going to the bar for drinks – lemon barley water for Harriet and Bertie, brandy and ginger ale for Clary: 'Your emergency drink,' he'd said, and been rewarded with a wan but grateful smile. They'd laid the children on their bunks and read to them for the rest of the night.

The morning was grey, with fitful glimpses of sun, and the long process began of unloading the cars from the boat. They had arrived in St Malo, and there to greet them was the welcome sight of a row of cafés. 'We'll all have a jolly good breakfast,' Archie had said.

Breakfast had been a success. The children loved croissants and very milky coffee, but the highlight had been an old man who walked slowly up and down past them with a cheetah on a lead. This naturally thrilled them and, seeing their interest, he stopped at their table. The cheetah turned out to be called Sonia, and he encouraged both children to stroke its head. Archie realised just in time that the man expected a tip, and as he had no change, it was rather a large one. However, it was worth it: the children were completely entranced.

But the rest of the holiday had been patchy. It had rained a lot, and Archie's bad leg had ached more than usual, and the caravan was not ideal as a place to be for hours on end. When the sun shone the children loved the beach with its rock pools and sand: they would each appropriate a pool, then spend happy hours catching shrimps.

He and Clary took turns on the beach, while the other tidied the caravan, tried to get their stock of towels dry enough for the children, shopped for food and made a picnic lunch. When Bertie once complained that his sandwich was scratchy, Harriet turned on him. 'Of course it is. Why do you think it's called "*sand*wich"?'

'They're not scratchy in England.' But he looked near to tears.

Clary took his sand-encrusted paw and wiped it clean, then shook his sandy baguette.

'There was a gigantic war in England, and Mrs Burrell at school said there were shortages of everything. So there would have been a shortage of sand, you silly ass.'

'I'm not a silly ass. You're horrible.'

'I'm nothing like as horrible as you.'

They glared at each other.

Archie burst into loud mock sobs. 'Why have I got

two horrible children? It must be your fault.' He glared at Clary, who took the hint.

'It's your fault. There's nothing horrible about me, it's you.' She started to sob.

Harriet flung her arms round her father. 'Oh, don't, Dad. There's nothing horrible about you – or Mummy.' She extended the caress to her mother. 'You love each other, really. You're upsetting Bertie. If you quarrel it spoils everything.'

Archie held out his hand to Clary and kissed it. 'I'm so awfully sorry, darling. I didn't mean it.'

'It's quite all right. I'm sorry, too.' And as the children watched this with relief and complacency, she added, 'And, Harriet and Bertie, you love each other as well, don't you?'

There was a pause, and then Harriet said, 'Up to a point.' She looked at Bertie's anxious, red, tearful face and relented. 'I do actually quite like you,' she said. 'Most of the time.'

Archie said, 'Well, give him a hug, then.'

When she had done so, she said, 'I did it, even though he smells horribly of sardines. Which you know I absolutely hate.'

Bertie, considerably cheered, said, 'I want an egg, a hard-boiled egg, but not in a sandwich.'

There were several more scenes of this kind – mostly when it rained and the children got bored with jigsaws and books in the caravan.

The worst thing from Archie and Clary's point of view was the evenings. Sometimes they went out to supper, but by about nine Harriet and Bertie, full of bathing and rockpool-owning and sun, became very ready for bed.

That was fine, but then they had to be awfully quiet because there was no division between the bunks and the rest of the van. He had tried making love to her once, but they had both felt constrained by the presence of their sleeping children. In the end they took two of the camp stools outside and sat drinking *marc*, smoking and talking quietly. Bertie was prone to nightmares – about a giant jellyfish with a sting, and about the cheetah, Sonia, which, he said, had secretly wanted to eat him.

All in all, they were both relieved at the end of the week. It had not been a real holiday for Clary, and he had done no painting at all.

LOUISE

Louise lay on her stomach in the garden of the villa her father had rented a few miles west of Ventimiglia. She had pulled down the straps of her bikini in order to have an even tan on her golden-brown back. The villa, when they eventually reached it, was large and full of faded velvet-upholstered furniture. Its drawbacks – not mentioned by the agents – included only one bathroom for the seven bedrooms and two lavatories that flushed reluctantly and sometimes not at all. The mosquito nets over the beds were full of holes, well known and found by the mosquitoes. The house, described as having a garden bordering the beach, was in fact cut off from the sea by a railway line that had to be crossed with care since a small train puffed along it, back and forth, at irregular intervals. The party consisted of Dad, Diana, their youngest child Susan, Diana's brother and his new wife, and Dad was paying for all of it. There was a cook and a gardener, so all Diana had to do was order the meals. In spite of that, there was a feeling of dissatisfaction in the air. Louise noticed that Diana seemed only to speak to her father to tell him to do something – 'The least you could do' was how she often put it. She also blamed him for the railway line, and the beach, which had practically no sand. However, Louise also noticed that in front of the brother and his wife, Marge, she presented a devoted front. With herself, Diana was icily polite and Louise felt unwanted.

She had recourse to the dusty leather-bound volumes that lived in a glass-fronted bookcase in the salon. At the moment she was reading a biography of Caterina Sforza, which contained a fascinating chapter on the poisons that Caterina recommended, each recommendation depending upon whether she wanted her victims to die at once or some time after they had left her palace.

'I hoped I'd find you. Don't overdo it, darling – you look rather red.' Edward picked up the bottle of tanning oil beside her. 'Like me to do your back?'

She sat up. It was lovely to see him without anyone else. 'I'd love you to.'

She watched him pouring the oil into his hands for a moment. He did not look happy, she thought. Was Diana being horrible to him, and might he want to confide in her?

'Where are the others?'

'They've all gone to swim.'

'But not you?'

'I didn't feel like it.'

'Something's worrying you.'

'Well – yes, it is rather.'

'Oh, Dad! You can confide in me. You know I won't tell anyone.'

'Darling! I don't mind telling you, but there's nothing you can do, I'm afraid. It's money. I'm running out of it. I'd no idea how expensive food and everything would be. I don't have to pay the servants, but I shall have to tip them, and then there's all the expense of driving back. I wasn't allowed to bring any more cash out than I have. So, yes, I am worried. I haven't told anyone else, even

Diana, because she'll think it's all my fault – which, of course, it is.' He put the bottle of sun oil down and wiped his hand on the grass.

Louise, who had been thinking furiously, had suddenly an idea for him. 'Dad! I think I know what we could do. My friend Stella is having her holiday with an uncle and aunt who live in Nice. She gave me her telephone number in case we went there. If I rang her, I bet she could get you money. Tell me how much you need, and I'll ring her.'

'Could you, darling? That would be marvellous.'

She got to her feet. 'Let's do it now.'

It all worked out wonderfully. Yes, Stella could get the money by the following day, and, yes, she would bring it herself – take the train from Nice to Ventimiglia, and could Louise meet her at the station?

Diana's voice from the bathroom: 'There's a bus to Ventimiglia that goes every hour Antonio says. She can take that.'

'I think I ought to drive Louise in this heat.'

'Oh, darling! I promised the others you'd join them at the beach. You didn't yesterday.'

There was a silence after that, and Louise, who had overheard them when she was leaving the bathroom, imagined him shrugging – and giving in. She hated the way her father seemed always to give in – hated it – but she was so excited at the prospect of seeing Stella that she decided not to think about it, and duly caught an early bus to be certain she was at the station by eleven.

∞ ∞ ∞

'Goodness! It sure is lovely to see you!'

Stella was wearing a black sleeveless shirt, a striped cotton skirt and, as always, her large horn-rimmed spectacles. She took a handkerchief out of her straw bag and wiped her face. Louise continued: 'It's jolly kind of you to come all this way. Really, Stella, you're such a good friend.'

'*De rien.* Honestly, it's quite a relief to get away from the family for a bit. All those heavy meals with aunts and uncles. And answering the same questions from all of them. Have I got a boyfriend? When will I get married? You know.'

They were walking towards the bus stop.

'We might have to wait a bit.'

'Let's get a cold drink. It was terribly hot on the train and I'm parched.'

'I'm terribly sorry, but I haven't got money for a drink. Only my bus fares.' Louise did not add, 'And not even yours,' because she felt so ashamed.

Stella gave her a quick look and said, 'It's OK. I've got plenty of money.'

They had Campari sodas at the station and, eventually, the bus came.

It was uphill out of Ventimiglia and the bus stopped about a hundred yards short of the villa. They trudged up the hill.

By the time they arrived they found everyone seated round the large oval dining-room table. Dad got up to greet them while everyone else stared at them in what Louise thought was an uncouth silence. When he had spoken to Stella, thanked her for coming and introduced his wife, Diana said, 'As you can see, there's really no room round the table so I thought you girls should have a picnic in the garden. If you go to the kitchen, Louise, Marie will tell you what to take.'

Without a word, Louise hooked her arm round Stella's and left the room. They went to the kitchen where Marie was dishing up a roast chicken. '*Ici votre déjeuner.*'

On a tray there was some cold ham, a baguette, a piece of Brie and some fruit. There was no wine, only a bottle of Pellegrino.

'*Bon appétit*,' Marie called, as Louise picked up the tray. They walked in the garden until they found some shade. Stella had been carrying the bottle to make the tray easier.

When they were settled Louise, humiliated and angry, managed to speak. 'I'm so sorry. So awfully sorry, and ashamed.' Tears came to her eyes. 'There's always been room for me round that bloody table, and they could easily have made room for one more.'

Stella handed her one of the paper napkins. 'Perhaps she doesn't like Jews.' She said it lightly, but there seemed a desolate wealth of experience behind the remark that made Louise feel worse.

'You're my best friend, and my father knows that, and you've wasted a whole day of your holiday to help them. I feel so ashamed. Your family have always been so kind to me.' There was a pause, and then, scarcely audibly, she said, 'I hate feeling ashamed of my father. Him being so weak and giving in to her all the time. I hate it. And I hate her.'

'Well, you can't change either of them. All you can do is accept them as they are, and don't let them hurt you.'

'Easier said than done.'

'Everything is like that.'

'Tell you what, I'm going to get us a bottle of wine. Marie is sure to have some in the kitchen.'

'Good thinking.'

How different families were, Stella thought, while Louise was away getting the wine. She frequently felt suffocated by her father's curiosity about her work as a political journalist while spasmodically berating her for not having read medicine at university. And the aunts and her mother went on and on about boyfriends and marriage. But at least in their exasperating way they cared. Poor Louise had to put up with a weak father, an embittered mother, and that predatory, hostile step-mother.

'There was a bottle of rosé in the fridge.' Louise plonked herself down so that they were facing each other. 'You should have started. I got two tomatoes as well.'

'Actually,' Stella said, as they began splitting the baguette, 'it's really nicer to have you to myself. This is a sight better than sitting in our baking little flat. London was a stew when I left.'

'I know. It's because all the windows face south, and there's not a tree anywhere.' She was chattering because she recognised Stella's tact and was afraid it might start her crying again.

'Have you heard from Joseph?'

'He hardly ever writes letters. It's funny to think he's just a few miles away.'

'Really? Where?'

'A place called Cap Ferrat.' A playground of the very rich, she thought. 'Of course, I can't write to him there – in London, I can write to his office. He spends six weeks

94

there with his family and lots of friends, and then he comes back all brown and guilty, and I try to be horrible to him about it but I never pull it off.'

'Well, I don't know about the guilty part, but you've certainly got the brown. You've gone a beautiful colour, my dear, but don't overdo it. You'd be surprised at the number of old lizards there are on the beaches round here. Trembling old things with dark, wrinkly skin the colour of conkers.'

They both examined their bodies. Louise was wearing an extremely short pair of shorts of a brilliant blue and a bikini top: the clothes showed off her golden-tanned frame – bony shoulders, a flat, concave belly, long slender legs and toenails painted the palest pink. She was certainly beautiful, Stella thought, with a pang of envy. Her own body was none of those things. It was as though someone had made and then compressed her, so that her neck was too short, her waist too near her breasts, her thighs and calves making for legs that could only be described as stumpy. And lying in the sun gave her a rash.

But her face made up for much of this: her wonderful hair, which was black and curled all over her head, her high cheekbones above which her grey-green eyes sparkled with curiosity and intelligence, and the mole that was set so well below her small but expressive mouth. She wore spectacles much of the time – couldn't read without them – but the moment she took them off she appeared much younger and more vulnerable. 'I sweat so much,' she said, as she became aware of Louise looking at her. 'Especially on my scalp.' She smiled apologetically.

The talk moved on to what they were reading. Louise

told her about Caterina Sforza, and Stella told her about the Florentine lady who had gone to France to marry the king and brought her cooks with her. 'It changed French cooking for ever.'

'How? By poisoning people?'

'No. Well, she may have poisoned the odd person, but what happened was she taught the French that sauces were meant to bring out the flavour of whatever they were eating, whereas before they'd simply used sauces to cover up the taste of rotting meat.'

'Are you reading about that, then? What an amazing—'

But Stella interrupted her: 'I read it somewhere ages ago. No, I'm on Bertrand Russell's *History of Western Philosophy*. My father was so incensed I hadn't read it that he sent a messenger to the flat with a copy. Louise, I think I'll have to go now. I must catch the train back in time for dinner. I'd better see your father to give him the money.'

So they piled up the tray and went back to the house. It was breathlessly hot, and the house was quiet as most of its occupants were having a siesta. Her father was snoozing in a chair in the salon. 'Sorry, darling. I must have dropped off.'

'Stella has brought you the money.' She stood unforgivingly before him – willing him to be Dad-without-Diana. He was.

'It's extremely kind of you to come all this way. I'm most awfully grateful to you. Do you know how much it is? So that I can write a cheque – if that's all right with your family?'

'It's the equivalent of five hundred pounds. And a

cheque should be made out to my father. He's Dr Nathan Rose.'

'Right.' He picked up his cheque book, which he had put in readiness on the table in front of him. 'Could I also have his address? I should like to write and thank him.'

'I've got his address, Dad. Stella's got to go now to catch her train back.'

'Well, at least let me drive you to the station.'

It was all right. He was being her charming, attractive father.

He put Stella in the front of the car and during the drive talked to her constantly, asking her about her holiday, inviting them both to dinner at his club in the autumn. At the station he walked with them both to the platform where the little train was already waiting. He shook hands with Stella, then leaned forward and kissed her cheek. 'You've saved my bacon. I can't begin to tell you how grateful I am. Please tell your family, won't you?'

'I will.'

She and Louise hugged. 'See you at Mon Débris.'

'Is that what you call your flat?' he asked, when they were back in the car.

'Yes. It does suit it rather.'

'Are you short of furniture and things like that?'

'Well, not really. We've got the basic stuff. Stella's father gave her things.'

'What could I give you?'

'Well . . .' She told him about their gas cooker, purchased for two pounds ten, but it had a hole in the oven door, and brown paper pasted over it didn't last. 'So we need to get a new one, a new second-hand one, I mean.'

'I'll see to that, darling.' He squeezed her hand.

Later, he said, 'Sorry about lunch. The thing is that Diana isn't herself. Change of life or something.'

'Oh.' Louise made a resolution that when she got it – which wouldn't be for years and years – she would be especially nice to everyone; it wouldn't be an excuse.

'How's your love life?' he asked, as they reached the villa.

'It's the same,' she said. 'It's fine.' But as she said it, she knew somehow that these two things were incompatible. 'He goes away for ages in summer, to the south of France, as a matter of fact, and he hardly ever writes letters. I feel a bit blue then.'

'Good thing you're with us,' he answered heartily. He hardly noticed anything, Louise thought.

'I'm afraid that being a mistress is much more difficult than having one,' he said. So he must have noticed some things, she realised.

Ten days later she was taken to the airport at Nice to fly home. 'Dumped' was her word for it. Diana simply didn't want a repeat of two nights in hotels with costly meals, and said there really wasn't enough room in the back for Susan, all their luggage *and* Louise. Her father gave her some money to buy scent at the airport, and she found her favourite, Bellodgia by Caron, and that made up for quite a lot.

On the plane she made a number of negative resolutions: never to have another holiday with Diana, never to go to dinner at their house, only to see Dad without her. They all seemed quite sensible, but they made her feel sad.

RACHEL AND SID

'Eileen wants to know if you would like lunch in the garden.'

'Would you?'

'If you would.'

'All right, whatever you say.'

She had been writing letters all that morning, all the week since the funeral, writing and often crying. So many people had written, she said, either saying what a lovely funeral it had been, or how sorry they were that they had not been able to come. She felt she must answer them all, but it had taken its toll, Sid thought, almost angrily. Her face was still pale and ravaged by grief and lack of sleep. Fresh air would be good for her, and after lunch she might be persuaded to rest. After tea, they might go for a walk. Sid was still feeling pretty ropey herself, but she'd finished the marvellous pills and was sure she was getting better. She must get better, if only to stop Rachel looking after her and worrying.

It was another beautiful day, the air full of lavender and bees and roses. The butterflies had come for the buddleia, which was only just starting. It could all be so idyllic if only . . .

Lunch was cold chicken and salad and raspberries, and each coaxed the other to eat well – to little avail. But Sid did manage to get a glass of sherry down Rachel, which had some effect. She longed to discuss their future, but Rachel was distracted, considering the desires of her brothers about Home Place, and much of their conversation was about that. Hugh definitely wanted them to keep the house, and Rupert had finally decided that he did as well. Edward was clear that he didn't, and there had been talk about his simply passing his share to the rest of them. Rachel had been left a little money by her mother that had come to her on her marriage and been safely and dully invested in Cazalets' to provide an income of four hundred a year. Otherwise, she had been left a large number of shares in the firm, which also produced an income. The Brig had left furniture and effects to the Duchy for her lifetime, thereafter to be divided into four parts for each child. Rachel seemed to have no idea how much money she had, and clearly did not care. Sid, on the other hand, owned the lease on her little house in St John's Wood, and had a small pension from the school where she had taught all her life.

There was no comparison. They had been through so much, and apart when they had wanted to be together, that it seemed only fair that now they should subside into tranquillity, a safe harbour of some kind where there need be no deceit, no charade about aching desire professing mere affection. Although, in their case, affection was the breath of love. It was affection that had enabled Sid to be patient, to be gentle, to treasure those first faltering assurances that Rachel had felt able to give: 'I'd rather be with you than anyone in the world', said in a tea shop in Hastings on one of the few occasions when she had lured Rachel from family duties. But that had been either before the war or when it had just begun, and there had been years after that of longing and frustration, during which she had been unfaithful with that needy girl Thelma. She and Rachel had been brought up so differently: Rachel to believe in her duties as a daughter, an unmarried aunt, to think nothing of herself, never for one moment to consider herself interesting, or attractive, her opinions – when she had any – meshing completely with what she felt was expected of her, on and on like that; it had been pathetic and sometimes irritating. Sid had been brought up virtually as head of her small family: a father dead when she was still a child, a mother wanting all the time to be told what to do, and a younger sister envious of her talent as a musician, and heartless with their mother. Money had always been short; she had always had to supplement her mother's pension, to try to find her sister jobs, to live with her and deal with her day-to-day jealousies. It was because of all this that Sid had had to renounce playing in an orchestra for a regular job teaching in a girls' school, supplemented by private lessons. All this had lent authority of a certain kind so she had taken to wearing mannish versions of women's clothes: the tweed skirts, the thick woollen stockings, the shirt with a tie, hair cut as short as a man's.

Her face, which had never known any emollient, had settled to a weatherbeaten uniformity: she looked as though she had spent much of her life in a high wind, or at sea. Only her lively pale brown eyes had never changed, and when she smiled, she charmed.

'It would be so sad for the children if we gave up the house.' This was the kind of thing Rachel said when she wanted to stop talking about it.

They had finished lunch, and Sid had lit their cigarettes with the pretty tortoiseshell lighter that Rachel had given her for her last birthday. 'You know what I'd like, darling.'

Rachel had been lying back in her basket chair, but now sat up. 'What?'

'I'd like to take you away somewhere for a quiet holiday. The Lake District, or anywhere you would like to go.' Then she added, with some cunning, 'I feel the need for something of the sort. To throw off this bug for good and all.'

She saw that this was having some effect. A flurry of little frowns puckered Rachel's face; she bit her lip and looked at her anxiously. 'How awful! Of course we must have a holiday – you need one. It really is bad to have a reputation for thinking of others and then not doing anything about it.' She actually nearly smiled as she said that. 'Where would you like to go, my darling?'

Sid wanted to get up and throw her arms round Rachel, but at that moment Eileen appeared with the trolley to remove the lunch.

'That was delicious,' Rachel said. 'Will you tell Mrs Tonbridge?' And Eileen said that she would. 'I ought to find out when the children want to come before we make any plans.'

Oh, Lord! Sid thought. If I'm not careful she'll say she can't go because of the family. 'They always come with parents,' she said carefully, 'and they know the whole place inside and out. I'm sure you could leave it to them to sort things out.'

'Well, I'll have to ask them.'

'Of course you will. And now, my dearest, it's time for you to have a snooze. Do you want it out here, or do you want to go to bed?'

'I think out here.'

When Sid had fetched the rug and tucked her up, Rachel said, 'We need to pick the sweet peas. You haven't forgotten?' Every evening, since her mother's burial, Rachel had picked a fresh bunch of the Duchy's favourite flowers and taken them to her grave.

'Of course I haven't. We'll pick them after tea and I'll come with you.' She stooped to kiss Rachel's forehead. 'I'm for my bed. I'll wake you at teatime.'

∞ ∞ ∞

I'm almost back to square one, Sid thought sadly. She had spent one night in bed with Rachel during the last week, and Rachel had clung to her and wept and sobbed in her arms, until, eventually, she had cried herself out and fallen asleep. Physical contact of any other kind had been clearly out of the question.

When we go away, she thought, if we go away, things will get back to how they were before. It is simply a question of patience and love. Although why either of those things should be regarded as simple was not clear to her at all.

POLLY AND GERALD

'If we sold another picture, we could.'

'We can't keep selling pictures.' His newly filled pipe had gone out, and he examined it despondently.

'We don't keep selling them. We've only sold six, one for each of the children and three to make our bit of the house comfortable. You wanted to give each of the children the proceeds of a Turner, and we needed to make the house OK to live in. But none of that means any income. If we did up one or two of the big reception rooms, we could do weddings and birthday parties.'

He muttered something about not wanting people tramping all over the house, and she simply looked at him and started laughing, so he laughed as well.

'Oh, Poll! How do you put up with me? Of course they wouldn't be tramping, and it wouldn't be all over the house. But do you honestly think that people would want to have their wedding party here?'

'Yes. Most people hire somewhere for that. I've made a rough plan of what we'd need to do.'

'You have? You've thought it all out. Darling, you are a marvel. How do you manage it?'

'Well, with Nan hounding me to put my feet up every day, it was something to do.'

She was lying on the yellow sofa, wearing her peacock-blue kaftan with her small white bare feet crossed at the ankles. It was evening and the room was suffused with violet shadowy light, excepting the lamp at her end of the sofa, which illuminated her hair. She looked, he thought, like a charming French painting.

'I'll just read you what I thought and you say what you think. We could use the big drawing room and the old library that leads off it for receptions. The old morning room could be turned into a kitchen or at least somewhere for the caterers to put their stuff. The dining room could have all the food and drink in it. We'd have to put some lavatories in, but if we do them on the north side, that fits with the plumbing. The guests could come in through the old front door. That's about it, really, but of course we'd have to get Mr Cossey to come and see what it would cost. What do you think?'

Of course he thought it was an amazing idea, but he still wasn't sure how many people would actually want to hire the place and what he and Polly might charge. Also, what about a car park, and facilities for the bride to change before going away?

They could park in the forecourt, she said, but he was quite right about having a place for the bride to change. 'We might be able to use that funny little room where Nan gave us our first lunch.'

'Supposing by a staggering chance that it's not raining or icy cold, won't they want to have drinks, et cetera, outside?'

'Oh dear, of course they would. But the garden's a wreck on that side of the house. We'd have to sort all that.' She sighed, then yawned.

'It's time for bed,' he said. 'I'm going to put a cloth on the parrot's cage.' He had once called her pretty Polly and she had said she certainly wasn't a parrot any more than he was a frog.

He helped her off the sofa and they went upstairs holding hands.

'I warn you, I'm getting fatter by the day.'

'Of course you are. We want a full-grown baby . . .'

Later, when they were lying side by side, he murmured, 'The parrot and the frog. It sounds like some ghastly craft shop kept by amateurs. Or a horribly twee story for kiddiwinks.'

'But it's all right for us – so long as it's private.'

'It is,' he said. 'All the best things about us are private.' He put his hand on her neck and turned her to face him. 'I've just thought of another private thing. How would you feel about that?'

'Happy to oblige.'

But when he had finished kissing her, he said, 'No – not tonight, Josephine. You're whacked. You needn't be so accommodating, sweetheart. I love you quite enough to be happy simply to have middle mornings with you.'

'Oh, I do hope not. After a month or two of that, I should begin to feel rather left out.'

'Spoons?'

'Spoons.'

She turned on her side away from him and he put an arm round her. They went to sleep holding hands.

HUGH AND JEMIMA

'She's agreed to divorce him. Apparently, she agreed over a year ago, and it's reached the decree absolute. And he's said nothing about it.'

'I suppose he just thought that you would try to argue him out of it. After all, Polly said that she's had two of his children. You can't really blame her for wanting to be married to their father.'

They were having supper on the small terrace outside the basement kitchen. Jemima's boys, Henry and Tom, were playing Monopoly in the drawing room, and Laura had been put to bed. An afternoon at the Round Pond in Kensington Gardens 'helping' Tom and Henry sail their boats had over-tired her, and she had cried at tea owing to an absence of Marmite sandwiches. But Marmite, to Jemima, smacked too much of the years of rationing, and she always tried to make the children's teas more varied and nourishing. The boys ate everything and always wanted more, like happy dogs, she thought, but Laura liked things to stay as they had always been, with the disastrous exception of the Kit-E-Kat: Laura adored Riley, the cat that Hugh had bought her, and was found trying to feed him and eating all the bits he scorned.

'I really love his food,' she had said, licking her greasy fingers, which she then wiped on her spattered frock.

'How did you stop her?' Hugh had said, laughing. Everything his daughter did amused and delighted him.

'I told her that it was very unkind to Riley. I said he had to have special food because of his fur. She stopped after that but, as usual, she had the last word.'

'Which was?'

'Oh, that she wouldn't at all mind growing fur all over her body and then she wouldn't have to wear clothes.'

'She'd make a wonderful cat.'

'I told her you would be miserable if she turned into one.'

Why are we having a light-hearted conversation? Jemima thought, as she removed the plates of fish and salad and fetched the raspberries. I know his head is bad, and he's awfully upset about Edward and worried about Simon not wanting to be in the firm – not seeming to want anything – and, of course, and probably worst of all, his mother dying. For a moment she thought of the funeral – the church full of flowers, and practically all the family, and Myra Hess coming, quite unexpectedly, to play 'Jesu Joy of Man's Desiring' on the awful little upright piano. That was almost the best part; all the Duchy's children had been so touched and delighted.

Afterwards, they'd all gone back to Home Place where Mrs Tonbridge had made a wonderful spread before attending the service, and an atmosphere of wary jollity had been upheld. All three brothers had made little eulogies in the church. It had been a good send-off. The smaller grandchildren had been left at Home Place – in Polly's case, at home with her husband. But Teddy and Simon, Louise, Clary and Archie, with Harriet and Bertie, who had had many happy holidays thanks to the Duchy, Zoë with Juliet, Lydia, who had managed a day off from

108

her repertory company, had all come. Only Roland had been absent, as Villy had refused her invitation on the grounds that she didn't want to see Edward, and she wouldn't let Roland go without her. Really, Jemima now considered, she had been afraid of meeting Diana, who had mercifully stayed away.

It was odd, she thought, how being content – no, happy – with her own life (Hugh was the most caring and loving husband anyone could have) made her anxious about everyone else. No, that wasn't – as most things are not – entirely true: her boys (her twins) had accepted the new situation with astonishing ease, no jealousy of their new stepfather, no discomfort about no longer being the centre of her life. They had relished having a father, in fact, and he had been a very good one. They had also been resigned to Laura, first a boring baby and chronically a girl. 'I suppose, Mum, there's no hope that she might change – you know, grow into being a boy?' But, disabused of this idea, they had settled down to her being endlessly rotten at catching a ball, having to be read the same soppy stories again and again, and not really understanding the rules of Monopoly or Racing Demon. They were certainly helped in this by her total, uncritical admiration for everything they did.

No, it was Simon she worried about. He was thirty now, but in many ways he seemed older than that. He had always been withdrawn, silent most of the time, an onlooker. He seemed not to have made any friends at either of the schools Hugh had sent him to or after he had left, and his dutiful letters home told them nothing. Apparently his school reports had been blandly noncommittal, excepting for his music master, who said that he had a talent to which he should pay more attention.

Recently he had expressed a wish to stay with Polly – the only person, she had noticed, at the funeral to whom he seemed visibly attached. So that had been arranged and he had stayed almost a month with her.

Then he had asked if he might spend a week at Home Place, and Rachel had said of course he could. 'After all, it has been his home for most of his life,' she'd added. But he must have heard talk of the house being given up now and Jemima guessed that this must disturb him.

She wouldn't talk to Hugh about it this evening: it would only upset him even more. But when she had finally assembled the tray with the fruit and the cheese, Hugh said that he was getting bitten by midges or something, could they finish the meal indoors?

He helped her as much as he could, clearing the supper table (it was astonishing what he could do with one hand), and they settled in the kitchen in a peaceable silence, broken by his suddenly asking whether she wanted another baby. At the same moment she became aware of the twins standing on the bottom step of the basement stairs.

'We came down very quietly so as not to frighten you,' Tom said, not meaning it at all.

'It's time you were in bed.'

'We know that. The thing is we don't think we'll sleep much as we're so hungry.' Henry smiled engagingly.

'You had an enormous supper.'

'We had a perfectly ordinary supper ages ago. You shouldn't exaggerate, Mum. Anyhow, now we're both starving.'

'It was only fish pie, and we don't count fish much as food.'

'And raspberries and cream are jolly nice, but you can't count fruit as real food either.'

110

'What would be real?' Hugh had lit a cigarette, and the question was asked in a friendly non-combative manner.

'Well, what we'd like now—'

'Need now,' his brother interrupted, 'would be something like bacon and eggs.'

'Or a smelly cheese sandwich, which would be less trouble.' Tom had spotted the Brie on the table.

'We could make it ourselves, Mum.'

Hugh looked at Jemima, who shrugged. 'OK. You win. Only bring me the bread and the bread board. You always make a mess of the loaf.'

While the sandwiches were being made, Henry said, 'You know, we actually need these because we're growing so much. You need more food when you're doing that.'

This was true. They already topped her by a head.

'If we feed you like this, about six meals a day,' Hugh said, 'you'll end up being nine feet tall.'

This delighted them. 'We could be in a circus as the tallest people in England.'

'The world, probably.'

Practically all conversations were carried out with both of them at once.

'Now take your food upstairs to your room, and don't wake Laura.'

'Wake Laura? You must be mad, Mum. We don't want to start hearing about her soppy bear. Of course we won't wake her.'

'It's good she goes to bed earlier than we do: it gives us a bit of grown-up time without her spoiling it.'

Perfunctory hugs and they were gone.

'Peace,' she said. Hugh stretched out his good hand

across the table. 'You have such exceptionally nice children, I just thought you might want more of them.'

'Do you?'

'I want what you want.'

'Oh, but past that!' He had such kind eyes that it was difficult to find the true person behind them. 'I mean, are you secretly wishing for them, or longing for me to feel the same? You remember we had a pact not to conceal things from each other? Well, I feel that you're beginning to do that. I want to know what you think, not what you think I want you to think.'

There was what seemed to Jemima a very long silence. He had withdrawn his hand, rubbing it now across his head, and seeing this, she said, 'Darling Hugh, let's talk about it tomorrow.'

'No. I wasn't concealing anything from you. The truth is that I don't know. Of course if we had another I would love it. But I'm not sure I could bear you going through all that again. When you had Laura, my chief fear was that I might lose you.'

There was another silence during which they both remembered the prolonged and agonising labour into which she had gone so lightly. 'I had the twins quite easily, darling, and we know there's only one this time,' she had said. She knew that Sybil had lost Wills' twin and that it had left an enduring mark. But hours had passed, and he had had to watch her strength and courage ebbing away . . .

Twenty-four hours later, Laura had joined them, bloodied, crying – and perfect. But it had been an ordeal for both of them. Custom had changed. He had not witnessed Sybil's labour, but with Jemima he had been present throughout. During those hours he had been beset by the nightmare of her not surviving, of possibly being left with a new-born baby, and her own children orphaned. When they were alone, while the baby was being bathed, he had held her hand with a small rocking movement. Though he was smiling, tears had streamed from his eyes – the relief had overwhelmed him.

'I think,' he said now, with difficulty, 'that I'm content to stay as we are. But only if you feel the same. Laura has enough cousins. She doesn't need a sibling. There.'

'There,' she repeated. She got up from the table and began to clear it of food. 'Better get on with this before they come down wanting another giant snack. You're so sweet to them, Hugh. They're nearly as lucky to have you as I am. No, you go on up, this won't take me a minute.'

'What does "there" mean?'

'It means I agree with you.'

'I thought it did. Just wanted to make sure.'

SIMON, POLLY
AND GERALD

He'd got through absolutely awful homesickness at his prep school, but when he'd had to go on to Radley, his public school, it had started all over again. One got used to muffled sobbing in the dorms at night but, except for the inevitable bullying, nobody said anything. It wouldn't have been good form – a mysterious state that seemed to involve a whole lot of things one didn't do or say. At home (Home Place) he had early learned that his mother dying had upset his father, and Polly and Wills – but how could *Wills* be upset – he couldn't remember her at all. Funnily enough, though, he'd told Simon he did remember feeling hopelessly sad – and you couldn't talk to anyone about that because they would simply think you were odd. The one great thing Simon had learned from his schools was never to stand out. Be as much like everyone else as you possibly could. Now he wondered whether that applied to the rest of life, too. Because trying to be like everyone else was not only tiring but dull. He had noticed recently that he was bored nearly all the time. Dad and Jemima were quite kind – well, very kind, really – considering he was an outsider: the twins had their own life and Laura was just a small girl. The house in Ladbroke Grove had never been much like home, not like Home Place.

The only house Simon liked to be in was Fakenham Hall because it had Polly in it. He loved her more than anyone else, and because of her, he had even felt quite good about Gerald, who had never asked him those awful stock questions like was he at university, and what did he want to be after that.

He had spent a month with them: Neville didn't need him and they were not going away anywhere because Polly had started another baby. They had decided to spruce up part of their huge, rambling garden, which meant rooting up a whole lot of half-dead shrubs and burning them. They hadn't asked him to help, but he did, and found that he enjoyed it. When the weather was bad, he played the old Broadwood piano that lived in one of the unused rooms. It had a satinwood case and was badly out of tune, but he could play it without anyone being there. Polly got a piano tuner to come and tune it for him, and he had secretly started to compose a piano sonata, which he was going to dedicate to her when he had finished it. But mostly it was a hot, sunny August and he had found that he no longer wanted to stay in bed in the mornings because he wouldn't know what on earth to do if he got up. Gerald had a book on gardening and together they started to take cuttings from the worn-out parterre of box, and then – more wildly – of various other shrubs. In between they had picnic lunches made by Polly and their old Nan – lovely food, cold sausage sandwiches and apple turnovers and figs and grapes from the crumbling greenhouses, with cider, and lemonade made by Polly. The children joined them for this, and once, afterwards, Eliza and Jane had insisted that they should all go and watch them practising for the gymkhana, their first.

And Andrew had cried because he hadn't got his own pony. 'But it would be no good, Andrew,' Jane said, and Eliza chimed in, 'There simply isn't a pony small enough for you to ride.'

And Gerald had immediately said, 'I'm a very small pony, you can ride me.' He had cantered about the field with Andrew on his back – done the bending poles and even attempted one of the small jumps. By then he was the colour of a tomato and completely out of breath, and Andrew was laughing in triumph, and begged to do it again, but Polly had said that was enough, and that Gerald was closed until well after tea.

'Closed? Like a shop, do you mean?'

'Just like one.'

'I don't think people close like shops, Mummy.'

She was sitting with her back against the shady oak, and Gerald had cast himself on the ground beside her. On inspiration, Simon had got his pen and written 'CLOSED' on a paper napkin and laid it on Gerald's chest.

'We can't read that word,' Jane said. 'We only read short words.'

'It says "Closed", and you could read it if you tried.'

'I can read it,' Andrew said. 'It says "Closed". I can read any word if I want to.'

In the end Simon offered to take the girls to unsaddle their fat, sweating ponies and turn them out into their paddock, and Andrew insisted on going with him. This earned him grateful smiles from the parents. 'I think we'll all knock off until five,' Gerald had said. 'It'll be cooler then.'

He had no sooner helped the little girls divest Buttercup and Bluebell of their saddles and opened the gate to the paddock, when Nan appeared, saying it was high time for the children's nap. There was a token clamour about this, the twins saying that Andrew should go first – 'He ought to have a longer rest than us.'

'You get those bridles off quick and come into the house. I'm not standing for any more of that palaver again. You'll do as you're told.' She watched while the tack was slipped off and the ponies trotted out of reach into the paddock. Then they all followed her meekly to the kitchen door – Andrew, whom he had prised off the paddock gate, firmly held by her hand. 'You can tell her ladyship that I've got them, and she should go and put her feet up.'

He said he would, but when he got back to them they were lying, hand in hand, asleep. He wanted to clear up the picnic, to start another bonfire, to root out another barrowload of weeds – he wanted, in fact, to astound them with his usefulness, to become someone they couldn't do without, so that he could stay there for ever . . .

Simon realised, then, that he wasn't – hadn't been – bored for weeks. He loved the gardening work but, above all, he loved being treated as an equal by Poll and Gerald. They had discussed their plans for turning the ugly old house into a place for weddings and other events with him, asking him what he thought, and thanking him if he had the smallest idea for their project. They treated him as a grown-up member of their family. Which, in a way, he was. And if they were really going to let parts of the house out for parties, there would surely be a lot of jobs that he could do. He decided to have a serious talk with Poll about it, and meanwhile he would try to get on with his piece of music. He thought then, suddenly, of the

Duchy. She would have been interested in his music, although – naturally – she would have noticed that he was nowhere near as good as the Three Bs, as she called them. This had made him wonder whether you could only get really good at something if you did it to the exclusion of anything else. That knocked out his becoming a composer because he certainly didn't want to spend his whole life glued to a piano and struggling with his awful hand on manuscript paper. Yes, he certainly must have a good talk with Poll, and see what she thought. Without Gerald there, though, he added to himself: he could only talk about something so serious as his whole future with one person at a time.

EDWARD AND DIANA

She had certainly pulled all the stops out. Once they were back from France, she had got in touch with a whole clutch of agents, and stuff about houses had poured through the letterbox every morning. He had only stipulated that the place must be within reasonable distance from London as he was going to have to commute.

Hugh had suggested that he go to Southampton to run the wharf there, but he suspected that this was simply Hugh trying to get him out of the way to avoid the ceaseless arguments about capital, income and, of course, the bank. The worsening relationship with his brother, to whom he had always been so close, cut him to the heart. He knew that Diana came into this: Hugh maintained (in Edward's view) a totally unreasoning prejudice. He had made no effort with her at all, refused – with transparent excuses – to dine with them, and never invited them to Ladbroke Grove. Bang went their quiet evenings of chess or bridge. They met occasionally for lunch at one of their clubs, but chiefly in the office, where constant interruptions seemed to mean that they went over the old ground again and again, without ever venturing beyond it. Supposing the bank ceased to wear their steadily increasing overdraft (him); what a dangerous difference it would make to their books if Southampton was to go (Hugh), and if they were to hang on

to Southampton, who should be put in to run it? He was
of the opinion that McIver was the best candidate: he'd
been with them for thirty years now – hadn't been called
up due to poor eyesight – and worked his way up from
office boy in Great Uncle Walter's time to managing one
of the London sawmills. But Hugh had insisted that the
place must be run by a Cazalet. Which would mean
Rupert, who, bless his heart, was not cut out for running
anything, or Teddy, who, though promising, was not
really experienced enough.

'We're nearly there, darling. Slow down a bit, it's a
very small turning.'

With a jolt, with relief, he was back in the present –
always his best place. They were going to look at a house
just outside Hawkhurst, and Diana had the agent's
instructions on her lap.

'Now! This is it. There it is!'

It stood on a small eminence above them, a rectangu-
lar stone house with a slate roof, and a portico with two
stone pillars each side of the front door. It was in what
might once have been its small park, but was now let to
farmers for grazing. He stopped the car for a moment so
that they could look at it from afar. A plain house that
had a kind of mini-grandeur about it that he knew she
would love.

'It looks marvellous. I can't wait to see inside.'

She had been very excited ever since she had been
sent the particulars, and this had made her more affectionate to him than she had been since before they'd gone
to France. He squeezed her knee. 'Off we go, then.'

It was a balmy September morning – the trees turning
but still well leafed. They pulled into a narrow drive that

had an open gate marked 'Park House'. Mr Armitage, the agent, was already there, his bicycle propped against the porch. He was happy to show them round, he said, but most clients liked a first viewing on their own. Just give him a shout if they wanted him. He unlocked the front door and went to sit on the shallow stone steps that led up to it.

'He looks as though he's got a hell of a hangover,' Edward said, and Diana answered, 'He probably hates working on Saturday mornings.'

The house was empty, which Diana said she liked. The wallpaper was marked where pictures had hung, soot had fallen in the grates of the pretty fireplaces and paint had blistered on the shutters; there were a large number of prosperous spiders' webs everywhere, the bathrooms both had green stains from dripping taps and the kitchen showed signs of mice. They saw it all: the bedrooms that were graded from the front of the house – grand then gradually becoming more and more spartan as they reached the back – the drawing room that had a double aspect, its large bow window looking out onto a walled garden, the dining room, with its serving hatch to the kitchen, the stone-floored larder, with its marble slabs and ancient flypapers studded with bluebottles, the ice-cold scullery and store room, and, at the very back, a dank little lavatory for servants.

'Oh, darling! It's perfect! Don't you think so? And a walled garden. All my life I've yearned for one.' She turned to him, her lovely hyacinth eyes glowing with excitement and pleasure.

'If you're sure you want it, darling.'

'Oh, I do. And you do too, don't you?'

'Of course I do. And if you want it, it's yours.'

She flung her arms round his neck. 'Our house! Our first real house.' She kissed him, and all his earliest feelings for her returned. He'd got the old Diana back.

PART FOUR

DECEMBER 1956–JANUARY 1957

HOME PLACE

' "O Pears" indeed! I can't think for the life of me why they call them that. More trouble than they're worth if you ask me.'

The trouble was, Tonbridge thought, that nobody was asking her. If you asked Mabel for anything, she would give it to you, whether it was a rock cake or a piece of advice – her mind, she called the latter. He wondered whether he might be so bold as to bring up the subject with Miss Rachel, and decided that he would have to wait until the right occasion presented itself. Which meant, he secretly knew, that nothing would induce him to bring it up at all.

He did his best to help. This morning, he had brought in the wood for the fires – the small ration of coal had gone by Boxing Day, if not the coke for the kitchen range. He had gone to Battle to fetch the meat and groceries, brought in the potatoes and onions that McAlpine had dug up, and fetched Miss Sidney's prescription from the chemist. Then it was time for a break before the family's lunch, which had been laid by Eileen – the dining room for the grown-ups, and the hall for the children and O Pears, two foreign girls, who had washed up breakfast, breaking two cups and a jug, and were now rather sulkily making the beds. It was Miss Rachel who had hired them; and she said it had been explained to them that they were required to lend a hand to anything that was needed. But they had to have a lot of time off, to learn English, and they seemed to spend most of that washing their hair, painting their nails and complaining of being cold.

The house was overflowing. In the old days one family, at least, would have been in Manor Farm, the place down the road, but it had been let. He counted them now. Mr and Mrs Hugh, with her two boys, the little girl and, of course, young Mr William. Mr and Mrs Rupert with Miss Juliet and the little boy with that rat. Mr Lestrange and Miss Clary, with their two children. And, of course, Miss Rachel and her friend Miss Sidney. It was a good thing that Mr Edward and the new Mrs Edward were staying in their own house with their lot, and Lady Fakenham likewise. Well, there simply wasn't room for them, although Mr Edward had brought some of the family over for Boxing Day tea. Mabel was a wonder, the way she went on producing meals for everyone, but her feet were something awful in the evenings now. He had to admit that the ladies all helped, though. Not like the old days. You'd never have caught Mrs Senior or Miss Rachel with a Hoover. Then there had been a proper staff, and ladies had simply sewed or gone for walks, played tennis and had afternoon rests – except for Mrs Senior, who couldn't keep out of the garden.

Better get going. He swallowed the last piece of cheese tart, brushed the crumbs off his trousers, and passed some wind before leaving the snug little room adjoining the kitchen that had always been Mabel's (many a nervous snack he'd had there, with him explaining the state of the world about which she, being a woman, knew very little . . .).

In the kitchen he found Mr Rupert's little boy asking what was for lunch.

Macaroni cheese and treacle sponge, she told him. She was beating up the sponge mixture in an enormous bowl.

'Oh, good! I love treacle sponge. The thing is,' he had climbed onto a kitchen chair next to her, 'I wonder if it would be all right for me to have a bit of cheese without the macaroni? Just a small bit?' He was stroking her arm. 'It's not for me. I love macaroni cheese – it's for Rivers.'

'And who is he when he's at home?'

'He's my friend. Actually, he's a rat, but he's not like most rats.'

'Don't you dare bring him into my kitchen.'

'I won't.' He quietly thrust his hand down into the deep pocket inside which Rivers usually travelled and kept it there. 'Just a small bit, and he doesn't mind rind.'

He had got one knee on the table, and was holding her arm and looking up into her face. It was too much for her. She put down her spoon and went to the larder. While she was getting the cheese, he put his finger into the mixing bowl and scraped out a finger-load, which he quickly ate. It was delicious, almost nicer than when it was cooked.

She came back with a generous piece of Cheddar. 'Now be off with you, and don't you dare bring that creature anywhere near me.'

'I promise. Thank you very much.' He scrambled off the table and was gone.

'Young monkey. The spitting image of Mr Rupert,' she added, to excuse her softness with him.

'You'd give anyone anything,' he said fondly, which provoked her.

'There are some things I can't abide, and one of them

is you standing over me when I'm working.' A huge kirby-grip fell into the bowl. 'Drat it! Now look what you've made me do!'

Injustice on this level was a serious warning sign. 'I'm off to clean the car,' he said, trying to sound offhand.

She sniffed. 'You and your cars,' she said. 'Just don't be late for your dinner. I don't want to send one of them O Pears to get you.' She had early ascertained that they posed no threat: he didn't like women with no flesh on their bones.

THE FAMILY

Christmas had been a success, although it had begun with the smaller children in tears because they had woken much earlier than seven, which was the hour when they were permitted to open their stockings. This was worst in the large room called the linen cupboard room because it had an airing cupboard, faintly heated by the kitchen range, although beds were observed steaming on the rare occasions when a hot-water bottle was put into them. This room now contained the twins, Henry and Tom, in sleeping-bags on the floor, Harriet and Bertie – Clary's two – Georgie, and, after much wrangling, Laura, on the understanding that it was for Christmas Eve only. She was told to do everything that Tom or Henry told her and, awed by having actually got her way, she solemnly agreed. The moment all the parents had left, Henry pulled his Monopoly board out from under the bed, switched on his and Tom's torches and they started playing. No, the others couldn't join in: there weren't enough torches and, anyway, they were in the middle of a game. Laura started sobbing, but they threatened her with shouting for Jemima and her being returned to her bed in the parents' room. Georgie was preoccupied with getting Rivers out of the cage and into his bed, but poor Harriet felt dreadfully left out. 'I am eight,' she kept saying, 'and I'm perfectly able to play that game.' Eventually she felt so tired

129

with sadness that she pulled the bedclothes over her head and went to sleep.

Downstairs they were all dying to go to bed. Rachel had already gone up, followed by Sid. They had spent most of the day decorating the large tree. Long ago, the Brig had decreed that the tree should be live, and the Duchy that there should be real candles, 'none of that vulgar nonsense with electric lights'. Zoë had carefully arranged presents around it, and the stockings – the long, thick ones used by the men for shooting and golf – were piled on one of the sofas, including a very small sock that she said was for Rivers. 'Georgie specially asked,' she said, blushing slightly. She was dotty about her son but didn't want anyone to think she was. Rupert put his arm round her, and Archie said jolly good idea. It was decided that everyone should help in carting the stockings upstairs, but only two people were needed to put them at the ends of beds.

Clary had gone to sleep on the sofa. When Archie woke her, she said how much nicer it was being a child than a grown-up. 'I used to lie in bed with my eyes tightly shut pretending to be asleep while you or Dad creaked about with my stocking.'

'I bet you opened them the minute my back was turned.'

'Certainly not! We were on our honour not to. So the only person who did was Neville. He said that when he promised his fingers were crossed so it didn't count. He slithered out of everything.'

'Bed,' said Archie, so firmly that everyone got to their feet and picked up their share of stockings.

'As the drawing room is out of bounds until after lunch, we'd better lock up.' Hugh turned the key and gave it to Jemima.

'I'll do the big nursery,' Zoë whispered. She wanted to make sure that Rivers's sock was in a prominent position.

Jemima did her boys and Rupert did Juliet and Louise, and that, for the night, was that.

∞ ∞ ∞

It was a short night for Jemima, because Laura was crying and had woken all the others.

'She wants her stocking, but she can't have it for another fifty-nine minutes. We've put it in the cupboard where she can't get at it, and I'm timing her for seven, Mum.' Henry and Tom were maddeningly self-righteous.

'It won't ever never be seven.' Laura wept.

'And now she's woken up when I was having a nice good sleep,' cried seven-year-old Bertie – only a year older than poor Laura.

'How about you come to Mummy and Daddy's room and have your stocking there?'

But this was no good at all. 'I want my stocking with the grown-up children.'

'Well, actually,' Henry said, as kindly as he could, 'we don't really want you here at all.'

This upset Harriet. 'But you're her brothers! You can't—'

'Yes, of course we're her brothers. But she's very, very small. When she's older, we'll take her to the zoo and nightclubs—'

Laura had stopped crying. 'What are nightclubs?'

'Clubs that go on at night, of course, stupid.'

'Don't call your sister stupid.'

'But, Mum, she is S-T-U-P-I-D.'

'Anyway, it's forty-nine minutes now.'

'Well, Laura, you have the choice of coming with me or staying and not crying any more. I strongly advise you come with me.'

'I strongly advise no.'

'All right. Boys, you behave yourselves.'

The silence after she had gone was momentary, and then the twins collapsed in fits of laughter. 'Behave ourselves. We can't behave other people. Honestly!'

Georgie, who had remained silent during the fracas, now beckoned silently to Laura to get into his bed. He had piled up his daytime clothes under the eiderdown to make a tent. The tent housed Rivers, who was busy unwrapping a very small parcel that he knew was cheese. His Christmas sock lay beside him. Georgie, whose kind heart extended well beyond rats, knew that watching Rivers having a lovely time would cheer Laura up and it did. By the time Rivers had explored – and in many cases eaten -- the contents of the sock, cleaned his whiskers and paws and finally gone to sleep in his favourite position round Georgie's neck, Henry and Tom had announced that it was seven o'clock.

Everybody scrambled for their stockings, but Laura wanted to have hers in bed with Georgie. 'Just this once,' he said. He didn't want to be stuck with her the whole day. The presents were received with whoops of joy, but there were one or two disappointments. 'A clockwork frog,' Georgie exclaimed in disgust. 'Surely they must have known I meant a real one!'

∞ ∞ ∞

'I'm really too old for this sort of thing.' Juliet was sitting upright in bed, trying to look bored at the prospect of a stocking.

'Are you? Well, I love them. Haven't had one for ages.' Louise was also sitting up and pulled her stocking towards her. She was wearing a white nightdress trimmed with blue chiffon. She looked like a film star, Juliet thought, with her long, golden hair streaming over her shoulders.

Juliet, who had insisted on pyjamas because her best friend wore them, now wished she had opted for a nightdress, too. But even that wouldn't have changed her hair from reddish brown to golden. Her breasts, she could see, were larger than Louise's: she wondered whether they were too large.

Louise was well into her stocking: tablets of Morny soap, a pretty silk scarf, a red leather pocket diary, a clutch of coloured linen handkerchiefs, a Mason Pearson hairbrush and a tube of hand cream had so far come to light.

'Come on, Jules. If you don't open your stocking, I will.'

Enough of adult indifference. She had been waiting to be told and, actually, she was longing to start. The beginning was not promising. 'Pond's Cold Cream! A pot of vanishing cream! And a tablet of boring old soap. Honestly! I'm not a baby!'

'You're bound to get some duds. I sort mine into two piles – good and no good.'

Things got better. A long, narrow box filled with neatly coiled silk-velvet hair ribbons in lovely unusual colours. A marcasite brooch in the shape of a butterfly.

'Aunt Zoë's got very good taste,' Louise said. 'Which is more than can be said of my mother.'

'Has she got bad taste?' Juliet was interested: she was not at all sure what bad taste actually was.

'She hasn't got any taste at all. You know, cream paint everywhere and wood-veneer pictures on the wall – that sort of thing.' She was remembering Lansdowne Road. She hadn't minded any of that at the time, but there had been other things . . . 'Awful clothes. She used to make me wear bottle-green silk when I was eight and everyone else had pink and blue taffeta. And bronze stockings.'

'Goodness! Poor you.' She was longing to ask Louise all sorts of questions about her life, which, from what she had been told, was both tragic and exciting. She had been married (she remembered that); she had had a baby that lived with its father and stepmother. She had been divorced and now lived in a rackety flat with her best friend. She was a clothes model, which, next to being a film star, was the height of glamour – Juliet had boasted about it at school. Sharing a room with her was simply wonderful, but she had been told not to bother her with questions so she tried not to ask too many. 'What shall we do with the no-good piles?'

'Wrap them up and give them to the au pair girls. And perhaps the soaps to Mrs Tonbridge and Eileen.'

'That's a wizard idea.'

They dressed, and Louise very kindly tied back Juliet's hair with one of her Christmas velvet ribbons.

NEVILLE AND SIMON

Neville had very nearly not gone down to Sussex at all. Having escaped Christmas Day on the grounds of work, he could easily have said that he had to work on Boxing Day as well. It was Simon who had stopped him.

'You said that if I worked on Christmas Day you'd give me a lift to Home Place today.'

'What's to stop you going by train like other people?'

'I don't have any money.'

'What happened to the bonus I gave you?'

'I spent it on presents. It wasn't nearly enough. Ten pounds! Anyway, you promised. And your dad will be very sad if you don't go. So will Clary . . . Think of the lovely free meals,' he urged, a moment later. 'There's always smoked salmon on Boxing Day, and fried Christmas pudding.'

Neville thought for a moment. 'All right,' he said at last. 'To please you.'

Simon, who knew that Neville never did anything to please anyone but himself, avoided pointing this out. They were going; that was the thing.

It had turned much colder, with fitful sun, and when they got to Sevenoaks, it had begun to rain. By the time they reached Home Place there was a steady downpour. Most of the children were engrossed in an enormous jig-saw puzzle laid out on the hall floor. 'It's the Changing of the Guard. Awfully difficult, all red coats and black horses and masses of sky. Hello, Simon and Neville.'

'I'm Uncle Neville to you. And to you, Harriet.'

'Hello, then, Uncle Neville.' She said it in a silly sing-song voice, and the others joined in.

Just then Eileen, who had been picking her way round the puzzle on her journeys from kitchen to dining room, announced to the people in the drawing room that lunch was ready, and they filed out, locking the door behind them. They seemed both pleased and surprised to see Simon and Neville. 'What about our presents?' Simon said, after he had been kissed a good many times.

'Presents are always in the drawing room.'

'Well, I want to put mine there.'

'I don't need to do that because everything I've bought is for everyone. I thought it would be a good idea.'

Simon knew that Neville hadn't bought anything: he'd simply wrapped all the things that rich clients had given him in newspaper – a side of smoked salmon, two boxes of extremely expensive chocolates, a bottle of champagne and another of apricot brandy, toilet waters from Floris and Penhaligon, a Smythson diary, a python-upholstered travelling clock and, finally, no fewer than six ties from Florence – he never wore a tie. All those expensive presents without his spending a penny, Simon thought enviously, as his own wretched contributions flitted through his mind: socks for Dad, a very small chiffon scarf for Jemima, a Mars Bar for Laura (then he had bought the same for each of the children), a little bottle that said 'lavender water' on the label but smelt of some-thing quite different for Aunt Rachel ... All of these things had come from Woolworths, and at that point his money had run out. Well, he would drown all these discomforts with cold turkey and all the delicious things that went with it. And when it got to New Year resolutions he would resolve to get frightfully rich and next year he would give everyone presents like fur coats and motor-cars, even the odd aeroplane or two, and they would all be amazed and he would be everyone's favourite person. He went into lunch feeling quite cheerful. It was lovely knowing exactly how everything was going to turn out when they were reassuring things like a Christmas-time feast.

∞ ∞ ∞

It would be the same old things – like getting the day-old drumstick of the turkey and trying to hide the chestnut stuffing and there not being enough bread sauce and the children all talking about their wretched presents and Laura crying because her Red Indian feather head-dress fell into her plate (last year it had been a gold-paper crown with pretend jewels) – all that old hat.

But it wasn't like that at all, not in the least, because on looking up from his plate, Neville saw opposite him – or, rather, he was struck by – a vision of such perfection, of such amazing beauty, that for an unknown amount of time he was paralysed; it was like being hit or stabbed to the centre of his heart.

After the unknown amount of time, he realised he hadn't been breathing, and then became anxious that some of the others, at least, would have noticed what had happened to him. The fog, the mist, that had shrouded them, sitting each side of her, now cleared and he could see Simon and one of the twins. He looked round the table, but everyone was busy eating and talking. The only

137

person he didn't feel sure about was Sid, who at one moment (was it when he wasn't breathing?) caught his eye across the table and then smiled – a small smile, as though they shared a secret.

He had always been secretive. All his life he would never forget the black despair that had taken hold of him when his father had been a virtual prisoner in France and had sent a message to Clary and not to him. From that time, he had cultivated an indifference coupled with a desire to shock. He had never known his mother, as she had died giving birth to him, and really he hadn't missed her because he had had Ellen, his nanny, and he had quickly discovered that being motherless made people want to be kind to him. After school, he had refused to go to university, choosing boring but well-paid jobs in order to buy whatever clothes he liked. He had also bought a camera, quite a modest affair, and begun taking photographs. He had instantly found that he enjoyed that, and talked his way into employment at a magazine by pretending he had worked in the States. His expensive clothes and his easy assurance, coupled with an entirely misleading air of modesty, had got him to the point at which he could choose what work he would do. He was reliable, creative and altogether professional, never out of his depth, and skilled, when necessary, at skating over thin ice. *Country Life* was running a series on 'How The Other Half Lives', which he was due to start in the New Year; he was looking forward to photographing the castles and grand houses that would doubtless come his way.

His social life was as full as he cared to make it. Girls were almost always attracted to him; sometimes men were, too. He had experimented with both, but had not got on with either. He hadn't enjoyed the sex and had nothing to say about it. It was just something he felt he didn't need.

And suddenly – out of the blue – here was Juliet. It must have been at least a year since he had seen her, and during that time she had grown from being just another gangly, round-faced schoolgirl, with unfortunate spots, he remembered, and her hair in tight pigtails, to someone altogether rich and strange: her hair was now styled so that its dark brown with reddish lights could be seen, drawn back and tied with a peacock velvet ribbon that showed her delicate ears; her face was transformed, with high cheekbones, her skin flawless, pale with a hint of rose, her long narrow eyes still Cazalet blue. He used to think her eyes were her one good feature.

At this moment of his reverie, she leaned across the table and smiled at him.

The thought occurred to him then that if one was in love one could not be anything else. This frightened him. He smiled hastily back – the sort of casual smile he would give a bus conductor or a waiter when they provided him with a ticket or a menu . . .

Best to concentrate on food, although he discovered that he was not in the least hungry. Instead he heard fragments of the many conversations round the table . . . 'Well, if the Astronomer Royal says the idea of space travel is bilge, it probably is.' Almost certainly Uncle Hugh.

'But we've planned to go into space. We've planned to go to the moon.' Tom and Henry.

'It'll be frightfully cold and you won't know a soul there.' Archie.

She wore a turquoise heart on a gold chain round her slender neck . . .

'And I can't help feeling very sorry for her.' Aunt Rachel.

'Who, darling?'

'Princess Margaret.'

Her dress was very dark green velvet, the bodice cut with a low square, the sleeves tight and finishing just below her elbows . . .

'Please don't say anything.' It was Georgie, who was sitting next to him. Rivers had escaped from his pocket and was trying to climb onto him, his nose twitching at the delightful smells. Neville instantly leaned over him, and wiped his face with his napkin, which shrouded Rivers long enough for Georgie to cram him back.

'That's better, isn't it?'

'Yes, thank you, Uncle Neville.' He had picked a piece of turkey off his plate and thrust it into his pocket. They exchanged glances – bland with conspiracy.

He wondered whether she had noticed, and thought that she had, since she smiled at him again.

The twins were told to collect the plates and put them on the sideboard, and Eileen appeared with the pudding plates.

He managed to eat his pudding at the same time as looking at her – unobtrusively, he thought, until his father, from across the table, asked him if he was all right. This made other people look at him, so he said he was fine, if a little drunk – on food, he added quickly. 'You should see what Simon and I live on when we're working. Tell them, Simon.'

'Baked beans, the odd pork pie, rather old eggs and spongy bread. Oh, and HP sauce on pretty well everything.'

140

But if Simon expected sympathy for this, he was mistaken.

'Nearly all my favourite foods,' Harriet said. 'But we hardly ever have them.'

'Are the old eggs Chinese?' Tom asked. 'Because Henry read in a book that they wait a hundred years until they're pitch black.' Henry did most of the reading for Tom and himself. Tom did the remembering. 'Because that would mean unless you lived to be a hundred and one, you'd never eat your own eggs. So your eggs can't be very old.'

'What's HP? I've never had it. Is it something wicked if it doesn't have a proper name?'

'It's a sauce. You wouldn't like it, darling.'

Laura turned to her mother. 'Bet I would. You said I wouldn't like black olives and I did. You don't know all my likes at all.'

'Time for crackers,' Hugh announced.

And while people were crossing their arms to take their own and a neighbour's cracker, Neville noticed that Georgie nipped some almonds from a dish on the table, thrust them down into his pocket and shoved his napkin on top of them. 'He might be frightened by the bangs,' he muttered to Neville, 'but he simply loves almonds.'

The crackers were really grand ones. They were large and beautifully decorated and, best of all, they contained extremely acceptable surprises. Things like little pencils with coloured tassels, a proper Dinky toy, necklaces and rings, a tiny red leather purse and so forth, plus, of course, the terrible jokes on thin folded paper that they all read aloud to a lot of contemptuous laughter. Some people got the contents of two crackers, some none, and

141

this had to be smoothed out by parents. A certain amount of swapping went on. Neville was one of the lucky ones. He got a scarlet linen handkerchief and a ring with a large green stone in it. Luckily for him, Juliet had been one of the losers: he rolled the ring across the table to her; she gave him an enchantingly grateful glance and put it on at once. A surge of pure joy possessed him. His first present to her and she had taken it.

∞ ∞ ∞

It was customary for everyone – or practically everyone – to go for a swinging walk after Boxing Day lunch. The exceptions were Rachel and Sid, Zoë, Laura and her mother. Laura made such a fuss about this that in the end Jemima compromised with a very short walk to the stables with food for McAlpine's ferrets (Laura loved feeding any animals). Archie, Rupert and Hugh took the older children up the road to Whatlington, then back through the fields and woods of Home Place. Tom and Henry, who had heard Simon and Teddy talking about the camp they had once made with Christopher, begged to see it.

'I shouldn't think there'll be anything left by now. It was ages ago,' Teddy said. He felt vaguely uncomfortable when he thought of it.

'You fought Christopher. It was his camp, really. And he was against people fighting.'

'Did you kill him?' Henry was fascinated: he had never met anyone who had gone in for murder.

'Good Lord, no. It was just an ordinary scrap.'

They had reached the hedge that bordered the wood;

142

Simon found the familiar gap in it and all four of them climbed through. They soon reached the little stream, and Simon stared at it. It was just the same, winding its way between mossy banks interspersed with stretches of wider, shallower water and flat, sandy beaches. If you looked long enough, you could imagine it being a great river: the ferns on the moss would be vast tropical trees, the sandy beaches would have people lying on them . . .

'Come on, Simon, let's find the camp. We both want to see it.'

That was the trouble with twins, he thought. They always seemed to want the same things, and when it came to choosing or voting for anything, they had a head start. He turned right by the stream and in a few minutes he reached the place where the camp had been.

'It was here,' he said doubtfully. The grassy patch where the tent had been was now overgrown with brambles; the place where they had made the fire still had a few blackened bricks – Christopher had tried to build an oven – and clumps of stinging nettles were thriving . . . 'It hasn't lasted at all.'

'It can't have been very well built,' said both twins, of course.

'It was a long time ago,' Teddy said. He wanted to be shot of it. He was remembering Christopher's white and desperate face as he had tried to defend the camp.

'It was Christopher's and my camp,' Simon said. He was remembering with some discomfort that he hadn't helped Christopher with the fight.

'Who's Christopher?'

'He's a cousin. He became a monk.'

'Oh. No wonder.'

'No wonder what?'

'Well, I don't think you'd get a single monk to be much good at building anything.'

'What do you know about monks? Either of you?' That was meant to pre-empt the twin thing.

Henry turned to Tom. 'What do we know?'

Tom thought. 'Well, they had a rotten time with the Tudors. They got turned out of their monasteries and burned at the stake, and the Catholic ones had to hide in cupboards in people's houses.'

Teddy, now thoroughly bored, suggested they all went home for tea and, in spite of the twins arguing about buildings and how long they could last if properly built – Stonehenge came into it, 'But you couldn't possibly live there!' – they sped through the fields, ending up in a race, won, of course, by the twins.

∞ ∞ ∞

The jigsaw puzzle had been cleverly towed away on its blanket to the kitchen end of the hall, the table laid for tea, and some people were already attacking the sandwiches. 'I have coffee and tea in my milk, please don't forget,' Laura was saying. She now wore a gold-paper crown that sat uneasily upon her Red Indian feathers.

'I think that's about everyone,' Archie said. 'We can all have a swig now. That was some walk!'

'It was too much for me,' Bertie said. 'I've got a sore heel.'

'That's because you wouldn't wear your socks.'

'Where's Juliet?' Zoë suddenly said. 'Didn't she go with you, Rupe?'

'I thought she went with Teddy and Simon.'

Henry said, 'And us. No, she didn't.'

Zoë, who had opted for a rest rather than a walk, now felt guilty. 'Honestly, Rupert, I thought you said you would take charge.'

Georgie looked up from his egg sandwich. 'I think she went with Neville in his car.'

'Oh, that's all right, then. She'll be quite safe with him.'

∞ ∞ ∞

'You aren't worried, are you? You're quite safe with me. Darling, beautiful Juliet.'

She looked at him quickly, then down to her lap. 'Darling', 'beautiful' – the words induced a kind of nervous excitement in her. The awful thought that he might be laughing at her occurred. 'Do you really mean that?'

'Oh, yes. I mean it. Don't laugh at me. We could have a pact not to laugh at each other. Yes?'

'Yes.' It was a relief to have that clear.

'But, on the other hand, if someone else metaphorically slips on a banana skin, we can laugh as much as we like.'

'I don't think I'd want to. Think of the poor person!'

'I needn't, because he isn't anyone. If you're hypothetical you don't exist.'

'Oh.'

He was silent. Things weren't going as he had imagined. He had thought that the worst problem would be getting her alone, but that had been the easiest part. 'You don't want to go for a freezing walk. Come for a drive in my car.' She had reached the age where several of her contemporaries boasted of boyfriends, but none of them owned a car. This would silence them when she told them about it.

That was fine. She agreed and together they slipped through the kitchen door and down the cinder path to the courtyard with the stables and garages.

It was when they were in the car and had waited for the crowd of walkers to turn left to go to Whatlington, and he had turned right for Battle, that he began to feel anxious – even shy, now he was alone with her. How could he tell her of the amazing thing that had happened to him? Should he treat the afternoon as just a jolly outing? Or should he try to tell her seriously how he felt? There was something wrong with both of these approaches. Anyway, he decided that he couldn't do any of it while driving. He would go past Battle to a place where there was a track into the woods. When they got there, he would suggest a short walk, and ask to take some pictures of her.

He told her this and she seemed calmly happy about it.

He started driving faster – he longed to get to the wood.

It was a real winter afternoon, windless, so that many of the leafless trees looked like elaborate armatures waiting for their sculpture of green. The sky was dense and leaden; a faintly orange sun was sinking unobtrusively, leaving a smear of dusk.

He found the opening to the wood, and they both got out of the car.

'If you photograph me, will you put it in a magazine?'

'I don't know,' he said. Then, seeing that she looked downcast, he added, 'I expect I might one day. Give me your hand. Goodness, you're cold!'

She was wearing her new winter jacket – olive green with a fur-trimmed hood, which made what he could see of her face even more mysteriously beautiful. I'll take some pictures of her, and then I'll tell her, he thought.

A few yards along the track there was a large Spanish chestnut that had fallen – or, more likely, been felled since it lay, with no sign of its roots, propped at a slant where the higher branches had been trapped by the branches of its neighbours. He put her on the thicker part of the trunk, got out the little pocket camera that he took everywhere with him and told her to take off her hood. The light was bad, subsiding gratefully into dusk, and he knew the pictures would not be much good, but she would not know that, and he would take many others that were likely to please her.

'Now, I'm going to be professional and order you about.'

'OK.' The great thing was to be cool about it. Most models looked bored, and she tried now to emulate them, but this only made him think she was frightened, and he became gentle and teasing, coaxing her to move her head, to shift her body, to position her hands as he wanted.

He worked until her teeth were chattering with cold and he was overcome with remorse. 'You should have told me, my darling! When I get stuck in, I don't notice anything. I'm so sorry.' He was putting her hood over her, chafing her hands, and then, with an arm round her, he helped her to the feet she could no longer feel, whereupon she stumbled. He picked her up and carried her to the car.

'Was I any good at it?' she asked, when she could speak.

'Good at what?'

'Being a model.'

'Oh, that! Yes, of course you were. A marvellous model. Couldn't ask for better.'

She gave a deep sigh of contentment.

He fumbled in a side pocket and produced a battered packet of Polo mints. 'They'll make you feel warmer.'

'Would you like one?'

'I would. Post it to me.' He slowed the car and turned to her – for a second felt her cold fingers touch his lips.

It was nearly dark, and large snowflakes had begun, with random indolence, to drop slowly out of the sky.

'How old are you?'

'Fifteen. Well, nearly sixteen, actually,' Juliet answered, in her cold, grown-up voice: she hated to be asked about her age, because so often it led to a sickening patronage. 'How old are you?'

'I'm twenty-six. A rather young twenty-six.' God, he thought. We shall have to wait years.

'You're ten years older than I am.' She said it with a quiet satisfaction. 'That's quite old. But, actually, you don't look especially old.'

She was beginning to enjoy his appearance, which, when looked at properly, was both dashing and romantic: his high forehead with the lock of dark hair that fell diagonally across it, his high cheekbones, his eyes that could change in an instant from a kind of teasing charm to something unknown to her. She loved the mystery of this.

The snow had speeded up, the flakes only becoming white as they reached the windscreen, but now they were lying where they fell; the verge, the hedges and the country beyond began to glisten. The windscreen wipers, from doing a casual, reluctant sweep, struggled with a protesting screech. The windscreen began to mist up on the inside from their breath, and they took turns to wipe it with their hands. By the time they were through Sedlescombe and had reached the turning to the left, which ended with the Battle road, a snowstorm had begun.

'Are you all right, my darling? I'm sorry it's not warmer.'

'A bit cold, but fine otherwise.' The whole thing was turning into an adventure. After a pause she asked, rather timidly – she didn't want to sound unsophisticated – 'Why do you keep calling me your darling?'

'Because that's what I've discovered you are.' He waited a moment before taking the plunge. How to begin? 'It started at lunch today, so it's quite new. The fact is, seeing you across the table today, I suddenly – I didn't expect it, of course – suddenly felt quite fond of you – well, enamoured. I loved you, actually – I fell in love. I see now why people call it "falling in love".'

He stopped the car in order to see her properly – to see how she had taken this.

She had been hugging herself, and now she turned to him with sparkling eyes. 'In love with me? Really and truly? Golly! Is that why you gave me the lovely green ring?'

'Yes, I suppose it is.'

'A kind of engagement?'

He nodded. He was realising – not for the first time that afternoon – that she was much younger than she looked. 'But I don't think we should tell people,' he said

– and she broke in: 'Oh, no! It's much more exciting if it's a secret. Mummy would be furious. She doesn't think I'm old enough for anything grown-up or interesting.'

Can't go any further, he thought. He held each side of her face between his hands, and gave her a chaste kiss on her soft red mouth.

'There. That's sealed the second pact between us. No laughing at banana-skin victims, and our secret from the family.'

She wiped the windscreen again and he drove them very slowly home.

On the way she said, 'The real Juliet was only fifteen in the play.'

'Well, things happened much earlier in those days. People died a lot younger.'

'Anyway, they weren't cousins,' she said.

He nearly said no, and nor were they, but stopped in time. He hadn't much of an idea what she felt about him, and it seemed dangerous to ask. But then, she said, 'Of course! You're my half-brother. You seem so much older. I hadn't thought of you like that.' There was a pause, and then, in a small, defeated voice, she added, 'So it's no use you being in love with me. Is it?'

'It's got nothing to do with that. Darling Jules, when you love someone, that sort of thing doesn't come into it. All that stuff about incest is just social bosh. Don't think about it for a moment. That's just stuffy old convention. Don't spoil our lovely secret. You can't stop me loving you whatever you do.'

'All right, I won't.' She didn't at all want her friends to know. They would discount it, and jeer – a ghastly thought. 'I won't,' she said. 'I promise.'

When they got back, tea was nearly over, but everyone

seemed relieved to see them. He was surprised at the composure with which she answered the various questions asked of the drive to Battle woods, Neville taking photographs of her, the snowstorm on the way back, which had made the journey so much longer; surprised, and a little sad.

EDWARD AND HUGH

'Well, if you insist on keeping Southampton, we ought to be seriously considering who is going to run it. It's a shambles as it is.'

'Oh, I don't know about that.'

Edward looked despairingly at his dear, bloody-minded, obstinate brother. He was finding it difficult to keep his temper.

They had been arguing for months about having too much capital invested in property, and each time Edward felt that he had got somewhere, but then, when the subject was raised again, he found that nothing he had said to Hugh about it seemed to have sunk in.

'What about McIver?' He was loyal, liked by the men under him and a native . . .

But while he was in the middle of pointing out these advantages, Hugh had interrupted, 'Oh, I know all that, old boy, but he's not a Cazalet. We must have a member of the family. We must have a Cazalet running the show.'

'Why on earth— Why?'

'Because we're a small private family firm.'

They were lunching at Edward's club, the Royal Thames in Knightsbridge, and he now suggested that they repair to the coffee room. Perhaps a spot of brandy might lower the tension. But when they were finally settled, coffee for both of them, brandy and a cigar for him, the club's port and cigarettes for Hugh, his brother said, 'Actually, I was rather hoping that you would take it on.'

A moment of sheer horror. God! 'Out of the question, I'm afraid. You know I've finally bought the house in Hawkhurst. I couldn't possibly commute from there, and Diana has set her heart on the place . . . How about Rupe?'

Their eyes met for the first time in indulgent conspiracy.

'You know, Edward, he's not the most decisive person in the world. I'm afraid it wouldn't do.'

'You're absolutely right, of course.' It was really good to have something they could agree on. They'd begun lunch with an argument about the Suez Canal: Hugh thinking that the British and French were right to try to hang on to it – 'After all, we and the French paid for most of it. The Egyptians contributed a mere ten thousand pounds.' But Edward had insisted that it was built on Egypt's territory and no attempt had been made for friendly negotiation.

'And they won't maintain it properly. I'm told by a yachting friend that they've already left the shark nets unrepaired, which means the Aegean is starting to fill up with happy, hungry sharks. He'd actually seen one, a large black fin cruising along at sinister speed – like a submarine.

'Well,' Hugh said, after an uneasy pause, 'perhaps this is the moment to promote young Teddy. He's been doing very well with clients, and I've been sending him down to our wharves there every week or so. What do you think?'

'He's a bit young for it, isn't he?'

'Nonsense. He's – nearly thirty-three? Just right, I'd say. And McIver will show him the ropes. You ought to be proud of him, Ed. I wish Simon was more like him, but there it is. God! Look at the time.'

Edward signalled a waiter for his bill to sign.

As they walked through a sudden, fitful shower to Edward's car, Hugh said, 'Come on, Ed. Surely you can agree with me about that.'

And Edward, relieved – he was indeed proud of Teddy – replied heartily, 'I think it will be wonderful for him. A jolly good idea.'

PART FIVE

SPRING 1957

SIMON AND WILLS

They had agreed to meet at Lyons' Corner House near Marble Arch. It had been Jemima's suggestion; she had mentioned it first during the Christmas holidays. 'Have you seen much of Wills lately?' she had asked, and Simon had said no.

'He keeps going off to stay with an old school friend, or else moons about at Home Place. I don't have much time. Neville's a slave driver.' He felt defensive about Wills, suspecting that his younger brother felt much the same as he did: aimless, stuck, bored a good deal of the time probably. Somehow he didn't want to be with people like that.

'Well, you know he's about to start national service.'

'I'd forgotten that. He'll hate it – like I did.'

'I just thought that perhaps it might be helpful if you told him about it. Look, you've agreed to babysit for us when Dad and I go to the theatre. Dad says you're to have a fiver for it. So you could afford to take him out to supper – give him a treat, like a good big brother.'

The idea of being able to take someone out, to give them something, appealed to him at once.

∞ ∞ ∞

157

A few days later they were sitting opposite each other at a very small table scrutinising menus and trying to look as though this was something they did every day. For twenty-five shillings a head they could get a two-course meal, plus one lager each and coffee.

'What do you feel like, Wills?'

'What about you?'

'I feel like all of it. Neville doesn't care about food, so we have awful grub or nothing. It's all very well for him. He gets taken out to posh places by art editors and the like and I just have to make do with a sandwich somewhere. Shall we have our lagers now, while we're choosing?'

'Good idea.'

Simon waved at the nearest nippy, who immediately signalled to the one he belatedly recognised had brought the menus.

She pulled her pencil from where it rested behind her ear while collecting her writing pad that was fastened to her white lacy apron. 'Now, gentlemen, what can I get you?' Immediately, they felt that they must place their order quickly. Simon asked what the meat pie was like, and the nippy said it was beef, very nice. And the shepherd's pie. That was very nice, too.

In the end they both hurriedly ordered the meat pie and two lagers.

'You could have soup, if you wish, as a starter.'

Wills said, 'I'd rather have pudding. An ice.'

Simon said, 'As a matter of fact I agree with you. What ices have you?'

She reeled the varieties off, ending with a Knicker-bocker Glory.

'That's for me,' Simon said at once. So long as he

didn't have to say the silly name it seemed OK to have one. Wills agreed. He had been afraid that Simon would think it childish of him, but if he was having one it must be all right.

They were both so hungry that when the meat pies came there didn't seem time for conversation. The portions were generous, accompanied by cabbage, mashed potato and carrots. By the time they got to the end of that, the lager was all finished as well.

Wills smiled. 'Thanks. That was smashing.'

This was the moment. 'I suppose you can't make any plans about what you want to do till you've got through your stint in the services?'

His face clouded. 'You bet I can't. I suppose it's more or less like school only worse. I can't imagine how, but I somehow know it is. What was it like for you?'

Simon skipped his first awful week: sleeping in a stuffy dorm with fifty-something other men; eating porridge (which he loathed), with dark brown tea (comforting until someone told him it was laced with something to stop them feeling randy); going for endless runs when you started perishing cold and ended up gasping and streaming with sweat, and all the time being yelled at by some petty officer who clearly despised the lot of you. The hours of standing to attention to be inspected, the awful watery stews and thick, gluey pies filled with root vegetables and one or two pieces of meat that people said were whale, more brown tea, tinned fruit and custard, afternoons spent learning to service radio equipment in planes, 'tea' at six – dried scrambled egg or slippery ham, fruit cake with hardly any raisins in it, biscuits and brown tea again. 'You get used to it,' was all he said. 'Which service are you going in for?'

'I haven't absolutely decided. I thought the Navy, but I remembered how awfully sick I felt in Uncle Edward's boat. Then I thought the Air Force because they have a lot of good musicians, or they used to have. What would you do if you were me?'

Simon tried to think. 'I'd do what I did. Though I warn you, the officers moult in the bath. You have to clean them,' he explained. 'The baths, I mean. The best thing about it is that it's only for two years.'

'But then what on earth shall I do?'

Goodness! Simon thought. He's just like me. 'I suppose you could go into the firm.'

Luckily, at this point their unmentionable dessert arrived, with wonderful long spoons that meant you could easily plumb the depths of the tall glasses. They demolished the ices with frank enjoyment, and when Wills started asking him about his life, Simon discovered that he really wanted to talk about it.

No, he didn't want to be a photographer, no, he had never wanted to go into the firm, had done three months because their father wanted him to; he had half wanted to be a musician, but he knew that he wasn't good enough; the girls he met were snooty, fussing about their appearances and their shape – on diets, most of them, which tended to make them short-tempered and tired.

But didn't the girls being on diets make them quite cheap to take out?

'Don't you believe it. They just want a dozen oysters, *truite au bleu*, and then whatever fruit is absolutely out of season. I only did it once and it cost me a month's salary. I'm more or less through with girls,' he finished morosely.

Wills was deeply impressed. At school some boys had

talked endlessly about girls; he was intelligent enough to recognise that a lot of the boasting was made up, but there was also a good deal of nervous speculation about what actually having a girlfriend would be like. One (foreign) boy, whose parents seemed madly rich, said he had gone to a brothel in London with an older brother, and had two girls on the same evening, plus two bottles of shockingly bad champagne, but his brother had paid for everything. Sex was much better if you paid for it. After all, if you married (which, of course, you had to do in the end in order to have sons), it was a meal ticket for your wife for life: you had to go on paying for her however boring you found her.

This sort of talk appalled Simon. It felt all wrong, somehow. He thought of his father when Sybil died: there had been no doubt that he had loved her to the end, and grieved for ages until he'd found Jemima, and it was clear that he loved her as well. Perhaps, he thought, it was a question of what country you belonged to, because he simply couldn't imagine any of his family believing that sort of rot.

To change the subject, Wills said, 'Oh, well, I should think anything I do when I come out will seem good after that.' He looked hopefully at Simon when he said this, and Simon hadn't the heart to warn him that it might not.

Instead they talked about their much-loved sister, Polly. 'How's Lady Fake?'

'Haven't seen her since before Christmas. She was fine then, except awfully fat. Of course you know she's having yet another baby.'

'Of course I do. It must be due any day now.'

'She's supposed to be having it some time this month. It takes a hell of a long time, doesn't it? Well, at least there'd be plenty of room for it in that house.'

At which point their nippy arrived to clear the table and present them with the bill.

'Thanks awfully for the meal. It was wizard.'

Simon nodded abstractedly. He was trying to work out the tip. In the end, he put down five shillings, and she thanked him. He hoped she was pleased, but he couldn't tell. He left Wills waiting for a bus. 'Let me know when you're off,' he said, and Wills said he would.

Simon crossed the road to reach his own bus stop, then changed his mind, deciding to walk to Maida Vale. He was not looking forward to Neville's depressing flat, which would either be full of dirty cups and glasses he was expected to wash up, or full of people he did not know. They would be whooping it up with records of the latest rock-and-roll bands played on Neville's awful gramophone so loudly that he wouldn't be able to sleep. It would probably be full of both, he thought. His talk with Wills had been disturbing. What the hell was he doing with his own life? This made him realise – with some discomfort – that he always thought about the things he didn't like without any consideration of alternatives. What did he really want? The answer came with the smooth ease of a ticket from a slot machine. He wanted to live with Polly, be her gardener – or learn to be – and, meanwhile, help with her plans for weddings at the house. He remembered that he had wanted that when he'd been staying with them but done nothing about it. He would write to Polly, to ask if he could stay for a weekend, and talk to them then. And he was amazed at how cheerful this made him feel.

RACHEL AND SID

It was their first proper row, and she felt really awful. True, they had had little spats, but nothing like this. All the way back from Hawkhurst to Home Place, Rachel had refused to speak – had retired into some icy calm of what felt like total indifference, a couldn't-care-less attitude – which had never happened between them before.

It had all started with Edward and Diana asking them to dinner. She, Sid, had not at all wanted to go: this was partly because she was afraid of Diana, but quite as much because she really did not feel at all well. For months now she had been having what she called tummy troubles, which meant her digestion was tricky, and she always felt rotten if she ate anything rich. And she guessed (rightly) that the dinner would be just that. But Rachel was hell-bent on trying to reconcile her brothers, and was convinced that meeting Diana was the first step. She had insisted, had even offered angrily to take a taxi if Sid didn't want to do the driving, but of course she couldn't accept that. 'A ruinous expense,' she had declared, and she wouldn't hear of it. So they had gone, Rachel armed with a bunch of violets from the Duchy's garden. They had both taken trouble with their clothes, Rachel wearing her best blue linen suit, and Sid in the trouser suit with a silk shirt Rachel had given her for her last birthday.

Park House was not easy to find, and they lost their way – had to stop and ask a farmer, whose tractor was towing a cart loaded with bales of hay. Eventually they found the narrow turning that led up the drive to the house.

'It looks very imposing,' she had said, but Rachel had replied, 'Oh, Ed has always liked large houses.'

They were greeted in the hall with varying degrees of enthusiasm by Edward, Diana and a yellow Labrador.

'It's so lovely to see you, darling – down, Honey, DOWN! This is Diana.'

'And this is Sid,' Rachel said.

'Lovely to see you, Sid.' She found herself briefly enveloped in lavender water and then the Lebanon cedar that scented all of Edward's clothes as he propelled them to the drawing room.

It was close-carpeted in a brilliant yellow, and had one window that looked onto the drive, and two that looked onto a garden, which had lawn, a cedar, and was bounded by three walls edged with wide beds of herbaceous plants.

While she was taking all this in, and Edward was opening a bottle of champagne, she heard the following exchange.

Rachel: 'I've brought a little bunch of my mother's violets. They're the old-fashioned kind, because she always thought they smelt the best.'

Diana: 'How sweet of you. It's such a pity that they don't really last when they've been picked, isn't it?'

Sid turned from the window to see Diana put the flowers on the nearest table. She wore a crêpe dress of emphatic purple with a row of black sequins round the low-cut neck. I'm never going to like her, Sid thought then.

Edward had poured the champagne into four glasses and was now handing it round. 'Here's to all of us.' He lifted his glass, and they all drank – in Rachel's case, sipped. She drank very little, but her family had always taken wine seriously and, naturally, she did not want to hurt Edward's feelings. Sid took an unthinking gulp; she used to love champagne, but the last two or three times it had given her violent indigestion. Oh, well, I won't have to drink any more because I'm driving, she thought. This excuse cheered her, and she wondered how much longer Diana would continue to avoid speaking to her.

By the time the champagne was finished, it was time to go into dinner. The dining room was dark red – damask paper made to look like rich material, crimson velvet curtains of a darker colour, and three pairs of sconces that produced a subdued electric light. The table was round, made of rosewood, and laid for what looked like an elaborate dinner. She had time to notice all this because Diana was arranging 'the placement', as she put it.

'Oh, come on, darling! It's quite simple. You sit in your usual place with me opposite and the girls between us. This is a family dinner – the Lord Mayor unfortunately couldn't make it.'

So they all sat as told.

'I think you forget, darling, that I don't know your family. Of course I've heard a lot about you – may I call you Rachel? – but I hardly know your name. Miss Sidney, isn't it? Like the Australian town. Do you by any chance come from there?'

'I don't. I'm strictly European. Jewish, actually.'

At this moment the soufflé arrived.

'I think I'd better serve it, Amy. You bring the plates quickly, and make sure they're hot. It's crab,' she explained.

While Sid was thinking wildly of how she could get out of eating any, Rachel was asking to be given very little, as she could not eat much. 'And I can see that there is more to come.'

'I'm rather like Rachel in that respect,' she said.

But Diana simply behaved as though neither of them had spoken, doling out mountainous spoonfuls of an equal size for all of them. Meanwhile, Edward was pouring a white wine into their glasses, telling them it was a special sauvignon in their honour. 'It's especially good with crab!' She had to eat some of the soufflé, and found that washing it down with wine was a help.

The conversation was clinging rather limply to the problems of the Suez Canal. Edward said that he could not imagine Nasser would accept an international body administering the canal. He must be stopped – indeed should have been opposed with force from the moment he seized it. Rachel deplored the way in which politicians regarded force as the best way of dealing with anything. Diana said that she entirely agreed with Edward, but it was a comfort that we had the French on our side.

Rachel had managed to move most of her crab onto Edward's plate and was now having a conversation with him, conducted so quietly that Sid could not hear it.

Diana rang a little hand-bell for the plates to be changed. She looked pointedly at Sid's, but said nothing. Indeed, Sid thought, they clearly had very little to say to one another, but she knew that Rachel needed to talk to Edward about Hugh, so she must somehow distract

Diana. The new house might be the most promising subject.

'It is a beautiful house. Did it take you a long time to find it?'

'Ages. Edward, darling, how long did it take us to find Park House?'

'Darling, I've no idea. Diana did all the work – she looked at dozens of places and sorted out three for me to view.'

'It had to be within commuting distance of London because Edward seems to have more and more work these days, since they sent Teddy to Southampton. The poor old boy comes home exhausted, and we both look forward to Friday night.'

The next course arrived. A venison stew, Diana explained, done in wine and brandy. Edward got up to collect a bottle of burgundy from the sideboard.

The casserole stood steaming in front of Diana; the smell made Sid feel queasy, and her back was starting to ache. She asked for a very small helping, and this time she put her hand on Diana's arm to emphasise her request. 'Rachel and I are used to a very light supper at home – an omelette or a bowl of soup.'

'Oh, Edward! Why didn't you tell me? You said you wanted an especially nice dinner for Rachel so, of course, I planned a bit of a feast. Pointless, as it turns out. You might have warned me!'

Rachel, who looked really distressed, said, 'Oh, Diana, don't take any notice of Sid. She's always worrying about food – particularly where I'm concerned. The venison smells simply delicious – I'm longing to try it.'

This mollified Diana somewhat, and she ladled a large amount onto a plate and handed it over the table to her sister-in-law. The maid had brought in two vegetable dishes that turned out to contain new potatoes and peas. 'Do help yourself,' she said.

Edward, who had finished pouring the burgundy, turned to Rachel. 'This was the Brig's favourite burgundy. It was left to me, and this is the last bottle.'

'Oh, darling Edward, how very sweet of you.'

When it came to serving Sid, Diana, underlining every movement, as it were, picked half a carrot and two very small cubes of meat. She then poured from the jug so much sauce that nothing on the plate could be seen and handed the plate to her. 'I hope you're hungry,' she said to Edward, in a threateningly quiet voice.

'Of course I am.' He was angry: things didn't seem to be going at all as he had expected, and he couldn't understand why.

Rachel made a desperate effort. Having taken a cautious sip of the wine, she said how good it was, stared at her plate, then resolutely began to eat. She shot a glance at Sid, which clearly meant 'do the same', but the fumes rising from the sauce were making Sid afraid that she might actually be sick, and after the terrible débâcle at Home Place, this paralysed her with terror. Here she did not even know where the nearest lavatory was . . . So, in the end, she simply did not eat.

From that moment Diana ignored her.

'What are you two talking about?' she called across the table.

'Oh – just family matters,' Edward answered.

'Well, I suppose I'm family now, so could I please join in?'

'Well, it's a bit complicated,' Rachel said. 'I was hoping to get Edward to have lunch with me and Hugh.' She was blushing. 'To sort something out. It's more to do with the firm than the family, really.'

She had stopped eating her venison, but had almost finished her wine.

Sid said, 'Anything to do with the firm is to do with the family.'

Edward, refilling her glass, said, 'It's no good, Rachel, old dear. Hugh's not going to change his mind, and he is the chairman, after all.'

There was a brief silence during which they all disliked one another. Then everything seemed to happen at once. Diana announced the pudding, which was to be a crème brûlée, Rachel wiped her tears with her napkin and seized Edward's hand, and Sid, draining her glass (for courage), said, 'It's getting late. I really think we should be going home.' Then, turning to Diana, she said, 'You shouldn't try to bully people about food. Leave it to them. Would someone please show me to a lavatory?'

'Show her, Edward. We don't want her throwing up on our new carpet.'

He took her and she was able to be sick in peace. Then, rather shaky, but relieved, she returned to find Edward in the hall, helping Rachel into her coat. She put on her own, and felt for the keys.

'Darling Ed, I'm so sorry we've been such a nuisance about food – and everything. I didn't mean to worry you about Hugh – and since Sid hasn't apologised about being so rude to Diana, after she had taken so much trouble, please tell Diana, please tell her now from me. And remember that you do love your brother, and everyone has disagreements from time to time.'

'It would help if he would be civil to my wife.'

'Of course it would, and I shall tell him.' She laid a

169

caressing hand on his shoulder and kissed him goodbye.
'Come on, Sid.'

∞ ∞ ∞

Sid started the car and drove it to the lane before stopping. For a moment she was speechless with rage.

'Why have you stopped?'

'Why did you betray me like that? Putting it all on me. Yes, I was rude to Diana, but she had been getting at me all evening. Did you know that she didn't condescend to acknowledge my presence until we got to the dining room and she started sniping about my origins? And when I asked if I could have a small helping of the crab – which you know I can't bear – she simply piled it on my plate.'

'She did that to both of us.'

'And when that nauseating stew arrived, she pretended to make a small helping for me, then deluged it with that rich sauce. She didn't do that to you because you sucked up to her, which simply made me look worse. I knew if I tried to eat any of that stew, I'd be sick. As for being rude, I thought a little plain speaking would do her good.'

'It's funny how people who are rude call it honesty or plain speaking. It's only other people who are rude. Do you think that I wanted a rich meal like that? You might have had the manners to put up with it. I'm sure she was trying to be kind, making all those complicated things. As it is, you've made the whole evening a fiasco.'

'There you are! Putting it all on me! It was all very well for you. You had Edward to talk to. I was stuck with her and she didn't in the least want to talk to me.'

There was a silence during which she realised that she

had a pounding headache and her back was throbbing with small dagger-like stabs.

Rachel said, 'I think you'd better get on with driving us home. I'm tired, and I don't want to discuss this any more. At least Diana didn't say anything horrid when you told her you were Jewish.'

'That was good of her, wasn't it? Really wonderfully good!'

Rachel did not answer. Nor did she reply to any of Sid's increasingly desperate attempts to engage her. In the end, Sid stopped trying, concentrated on her driving (she had an uneasy feeling that she might be a bit drunk), but she was also confounded by this very different Rachel, who, until now, she had never encountered. The remark – no, the gibe, surely – that Rachel had made about Diana's non-reaction to Sid's saying she was Jewish, with its hostile inference, had really hurt her to the quick. Curiously, it had wounded her far more than the allegations about manners and rudeness. Rachel, who had once said, 'I would rather be with you than anyone in the world,' had painfully turned into the world. Tears stung her eyes, and as she covertly brushed them away, she glanced at Rachel, but she was leaning back in her seat, her eyes closed.

Back at Home Place, she parked the car, woke Rachel, who said she had not been asleep, and unlocked the front door. Rachel went ahead of her. 'I'm going to sleep in the Blue Room,' was all she said, and Sid followed her up the front stairs where they parted without touching each other and in silence, Sid going towards the room they usually shared, and Rachel to the opposite passage.

Sid took a painkiller, ate a water biscuit to allay her stomach, undressed and got into bed. She fully expected to lie awake all night, but in fact she was so exhausted that she fell almost at once into a deep, dreamless sleep.

∞ ∞ ∞

She was woken in the early hours by a tearful, contrite Rachel kneeling by the bed and imploring forgiveness. 'Darling, I was so horrible to you. I'm so sorry – must have been a bit drunk. I had far more than I'm used to. But I'm not excusing myself. I was an absolute beast. I knew Diana was being awful to you and it was cowardly of me not to stand up for you – I was so disappointed in Edward being so obstinate about Hugh – no, I wasn't just – I was angry. I was actually furious with him about everything, and then I thought, Whatever Diana is like he has married her, and I must try to see the best in her because of him. But you, my poor darling, you had the worst of it. You didn't want to come anyway – only did it to drive me. Please, please, forgive me!'

'Get into bed or you'll freeze.

'And of course I forgive you,' she said a minute later.

After they had kissed and Rachel lay in Sid's arms, she said, 'The worst thing I did was that monstrous gibe about it being a good thing that Diana hadn't gone for you being Jewish. I said that to hurt you. I think when people are angry they pick on anything that will hurt, and that's what I did. I take it all back, of course.'

'You're not very good at anger, my treasure. It's never been your strong suit.'

And so they made it up.

∞ ∞ ∞

It was some weeks before she could bring herself to ask (casually) whether Rachel actually minded her being Jewish, and was blessedly assured that of course she did not.

LOUISE, JOSEPH
AND EDWARD

She felt very grown-up in her new black corded silk dress that Mrs Milic had made her, the bodice cut low with a deep, rounded neckline that showed off the gold chain Edward had given her for her birthday. She also felt a sense of triumph: although it had proved surprisingly easy to get her father and her lover to dine together, it was more fun to feel it had required intense diplomacy. Her father had fetched her from Blandford Street and they had arrived at L'Étoile before Joseph, were shown to their table by the *patron* himself and presented with glasses of champagne.

'Darling, you do look wonderful. You get less and less plain by the week.'

He was looking rather haggard – poor Dad – and she bet that living with Diana was no bed of roses. 'How is your new house?'

'Oh, splendid. You must come and visit us – we'd love to have you.' But he said it without much conviction, and they smiled at each other to cover the insincerity.

'Here's Joseph,' she said, with some relief.

And Edward saw a tall, dark-haired man, impeccably dressed, with an Old Etonian tie, moving gracefully towards them. He shook hands with Edward and picked

up Louise's hand to kiss it. 'How good of you to come.'
A glass was produced for him at once, with menus for
them all.

The menus were the kind that omitted prices on those
given to the guests, and just as they were settling down
to choose, the oldest waiter, with white hair and a tragic
expression, wheeled a trolley up to them that contained
a magnificent fish salad and they all decided that they
would start with it. 'It's absolutely delicious,' Louise told
her father. She was famished – hadn't eaten properly
since her dinner with Joseph the night before.

Joseph, who had been studying the wine list, said,
'How would you all feel about a rack of lamb to follow?'

Louise said good, and Edward said perfect.

'I must say you are the perfect guests: no fussing and
changing your minds.' He ordered two bottles of wine.
'The red may be a bit of a gamble. It's a 1934 Mouton
Rothschild, and it may not have come round. I keep
trying it every six months or so because it's such a great
wine, and last time it was so nearly there that tonight I
feel we might just have hit the jackpot. Meanwhile I
thought we'd start with a Pouilly Fumé. Your daughter
told me that you feel about wine much as I do.'

The white napery and sparkling glasses made for an
atmosphere both festive and cosy, and the mirror glass
in the back wall reflected an infinity of little red lamps
around them.

'Well, now. Louise has told me that you have a family
business selling timber, and that you own three wharves,
two in London and one in Southampton. Plus a London
office in a pretty posh part of Westminster.'

'Yes. But in the last few years we haven't been making
enough money.'

'Ah.'

There was a pause as they each started on their meal, and then Edward continued, 'We specialise in unusual hardwoods – my father was the first timber merchant to import them. We used to do quite a lot of business with private railway companies, but since nationalisation that's got much harder because there aren't the number of buyers there used to be.' Something about Joseph's attentive and intelligent expression gave him confidence: he looked the sort of chap who'd understand.

'We're not simply making too little money, we're losing. We're heavily in hock to the bank, and I don't think they'll stand for much more. I think we should sell off at least two wharves and find a cheaper office, but my brother, who is the present chairman, is dead against it. Any of it.'

Louise noticed, when she looked at her father, how careworn he seemed – years older than the gallant charming Dad she was used to.

'Of course, selling off property is an option. But have you considered a third one?'

'What would that be?'

'Going public. Ceasing to be a private firm. Of course you would still be running it, but you would no longer be responsible for its finances. There would be people put in to deal with that. The accountants would also need to be assessors. They would be responsible for assessing all the capital value, as well as the debts, plus the goodwill is sure to be considerable, and when a new board of directors is formed, the shareholders would need to be represented. But if you decide to go public, your present directors could walk away with substantial sums of money, plus a number of shares in the new company.'

There was a silence while the wine waiter poured a small amount of the burgundy into Joseph's glass and he tasted. Then, to Edward, he said, 'I shall be most interested in what you think of this wine, as I know from Louise that you're an authority.'

So Edward went through the ritual: swirling the wine gently in the glass while he inhaled it, taking a sip and rolling it round his palate before finally swallowing and waiting for its aftertaste. 'Yes! Oh, *yes*! Full marks from me.' And he smiled at his host.

How clever Joseph is, Louise thought. Her father had been looking somewhat overwhelmed by Joseph's radical suggestions; now he was feeling really good because Joseph had deferred to him about the boring old wine.

'My friend does not like her lamb too pink. Give her the ends. I'm so glad you like the wine. It's taken a devil of a time to come round, but here it is at last. Here's to the future of Cazalet Brothers.'

It was then that Edward, who was clearly much impressed by Joseph, started to tell him more about his brother's attitude to change of any kind, and the stalemate consequences.

'And the rest of the board? What do they think? And, by the way, who are they?'

Edward, for the first time, looked uncomfortable. 'Well, they realise that things haven't been going well lately, but otherwise they're rather in the dark. At meetings this has not been discussed. Except by my older brother and me. Hugh is the chairman.'

'Yes, so you said. But who are the others?'

'My second brother, Rupert, my son Teddy, who has only just been appointed, and our sister, Rachel Cazalet. Our father was adamant that only Cazalets be appointed. Rachel is not a very active member: she lives in the country.' He stopped there to take a refreshing swig of the wine.

Joseph, who had been regarding him steadily, said, 'My dear chap – may I call you Edward? – I'm afraid I've been spoiling your dinner. Putting you in the dock, as it were. Louise and I went to the Royal Court last week to see Laurence Olivier. He gave a cracking performance, didn't he, darling?'

'Oh, yes! He played the part of a clapped-out music-hall turn. He was wonderful, so seedy and vulgar – and sad! It was marvellous. You should go, Dad – you'd love it.'

She was about to suggest they go together when he said, 'I think Diana would enjoy it. She loves the odd night in town – stops her getting bored in the country with me away all day.'

Joseph, who had been told at length about Diana's behaviour in France, now fleetingly caught Louise's eye, which stopped her feeling sad and made her simply want to laugh: When people marry awful people, just be grateful that you aren't them – either of them.

Edward had finished his lamb, and pudding menus were presented. The men opted for cheese because of the burgundy, but she was free to have a lovely large ice cream.

'I can't think where she puts it all. She eats like a horse and stays as thin as a rake,' Joseph said fondly. He had no idea how little food was consumed at Blandford Street. Stella regarded food simply as fuel and they rarely had time to cook. Stella – who was always too late to catch buses – spent her money on taxis and Louise spent hers on beautiful material for her Polish dressmaker to make her clothes. They also splashed out on a cleaner three mornings a week, a large, mournful lady, who said she started each day on ten aspirin, and Stella said looked unnervingly like Katherine Mansfield.

The men were still talking about business. She caught Joseph saying that perhaps Edward's brother might be consoled by the fact that going private would take at least two years, during which property would have to be sold off to pay back the bank and trading would need to return to profit – otherwise nobody would want to buy shares when, eventually, they came on the market. 'But I do urge you to think seriously about this. Now is the time. If you leave it much longer, it might be too late. In the meantime, in spite of our delightfully urbane prime minister, one cannot be sure how long anything will last. Busts tend to succeed booms, although people never seem to think they will at the time.'

The wine waiter arrived with his trolley, and another with their coffee.

'Brandy? I prefer Delamain myself, but do choose what suits you.'

Edward said that Delamain would be fine.

'Dad, you're not driving all the way to Hawkhurst, are you?'

'I told Diana I'd be back.'

'Oh.'

'What about you?'

'Jo will drop me off. Couldn't you stay the night with Uncle Rupe?'

'I expect I could, but I'd rather get back. The roads are

clear at this time of the evening – it will be easy.' He finished his brandy and stood up. 'I have to thank you for the most delicious and helpful evening.'

'Not at all. If you ever want any more advice of the kind I can help with, just let me know.' He pulled a card out of his wallet and handed it to Edward. 'That will find me.'

Edward stooped to kiss his daughter, who put an arm round his neck to kiss him back.

'Drive carefully, won't you?'

'Like a racing snail,' he said, and then he was gone.

'Did you like him?'

'Darling, what a silly question. Of course I liked him, and I can see that the poor chap is caught in the usual trap of small family set-ups. A clash of personalities between a group of people who aren't really cut out to be in business anyway. But if I'd loathed him, would you seriously have expected me to say so? Would you, my foolish little rabbit?' He signed the bill, and they were shown out by the *patron* who still kept offering Louise a free lunch every day if she would sit at the window table to eat it. 'But I can't possibly eat by myself in a restaurant!' and Joseph had laughed and said of course she couldn't.

∞ ∞ ∞

They drove back to Blandford Street, and he was undressed and in her bed before she had finished removing her make-up. She felt strongly that going to bed with any of it on was squalid, so every night he contained his impatience and watched until she, too, was naked.

CLARY AND ARCHIE

Clary found herself crying over the washing-up of last night's supper and that morning's breakfast. She was alone, as usual. The children had gone to school, and Archie had one of his teaching days. She wiped her eyes crossly on the already sopping teacloth and sat down at the kitchen table to try to sort things out. Why on earth was she crying? On the face of it, things had got much better: Archie taking the teaching job at Camberwell meant that a little money was reliably coming in. She could cut down her freelance proofreading and get on with her novel. The trouble with that was that she wasn't getting on with it: she was stuck, bored with the people she was writing about and fed up with their silly antics. She was ground down by the endless household chores that seemed to need redoing as often as meals had to be prepared and demolished. The children were doing fairly well at school, although Bertie had had to have an expensive brace for his front teeth, which had to be adjusted. She had taken to giving him a treat of some sort after each dental visit, but this meant taking Harriet as well, which made it more unfair than ever, according to Bertie. Harriet resorted to sore throats as a way of qualifying for the treat. But this was all minor stuff; the children were fine, really, and Archie was a good, involved father.

Archie had begun at Camberwell by saying how much he loathed teaching, but lately he had come back after his teaching days apparently much happier, although he told her less and less about them. She had asked him once whether he thought any of his students were promising, and he had answered shortly that one or two might be. He came back from those days too tired, he said, to fuck, but wanted a really good cuddle in bed, and she enjoyed that.

It was Monday, a day when he was teaching, and the day when she went every week to clean and clear up his studio; he was a very messy painter and left everything not where he had found it. Afterwards, she would go and have coffee and a sandwich at a nearby café.

It was a bright day, with a cool wind, and she noticed at once that he had left his leather jacket hanging on the back of the easel.

When she had finished the cleaning, she pulled the jacket off the easel – it got stuck, she tugged it, and as it came free, an envelope fell to the floor. The envelope said 'Melanie' on the outside, and had not been stuck down.

Although a part of her knew she should not do so, she pulled out the letter inside and read it.

Half an hour later, she was sitting in the café with coffee and a sandwich that she found she could not face with the letter, open, beside her. She felt dizzy, and her cup shook in her hand so that she kept spilling it. Phrases from the letter kept repeating themselves in her head: 'the most difficult letter I have ever had to write', 'your incomparable beauty – you have a face that Holbein would have delighted in', 'you are twenty, my dearest, at the beginning of your life, and I am an old man in comparison, a married man with two children, quite the wrong person – though, God, how I wish it was other-wise . . .' And then a whole paragraph about how their love for one another must stop, 'for Clary's sake and the children's'. She must transfer to another class, must never come to the studio again, must not write to him. He would keep faithfully to his side of the bargain, and he knew, with her tender heart, she would understand and comply. Believe him, she would get over it, and however hard the struggle was, he would do the same.

She had read the letter so many times that she almost knew it by heart. Heart! She felt as though it had been stabbed so many times that it was like some great bleeding bruise, unable now to withstand repeated blows.

She left the café and walked to Hyde Park to find some quiet bench where she could cry and try to get over the shock.

She remembered at their beginning that she had hardly been able to believe that he really loved her, how long it had taken to restore her trust, and how patient, how gentle he had been about that, and how her pleasure and joy in the general affections of family life had finally beaten her rotten opinion of herself, and her uncertainties had receded to periodic shortages of money, worrying about her novel and having to cook so much.

And now – this. This ambush; this monstrous, horrible cliché. Middle-aged married man falls for young girl whose breasts would not have sagged from breastfeeding two babies, whose (no doubt) flawless complexion would not have fine lines or blue shadows under her eyes from months of sleepless nights, who was probably over-whelmed by the attention of an older, attractive man, who most likely regarded her situation as uniquely romantic, who had possibly been egging him on to run away with her . . . How long had it been going on? He might well have been writing letters of this kind for months, letters in which the resolution was easily broken down by her pathetic frantic replies . . . Which meant that he had been lying to Clary for months . . .

When she had sobbed herself dry she began to feel angry; very, very angry. He couldn't love her and write that sort of letter. She appeared in it simply as a duty – a responsibility, with the children. The thought of them further enraged her. How could he do this to them?

By now, she had convinced herself that he would leave her to cope for the rest of her life with two unhappy children, not enough money to do more for them but scrape by, trying to mask her broken heart from them, trying always to speak well of their perfidious father. Life would be lived alone once the children were old enough to leave her. But the future, however terrible and bleak, was nothing compared with the present. For how long had she been so bloody certain that he loved her when he had really loved someone else and lied to her about it? How long had she been humiliated in this way? Did the whole class at Camberwell know – or, at least, guess – what was going on? How could she have been so insensitive not to feel the change in him? And how did she now feel about him – about Archie?

Saying his name to herself brought on a fresh agony of tears – Archie, Archie; repeating it made her realise that she still loved him. Of course! That's why it hurts so much. I still love him – have no idea how to stop that. He's selfish, a liar, he's despicable, he's not thinking for a moment about poor Harriet and Bertie – or me, come to that: how can I love him? She had run out of paper handkerchiefs and had to use her long cotton scarf. She got up from the bench and started to walk north up Park Lane. She would have to confront him as soon as he came home, but it couldn't be in front of the children. She walked as far as Marble Arch and, when she had found a shop, bought herself a packet of cigarettes. It was noon, and he would not be back until after six.

∞ ∞ ∞

Archie, who had been dreading it, had a day that had lived well down to his expectations. For a start, it was surprisingly chilly, and he had left his only warm jacket yesterday in the studio. Then, when he walked into the studio where he taught, she was there. His heart gave a little jump at the sight of her, which he quelled to an ersatz irritation. Either she had disobeyed his instruction, or she had not got his letter.

He had oh so painfully prepared himself for her absence that seeing her – in her paint-bespattered blue overall, with her lovely red-gold hair tied severely back into a ponytail – was almost more than he could bear. Two whole hours of it, during which he must concentrate on teaching the rest of the little buggers. He felt her eyes upon him, and gave her one stern, unforgiving glance. He posed the model and told them what he wanted them to do.

When, after the first break, he did the rounds, he left her until last. He bent down, as though to examine her drawing more closely, and said, 'Why are you here? Didn't you get my letter?'

'What letter? No. What letter?' She looked very frightened.

'I can't explain that now. But no coffee this evening. I

have to get back.' And, as he said this, he suddenly remembered quite clearly that he had put the letter in his leather-jacket pocket, meaning to post it yesterday on his way home. And, of course, he had forgotten the jacket. It had not been posted. What a fool! 'You mustn't worry,' he said more gently. 'I simply needed to write to you. I'm afraid I forgot to post the letter.' He was feeling deeply ashamed of himself now. It was surely a cowardly way of saying goodbye to her – but it had had to be done somehow, and it had cost him so much agony of mind to make the decision, then to write it down. There was no kind or good way of ditching someone, he kept saying to himself, as he struggled through the afternoon.

He had written because he simply didn't trust himself to stick to his decision if she was there – weeping, no doubt, arguing, wanting to talk about their love – throwing her arms round him, imploring him to think again, saying that she didn't care about marriage, would be content with so little, provided she could be with him sometimes. These last promises he knew to be untrue, knew also that she did not know that.

He was her first love, and he knew – or could remember – how potent, how unique that situation was for those so entrapped.

She would get over it – probably a good deal sooner than he.

But at least, by this decision, by putting it down on paper, he had spared his darling Clary any pain. Because, of course, he loved her, too.

It was all nonsense that people were unable to be in love with more than one person at a time; possibly this might be true for a woman, but clearly not for a man. 'I wasn't searching for someone to be in love with; it simply struck me – out of the blue.' Part of him longed to tell Clary this – to show her how much he must love her to sacrifice so much for her. But this would be a mistake: Clary's equilibrium was too fragile for even mild shocks – after all, the whole point of the letter was that the affair (which it had never physically been) was over. All he had to do now was to try to stop thinking about Melanie until she faded into the past. This made him think about her the whole of the long bus ride home. He decided to stop at the pub in Abbey Road before facing the family. A drink would warm him up; he felt perished, and the pub would provide a kind of no man's land between Melanie and Clary.

∞ ∞ ∞

'But you weren't going to tell me, were you?'

'I wasn't going to tell you because it's over, finished, done with.'

'So all these weeks of lying don't count for anything.'

'They count, of course, to me. But I desperately didn't want to upset you.'

'Upset me!' She tried a hard little laugh that turned into a sob. She wasn't wearing her usual house clothes but the grey corduroy pinafore dress with a shirt of a paler grey. And she had brushed her hair. She must have been waiting all day to confront him, he realised, and she had clearly been crying a good deal. He felt a rush of pity for her. She had sent Bertie and Harriet away for the night so she had had hours alone with the bloody letter. He, more than anyone, knew what she had already suffered.

'Dearest Clary – I know you may find it impossible to

believe, but I do love you. I am so, so sorry that I have exposed you to all this. It's my bloody carelessness—'

But she interrupted: 'Upset! It's not your bloody carelessness – it's what you've done. You've fallen in love with someone else and lied about it. Surely you can see what that means . . .'

'But you can see from the letter that I'm giving her up! You don't seem to have taken that in.'

There was a pause, and then, with some difficulty, she said, 'Being responsible, duty and all that, doesn't change your heart. You are in love with her "incomparable beauty – a face that would have delighted Holbein". You do love her.'

'And I love you, dearest girl.'

'There you go again! You cannot have two dearests.' She picked a cigarette out of the nearly empty packet and lit it with shaking fingers.

'It's something I've discovered,' he said, speaking awkwardly – everything he said seemed to have a double edge to it. 'Actually, you can love two people. I didn't know that until now.'

She met his eye as she answered steadily, 'I couldn't. I could never love two people at once. I don't believe that.'

No, she would not. He realised then that she would want to know something desperately important to her, something that she would be too proud to ask. 'You might like to know that I have never slept with Melanie. Nothing like that.'

He saw the tension in her shoulders relax a little, as she replied, 'There isn't anything "like that".'

'No,' he agreed. 'But I thought you might like to know.' He wanted to take her in his arms, but she was not ready to be touched. Instead he said, 'Shall we have a glass of wine?'

'If you like.'

When he came back to the table with a bottle and glasses, she had packed the letter into its envelope. He poured the wine. 'By the way, nobody knows anything at all about this.'

Much later, he said, 'Why do we always sit at the kitchen table when we have a lovely studio looking onto our nice wild garden?'

'It began when Bertie started walking. He was fascinated by your paints and pulled your palette down one day and did an extensive finger-painting all over our old sofa.'

'You never told me that.'

(A faint smile.) 'I didn't dare.'

'Bring your glass.' He tucked the bottle under one arm and took her hand. 'I'm leading you – I don't want you to lose your way. You know what you're like with maps in cars.' He felt her hand trembling in his. He thought, I'm glad I love her so much.

They sat side by side but with a gap between them on the battered old red velvet *chaise longue*. The bottle and their glasses were perched upon his painting stool.

'Well, at least we've got some daffodils in our garden.'

'I don't really like daffodils. They seem to me rather heartless flowers – except the very small timid ones.'

'I'll get you some of the cowardly little creatures to plant for next year.'

'Next year. Oh.' She glanced at him, then quickly looked away.' Her poor face was ravaged by her prolonged weeping: unlike heroines in books, she had a sort of greyish white pallor, with a bright pink nose and her lovely eyes red-rimmed. Usually, he could have made her laugh about this, but not now. Now she wanted comfort, reassurance, and he was unsure how to give it. Time – she needed time.

'What are we having for supper?'

There was a pause, and then she said, 'I was trying to think. I'm afraid there isn't anything. I was so busy packing the children off to Dad and Zoë – and I didn't think . . . You might not have been coming back—' Her eyes were filling with tears again, and again he realised, with fresh humility, how much she had been through, how much she did, in fact, love him.

Love, for Clary, had always been a wholehearted and serious matter. Losing her mother, then her father, Rupert, being missing all those war years, not just missing, presumed by the family to be dead: everyone had supposed that excepting her.

'I could take you out to dinner,' he said. 'Would you like that?' But she shook her head.

In the end, he went to the small Indian restaurant near Maida Vale tube station and got them chicken curry, dhal, rice, and some poppadoms that broke into pieces in their paper bag. During the walk, wait, and walk back, he decided a dozen times not to think about how Melanie was feeling, which made him – each time – think about her more.

She certainly knew that all was not well; she would be fearful, anxious and miserably imagining what the dreaded letter might contain.

He had addressed, sealed and stamped the letter – had had to ask Clary for a stamp, which she had produced without looking at him. (The letter was now safely posted.)

I've behaved like a shit to her, and I suppose that means in a way that I am one. Turning over a new leaf was so difficult because one never knew what would be on it. He thought again how glad he was that he loved Clary so much. At least he was sure of that. This made him think how completely awful it must be for husbands who fell in love with someone they weren't married to and who didn't love their wife in the first place. He couldn't think long about that, but his incredible luck made him feel humble.

All very well, but supper wasn't easy.

It began all right, because the children had rung up while he'd been out. They were fine, Clary said, except they were hell-bent on having a white rat – two white rats, like Rivers. 'Georgie says it has changed his life having him. And we want our lives changed.' They were seizing the telephone from each other in their eagerness to express the idea.

'What did you say?'

'I said I'd think about it, and Bertie said, "That means you won't do anything." I remember how maddening I found that think-about-it stuff – it's just a weak cop-out. The trouble is, Archie, that I don't really like rats. In fact, I'm slightly afraid of them.'

She had said his name – a small step?

'Why don't we get them a kitten?'

'Two kittens, they'll want one each.'

'Well – two. We could get them when we go to Home Place at Easter. Mr York, that nice farmer, is bound to have some.'

But after that, constraint set in. They were both trying to be normal, but the trouble with normal was that the moment you tried to be it, it wasn't possible. In the end, bed had to be mentioned: they were both bone tired and longing for oblivion.

In bed, he told her he loved her, and she was still while he said it, but when he tried to kiss her face, she turned away and he only managed the side of her forehead.

He woke in the night because she was crying. He put an arm round her shoulders and soothed her awake. 'Only a dream, my darling, just a sad dream.' He felt her trembling – repeating the dream in her wakened mind as one does so often with nightmares. When she had finished, he pulled her close to him. 'You are my dearest girl.'

And he knew she was better, because she murmured in a soft furry voice, 'Buttering me up,' and was instantly again asleep.

PART SIX

SUMMER–AUTUMN 1957

TEDDY

He had been very excited when Uncle Hugh had told him that he was to manage the Southampton wharf and mill. Excited and – although he did not admit it to anyone – very nervous. In London he had always had Dad to ask about things; now there would only be a man called Hector McIver, and although he had been working at the firm for what seemed for ever, he still felt a bit awkward asking an employee – not even on the board – for help.

Add to this the fast-discovered fact that poor-sighted McIver was also extremely deaf – you really had to face him and shout. He spoke so quietly and, with a Glaswegian accent, that Teddy had to repeat nearly everything he said. He was courteous, hard-working, and he worshipped Teddy's father, which made a good start. He found Teddy lodgings in a house kept by a naval widow, who was prepared to make his breakfast and supper and see to his laundry, all for six pounds a week. This was a piece of luck for Teddy, because although his salary had been increased, he could no longer count on meals with the family, and also they had taken his car, which they'd said he would no longer need. He felt injured by that: it made a huge difference to finding a girl, and having any outdoor fun with her if he did. He determined to save up for one: you could get quite a decent car for five hundred quid. He could get to the wharf by bus or foot and he was expected to be in his office by nine when a Miss Sharples would come in with his mail and, each week when it came out, the *Timber Trades Journal*. He was supposed to read this from cover to cover, and it proved to be diabolically dull. As a result, he did not learn very much from it. Outside, he was struggling to identify and remember the exotic names of the hardwoods that were imported largely to Southampton – pyinkado, Andaman padauk, the endless mass of boxwood, rosewood (nothing to do with roses), laurel, acacia, walnut, lime, cherry, elm, oak of varying kinds, chestnut, ash – not to mention softwoods that arrived in regular batches, and had to be unloaded, then floated in the river until space could be found for them in and around the sawmill. Miss Sharples brought him mail that contained orders, often couched in – to him – unintelligible language. Then there were a rising number of complaints that orders had not arrived on time, or were not supplied in the quantity asked for, and in some cases simply the wrong timber, or no timber at all.

'We really don't have the requisite number of lorries, Mr Teddy. That is our quandary. Perhaps you could have a word with your father about that.' Costs were rising all the time, and orders were not keeping pace with them. Teddy found a great deal of it tedious. And when he thought about the lives that his father and uncles enjoyed, he felt that something was wrong somewhere. He had taken to skipping Mrs Malton's suppers: they generally consisted of grey oily mince with a great deal of lumpy potato, followed by tinned fruit and custard. He tried several pubs and settled on one that was in walking distance of Commodore Villa – the House of

Mince he had come to call it: his hostess minced as much as she made it.

The pub had been half-heartedly made to look old-fashioned, with horse brasses and a large stone fireplace piled with logs that were never lit and sconces that had small shades covered with sailing ships. However, just as he was going to give it up, it proved to have one great asset: a buxom young barmaid, who wore rather carelessly buttoned shirts under her apron, bewitching black stockings and pointed high-heeled shoes. She had red hair that was a riot of curls, a milk-and-roses complexion, and a soft Irish voice that enchanted him. They started to have conversations while she drew his beer, frequently stopping to serve other customers, he soon realised, to prolong them.

She had been in England only for a month, she said; came from Cork where her family had a small farm that her father managed with her uncle but they didn't hit it off, and her mam was worn out with the children and the fights on Saturday nights. As soon as she could, she had got away to earn some money and see the world. She was eighteen, she said, but later confessed to being a year younger. A friend had told her that work was to be had in pubs and clubs, especially in ports, so she had come over with four pounds and a bed with her friend Louie.

'Here I am, so.'

He asked her name. She was Ellen. He asked her if she would come out with him.

She only got a half-day a week, she said, 'But I'd really like to come.' She was blushing deeply. She was a most charming blend of seductiveness and innocence.

Her half-day proved to be Wednesday.

They arranged to meet where the ferry left for Ryde, on the Isle of Wight. He asked McIver if he could possibly borrow one of the firm's cars for the day – he had a relative on the island who was ill and anxious to see him. McIver was easy to take in, and agreed 'just this once'. He cashed fifty pounds and the following Wednesday watched her walking down the quay towards him with true excitement. It was a balmy day, and the ferry was not crowded at all.

'You have a motor!' she exclaimed, when she reached him. She wore a tight black skirt, her high heels and carried a mac over her arm. Her shirt was of grass-green satin, cut so low that the cleft between her milky breasts was immediately apparent. She looked at him with her cloudy grey-green eyes and started to blush. 'I've never been out with a gentleman,' she said.

She had not, he discovered later, really been out with anyone.

'Where are we going?'

To the island, he said. He'd never been there and thought it would be fun.

They both enjoyed the ferry, had a soft drink at the bar, and then went on deck. The sea was behaving like it did in a watercolour hung in the drawing room at Home Place: gentle blue water, with little creamy waves, dotted with the sharp bright white triangles of the many sailing craft that scurried to and fro upon it. He put his arm round her. 'Don't want you falling in.'

'Nor I. I can't swim no more than a wheelbarrow.'

'I would rescue you,' he said. He felt full of tenderness towards her. She was the opposite of his ex-wife Bernadine and the most recent girlfriend he had left so easily in London. 'I would protect you from anything,' he said.

He bent down to draw her towards him, lifted her chin to kiss her inviting mouth. She gave a little gasp, then pressed herself to him. When they drew apart, she said, 'I feel kind of funny – must sit down.'

He led her to a bench and they sat in silence for a minute or two. Then she said, 'I thought I was going to pass out. Sorry. Never felt like that before.'

'Like what, darling?'

'Kind of watery – weak.' Then, almost inaudibly, she added, 'Weak and eager.' Then, she said, 'What's your name when you're at home?'

'Oh. Sorry, I thought I'd told you. Teddy. My name is Teddy – short for Edward, after my father.'

'Mr Ted. Or Mr Edward, I suppose.'

'That's my first name. I'm Teddy Cazalet.'

After a moment she said: 'And I'm Ellen. Ellen McGuire.'

They were approaching land; the port seemed jammed with traffic and people, the sun winking on the windows of houses and cars. It was midday, and Teddy felt hungry.

'Where are we going here?'

'We're going to find some lunch, and then we'll go exploring. Would you like that?'

'Oh, yes! I'd like anything we do really, Mr Ted.'

'I'm not Mr, darling, just Ted or Teddy.'

They found a quiet pub outside the town where a few people were eating in the garden. 'Do you like lobster?'

'I've never had it. When they caught any, the fishermen sold it to Dublin for tourists.'

'Well, today we're tourists. We're on holiday. If you find you don't like lobster, you can have something else.'

But she did like it, and once he'd shown her how to

crack the claws and pick out the meat she was better at it than he. 'It's the best food I've had in me life.'

He leaned across their table to wipe her face with his paper napkin, and she kept trustfully still while he did so. They drank bottled beer with the fish – 'You can't trust the draught if you don't know the pub,' she said, and he didn't feel up to choosing wine. He offered her an ice for afters, but she said she couldn't fancy another thing.

She announced – in a stage whisper that caught the attention of a couple sitting near them – that she was going to find a toilet, and he called the waitress for the bill, which was surprisingly reasonable.

They drove inland to pretty and sparsely populated countryside. They both felt sleepy after the meal, and he said he was going to find somewhere they could have a nice snooze.

In due course he found the perfect place: an opening with a gate into a small field. On the far side of the hedge was a delightfully dry ditch. There was an old tartan car rug on the back seat, and he took that with him and laid it in the ditch. She had kicked off her uncomfortable shoes and joined him in their makeshift bed without a qualm. Soon they were lying side by side, out of the breeze with the sun on their faces. He had taken off his jacket and made a pillow for her head.

'Comfy?'

She nodded, and gave a pretty yawn, which showed her small white teeth.

But as soon as they were set for the sleep, the desire for it vanished. Instead he was undoing her blouse, exposing a tantalisingly inadequate brassière that hardly restricted her firm white breasts and rosy nipples. The moment he took one in his mouth she moaned, and the nipple hardened. He took his hand away to tear at the zip of his trousers, but she did it for him. 'Oh, Ted. Oh, Ted!'

For a moment it occurred to him that she had done all this before, and a mixture of disappointment and relief overcame him. 'So you want me, darling?'

'Oh, I do, Ted, I'm yelling for you, whatever it is. Wait just one moment.'

She pulled down her skirt and then the white pants until her whole body was to be seen. Her nipples were like the furled centre of a dark pink rose.

For an unknown amount of time he had her, as many times as he could get a fresh erection.

She had not done it before – she cried out the first time – but her arms tightened round him, and when he asked her if she was all right, she kissed him with surprising strength. In between these bouts of passion, he stroked her hair, murmured to her, kissed her throat and told her how lovely she was. 'I love you,' she said.

When eventually he parted from her he realised that she was bleeding heavily; the rug was soaked under her legs, which had more blood running down them.

'I must have hurt you – I didn't mean to.'

'No hurt,' she said. 'Only a smidgen. Nothing to fret about.'

But there was. There was nothing to clean her up with, so he got up and looked wildly round for water – a stream or a pond – but there was nothing in sight. He knew from his map that even if they managed to reach the sea it lay at the bottom of steep cliffs. They had to get back from the island somehow, but for a few panic-stricken moments, he could not imagine how this was to be accomplished.

'I think it's stopped,' she said. 'Give me my stockings.'

She rolled them up and stuffed them between her legs. She was sitting up now, and held out her hand for her diminutive white knickers, and he helped her pull them up. Then she sat on the edge of the bank while they tried to scrub her legs with the rug. This was not really successful as the blood had dried, and the result merely looked rusty. 'I don't mind,' she said. 'I don't care about anything but you.'

Somehow, he finished dressing her, hooking up the bra, pulling on her small black skirt and the green shirt, whose buttons he fumbled with. 'I didn't know bleeding was involved,' she said. 'People don't tell you anything where I come from except it's wicked, unless . . .' Her voice tailed off, until, in a quite different tone, she said, 'Oh, Ted, will I be having a baby?' Terror. She was terrified, he could feel.

'Of course not, darling. Of course you won't.' But this lie frightened him.

'Anyway, it would have happened when you kissed me on the boat, yes? It would have happened then?'

He was able to reassure her: no, that was not possible. Desperately not wanting her to pursue the matter, he looked at his watch and said they must be getting back so as not to miss the ferry.

He picked up her shoes, but she said she didn't want them until they got back. 'They kill me,' she said, 'but I don't have another pair.'

The journey back was more or less silent. He attended to her – got her a cup of tea on the boat and brought it to the same bench on deck that they had used before. He found that if he sat with his arm round her, she seemed content and, burdened with the lie he had told her, he didn't really want to talk at all.

They parted on the quay where he wrapped her in her mac. Silently, she held up her face and he kissed her trembling lips. She was trying not to cry. 'I'll see you tomorrow,' he said. 'It's been a wonderful day.'

'All the best,' she said, then went bravely stumbling in her shoes down the quay and out of sight.

∞ ∞ ∞

Alone, he sat in the car for a while, trying to sort out his feelings, but he couldn't and felt suddenly too tired to try. Better get the car back but, no, he would have to take the car rug to the cleaners and they would be shut now. He went to his lodgings, needing to wash and find a fresh shirt.

But when he got back, he was confronted by his landlady in a state of high excitement.

'There's two gentlemen been calling for you. I told them where you work, but they told me to pass on the message that they'll be expecting you at the Polygon Hotel before eight o'clock. It's ever so nice at the Polygon. My late husband's niece had her wedding reception there. She married an accountant, you know – they went to live in Canada so, of course, I don't see much of them. Two little girls they had, Sally Ann and Marylyn. I've ironed your best shirt and pressed those suit trousers for you.'

He thanked her, with a sinking heart. Somehow he knew that the appearance of uncles and/or his father boded no good.

It did. They were waiting for him at the bar and beckoned him to a table in a far corner.

Uneasy greetings.

'I wish you'd told me you were coming.' It felt the wrong thing to have said the moment he'd said it.

'McIver told us that you'd gone out for the day.'

'Yes – yes, I did. I felt I needed a day off.'

Hugh said, 'He told us you'd gone to see a sick relative on the Isle of Wight. He apparently lent you his car.'

'It was very kind of him.'

His father said, 'You know perfectly well that is not on. This is a weekday, and you're supposed to be running the wharf and sawmill. So your grandmother's funeral ploy won't wash.' He beckoned a waiter and ordered a second round.

That was just the beginning of it. They had been looking at the books – the correspondence, the lack of sales, the muddles and complaints. Did he know that a large order for teak had been transferred by the vendors to Maxwell Perkins, well known to be a highly competitive rival? And what had possessed him to order a large quantity of softwood to be dumped in the river?

When he said there hadn't been enough room on the land his father had exploded. 'Balls! You know perfectly well that soaking softwoods renders them unsaleable for weeks – even months – after you've taken them out.'

At this point a waiter said their table was ready in the dining room.

They chose their meal – at least, his father and uncle did – and he said he would have whatever they had chosen, which turned out to be lobster. He drank some of the wine, which was waiting for them in a misty bucket, and wondered how on earth he was going to get through the evening without blubbing or throwing up. At one moment, when his uncle went to answer a telephone call, his father leaned towards him and said, 'Listen, Teddy. You took some girl off with you for the day, didn't you? Hugh won't understand that, but I do. It's all very well for you to have some fun sometimes, but you really should be more sensible about how you go about it. And the one thing I won't stand for is you lying – to me or anyone else. You let the whole family down when you do that.'

His eyes filled with scalding tears and Edward whipped out one of his immense silk paisley handkerchiefs and proffered it. 'Blow your nose, and pull yourself together.'

'Sorry, Dad. I truly am. You see, I don't know if I can do this job – if I'm up to it.'

'Nonsense. You just need to learn more, work a bit harder at it. It's time you got married again, Teddy. I know you made a bit of mess with whatsername—'

'Bernadine.'

'Her. You need to find a nice girl, settle down and start a family. Lots of people don't have a good job they can walk into as you do.'

There was a pause while Teddy watched him put mayonnaise onto a mouthful of lobster. He looked then at his own plate, and pictures of the sunlit lunch with Ellen flickered and went out. He had lied to her, too. Well, a kind of lie. He supposed time – nerve-rackingly inexorable – would tell about that.

'Could I have some more wine?'

'Help yourself, and give me some. Hugh doesn't seem to drink much these days.'

A sudden passionate wish to confide in his father about Ellen invaded him. He would feel better if he could tell someone – especially if he could get some advice. But at that moment Hugh came back. 'Sorry, chaps. It was Jem. Her boys have got measles, and she feels she ought to send Laura away until they're out of quarantine.'

He looked only mildly worried; the ghost of a tender smile was there, as it always seemed to be whenever he spoke about his wife. He adored her – and it was mutual.

Edward suffered a twinge of jealousy as he thought that. Not, of course, for Jemima but for their situation.

'I told Jem we were gorging on lobster, and she said you know it gives you gyp, but from time to time it's worth it. I've ordered another bottle of Sancerre, so let's not talk shop for a bit and enjoy ourselves. You're not much of a trencherman, Teddy, are you?' But he said it kindly.

He listened while they talked about the state of the country – about what a good thing it was to have Macmillan rather than poor, worn-out Eden. Hugh didn't like the way 'we seem to be giving away our empire', but Edward said it would be a relief: there was always going to be trouble all over the place and we would be far better off keeping out of it. 'After all, he says we've never had it so good, and he's right.'

Trying to do his bit – he sensed that the brothers were on the edge of some argument that could turn acrid – Teddy said, 'But people are going to fight about things anyway, aren't they? They said that your war was the one to end all wars, and wars broke out all over the place.' He had speared a piece of lobster on his fork in the hope that if he concentrated on the conversation he might not notice eating it. Not so: he swallowed it whole, and it stuck in his throat precluding any further traffic, excepting wine, which he gulped in an effort to clear the way.

Eventually the meal was over, with coffee and a glass of port each on the table. A cigar for Edward and gaspers – as Hugh called them – for himself and Teddy.

They were both staying at the hotel, but Edward saw him off in McIver's Vauxhall.

'We'll expect you in the office at nine sharp. Don't be late. We have things to go through and discuss. Good night, old boy.' He clapped him on the shoulder and went back inside.

Teddy dragged the car rug out of the back seat and crammed it into the boot. It occurred to him with a kind of dull fear that the cleaners might not be open before nine in which case he would be in further trouble. It's as if I'd committed a murder, he thought. He felt rather drunk and really tired.

He crept into bed with the last thought that if the worst came to the worst, which it seemed to be bent on doing, he could chuck the wretched rug into the river. He set his alarm for seven thirty in the hope that there would be some warmish water for a bath. Then he tried to work out what he actually felt about sweet Ellen – a jolly romp? Love? Marriage? But somehow he was unable to feel anything. He was a creep, a liar; he could find nothing to justify his behaviour – to her or anyone else, come to that. Sleep rescued him from having to be alone with someone he could not like.

RUPERT AND FAMILY

'The thing is, Mum, now that I've got to eight, I'd rather stop getting old. I don't *want* to be like the rest of you. I just want Rivers and my zoo. So there's no point in my going to school.'

He was sitting on the kitchen table and Zoë, who was ironing, looked up. 'Georgie, I've told you dozens of times that you can't choose your age. You simply get older every time you have a birthday. And you wouldn't like not having them, would you?'

'I wouldn't,' Georgie conceded. 'But you could still make a non-birthday cake and give me the same presents.'

'But eventually you're going to need some money to buy food and things. You have to work to earn that.'

'I don't. I'll charge for the tickets to my zoo.'

'But where will you have the zoo?'

'There's plenty of room in the garden if you give up growing flowers.'

She spat on the iron before saying, 'But you won't be living here when you're grown-up. You'll have your own house and family.'

This shook him. 'But, Mum, I don't want to live anywhere without you! You, and Rivers. Dad could live with Juliet. I don't mind at all living without her.'

'And what about poor Dad?'

'If I have the zoo in the whole garden he can stay.' He had been chopping up the outside leaves of a lettuce for his tortoises with a very large knife, and now cut himself.

'Oh, Mum, look!' He held out a dirty hand on which a row of beady red blood was neatly ranged.

'I told you not to use that knife. Go and wash your hand – both hands.'

'It won't stop the blood, Mum. It needs a plaster.' But he jumped off the table and went to the sink.

'Use the soap, Georgie.'

'Now will you bandage it up?'

He loved Elastoplast and practically always had one or two plasters stuck on arms and legs. Some of them stayed for weeks after they were needed and she could only remove them by stealth – in the bath, or when he was seriously occupied with Rivers.

It was Saturday morning, and Rupert had been asked to meet Edward and Hugh at Hugh's house. There was no sign of Juliet, who alternated endless conversations on the telephone to her friend Chrissie with long sessions in bed, or trying on and discarding heaps of clothes that she claimed had become unwearable. She had really become a nuisance, Zoë thought, sulky, remote, sarcastic and wanting always to go shopping at weekends.

In spite of her tiresome manners, or lack of them, she continued to become prettier – had none of the teenage disadvantages, only the compulsion to play her pop music at full blast. Rupert had given her a cheap gramophone, so at least the music was confined to her room. Was I like that when I was her age? Zoë wondered rather uneasily – she felt guilty whenever she thought about her mother. She would never forget her on the telephone, when the cancer was killing her, saying that the last few years with her friend on the Isle of Wight had been the happiest of her life. Even that had upset her: those years should have been with me, she often began to think, then made herself stop, because that was simply further self-ishness on her part.

So, Juliet's behaviour was almost a way of making her pay for how she had been.

As Rupert was out, she would make sandwiches for herself and the children and they could have toad-in-the-hole for supper.

The telephone rang, and when she picked it up, Juliet was already on. 'It's Dad, for you,' she shouted – her bored shout: what could be duller than Dad ringing up Mum?

After confirming that he wouldn't be back until late afternoon, there was a pause, and then Rupert said, 'Could you get Jules to babysit Georgie tonight? I want to take you out to dinner.' He was using what she knew was his casual voice, which meant he was serious.

'I think she has a plan to stay with her friend Chrissie.'

'Tell her to have Chrissie over to us, then. Or I will, if you like.'

'I think I would like. What's up, darling?'

But he simply said, 'Put Jules on the phone, please.'

So she shouted and finally went up the stairs to attract Jules from the daily clamour of her music. 'You can take it in our room,' she yelled, above the din.

Georgie had gone into the garden with his tortoise food. The house, bathed in sunlight, seemed worryingly shabby: the stair carpet badly worn, the tiles on the kitchen floor chipped; even the pots of herbs on the windowsill were dusty. Her cleaner, who came two mornings a week, simply banged the Hoover about and then had a prolonged middle-mornings snack. She found herself thinking with nostalgia of the comfortable flat they had had in London, where everything had been well built and easy to maintain. This old and romantic house, with its ancient boiler and endless draughts, had fewer charms for her than it had for Rupert, who blithely ignored or dismissed the drawbacks. Its wonderful view of the river, its lovely eighteenth-century windows and panelled doors, its wide-boarded elm flooring and its pretty staircase were the things he loved. Oh, well: she knew that he had never wanted to stop being a painter and go into the family firm, and the house was his consolation. And, of course, it was nice to have more money. It was only that there now seemed to be so many more dull things to spend it on.

Still, it would be lovely to be taken out, not to have to cook dinner and play Racing Demon, Jules being bored and impatient with Georgie, who was rather slow at getting the hang of it. On Sunday, Clary and Archie were coming to lunch with their children and she decided to make a lemon meringue tart for pudding. While setting out the ingredients, she began to think what she would wear for the coming evening.

Juliet came down in her pyjamas to hack a piece of bread off the loaf and spread it liberally with Marmite. 'Dad said he'd collect Chrissie on his way back to pick you up. Half past seven, he said.' She seemed mollified at the prospect.

'Jules, it's nearly lunchtime – don't eat any more bread.'

'Lunch! I don't want lunch.'

And Zoë decided not to pursue the subject.

∞ ∞ ∞

Nearly eight hours later, after a trip to the pet shop with Georgie for him to gaze at the budgerigars and grass snakes, an early supper (Chrissie and Juliet were going to eat later), after bathing him, reading a story from *The Jungle Book*, after asking Juliet's advice about which dress she would wear (this in order to be able to implore her to be nice to her brother – she loved her mother asking advice and gave it freely: 'You can't possibly wear that, Mummy, you look awful in it'), after settling in the end for the old Hardy Amies that never let her down, after showing Juliet where the supper was in the fridge (she had had to buy things – 'Toad-in-the-hole is disgusting, Mummy. Chrissie couldn't possibly eat it'), after combing out her newly washed hair and putting on the old paste earrings she'd had for years – the first present she'd had from Rupert – after waiting only a few moments for him to arrive, after the pleasant drive into town, they were ensconced on the first floor of Wheeler's restaurant in Old Compton Street, sipping white wine with two large platters of oysters between them.

'So how was your meeting?' she asked. Get that out of the way and then we can talk about serious things, was how she secretly put it to herself.

He took a deep swig of his wine, then stretched out his hand on the table to touch hers. 'Sweetie, prepare yourself for a bit of a shock.'

She looked into his anxious eyes and her heart sank.

'Do they not want you in the firm any more? Darling, is that it? You know I support you in whatever you want to do.'

'It's nothing like that. It's— Well, apparently, Teddy isn't really up to running Southampton—'

'Well, surely it's a very good position. Hundreds of people would jump at the chance.'

'Yes, but unfortunately hardly any of them are called Cazalet.'

'You mean Hugh wants you to do it.'

'They both want me to.'

She stared at him for a moment, then said, 'But you can't. No, really, you cannot possibly do it. Commuting from Mortlake every day – you'd spend half your life travelling, you'd be utterly exhausted. Oh, darling, and you never wanted to do any of it in the first place.'

'We'd better get on with our oysters or our sole will be spoiled . . .

'The thing is,' he said, moments later, 'that of course it wouldn't work if I commuted. What it does mean is that I would have to live there – that we would have to move.'

'Leave Bank House? When you love it so much? What about the children? What about their schools?'

'We'd have to find new schools. We needn't live in the city. We could find some lovely village outside but not too far away. We could let Bank House, and rent the village one. It wouldn't be for ever, sweetheart, a couple of years perhaps . . .' But her face had resumed the expression that it had so often worn in the early years of their marriage. She had been years younger and it no longer became her.

'Darling! It's not my choice – you know that.'

'Of course I know it. So why should your brothers boss you about like this? Why doesn't one of them do it?'

'Well, I haven't talked about this because he doesn't want people to know, but Hugh isn't feeling so good these days – Edward doesn't actually think he would be up to it.'

'What about Edward, then?'

'I did ask him about that. But he's worried sick about Hugh's management. He said he simply couldn't leave him on his own in London. He told me he'd spent an evening with some banker chap who said we should aim to sell out – go public after we've got our bank loan down to acceptable proportions. He said the whole business could take at least two years, and that we should get on with it. Edward thoroughly agrees, but shifting Hugh is not easy. He still thinks that our father's methods are the only right ones. He simply won't accept that times have changed – are changing. Darling, you don't want to hear all this.'

'No, I don't. All I can hear is two selfish old men wanting their own way, and expecting you to pay for it. You should stand up to them, Rupe! Stop being so amenable!'

The waiter arrived to remove the oyster plates, and stopped when he saw that she had eaten only four of hers.

'I don't want them,' she said.

There was silence while their soles, Véronique and Colbert, were put before them and more wine poured.

'Don't tell me you've agreed to this.'

'I said I'd think it over. And talk to you.'

'Well, you have talked to me. And as you usually

seem to agree with the last person you talked to, the thing should be settled, shouldn't it?'

This last snipe really hurt him: it was nasty, and he also knew that it was uncomfortably true, but he could not bear it coming from her – his Zoë, his wife. 'I know,' he said, trying to smile. 'I know I'm supposed to be an indecisive person. Well, I am one. I can't help seeing the other person's point of view. Hugh has never recovered from the wound in his head, still suffers from appalling headaches that lay him out. His loss of a hand is nothing to that. And Edward, well, I sometimes think that Edward knows he made a mistake with Diana, and Rachel says that he's very unhappy about the rift with Hugh. I think he also misses the family life at Home Place. Rachel keeps trying to mend the rift, and Edward would be all for that, but he knows that Hugh disapproves of the marriage with Diana, which puts him on a sort of moral high ground that Edward can't swallow.'

After a pause, she said, 'But this is all about them. What about you?' Then, she added, 'That was a horrible thing to say. You have a much nicer character than I do. You worry about other people and all I care about is you and our children.'

The temperature had gone down a bit, he thought gratefully – and, after all, she had a point of view, which he absolutely had to take into account.

'I think we've talked about it enough for now,' he said. 'Shall we make a great British effort to enjoy ourselves?'

So it wasn't until they were driving home, and she was sleepy and content after her second rose-impregnated Ghul, which was the only liqueur that she really loved, that he said, in a carefully casual way, that perhaps while they were making up their minds, it might be useful – even fun – to pop down to Southampton and explore the villages nearby.

But she made no answer to this, and he realised that she was fast asleep.

SIMON AND NEVILLE

'Well, all I can say is that you're a fool.'

Neville was running through strips of negatives, holding them to the light, and every now and then chalking the possibles, with Simon standing awkwardly behind him. When Simon didn't reply, he said, 'As a matter of fact, I was on the point of arranging for you to go with me to Venice for a shoot, and now you'll miss all that.'

'I honestly don't care. I'm not getting anywhere working for you.'

'You're training. If you bothered to learn—'

'What? I've learned to be a dogsbody, if that's what you mean. I don't want to be a photographer, if *that's* what you mean.'

Neville, who had so far conducted this conversation with his back to Simon, now turned round. 'Well,' he said, 'what do you want to be?'

And before he could think any more about it, Simon said, 'A gardener. I want to be a gardener,' and as he said this, he realised he had been saying it to himself for months. It was Neville's look of extreme condescension that had goaded him to commit himself aloud to someone else. 'A gardener,' he repeated.

There was a short silence while Neville lit a cigarette, then said, 'Oh, well, I suppose you know best.'

He sounded unconvinced, which made Simon say, 'So

I'll be handing in my notice as from now. You owe me nine pounds,' he added.

'You ought to be giving me a month's notice. It's the least you could do.'

'I'm sick of doing the least I could do. I'm leaving now. So cough up.'

'It isn't nine pounds because you borrowed a fiver off me last week. Remember?'

'OK. Whatever it is, then.' By now he was stuffing his few belongings into his rucksack – no more sleeping in a cupboard.

Neville had followed him to watch this, and now fumbled in his threadbare velvet jacket – the one he only wore in the flat – for a handful of notes. He counted them out and added two fivers. He was starting to feel rather a shit.

'Bonus,' he said. 'A Golden Goodbye.'

'Thanks very much.' Simon was clearly pleased. They parted more comfortably than either of them had expected, shook hands and wished each other good luck.

∞ ∞ ∞

With Simon gone, the flat seemed surprisingly desolate. He had no assignment until he was to go to Venice for the weekend. In the end he did what he often did when alone: made some proper coffee, settled into the sagging armchair that never stopped leaking feathers and looked at his pictures of Juliet. They were stunning. She was a natural model, difficult to take a bad picture of her, and since last Christmas he had accumulated quite a stack.

Their relationship – precarious at best – was at once kept alive and impeded by secrecy. He knew that the family would come down on him like a ton of bricks if they knew about it, and she would be badly affected. He managed to see her by making his arrangements with Rupert or Zoë, who simply thought how nice it was of him to ask her to the theatre or cinema, or for walks in Richmond Park. Twice he had taken her out to lunch after a shopping session, which she'd simply adored, never questioning him about his choice of clothes. Every time they met, he was struck by her beauty, sometimes trying other words to describe her: lovely, pretty, attractive, ravishing, perfect – all these descriptions fitted her appearance, and no single one seemed enough.

On the whole, his situation with her (she had no idea how serious he was) suited him. He would have to wait for her to be old enough for him – as he put it – to carry her off, but this would give her time to grow up and for him to get his life together.

He would give up this grotty little flat and get himself somewhere far better and more suited to their future life together, and meanwhile the romance, the sheer amazing chance that he should have met her before anyone else had staked a claim, was enough for him to be going on with. His energy, emotional, sexual, whatever it was, had to be largely spent upon his career. He was known, but he needed to be famous; he needed to be one of the half-dozen top photographers in his field.

He opened the last tin of baked beans and ate them with a spoon, while he imagined finding somewhere marvellous and unusual – a boat moored at Chelsea, or a wharf on the river with a roof garden – to live, eventually, with his radiant love.

For the rest of the day, while he was checking and packing his equipment for Venice, calling his editor to find a replacement for Simon, searching for a clean shirt and trying to remove some mysterious mark from his newest velvet jacket, these glinting thoughts of his future began to make him feel isolated. He would drop in on Clary: she would give him supper, and she would help him with his blasted jacket.

He bought an evening paper, two gobstoppers and a small bunch of chrysanthemums before catching a bus up Edgware Road. Archie would have to do without a present.

The flat was the ground floor of a very large house, and its garden might once have been an orchard as it contained apple, plum and pear trees set in rarely mown grass and stalwart weeds such as loosestrife and dandelions. The studio looked onto the garden, which made the place seem like a piece of country. He had time to see all of this because the front door was not locked, and when he shouted for Clary, she shouted back that she was in the kitchen washing her hair.

'I suppose you've come to supper,' she said, after she'd given him a rather wet hug.

'I think I have. These are for you.' He proffered the chrysanthemums.

'Goodness! Thank you.' She looked wildly around for something to put them in, and settled on a jam jar stuffed with Archie's paintbrushes.

'Won't he mind?'

She shrugged. 'Not very much. There isn't a great deal of room in this flat for things like flower vases.'

She had been towelling her hair and now gave it a shake, so that spots of water fell everywhere. 'I've got a comb somewhere – oh, yes, I think it's on the draining board. Please get it.'

He wanted her to clean his jacket so he did as he was told. She wrenched the comb through her tangled hair for a minute or two. 'See if you can find an elastic band, unless you happen to have one on you. I must get the children in for their bath.'

The children turned out to be in the garden, and came plodding in carrying a heavy bag between them. 'Here are your horrible pears. Please don't make us eat them. They really are horrible.'

'Say hello to Uncle Neville.'

'Hello, Uncle Neville. Mum, I had a good idea about the pears.'

'Actually, it was my idea.' Bertie was a year younger than Harriet, and made the most of it.

'OK. Tell us your idea, then go and have your bath.'

'Oh, Mum! We had a bath yesterday!'

'We simply aren't dirty – except my knees. You can't count knees as being dirty.' They had dumped the bag on the floor, whereupon it fell sideways and a number of small green pears fell out. 'She stews and stews them and then we have to have them as pudding,' Bertie explained to Neville. 'And there are millions of them.'

'Anyway,' Harriet said, 'you know that story when an old woman builds her house of pear seeds? Well – that's the idea. That would use up all the pears and we would have a proper house instead of the leaky old tent in the garden.'

'It sounds an interesting idea, but quite difficult to do,' Clary said.

'Dad will help us,' Harriet said. 'You can, too, if you want to, but honestly I think it's the kind of thing that Dad would be best at.'

'Right. Up you go now.'

Neville said, 'If you go now, I've got a present for you when you come back.'

'What?'

'It will be a surprise.'

They went, of course. When they had gone, Neville said, 'You're very good at being a mother, aren't you?'

'Am I?' She looked surprised. 'I don't feel especially good at it. I get ratty sometimes and want to scream at them. It's the going-on-ness of family life, you know – all the meals and washing clothes, clearing up whatever happened last and getting ready for the next thing.'

'But you like it, really, don't you? And you have Archie.'

'I have Archie,' she repeated, but for a moment her face clouded – something sad and determined occurred and went. 'If you want to go on talking we must sit down. Also, it's time you told me what you've come for.'

'How do you know I've come for anything?' He felt aggrieved that she was so sharp.

'Because you always do. I don't mind in the least. What is it?'

'Well – I felt like seeing you. Your company.' This, he discovered to his surprise, was completely true.

The kitchen was fairly tidy for Clary, he thought. The table had rather a lot of flour on it and there were vegetables waiting to be prepared on the draining board alongside a bottle of shampoo.

'Darling Neville, what else?'

'It's a tiny thing, really. I've spilt something on my only good jacket and I'm off to Venice this weekend, and I thought you'd know how to get the mark off. You used to spill so many things on your clothes, I thought you'd be an expert.' He smiled winningly.

This did not go down well. 'When I spilled things they tended to stay there. It was Poll who showed me what to do.' It was a tart reply. However, she looked at him, and then said, 'Show me the jacket. What did you spill on it?'

'I haven't the faintest idea.' He had pulled it out of the carrier bag. She took it to the draining board. 'You should have had it dry-cleaned.'

'I know. But it's too late for that. I only noticed when I was packing.'

'I'll have a go, if you like, but I warn you, it may not work.'

While he watched her spread the stained cloth on the wood, put some washing-up liquid on her finger and rub it carefully round and round, he had a sudden mad desire to tell her about Juliet, to say, 'I'm in love with my half-sister – no, it's really serious – I know she isn't old enough to marry me, but she will be and then I shall.'

'When will Archie be back?'

She looked at her watch. 'Any minute now. It isn't one of his late nights.'

Not a good moment then. He knew she would protest, and he needed time to field any objections. His urgent secret withdrew, like a snail. 'Tell me what's been happening to you.'

He saw her shoulders stiffen for a second, then she turned to look at him (she had marvellous eyes, he noticed now, because he was not used to them). In a very calm, flat voice, she said, 'The chief thing is that I'm writing a play.' A very large tear dropped onto the black velvet.

At that moment, there were sounds of Archie's arrival.

'Please don't mention the play,' she said, then called out, 'We're in the kitchen. Neville's here.'

223

Archie was pleased to see him. He looked awfully old, Neville thought. His hair was partly white and there was less of it. He seemed tired. He dumped the satchel he had been carrying and turned Clary from the sink to kiss her. 'How's Mrs Beeton been doing? Darling, your hair is soaking!'

'Better not come near me, then.'

'Clary's very kindly cleaning my jacket.'

'I'm afraid I've got a bit behind with supper.'

'Never mind. I've brought a bottle of wine back. We can all have some while we're waiting.'

'It won't be just waiting, I'm afraid. There's the potatoes to peel and carrots to scrape. And the children to get out of the bath. I've made the fishcakes, though.'

'Oh, good. She makes lovely fishcakes.'

'I don't. Either they're too full of potato and don't taste of anything, or they go all crumbly when I fry them.'

Archie, who had been fumbling in a kitchen drawer, said, 'Where the devil has the corkscrew got to?'

'It'll be in the sink, concealed by suds. I was using it to try and open a bottle of hair stuff. Sorry.'

Neville became conscious of effort in the air, but other than not being there, he couldn't think what he could do about it. 'Are we going to have the wine now, or save it up for dinner?'

Clary, who had begun peeling potatoes, said irritably, 'I don't care. You do what you want.'

But that was his cue. 'I meant to bring you some,' he said. 'Where's the nearest off-licence? No, really, Archie, I want to.'

And Archie was persuaded.

During his walk, he reflected that he had not told

Clary about the most important thing in his life, and then
– a sudden and perhaps tardy notion – that she had not
told him either. The play she had said she was writing,
the momentous tear that had fallen onto his jacket, her
saying not to mention it when they heard Archie . . .
Something was going on. She had not made the slightest
effort to tidy herself, to change from the fraying green
shirt, to don an apron not so spattered with previous
cooking, and she had been distinctly ungracious about
whatever Archie had said to her. They must have had
some married couple's tiff. Well, he certainly wouldn't
ever have any of those with beautiful darling Jules. In the
end, he bought two bottles of champagne and walked
quite briskly back, through the dusk turning to dark, and
returned to a far more cheerful scene.

Archie was laying the table, Clary was frying fishcakes; they had not drunk the wine – 'Waiting for you' –
and the children were showing their father a drawing
Harriet had made for the pear-seed house. His jacket
hung from the plate rack. 'The best I could do,' Clary
said, and Archie added, 'She used her own toothbrush to
stroke up the nap.'

The champagne was greeted with delight and even
some awe.

'I thought people only had it at weddings,' Bertie said.
'Can we have some?'

'You can have a sip,' Archie said.

'A very small sip,' Clary amended. She began dishing
out the food for them.

'I should like a very large gulp, several gulps, because
it might take me time to see if I like it.'

'You'll have exactly the same.'

Neville uncorked a bottle that fizzed, pouring the

champagne quickly into the glass that Archie held out for him.

'Smoke comes out!' Harriet shouted.

When they had had their sips, she said it was too prickly whereupon Bertie said he loved it.

'Aren't you having supper with us?'

'We're going to have a drink first. You don't usually have supper as late as this. Eat it up or you won't get Uncle Neville's surprise.'

'Carrots as well, Bertie,' Clary said, some minutes later.

'Mum, I really have told you and told you I don't actually care for carrots. I can't see the point of them.'

'The point of them is that they're orange,' Harriet said complacently. She had cut hers up into small pieces and was mashing them up with her potatoes. The fishcakes had disappeared in a flash.

They were delighted with the gobstoppers. Harriet had never heard of them, but Bertie said a boy at school had had one, and let his best friends all have a go to change the colour. 'But then a stupid boy swallowed it when it had gone green and he got turned upside-down and banged on the back until the gobstopper fell out.'

'Well, you're neither of you to share yours with anyone. You can keep them at home. In fact, one more colour each and it's bedtime.'

'She's in one of her firm moods,' Harriet said. 'And, Mummy, I wouldn't dream of sharing mine with anyone. I think it's disgusting.'

'Right.' Archie got up. 'Go now, and I'll come to see if you're in bed in five minutes, teeth cleaned and all. Say goodnight to everybody and be off.'

So they did as they were told, and went.

The peace in the kitchen was such that they could hear the cold tap dripping in the sink. Neville opened the second bottle while Clary dished out their dinner. During this, Archie went to her and gently untied her dirty apron, put his arms round her and kissed the back of her neck. She turned to him and smiled. 'What are you buttering me up for now?'

'To get the most fishcakes, of course.'

Neville, whose eye was sharp and practised when he wanted it to be, felt then that nothing escaped him. They had had a row of some sort, but it seemed to be cleared up. He was ravenous.

Archie duly went up to – as he put it – bottle the children. 'Can we start?'

'Of course. If we drink any more without eating we'll all be tight.'

They ate in companionable silence.

Then Clary said, 'Venice will be lovely, won't it? Tourists mostly gone and still good weather.'

He shrugged. 'The trouble is that when I'm working there's no time. You start practically at dawn and you go on all day, going to different places, setting up shots that don't work because they don't show off the clothes enough, and you have to do it all over again, with a whole lot of wardrobe and make-up people fussing about idiotic detail, and then the girls get cold and cross and want hot coffee and a sit down.'

There was a pause, and then Clary said, 'Well, I'd love to go to Venice any old way.'

Then Archie came back; he looked weary, the lines on each side of his nose more deeply indented.

'Are they settled?'

'Yep. I had to threaten them with Dr Crime. They want you to say goodnight to them, darling.'

'Who is Dr Crime?'

'He's a nasty character who writes down all the bad things they do. They love him, really. He goes about at night doing wicked things.'

'Well, Neville, what do you think of the state of the world?' Archie asked, when Clary had gone upstairs.

Surprised, he answered, 'I suppose I don't think about it much. I can't do anything about it, whatever I think. Things don't change much, really – do they?'

'Some things do, albeit slowly. Liberalising the laws about homosexuality, for instance. Are you in favour of that?'

'God, yes! I'm all in favour of liberalising everything.'

'Have you told your MP that?'

'I haven't the faintest idea who he is. So no.'

'It's something you could do.'

'Really, Archie, what difference would that make? One person. And don't tell me that if everyone did as you say it would make a difference because they won't.' He felt irritated and got at. Luckily, just as Archie was agreeing with him, Clary came back, and he said he must be off. He put on his newly cleaned jacket and pushed his old one into the carrier bag.

Clary kissed him.

'It was lovely you came,' Archie said. 'Sorry to rile you – marvellous champagne,' and the evening ended peaceably.

When he had gone, Clary began clearing the table, but he stopped her. 'I'll do it in the morning. It's my morning, remember, and your lie-in. Come with me now.'

On the stairs, she turned to look at him, a searching, anxious look.

'What is it?' he asked.

'Nothing. Only I'm afraid you're so sad.'

When she said anything like that, the weight of his abstinence enveloped him. He still saw the girl sometimes at the school – always at a distance – and each time could tell himself that it was easier. What he could not bear were these allusions: however discreet, it was the only thing that made him feel angry – no, impatient – with her. 'I'm fine,' he said. 'I love you, and I'm fine.'

POLLY, GERALD
AND FAMILY

'Basically, Lady Fakenham, basically, the idea of hosting wedding receptions in your beautiful mansion is a viable one. It's simply that some adjustments need to be made before you get the clientele that you want. By that I mean people who are prepared to pay.'

Mrs Monkhurst, dressed impeccably in autumn tweeds, cashmere and pearls, re-crossed her navy nylon legs and hoisted herself more upright in her chair. 'Now,' she said, 'perhaps we should start with what you think went wrong with your do last week.'

Polly, who felt rather slovenly beside her – she was wearing an old skirt that had been made of curtain material and a shirt that made it easy to feed Spencer – picked up the list she had made. It was she who had asked Mrs Monkhurst to come, as she ran some kind of agency for organising parties in large houses, but she was beginning to feel bossed and humiliated. 'Well, to begin with, it rained, almost the whole time. So people couldn't go into the garden. The marquee leaked, which wasn't our fault, but it made a mess, and the guests were not warm enough. Then there were perpetual queues for the lavatory on the ground floor here.'

'You only have one?'

'I'm afraid so.'

'But, Lady Fakenham, you cannot have expected over a hundred people to make do with one!'

'It was all so expensive, you see.'

'I hear that the music wasn't quite up to the mark.'

Polly spoke stiffly. 'We moved the piano into the marquee and my brother played, except when there were speeches on. He's very good at it.'

'I'm sure he is,' Mrs Monkhurst replied, with tones of exaggerated conciliation and disbelief. 'But they were expecting a three-piece band at the very least.' She was riffling through the pad on her lap. 'Is that all?'

'I'm sure it isn't, but I can't think of anything else. Off-hand,' Polly added, to be on the safe side.

'Ah! This is the feedback I have procured for you. Apart from what you've mentioned, there was some dis-appointment with the catering, I believe.' She looked enquiringly at Polly.

'I don't understand that. They chose the menu them-selves.'

'Yes. But the salmon and chicken were overcooked, the mayonnaise was salad cream out of a bottle and the canapés tasted, I was told, as though they had been made days before. You know what the answer is, don't you, Lady Fakenham?'

'I'm afraid I don't.'

'You chose the wrong help. Neither the marquee firm nor the caterers were what we should consider first class. I could put you on to people who would never make such mistakes. Of course, they cost a bit more but, believe me, they're worth it.'

'But we didn't have any more money! As it is, we've made a small loss.'

Mrs Monkhurst regarded her with a short mournful silence. Then, she said, at last, 'I'm afraid that means you're a tiny bit under-invested. If you're interested, I could do an estimate for you, which would include our costs for finding you clients.'

∞ ∞ ∞

'That was what she came for. When I asked her, I thought she was simply going to give us advice.' Mrs Monkhurst had finally driven off in her Humber and Gerald had emerged to hear the news. 'She was just after business.'

'If she's a businesswoman I suppose she would be.' He was in one of his mild moods, which alternately maddened and alarmed Polly: in one of them he would agree to anything.

'But, darling, she wants us to spend a whole lot of money that we haven't got. And, if she finds us clients, she wants fifteen per cent of the profit. It's hopeless!'

'Not hopeless, darling. Let's wait and see what she proposes. Here's Spencer, wanting his lunch.' Nan had come in carrying a cross red-faced baby. He was arching his back and his cries came in short staccato bursts, like gunfire. He was so beside himself that even after Polly had unbuttoned her shirt he banged blindly against her breast until she guided him to the right place, whereupon he latched onto her nipple, his slate-blue eyes regarding her with reproach.

'He's teething, bless him,' Nan said.

Gerald watched him fade from scarlet to a comfortable rose colour. Content was in the air, he thought, and it was all due to Poll. 'How I love to see you both,' he said. 'Now, you're not to worry about a thing. If the worst comes to the worst, we can always sell another picture. I must go and help Simon.'

Polly knew that she was meant to be reassured by this, but was not. She sighed as she winded Spencer and changed sides. You should think of good things when you're feeding babies, she thought. Dad is coming to stay, and nice Jemima and rather spoiled, sweet little Laura. And Simon is a great help. This afternoon I must make some food for them. She yawned; too many interrupted nights with Spencer. We simply have to earn some money somehow, she thought. Perhaps Dad will have a good idea, he is a businessman after all.

A few minutes later, she went in search of the pram, which was in the kitchen, where she found Nan making sandwiches. 'Tea's not quite ready, your ladyship, and I think those twins have eaten the cake.'

Oh dear! It had happened again. 'Nan dear, we need to have a bit of lunch now. Teatime is later, when the children get back from school.'

Nan stared at her for a moment, then said, 'Well, that's a relief.' But she did not look as though it was, at all.

'Would you like to go and call the men?' She knew that Nan loved telling people what to do and it would distract her. 'Take the bell with you, Nan. I think they're planting trees in the avenue.'

After she had laid the sleepy Spencer in his pram, and was stirring the soup, she wondered what on earth they would do if Nan's memory got worse – or, rather, when. She would have to be looked after, and Polly would have to employ someone to help with the children and there would be more housework than the girl who came one morning a week could possibly manage.

And they were planting new trees in the old avenue that was studded with stag oaks and splendid old elms, when there was so much else to be done where the results would not take thirty years to show! She cleared the table of tea things and collected the cheese and bread from the larder. She decided to get on with preparing the venison and vegetables for the stew for supper. Pheasants for tomorrow night, she thought. The family got sick of them at this time of year, but Gerald shot and hung them and they cost nothing. And Dad loved game. All I've got to do before they come is check their bedroom, make a chocolate cake for tea and some sort of pudding from our plums – a crumble would be easiest – and perhaps get Nan to make one of her treacle tarts for tomorrow . . .

By the time Gerald and Simon appeared, very pleased with themselves – 'We've planted twelve trees and run out of stakes for the others' – Polly had soaked the prunes in warm water, and finished scrubbing the Jerusalem artichokes, both intended for her stew.

∞ ∞ ∞

'I want to sleep with Andrew.'

'I don't want to sleep with her at all.' He looked at Laura with distaste. 'She was sick in the car. I don't want to sleep with a sick person.'

'I told you, I'm only sick in cars. Mummy, do tell Andrew I'm only sick in cars.'

'Darling, when you stay with people, you have to sleep where they say.'

Eliza and Jane, who were polishing off their share of the chocolate cake, surveyed Laura with disapproval.

234

One of them said, 'And you shouldn't talk about sick at meals.'

And the other said, 'No, you shouldn't. It's disgusting.' Laura looked at them both, and her eyes filled with tears.

'I'll give you some carrots,' Polly said, 'and, Eliza, you could take Laura to see your ponies. But only if you promise to look after her carefully. Laura is your guest.'

And Jane immediately said, 'I'll take Laura. I should like to.'

'OK, but everyone finish their milk.'

'And ask to get down,' Nan added.

When they had done all of this, Simon got up. 'I'll go with them.'

'Oh, thank you, Simon.'

Gerald then offered to show Hugh what they had achieved with the back garden, and he accepted gratefully.

∞ ∞ ∞

'If you go through to the sitting room, my lady, I'll bring the baby to you. It's time for his feed.'

'Shall I come with you, or would you rather be on your own?'

'Oh, come with me, Jemima. I haven't seen you for ages.'

Polly had been shocked by her father's appearance. He looked not only dead tired but somehow diminished. Jemima looked tired also, but she was always so neat in her appearance that her fatigue was not so apparent: blonde hair simply cut, a straight serge skirt and white shirt, with a tidy polished belt round her very small waist. She wore dark blue mesh stockings, and shoes as much polished as her belt. Her expression seemed to have settled to some sort of anxiety that had not been there the last time Polly had seen her.

'How are things?' she asked, after Spencer was settled at her breast.

'I'm worried about your father. He and Edward are not getting on, and that distresses him. Far more than it does Edward. Your dear father can be – well, once he's made up his mind, it's almost impossible to get him to change it.'

Polly waited a moment. Then she asked, 'What do you think he should change his mind about?'

'Accepting Edward's wife for one. I think Edward resents him about that, and I don't blame him. I mean, it's happened. He's married to her. But Hugh's still very loyal to Villy. He goes to see her regularly and every now and then we have to have her to supper. I know I shouldn't say it that way, but they are awful evenings: Villy always gets round to asking questions about Edward and she calls Diana "The Destroyer" and makes bitter remarks about her. And she won't let poor Roland go to Home Place without her, and she won't go unless Edward's there without Diana. So Roly hardly ever sees his cousins; he's being brought up as though he were an only child. By the way, Spencer's a lovely baby.'

Polly, who had him over her shoulder, smiled. Spencer was dribbling; he belched, and Polly stroked his head. He had worn a bald patch bashing his head about when he was in a temper, but his glistening red hair was growing quite long at the back. 'He's going through his unsuccessful-composer stage,' she said fondly.

'I wondered whether you could talk to him. I've tried,

236

and I know that Rachel has, but he adores you. It would be marvellous if you could make him see . . .'

'Well, I could try, but I don't think—'

Here they were interrupted by an influx of children.

'We fed both of the ponies. They simply love carrots – they have lovely soft noses and they smell really nice. I think I ought to have one.'

Eliza and Jane were clearly softened by Laura's enthusiasm. 'We're going to give Laura a riding lesson tomorrow.'

'Where's Andrew?'

'He got stung by some stinging nettles and cried.'

'I don't get stung by stingy nettles because I know what they are.' Laura was so happy that she felt like boasting about anything that came up.

'Did you give him a dock leaf?'

Jane looked sulky. 'Can't remember.'

Eliza said, 'We told him about them but I don't think he listened. He's only six, Mummy – he's still pretty stupid.'

'I'm seven and I'm not in the least stupid. I can play "Three Blind Mice" on the piano, and skip twenty-two times, and read some books, and walk two miles with Daddy—'

'Laura, darling, that's enough. It's time for your bath now.'

'I want to have my bath with Andrew.'

At this point Nan appeared. She seemed refreshed by more children. 'You're coming with me, Miss. You and Andrew, then the girls, or you won't get any supper.' And she took the unresisting Laura by the hand and led her from the room.

'Goodness!' Jemima said, in admiration.

'There's nothing like Nan when she's on form.'

So Jemima went to unpack, and Polly to change Spencer's nappy and put him in his cot.

∞ ∞ ∞

The long weekend (it was half-term) ran its course. Simon managed to tell his father that he had decided to become a gardener and, to his surprise, his father made no demur – even seemed relieved that he had settled on something. 'Don't you need to do a course or something to get qualifications?'

'Well, I suppose it would help if I needed to get a job somewhere different, but I like working here with Gerald and Polly.'

And this had been seconded by Gerald, saying what a marvellous help he was and how hard he worked.

Andrew settled for Laura, as she would do anything he told her to do and it made a nice change from being bossed about and snubbed by the twins. Spencer cut a tooth and was very smiley.

Polly, with the excuse of asking Hugh's advice about Mrs Monkhurst's suggestions, managed to get him to talk about his rift with Edward, and very carefully brought the conversation round to Diana. 'Dad, how would you feel if the family had refused to have anything to do with Jemima?'

Hugh stared at her, but she noticed that his usually kind eyes became hard, like marbles. 'I wouldn't stand for it,' he said. 'In any case, they all love her.'

'You see, I sometimes think that poor Uncle Edward may feel like that about Diana, too.'

There was a short, uncomfortable silence.

'I mean, darling Dad, it isn't so much what *you* think of her, it's how he feels about her. He has married her, after all.'

'And what about poor Villy? What about his ruining her life?'

'That's happened, Dad. It can't be changed. It wouldn't actually make the slightest difference to Villy if you met Diana, but I think it would make all the difference to Uncle Edward. Darling Dad, you're usually such a kind person – think how awful it would be for me if you didn't approve of Gerald. I'd be miserable. In the end, I'd stop loving you so much.

'Or, I might,' she added, seeing that this had really shocked him.

'Well,' he said at last, 'I'll think about what you've said. But, you know, it's not simply the Diana issue. The firm is having a bad time, and we don't agree at all on what we should do about it. We've reached a point when it has become almost impossible even to talk about it.'

They had been walking back up the avenue, having duly admired the new planting, and now he hooked his arm in hers. 'You know, Poll, when you talk like this you remind me of your dear mother – of Sybil.' He gave a little dry laugh to get rid of the terrible picture that recurred to him still of her dying – the slow certainty of it, the agony of watching her pain, his utter helplessness to save her from any of it.

Polly (and this would have surprised him as, like many people, he had been selfish in his grief) also had vivid and painful memories of her mother – her cries when the pain became unbearable, seeing her for the last time when she was conscious of nothing, how she had been allowed one unreciprocated kiss and then was banished. These separate griefs came to them now as they walked slowly up the drive, rich copper oak leaves falling gracefully to their feet and, above them, a sharp blue sky and cold yellow sunlight.

When the house came into view, with its monstrous façade of greyish-yellow brick ('lavatory brick', Gerald called it) and each of its many windows framed by architraves of an uneasy red, Hugh stopped to look at it.

Polly, watching him, said, 'Gerald says it has pomp without any circumstance.'

'Have you ever thought of selling it?'

'I used to. But Gerald is devoted to it. It has become his *raison d'être*. And I have grown fond of the place. We've simply got to make it earn its keep. And ours.' And she told him about Mrs Monkhurst and all the extra money needed, ending by asking him what he thought about sinking a lot more capital into the place.

'How much more?'

'She hasn't told us yet. But I bet it'll be another Turner.'

'Poll, I don't think you should keep selling those. They're a capital asset.'

'It's all right, Dad. We've still got a good many. We sold two to get the roof mended and a few other vital things like that. And Gerald sells one for each baby so that we've got money for their education.'

They returned to the house to be greeted by the twins. 'We're awfully sorry, Mummy, but Laura fell off Bluebell and she's probably broken an arm or a leg or something.'

'Where is she?'

'Jemima's taken her to the vet.'

'Not the vet, the doctor, silly.'

'It wasn't our fault, Mummy. She didn't want to be on a leading rein.'

Andrew said, 'Now you can see why I don't ride. I need my arms and legs – or how could I climb my trees?' He had not at all liked the twins appropriating Laura.

'You know perfectly well that you should have kept her on the leading rein. In fact, you should have led her yourselves. Where was Simon while all this was going on?'

'He said he had to get more wood in for the fires.'

'He made them promise not to trot or anything, but as soon as he'd gone they trotted. Jane was on Buttercup, anyway, so she wasn't much use.'

'Andrew, you're a horrible little sneak.'

'Yes, you are. I think you're the worst person I know.'

'Yes, I agree. Quite the worst person.'

Andrew's face puckered. 'I'm not the worst. I'm a good person. You're the ones who let Laura fall off. You're the worst.' He was in tears now, sniffing hard and rubbing his eyes. At that moment, Nan appeared with Spencer, who was also crying.

'He's worse than me. He can't even eat.'

'He's hungry. You're a bit late, my lady.'

'Sorry, Nan.' She took Spencer and suggested that her father followed her to her sitting room.

'And you, Master Andrew, will go upstairs and wash yourself for lunch. Not just your hands, your knees as well.'

'How can my knees have anything to do with lunch?' they heard Andrew saying. 'I don't eat with my knees . . .' His voice faded until they shut the door on him.

241

'Dad, do settle down. The paper's on the sofa table. They'll soon be back.'

But Hugh could not settle. He wandered about the room, peering frequently out of the window that looked onto the drive. 'I can't understand how we missed them in the avenue.'

'They probably went along the back drive – it's quicker. Simon will have told them.'

'And how far off is the hospital?'

'Only about ten miles,' she said off-handedly, trying to make it sound nearer.

Spencer was gulping his milk so fast that when she winded him, most of it came up again. It's time I started weaning him, Polly thought. She was becoming tired of a life dominated by her breasts.

'Do you want to wait for lunch until they come back, my lady?'

'No, Nan, I think we'd better go ahead. But first will you send Eliza and Jane in to me? I'm very cross with them.'

There was a gleam of admiration in Nan's eyes. 'Quite right, your ladyship. His lordship's too soft with them, the naughty monkeys.'

As Nan took Spencer, Polly said, 'Shall we give him some Farex and honey? He can sit on my lap and I'll feed him.'

'Very good, my lady.'

Eliza and Jane arrived, still in their jodhpurs. They looked nervous. Hugh had tactfully left the room, and Polly had got off the sofa and was sitting very upright in a chair.

'I'm very disappointed in both of you. You have behaved in a most irresponsible manner. You are two

242

very selfish, stupid little girls. Laura might have been killed by your idiotic behaviour. Do you realise that?'

They shook their heads. When they looked at her she could see that she had shocked them. 'Mummy, we never meant to hurt her – honestly.'

'Of course you didn't mean to. But you didn't take the trouble to see that she would be safe. As it is, we don't know how much damage you've done. When she comes back, I want you to apologise to Laura and to both her parents.'

'We will, Mummy, we promise you.'

'Right. And your punishment is no riding for either of you for the whole of half-term.'

'Oh, Mum! That's not fair! We promised Laura another lesson! After she fell off, she said she still wanted to ride.'

'Did she indeed! Well, that will be up to her parents to decide. And before you go, I should like to remind you that you didn't keep your promise to Simon.'

'What promise?'

'You tell me, Eliza.'

There was a pause, then Eliza said sulkily, 'Not to trot.'

'But, Mummy, we couldn't stop her!' Jane protested. 'She dug her heels into poor Bluebell's sides so of course he trotted. She was quite naughty, you know.'

'All right. That's enough. You must apologise to Simon, as well.'

'Mum, I do think you should speak to Andrew about his sneaking. When he can't find a true thing to sneak about, he makes things up.'

'That will do, both of you. Do you know where your father is?'

243

'He took them in the car. May we go now?'

When they had left, Polly went to the window that looked onto the drive and beckoned her father to come in.

'It's all right, Dad. Gerald took them. He knows the way, and he's marvellous with nurses. Come and have some lunch.'

∞ ∞ ∞

They got back at three. Laura had broken her right arm, and her left leg. She was in a state of high excitement. 'I've got two bandages – hard ones that people can sign their names on.'

'Laura was very brave.'

'I was. Very, extremely, triffically brave.'

Gerald was carrying her into the kitchen where Jemima arranged a chair with sidearms and cushions, and Nan fetched a footstool for her leg.

'They had to pull my bones together, and they told me it would hurt and it did – awfully both times – and then they did some ordinary bandaging, and then . . .' she paused dramatically '. . . they put some soft white smeary stuff all over the broken bits and said we had to wait until it was dry, but I didn't mind because Uncle Gerald kindly gave me a chocolate biscuit. And now the stuff is all hard. I have to have it on for weeks, so I won't be able to have baths, and I never really cried – only about five tears, wasn't it, Mummy? And Mummy held my hand all the time, and I trotted on Bluebell but I don't think I can have another riding lesson until the stiff stuff comes off.'

'Now then, Miss Laura, eat your lunch.'

Nan had put a dollop of shepherd's pie in a bowl with a teaspoon. But Laura was not very good at eating with her left hand and the food went everywhere – rather like Spencer, Polly thought. The Farex, when she put a spoonful into his mouth, made him screw up his face with distaste, and he let it slide out. In the end Hugh fed Laura a few spoonfuls. She didn't want food, and suddenly started sobbing. 'I don't want anything at all! I don't want horrible pie!'

'Reaction,' Nan said audibly, if under her breath.

Hugh picked her up and, followed by Jemima, carried her away.

'She needs a good rest, that's all she needs. She can have her tea later. And you, Eliza and Jane, you shouldn't stare at people. It's rude.'

'Rude,' Andrew repeated, with some satisfaction. For the rest of the weekend, he was very good to Laura, playing Snap and Old Maid with her, and helping her to do a small jigsaw that had wooden pieces. Gerald converted a very old pram that had been bought for the twins into a makeshift wheelchair, and everybody wrote their names and messages on her casts. Jemima arranged one of the tea trays so that she had a place to put cards or the jigsaw, while Eliza and Jane took turns reading to her. She insisted on an expedition to feed carrots to the ponies, accompanied by her anxious parents. She stroked their velvet noses and tried to kiss Bluebell. But he tossed his head and cantered out of reach. When the carrots were finished neither pony saw the point of hanging about. Everyone apologised to everyone else, and everyone felt better for it.

'You won't forget about Uncle Edward and Diana, will you?' Polly whispered to her father, when he hugged her goodbye.

'I won't, Polly, darling. I'm so proud of you.' Then, with Laura ensconced in the back, he got into the car, and Jemima hugged Simon, which made him blush with pleasure.

PART SEVEN

NOVEMBER–DECEMBER 1957

PART SEVEN

NOVEMBER-DECEMBER 1992

RACHEL AND SID

'The Duchy adored Gregory Peck.'

'I know. I remember her saying once that she would gladly marry him.'

Sid had enticed Rachel to spend a week or so in London, on the grounds that they could enjoy going to the theatre, concerts and the cinema. But in spite of a fairly constant round of these pleasures, the visit was not going well. Rachel was restless, and constantly ruminating about Home Place: whether the builders, whose estimate Hugh had agreed to, had started mending the roof or not. Sid recognised now that her own pessimism might be because she felt so tired all the time. Quite soon after she had got up in the mornings, her back started to ache, and became progressively worse during the day. She managed to conceal most of this from Rachel, or thought she had, until the morning after they had seen *Roman Holiday*, when Rachel said at breakfast, 'Sid, darling, I'm taking you to see Dr Plunkett today. There is clearly something wrong with your back, and I know that, left to yourself, you will simply suffer in silence. Your appointment is at ten thirty. And I am coming with you.'

She sounded so calm and determined that Sid could only feel grateful to have the matter organised for her.

∞ ∞ ∞

When they were sitting in the waiting room (flock paper, a collection of incredibly dreary prints, and magazines), Rachel said, 'Would you like me to come in with you?'

No, she wouldn't. Just then, a nurse called her name, and Sid followed her, down a passage, to the doctor's room. He rose from his desk to shake hands with her and then proceeded to ask a great number of questions, taking notes as she replied. He went into all of it: took her blood pressure (on the low side), her temperature (she had one, not high but he suspected always there), and finally he made her lie on his patient's bed while he examined her back. Then he said, 'Miss Sidney, I have an X-ray unit in the basement, and I should like to take some X-rays of your back. I should like them to be taken now, if that is agreeable to you. Yes?'

'Yes. Only could I go straight down from here? I don't want my friend to know.'

'Of course. The nurse will take you and bring you back here when they have been developed.'

So the pictures were taken, and by the time she got back to his room he was looking at them. 'Do sit down, Miss Sidney. I'm afraid we've found something.'

She had a tumour very near her spine. It was possible that there were others but they would need further tests to find out. 'It's a great pity that you didn't come to us earlier, but there it is. I shall send you to the Marsden for more tests. Meanwhile, are you taking anything for the pain?'

She told him about the aspirin.

'I think I can do better than that for you.'

He scribbled on a piece of paper and handed the prescription to her. She put it into a pocket. She felt stunned, unable to move or speak. Dr Plunkett was used to this, and he had learned to be kind about it. He got up from his desk and went to her. 'I know it is something of a shock, but you must be of good heart. The cancer may not have spread.'

'May I tell my friend that these other tests are for my heart or something? I can't tell her the other thing. I simply can't.'

'My dear, you can tell her anything you like. Do you live alone, or are you sharing a house together?'

'We share.'

'Well, sometimes, you know, people are better off with the truth. But it's up to you, of course.'

He shook hands with her and the nurse accompanied Sid back to the waiting room.

Rachel looked up from the magazine she had been trying to read, her face full of anxiety and affection. There were three other people in the waiting room, so she simply helped Sid into her coat and they left. They both thought they were smiling at the other.

'What would you like to do now, my love?'

'Coffee would be good.' Her mouth was so dry that she could hardly speak.

'Right. There's a good place round the corner in Marylebone Lane.' She hooked her arm into Sid's and they made their way.

In the coffee place she asked for a glass of water and drank it all. Rachel, trying to sound casual, said, 'How did it go?'

'He was extremely thorough. Did an X-ray on my back. He wants me to have a few more tests, and he's arranging that with a hospital. And he gave me a prescription for when I have pain. He was very kind. It all went very well.'

251

'Oh, good.' They were not convincing one another.

'I think it means I'll have to stay in London until I've been for the other tests. But you go down as we planned, and I'll join you.' If I could have just a little time on my own, she thought, I might manage to sort things out. Face it, if I have to, and find the right way to tell Rachel, the poor darling.

'I wouldn't dream of leaving while you're having the tests.'

'You said you have to cope with the builders. I'd much rather you go, and I'll join you the minute I can. As a matter of fact, I'd rather be on my own. You know I can't bear fussing.' She could see that this hurt Rachel, but she persisted, and Rachel eventually agreed.

'I wouldn't fuss,' she said sadly, but Sid knew that this was not true.

∞ ∞ ∞

Somehow she got through that first awful day. She said she would like to lunch at a Turkish restaurant where they picked from a large tray of mezze, which suited them both since neither of them ate very much. They collected Sid's prescription and then Sid suggested that they see an old French film showing at the cinema in Baker Street, *Le jour se lève*, with Jean Gabin. Sid fell asleep, but she had taken one of Dr Plunkett's pills, and when she woke, her back was hardly hurting at all. It was Rachel who looked exhausted, so they went home in a taxi.

Hugh rang up that evening to say that he would go down to Home Place to see what was going on with the roof, and would Rachel like a lift? He called for her the next morning.

She saw them off, promised to ring when she had her date for the hospital and watched them drive away before she shut the front door.

She was alone at last. She could think about her horrible future – whatever there might be of it – because she sensed that Dr Plunkett had known that she was almost certainly going to die. And that would mean leaving Rachel alone and grieving.

And before she died there would be awful things to endure: radiotherapy, chemotherapy, operations that would possibly only halt the disease rather than cure it. Why on earth hadn't she been to a doctor earlier? Because she had always been afraid of what they might say. Her mother had died of cancer; so had Hugh's first wife, Sybil. Alone now, she could admit to being terrified of severe pain. She could admit to being a fearful coward. With no Rachel present to deceive she could think of these last months, when she had been afraid that something was seriously wrong and had used what energy she possessed to conceal her wretchedness from Rachel. It had not been very difficult: Rachel suffered chronically from a painful back herself, and while she diligently applied her remedies for both of them – rubbing with arnica, stretching exercises, hot-water bottles – she had been tender and sympathetic, but not alarmed. They had been so happy. After years of secrecy and frustration they had finally been able to live more or less together, even with the Duchy alive. Rachel always said that her mother's extreme innocence meant that she had just accepted Sid as Rachel's best friend, but Sid had sometimes thought that the Duchy knew more about them and wisely kept her perception to herself. 'Am I to die? When we have been so happy together!' Charlotte Brontë's last pathetic cry to her husband had brought tears to her eyes; now, recalling it, she broke down and sobbed – stumbling upstairs to their bedroom to cast herself upon her and Rachel's bed. The sheets still held the Rachel scent of violets – the scent she had always worn after Sid had said she loved it so much.

She wept until she was dry of tears, mopping her face with the sheet, and then lay for a while, exhausted, but also curiously relieved – as though she had got rid of something that could not be borne.

She was woken by the telephone: it was Dr Plunkett's secretary with an appointment for two days' time. I have nearly two days to pull myself together, she thought. I must eat meals and rest and tidy up this shabby old house. I might even play my fiddle a bit – some unaccompanied Bach would be just the ticket. I must do things – any sensible thing I can think to do. And when Rachel rings I will sound light-hearted and casual. It would be pointless to tell her anything until I know the worst.

LOUISE AND JOSEPH

'Are you free on Saturday morning? I want you to help me with my Christmas shopping.'

Joseph hardly ever spent a weekend away from the beautiful house he had recently bought in Berkshire. She knew what the house looked like because, just after he had bought it, he had taken her there one late-summer evening. It was a small Georgian mansion overlooking the river, with four reception rooms, six bedrooms on the first floor, attics above, and a huge basement with a Victorian kitchen, wine cellars, larders, a pantry and other anonymous quarters. It also had several cottages, a walled garden, a rock garden and quite a lot of land, and could be approached by two long, winding drives. He had shown her all over it: 'Completely unspoiled,' he had said. 'The whole thing was only eight thousand.' It clearly excited him. She sincerely thought it was beautiful and said so. She also thought, rather sadly, that this was the only time she would see it; she would only be able to imagine his wonderful weekends spent there.

So when he asked her to go shopping with him, she agreed at once. She was enough in love with him to feel that any time spent with him was better than being apart.

'We're going to Cameo Corner first,' he said, when he had picked her up in his Bristol. 'Do you know it?'

She did indeed. She had, in her more affluent times,

bought earrings there, and Mosha Ovid would lend her amazing necklaces when she'd gone to grand dinner parties with Michael. She was particularly fond of Georgian paste, of which Ovid had a large collection.

Joseph clearly liked it, too, and picked out a necklace of peacock blue, large, simple stones set on a chain. 'Do you approve?' he asked.

What a wonderful present, she thought. I should want to wear it all the time.

'We'll have it,' he said. 'Have you a box for it?' They had.

'Now, which is the best material shop?'

'Jacqmar,' she said.

There he chose the most expensive green satin embroidered in gold and green sequins. 'How many yards for a long dress?'

The assistant told him. 'I'll take it. What do you think of my choice?'

'It's awfully grand – you know, for going to the opera.'

'Yes, I thought that. Glyndebourne, that sort of thing. Now we'll have some lunch.'

When they were back in the car, he said, 'That's Penelope sorted. You've been a great help.'

She could not think of anything to say. She knew that Penelope was his wife, hardly ever mentioned but always there. She wanted to cry. But pride forbade it, and she latched onto a gust of rage that he should have made her feel greedy and acquisitive, had probably been teasing her – not mentioning Penelope all morning. I suppose he feels guilty about her, and the presents are to make him feel better.

He took her to Bentley's for lunch and ordered oysters

and champagne, followed by poached turbot, but she couldn't get far beyond the oysters.

'How's your nice father getting on with his intransigent brother?'

'I have no idea. I haven't seen him since that evening. I could find out, if you like.'

'It might be worth telling him once more that time is running out. The business is trading at a loss now, and if that goes on it may be too late to sell.'

'How do you know about trading at a loss?'

'Oh, there are ways of finding out that sort of thing. Do you not want your fish?'

'I'm full of oysters. I can't eat any more.'

'Right. I'll take you home.'

'Are you going to stay with me?'

'Darling, I can't. Penelope is in London this weekend. Togetherness begins at six.'

She said nothing. She felt confounded by his indifference to her feelings, and humiliated by her position. She was a mistress, 'the other woman', and she had either to stop caring about him, or put up with being a spare-time person, forced into fitting in with any casual plans he had for her.

'Thank you for lunch,' she said, as she got out of the car, and practically ran down the dark passage that smelt always of the grocer's darker practices. The shop was on the ground floor, and the basement was where they plucked and dressed birds. Usually she hardly noticed the odour of singed feathers, decaying innards and over-ripe bacon, but today she hated the squalor. It was why the flat was cheap, and cheap was what she could afford. Perhaps Stella would be in: she would have a long talk with her about Joseph, and take comfort in her sardonic affection. They'd had these talks before. 'He's taking you in,' Stella would say. 'You want him to do that, though, don't you?'

But Stella had left a note outside her room that said: 'Have migraine. In bed. See you later.'

So there was nothing for it but to lie on her own bed, overcome by unhappiness and champagne, have a good cry and fall asleep.

HUGH AND JEMIMA

'I've been thinking.'

It was after supper, which they had eaten alone as the boys were still at boarding school, and Laura was – at last – asleep. Jemima had made a chicken pie, which Hugh particularly liked, and they were now finishing their bottle of claret with cheese and celery. Outside it was raw and raining, but the kitchen, with the new yellow velvet curtains that Jemima had made, felt cosy from the Aga's warmth.

She knew what he was going to say, because Polly had confided in her, but she waited to hear it from him. 'Tell me,' she said.

'Polly was talking to me about Edward and Diana, and I think it would be a good thing to ask them to dinner. How do you feel?'

She pretended to consider for a moment. 'I think it would be an excellent idea.'

'Good. Do you think we should take them out, or should we dine here?'

'Oh, much better to have them here.'

'I do love your decisiveness, sweetheart. Finally, should we ask some other people?'

'Oh, no! The whole point of the evening is for us to get to know Diana.' Jemima did not add, 'And for you and Edward to be better friends,' but that was really the point. Being nice to Diana was simply a first step. And Hugh had been looking so drained and unhappy of late that she had begun to worry about him.

'You ask him, darling. I think any Saturday would be good.'

∞ ∞ ∞

'Hugh and Jemima have asked us to dinner, darling.' He had waited until their second Martini had been drunk – was nervous about it. When he thought of it, the awful evening with Rachel and Sid still made him feel angry, ashamed of Diana's behaviour and, worse, his failure to tell her so. The truth was that he had been really shocked, seeing her in a new and most unwelcome light, but he had taken refuge – as cowardly people will do – in sulking and refusing to make love to her after Rachel and Sid had left. This had worked, up to a point. The next evening she had been full of excuses – she had tried so hard with the food and they had spurned all of it; Sid had been rude to her in her own house, and Rachel had spent nearly all the evening talking to him, until, she – Diana – had simply felt like a servant.

Seeing her blue eyes – they were more like dark hyacinths than bluebells – fill with tears was too much for him; he didn't want to argue any more, and she had apologised, so it had been a kind of a victory. He finished by saying, 'All I ask is that you'll be on your best behaviour with Hugh and Jem.'

'My best,' she promised, dabbing her eyes with his large silk handkerchief.

And so it was that the following Saturday he picked

her up from the Lansdowne Club, which she used on her shopping expeditions to London, where she had changed into the little midnight-blue velvet that he had agreed she should wear, with the amethyst necklace he had given her years ago before they were married.

∞ ∞ ∞

Jemima also was nervous. She consulted Hugh about the menu, and they settled upon potted shrimps (only the toast to do), followed by *poulet à la crème*, a dish she had found in Elizabeth David, one she knew she did very well, and ending with *tarte tatin*.

'I do think, Mummy, it isn't fair when you have party food that I should just have fish fingers,' Laura said, as she sat in front of her early supper. She had been watching the preparations all afternoon: the laying of the dining-room table, which was used only for parties, the candles, the arrangement of yellow and white freesias, a cluster of Dad's best glasses on the right-hand side of each plate, napkins as white as toothpaste, she thought, and masses of knives and forks and spoons arranged in military rows, much of this reflected in the beautiful shiny table made of walnut, Dad's favourite wood. She had helped to lay the table, and Mummy had told her how to do it, but she'd had to start again twice ... 'After all my helping,' she said tragically, 'you would think that that would make a difference.' Her arm was out of plaster, but she still hobbled about with the cast on her leg and had become astonishingly agile with her crutch.

'Darling, I promise you shall have chicken tomorrow for lunch.'

'And shrimps? And the upside-down tart?'

'Only if you eat your supper now, quickly, because I've got to change.'

Mercifully, Hugh arrived at this point. 'Go and have a lovely hot bath, and I'll see to Miss Horrible.'

Laura adored it when he called her names. 'How horrible am I?'

'Absolutely horrible – all over. Speaking when your mouth's full shows that.'

'I have to speak sometimes and I've been told to eat. That's two things at once.'

'Well, you eat and I'll tell you how horrible you are.'

She smiled contentedly, and began to demolish her fish fingers.

∞ ∞ ∞

He had just had time to make Martinis when their guests arrived. They had the drinks in the drawing room, which had not been changed since Sybil's day: the same Morris wallpaper, the same chintzy loose covers, and curtains to match the honeysuckle on the walls.

Jemima heard Hugh greeting the guests in the hall as she stood trying to get warm by the fire she had lit too late. She felt unreasonably nervous and, when Edward and Diana came into the room, realised she was not alone in that. All three of them looked as though they were going to the dentist, she thought. Edward greeted her with a kiss, and then said, 'This is Diana.'

'Hello, Diana, I'm so glad you could come,' and Diana smiled and said how nice it was for them to be asked.

Hugh was quickly pouring what turned out to be particularly strong Martinis; cigarettes were lit, conversations started uneasily about current news. Diana said what a pity it was that the Queen was abolishing presentations at Court for debutantes, and then asked Jemima if she had 'gone through all that'?

'Oh, no. I've never been quite sure what was involved, but in any case it sounds too expensive. My family could never have afforded it, even if they had wanted to. But I'm sure that for some girls it must have been fun,' she added, in case Diana had been one of those girls, and would think her rude. 'I'm off to make the toast.'

'Here comes the other half,' Hugh said.

'I must say, old boy, you do make a powerful Martini.'

'I've never liked weak drinks. I knew someone at my club who used to dip his finger in gin, run it round the rim of a glass, fill it up with tonic water and give it to his mother.'

'What a horrible trick! I'm sure neither of you would ever have done that to the Duchy!'

The brothers exchanged their first affectionate glance.

'No, we wouldn't. She liked her gin with Dubonnet.'

'But only one. She was very sparing about food and drink – for herself.' Hugh turned to Diana. 'What do you think about this plan to reform the Lords? Admitting women, and doing away with hereditary peers?'

'Well,' she needed time to think, 'I'm all for women having more say, but I don't know much about the other part. You aren't necessarily bad at a job because you were born to it. What do you think, darling?'

'I'm a Tory, darling. Not keen on change of any kind.'

'Yes, you are, Ed. You know you are. Look at the firm!'

At this point, Jemima called from below to say that dinner was ready, which was a relief for all.

'Let's not talk shop tonight,' Edward muttered to Hugh, as they were going downstairs.

∞ ∞ ∞

'I hear you've found a lovely house in Hawkhurst,' Hugh said, as he was pouring the wine, after he had settled Diana in her chair.

'Yes. It really is rather a dream home, and you love it too, don't you, darling?'

'I do indeed. Bit of a commute, but you can't have everything. Diana's a great gardener.'

'I wouldn't say that. I do simply adore it, though.' She turned to Jemima. 'Are you a gardener?'

'Not really. I try to keep our little patch at the back tidy, but I don't seem to have much time for more. Although,' she added, 'I suppose if I loved it I would find the time. It's a bit like people saying they don't have time to read. When, really, they simply don't want to.'

'Laura takes up a huge amount of time even though she goes to school,' Hugh said. 'And then there are the twins in the holidays.'

'Oh, I know what you mean. Poor Mrs Atkinson gets absolutely worn out producing huge meals for my boys. And then there's Susan and Jamie. Fortunately, the big boys are hardly ever with us – they prefer Scottish gambols with their grandparents.' There was a slight pause: Jemima took the shrimp plates and went to serve the chicken.

'Jem does all the cooking,' Hugh said. He was trying desperately not to disapprove of Diana, whose attitude to her older children had shocked him. 'Ed, could you deal with the wine? I'm just going to give Jem a hand.'

Edward walked round the table filling glasses; when he reached Diana, he gave her a kiss on the back of her neck. Her *décolleté* produced in him a twinge both of lust and anxiety: it was more suited to an unquiet evening at home than the present occasion.

'How am I doing?'

'Fine. You're doing fine. Not so difficult, though, is it? Jem is a sweetie.'

In the kitchen Jemima ladled out the chicken and Hugh added vegetables: they looked at each other, Jemima anxious and Hugh reassuring. Nothing they wanted to say to each other could be said. They carried two plates each through to the dining room.

The chicken was a success; Diana praised it extravagantly. She had become aware that anything nice she said about Jemima seemed to please Hugh. They all drank a lot, and gradually the atmosphere became less charged. Hugh admired Diana's necklace, and the women talked about the various boarding schools that Jemima's twins and Diana's two youngest, Jamie and Susan, attended. Hugh interrupted at that point by saying that they were not going to send Laura away anywhere – he didn't approve of boarding schools for girls. 'I'm not sure that I think they're a good thing for anyone,' he ended.

'I think the boys are quite happy at their school,' Jemima said, 'but of course I agree with you about girls. I should hate Laura to board.'

'Susan couldn't wait to go,' Diana said. 'And, of course, Jamie simply loves Eton.'

'He was pretty homesick his first year.' Edward, who had loathed all of his schooling, had secretly sympathised with the sobbing telephone calls on Sunday evenings, leaving Diana to cope with them.

'Oh, but, darling, they all go through that stage. It doesn't last. They get used to it.'

'I can't say I did. Nor did you, Hugh, did you?'

'No. That's what I mean. Most men I know didn't at all find school the best days of their lives. Most of them said they had a bloody awful time, so why are they – I suppose I must say we, since Simon went – so keen on exposing their sons to the same misery?' He turned to Jemima, who had begun collecting their plates. 'It's fine with the twins, I know: they've got each other. Edward and I didn't go to the same school. And we certainly weren't allowed to telephone home. We were left to the bracing uncertainty of matrons. You had a particularly horrible one, didn't you, Ed?'

'She smelt of pear drops and had rocky false teeth. I bit her and she was extra horrible to me after that.'

'I'm not surprised!' Diana, Hugh could see, was shocked.

'I had a boil on my neck and she squeezed and squeezed until it hurt like hell,' Edward explained.

'My marvellous resident chef has made you a *tarte tatin*.'

Jemima had brought in the pudding and set it on the table. 'I'm afraid I burned it. So it's lemon tart instead. I've cut it up, but I thought you might like to help yourselves.'

They did, and Hugh uncorked a half-bottle of Beaumes de Venise. 'It's all I've got left of it, I'm afraid. There's Calvados, though.'

'I hear you're having a bit of trouble with the roof at Home Place,' Edward said.

'Who told you that?'

'Rupert, I think.'

'The trouble was that Rachel employed Brownlow's

because the Brig had always used them, but I think old Brownlow has got too past it to go scampering over roofs. We've had to find new builders, get a new estimate. You know how long it all takes. It's going to turn out rather expensive, I'm afraid.'

'And who is paying for it?'

'Well, Rachel and I will be paying some of it, and Rupe, I hope, but the rest will be paid for by the firm. After all, it is Cazalets' property. It's part of the firm's assets.'

'Not a very profitable one, it would seem.'

'Ed, I really don't see why you should beef about it. After all, you got out of it.'

'Not if the firm is paying the major part. I'm still a member of the firm, and you know what I think about these so-called assets we have. We're losing money on all of them.'

'Not on the hardwood veneers. And Southampton will pay its way. We simply gave Teddy too much responsibility too soon.'

'Edward, darling, I really think we should be getting back: it's quite a long drive.'

Both women had stopped trying to talk to one another, and the atmosphere had become distinctly uncomfortable. Everybody got up from the table and Hugh led the way upstairs, where Diana collected her fur jacket. She was profuse in her thanks to her hosts for 'a most delicious dinner' and told Hugh how much she looked forward to them coming to Hawkhurst. Edward said he was sorry about talking shop, and Hugh said it didn't matter, which clearly it did.

'Oh, Lord!' Jemima, having given a final wave, shut the front door.

Hugh put his arms round her. 'You did awfully well. What did you think of Diana?'

'Well – I ended up feeling sorry for her.'

'What about Ed?'

'I felt sorry for him as well.'

They had begun to go downstairs. 'Don't let's clear up tonight. Let's go to bed.'

'I just have to blow out the candles and put the food away.'

Later, when they were in bed, Hugh said, 'Why are you sorry for them?'

'Oh. They have such a dull relationship. It felt sort of unreal. As though they were putting up with each other. Disappointment, I suppose. She has very ugly hands,' Jemima added.

'I didn't notice them.'

'Too taken up with her enormous breasts. I felt quite jealous of them.'

'I kept wondering if they'd fall out. Like that woman dining at the Berkeley – a waiter popping them back, and the head waiter reproving him, "Here we use a slightly warmed tablespoon."'

'Is that true?'

'I haven't the slightest idea. She just made me think of it. Anyway, I much prefer yours.'

'Do you really?'

Some time later, Hugh said, 'It was good to see Ed, but I can't understand why he got so worked up about Home Place.'

'Perhaps he thought that Diana wouldn't like to be jammed together with all the family.'

'More likely that they wouldn't get on with her.'

'She did say to me that their new house was the first real home she'd had.'

'Nonsense. They had that huge house in West Hampstead. Also, she's been married before. She must have had homes then.'

'All right. You don't like her much, but she is married to your brother, and you do love him.'

'So?'

'So you want him to feel OK. You'll have to talk to him, darling. How you feel about Diana isn't nearly as important as how you feel about him.'

'I suppose it isn't,' he said slowly, discovering this.

Jemima gave him a flurry of light little kisses, then yawned.

'Am I as boring as that?' But he stroked her hair back from her face and gave her a long, affectionate kiss. 'Poor little Jem. Nothing is as tiring as peacemaking. Sleep now.'

She was asleep in seconds, but Hugh lay awake, trying somehow to reconcile the deep rift between himself and his brother.

∞ ∞ ∞

'That wasn't too bad, was it?' Diana had taken his overcoat to spread over her knees; it was very cold and starting to rain.

'It was fine, I thought. What about you?'

'I thought it went well. I did my best, anyway.'

'You were marvellous, darling. The heat will come on in a minute. Light me a fag, will you? They're in that front pocket.'

'Jemima made me feel rather overdressed,' she said, when she had done so.

'You looked lovely, sweetie. Jemima never dresses up. I thought she looked very pretty.'

'I don't think Hugh liked me.'

'Oh, darling, of course he did. He always takes time to know people.' He had now said three things that she wanted to hear but were not really true. 'Why don't you have a little sleep?'

'I think I will. I feel quite woozy after all that wine.'

So Diana slept and he drove, wondering hopelessly how on earth he could break through his brother's obstinacy, his refusal to see the rocks ahead . . . Perhaps he could persuade him to meet that banker chap Louise had produced.

Could he? Well, he supposed he could try . . .

ARCHIE AND CLARY

'Why aren't we going to Home Place for Christmas?'

'I've told you, Bertie. The roof is in a bad state – rain coming in, builders, all that.'

'I can't see why that means we can't go.'

'We could take our tent,' Harriet suggested.

'Yes. We could take our tent. And you and Dad could sleep in one of the loose boxes.'

'And we could tell all the others to bring their tents, and their mothers and fathers could sleep in the other two boxes. Easy-peasy.'

'That's all very well,' Archie said. 'But you'd need some food from time to time. We're definitely not going. But we can have a very good Christmas at home.'

Harriet burst into tears. 'I want a Christmas in the country with snow. I want it more than I can say.'

'If there is snow there'll probably be some in London, too.'

'Snow is no good in London. It goes all grey and slushy in a minute.'

'Besides, there may not be any,' Clary said. 'Harriet, if you're going to go on crying, will you please stop eating. Your face is covered with porridge.'

'It's not covered,' Bertie said. 'Just a few drooly bits on your chin. You do exaggerate, Mum. It's quite annoying.

"You're filthy dirty", "You're boiling hot", when it's only my knees or I've been running.'

'Would you like some more coffee?' Clary asked Archie, in a muffled voice – she was trying not to laugh and Archie noticed, rather sadly, that their relationship was much easier when the children were present.

The holidays had begun for both of the children and for him: three weeks of trying to make the holiday good. He was taking his lot to the zoo where they were to meet Rupert and Georgie. And then Rupert would drive them to pick up Clary and go on to lunch at his place: a nice day. He had tried to get Clary to go with them to the zoo, but she'd said she had things to do.

When they were safely gone, Clary took the letter that she had received the day before, lit a cigarette and sat down at the kitchen table to read it for the third time. It was from the management of something called the Bush Theatre Company, and said that her play *Three Is Not Company* had been read by several members, including their resident director, Matt Corsham, and while it was thought that parts of it needed a rewrite, they would be interested in discussing a possible performance. Perhaps she would call to make an appointment for them to meet.

It was true. She had done it! The first time she had read the letter, she hadn't been able to believe it. The second time a wave of exhilaration and joy had possessed her. It was amazing, and true: she was a playwright. Fantasies unfurled of the first performance being such a resounding success that in no time West End managers were planning a production with Peggy Ashcroft, Dorothy Tutin and Laurence Olivier as the star cast . . .

But there was one very large and nerve-racking fly in this ointment. She had said nothing to Archie about it.

He had assumed that she was writing another novel; she had said nothing about a play. To begin with, she had told herself that it wasn't necessary as she might not be any good at playwriting. In which case she could burn it and nothing need ever be said. But it had turned out unexpectedly well: once she had got the structure in her head, she could concentrate upon her three characters, and the more she did that, the more she got caught up with their points of view. But now she would have to tell Archie, try to explain to him what had driven her to write this particular play.

At this moment, the telephone rang. Polly had heard that Christmas at Home Place was off, and wondered if she and the family would like to spend Christmas with them. 'If you come dressed as Eskimos, you'll be able to survive. Gerald and I would love it, and Simon will be here, and I haven't seen you for so long, Clary, it would be a real treat.'

'We'd love to come, Poll – if it isn't too much for you.'

'Of course not. Gerald is always complaining that there aren't enough children, although if anyone's been a fruitful vine it's me, four grapes. Oh, Clary, it would be so good to see you – and darling Archie. Come the day before Christmas Eve – the traffic won't be so bad. I'm longing to hear about your new novel. Dad said you were writing a lot.'

They chatted a bit more, and then Polly said, 'By the way, Nan has got a bit dotty, but not where the children are concerned. Thought I'd better warn you.'

After Polly's call Clary plucked up enough courage to ring Matt Corsham – whose signature could have been anything from a child trying out a pen to a road sign – but whose name was mercifully printed on the paper.

She explained that she would be unable to meet him before New Year, but that any date after that would do.

A date was agreed, for Friday, 3 January. 'If there's any hitch our end, I'll be in touch,' he said, before he rang off. He hadn't noticed that there was no telephone number on her letter, thank goodness, but then she realised that she would have had to tell Archie about it well before then.

∞ ∞ ∞

'Honestly, Clary, I don't know what to do. We spent a weekend down there looking for a decent house to rent, but we don't even agree about that. Your father wants a romantic Georgian manor house in some distant village where schools for the children will be miles from any-where, and I'll be stuck being a chauffeur all day. If we have to go, I'd far rather be in Southampton where at least there's some transport, and things going on.'

Lunch was over and Archie and Rupert had taken the children to Richmond Park, 'to work off some of their fiendish energy,' Archie had said. Juliet had refused to go with them; when pressed by her father, she had burst into tears and protested that at her age she should decide how she would spend the afternoon. 'Anyway, I loathe fresh air,' she'd said, fled upstairs and banged the door of her bedroom.

'Well, we don't need her. She's not interested in us,' Harriet had said, but without any conviction.

'And the worst of it is that poor Rupe doesn't want to go – not at all. He says he's always hated being in charge of anything, and he loves this house and refuses to sell – says we'll have to let it, but the thought of clearing it up enough to have tenants makes me want to faint and scream.'

'I'll help you,' Clary said. She was rinsing plates and Zoë was drying them.

'And, of course, you know about Home Place. The children are terribly disappointed about that – especially Juliet, funnily enough. Thank you for saying you'd help, though. I was wondering whether you'd like to have Christmas with us here.'

'Oh, darling, that would have been wonderful, but Polly rang this morning and asked us and I said yes. My lot were so disappointed about not going to Home Place because they love being in the country, and going to Poll will mean that they can be. And Archie and I need a rest, or at least a change.'

'I should have asked you yesterday. Oh, Clary! Why don't you wear gloves?'

Clary had been pushing her hair back from her face with a soapy hand. 'Can't be bothered. I know my hands are awful,' she added, 'all puffy and wrinkled and red, and I've only nearly stopped biting my nails, and if I put stockings on, my skin is so rough that I ladder them immediately. Archie doesn't like them at all.' Her eyes filled suddenly and she turned to Zoë. 'Do you sometimes feel that marriage is a profession? Where you don't get time off and whatever awful things happen you just have to bear them?'

Zoë pulled a chair out from the table, made Clary sit down, and pushed a packet of Gauloises and matches to her before answering. 'I think in the early days I felt rather as though I'd joined the wrong club. I adored Rupert but I couldn't understand why he was so keen on painting when he could have a much better job in the

275

firm. I felt inferior to Villy and Sybil, and that made me aggressive and demanding with Rupe. So I think I know what you mean. Oh, Clary, are you having a bad patch?'

'It's all my fault.' She lit her cigarette and inhaled gratefully. 'Absolutely mine.'

'It's never one person's fault,' Zoë said quietly. 'I learned that at the end of the war. We both fell in love with another person, you see. We both had a hand in it.'

'What happened?'

'My love died. And Rupe left his girl – woman – in France. In a way I think it was harder for him. But you have to talk about things, Clary, to get it right.'

'I know. But I dread it so much and I don't know how to start.'

'Have you fallen in love with someone else?'

'Oh, no. I could never do that. I love Archie.'

And then she told Zoë all about it, about his giving the girl up, and clearly suffering for it. She told her about the play, too, what it was about, and what was happening to it.

'And he doesn't know anything. He thinks I've been writing another novel, but the idea of making a play out of our particular triangle fell into my mind and I felt compelled to write about it. And, surprisingly, it's made me so much more understanding of what it's been like for the three of us.'

'You'll have to tell him. Give him the play to read. This evening, Clary. I'll have the children for the night so you have some time and peace to do it. Now I must go and give Rivers his carrot or Georgie will never forgive me.'

Clary began to thank her.

'Don't thank me – Georgie will be delighted and Rupe will bring them back in the morning.'

And she sped away, wanting to give Clary some time to recover. Her confidences had raked up the feelings that she had never quite lost for Jack Greenfeldt. Over the years they had diminished, become not only more distant but familiar and therefore less shocking. Speaking of him – usually to herself, but now to Clary – the same pictures reeled across her mind: the last time she'd seen him, when he'd turned up at Home Place; clearing out the studio that had been their secret place; the anguish he must have endured at the death camps that had led to his suicide – an act that she could now perceive to have been one of courage and love. These images recurred and still had the power to pierce her heart with their original pain . . . It was she, Zoë realised, who still needed time to recover, as much as Clary.

Rivers did not seem at all interested in the carrot, acted put out that she had simply interrupted the rest he so badly needed. At least, Zoë thought, as she mopped her face, Juliet will never have a war to contend with, will never have to endure what I went through.

∞ ∞ ∞

Juliet lay on her bed. She had sobbed herself dry and now twisted herself round so that she was on her back, staring at the ceiling. It felt like the end of the world. She had not heard from Neville for four weeks, three days and fifty minutes. The last time had been when he had taken her to the theatre, where they had seen an awfully depressing play (but he'd said he liked it so she had agreed with him that it was frightfully good). Then they had gone to a Chinese restaurant where they had had lots of little dishes of delicious things, like fried dumplings and prawns wrapped in dark green leaves that you didn't have to eat. He ate with chopsticks, but she had to give them up as she kept dropping bits of food from their slippery ends. She had worn her new navy blue dress, bought in a sale from Fenwick's, and had spent ages doing her make-up – had to keep scrubbing it off and starting again. She ended up with green eye shadow and a pair of false eyelashes that felt so heavy she could hardly keep her eyes open, some pale foundation and finally a lipstick of pillar-box red with which she had enlarged her mouth. I certainly look different, she thought, with uncertain satisfaction.

But when Neville came to fetch her, he burst out laughing. 'You look like a cross between a baby panda and a little green ghost. Why did you let her do all that?' This was addressed to Zoë, who shrugged and said, 'I don't organise her appearance any more.' In fact, she had protested and been snubbed.

Neville had seized her hand and dragged her upstairs. 'I won't have you spoiling your heavenly face with all that nonsense. Let me deal with it. I'm an old hand at make-up.'

Speechless with anger and shame at being made to look so foolish in front of her mother, Juliet collapsed in tears on the chair before her dressing table. Her room was strewn with discarded clothes, her bed was unmade; it was all exactly not what she had wanted anyone else to see – and especially not Neville.

'Darling, if you go on crying, you'll look more like a panda than ever.' He wrapped her up in her pyjama jacket. 'Must protect your pretty dress. Now. First I'll get these things off. Best if I do it quickly.' In fact, he was so gently deft that it didn't hurt at all and the false eyelashes lay on his hand like some horrible ancient insects. He chucked them into the overflowing wastepaper basket.

For the next half hour he cleaned her face, telling her at intervals how much prettier she was becoming, and she stopped feeling awful and revelled in his touching her and telling her that she was far too beautiful to use any make-up. 'And think how awful it would be if it was the other way round,' he said, when he had finished. 'Now, my darling Juliet, we must go or we'll miss the beginning of the play.'

It had been a heavenly evening, and for a while she was happy simply going over it all, and boasting to her best friends at school about going out with someone so glamorous. She could write to him at his flat – he had recently moved to a nicer one – but he would not write back to her. It was too dangerous, he said. They must wait until she was older. She did once ring him at his flat – she often tried whenever she had the house to herself – but on one occasion he was there and answered the call. He did not seem very pleased that she had rung, and soon she found nothing to say. There were sounds of music and then a girl's voice: 'Nev? Nev!'

'I've got to go, I'm working,' he said, and before she could ask him anything, he had rung off.

Then, at lunch today, she had asked (very casually) whether there was any news of Neville, and her father had said that he had found a new model whom he was very taken with: a magazine had done a big piece on Christian Dior, who had died in the autumn, and Neville had done the pictures, six plates of Serena wearing Dior clothes, and Archie had said, yes, he'd seen them, they were stunning, 'almost worth going to the dentist for'. Someone else had remarked that if Neville wanted to make a model as famous as Suzy Parker or Bronwen Pugh he would certainly do it. 'Especially if he was in love with her.'

She had managed to sit through the interminable minutes while the subject got changed, and then, affecting a choke, she'd excused herself and fled upstairs. Weeks and minutes were nothing to this. The whole of the rest of her life had somehow to be spent in secret, unbearable agony. Nobody would ever understand what it was like to love someone as she did, and then to have them torn out of her heart. And he had not told her! Had she not asked that casual question at lunch she might never have known until an announcement of marriage appeared. But surely she would have sensed the change in him. He had sounded different on the telephone – and then the music and a girl's voice, Serena's, it must have been.

She began to imagine what the rest of this grief-stricken life would be. She had once read in an historical novel that the heroine, on being been torn from her lover, had become a nun, had remained shut up in a convent for the rest of her life, had worn a hair shirt, and prayed constantly for forgiveness for loving her married lover. If she did that, Juliet decided, she would become known for her saintly disposition, fasting in order to give her bread to the birds, nursing the sick, welcoming any humiliation that came her way. In spite of the fact that all the other nuns looked up to her as an example of piety, and the reverend mother always called her 'my dear, dear child', she remained humble, and when she died everybody in the convent wept for their 'little saint'. But some fantasies go too far, and this one, like a half-cooked sickeningly sweet meringue, had passed the point of the slightest credibility. Now it induced a few hoots of hysterical laughter and relief. The future was not that bad. She did not live in an age when cruel parents shut their children up in convents if they failed to make the right marriage. Once she'd got through school, she could really start her life. Naturally it would be a sad one, but she felt it must deepen and mature her character. Almost at once she fell into a deep, peaceful sleep.

RACHEL AND SID

It was a week before Christmas and they were in London. Sid had just finished her course of chemotherapy, and was coming out of the Marsden, the hospital where she had been sent by Rachel's doctor. She had managed to keep the treatment a secret from Rachel, and this had entailed not telling her about the Marsden. She was so fierce with Rachel about wanting to go for her appointments by herself that Rachel had retreated, quite frightened by her severity. The last four weeks had been extremely hard for both of them. The chemotherapy made Sid nauseous and it was increasingly difficult to find anything she could bear to eat. Dry biscuits were the safest, but after one or two she had to give up, go to the lavatory and throw up. She hated being sick so much that she was usually sick a second time. The only thing she actually enjoyed was a cup of very weak China tea with a slice of lemon in it.

She had decided not to wait for a bus and to treat herself to a taxi. But she did not have to wait for anything because there was Rachel, sitting in a taxi and waving to her.

'How did you know I was here?'

'It's where you came the first time. I realised you must be here.'

They were sitting side by side, and now Rachel took

one of Sid's hands in both of her own. 'It's all right, my darling. I know. You don't have to pretend with me any more.'

Extraordinary relief. She couldn't speak, and she did not want to cry.

'You've been so brave, shielding me from this. But I'm glad to know. Now we can fight it together. It will be far better like that. I've been reading a lot about cancer, and the fact that you've felt so ill with the treatment doesn't mean that it won't have worked. So, my dearest one, no more hiding clumps of your hair in envelopes. I should love you if you became totally bald. Meanwhile, before you go for your next check-up, we've got to find things for you to eat. You'll have to help me with that. There's a pill you can take that will stop you feeling so sick. We're going to Home Place this afternoon, and Mrs Tonbridge will cook for us. You know how she loves to feed people.'

'What about the family, Christmas and all that?' She had been dreading the influx and letting everyone down.

'They aren't coming. The roof is still being done. It will be just you and me – really cosy and nice.'

Rachel was so calm and smiling, so much in command as well as being so comforting that she actually felt better than she had for weeks. 'Oh, darling! I do love you.'

And Rachel turned her head away to look out of the window. 'Same here.'

ARCHIE AND CLARY

'. . . and I wanted to talk to you.'

There was a pause, during which he felt his heart sinking.

'. . . without the children interrupting us.'

They were sitting in the car outside their studio. The darkness was only broken by a weak yellow streetlamp, and she sat now twisting her hands nervously in her lap. Her hair was hanging round her face so he could not see it. Her mood was contagious – he was feeling pretty shaky himself – but his old habit of protecting her won out, and in a gentle but matter-of-fact manner, he said, 'Come on, Clary. You'll feel much better if you tell me what's the matter.'

'Yes. Well, all these weeks I haven't been writing a novel, I've been writing a play.' She gave him a quick look.

He was smiling. Such relief. 'Why on earth didn't you tell me before?' was something he managed not to say. For some reason she was in a state about it and, like animals and small children, she liked to be taken seriously.

'And,' she continued, 'I sent it to the management at the Bush Theatre, and it looks like they might do it.'

'I can see that this is a tragedy, or at least you sound as though it is. I think it's marvellous.' He pushed her hair out of the way and kissed her cheek. 'Why are you being so gloomy about it?'

'Archie, I haven't told you what it's about yet.'

This was the crunch, he supposed. 'Tell me,' he said quietly. 'I expect it's about a man marrying a girl far younger than he, having children and not enough money to give her a good life.'

'Oh, no! It isn't like that at all. It's about a married couple, but he falls in love with another girl, and it's what happens to – to everybody after that. Nothing is the same, you see – after that. For any of them.'

'But he gives her up, doesn't he?' God! He hadn't gone through all that for nothing, had he?

'Yes, he does. But I've found that even if you do what you think is right, it doesn't change your feelings about it. In fact, it seems to make things worse. The damage is somehow done. I had to write about it. I had to try to imagine what it's like to love two people. I had to imagine what it's like to be the poor girl – suddenly cast out by the first person she falls in love with. And, of course, I had to find out what it means to be someone like me. But I became more and more afraid that you'd hate me for doing it.' Then, so quietly that he could scarcely hear her, she said, 'I have tried to be fair.'

'Clary, you know I would never try to stop you writing anything. Remember our cottage by the canal?' He had taken her hands and now he gave them a little shake. She nodded, and a tear fell onto his finger. 'I love you. I shall never stop loving you and that – other thing – it needs time, you know. It is passing, but damage always needs time. For all of us. It will slip into being a small incident in our lives, you'll see.'

Later, when they were in bed, he said, 'I should very much like to read your play.'

'But not tonight?'

'Certainly not tonight.' He was exhausted – light-headed with relief. Time to wind down. He settled her against him. 'I expect that, in the near future, you'll become famous, and I shall accompany you to first nights, red carpets and champagne, both of us dressed to the nines . . .'

'I don't think I'll ever be those things, famous and *soignée* and all that.'

'No, sweetheart, I've never thought of you as *soignée* . . .'

'I forgot to tell you. Polly's invited us all for Christmas.'

'Oh, good. Harriet and Bertie will be so pleased. How nice of Poll . . .' But he realised that she had already dozed off. He shifted his arm carefully from under her shoulder in case it went to sleep before the rest of him did.

VILLY AND
MISS MILLIMENT

Villy had always dreaded Christmas, except during those halcyon years when the brothers had taken it in turn to look after the children while some of the family went skiing. That had come to an end, of course, with the war. But the war years at Home Place hadn't been so bad either when she looked back at them. Compared to now, they seemed much better than she had thought at the time. After the frightful blow of Edward leaving her, everything had fallen to pieces: she remembered telling Miss Milliment that she would gladly have put her head in a gas oven if it weren't for Roland. That had been the time when she had taken a bit too much gin, a habit she dropped as soon as she realised she had acquired it.

For years now she had been trying to make Christmas merry for Roland. He was now eighteen, and she had just learned from Zoë that no one was going to Home Place because of repairs, and when, unable to stop herself, she had retorted that it didn't make any difference to her, Zoë had asked if she would like to come to Christmas lunch. 'With Miss Milliment, of course, and Roland – we haven't seen him for ages.'

Villy had accepted, very gratefully: it would be one

nice holiday event for Roland, and, if she was having a good day, for Miss Milliment, too.

Miss Milliment. She was becoming a real anxiety. It was easy when she was in her right mind – a trifle forgetful sometimes, but that was natural at her age. She had a whole series of other minds, though, the consequences of which were wholly unpredictable. They nearly always involved action of some kind – getting up at three in the morning and trying to make her own breakfast, boiling milk all over the stove and the saucepan burned. 'Oh, Viola, I wanted you to have a good lie-in this weekend.' This had happened in varying forms more than once. Another time, when she seemed to have disappeared, Villy found her in Abbey Road, in pouring rain and in her nightgown. 'Oh, Viola, I simply have to get somewhere but, do you know, I'm not quite sure where it is. I'm so afraid I'll be late.' And she had clung to Villy, her sparse grey plait streaming from the rain, her spectacles awry and her heavy flannel nightgown already dripping small rivulets at her feet. It had been early evening, and the road was empty except for a few people hurrying home to get out of the rain.

She had led her slowly home, sobbing, apologising, but beneath the confusion, Villy had sensed real fear – even terror – and she did her best to be gentle and reassuring.

When they got home, she changed Miss Milliment's nightdress, adding a bed-jacket, the scrambled egg upon which had become distressingly crusty, got her into bed with two hot-water bottles and finally brought her a mug of cocoa, then sat with her while she drank it . . .

'My dear Viola, I have a confession to make.' She was

regarding Villy intently. 'I fear that I have recently become rather forgetful.'

'Well, dear Miss Milliment, I think we all forget things when we get older. The great thing is not to worry about it.'

Miss Milliment was silent, and then she said, as though to herself, 'That would be the great thing.'

But later, long after Miss Milliment had dropped off, Villy lay in bed worrying. When she had offered her a home, she had not envisaged looking after a demented person, and that was what she now realised Miss Milliment was likely to become. She would have to keep the front door locked at all times, conceal matches and cigarette lighters to prevent combustion in the kitchen – and what else? Soon it would be unwise to let her be alone at all. But the worst would be feeling guilty and anxious whenever she did leave the house. She had planned to take Roland to *The Bridge on the River Kwai*, the new film with Alec Guinness, and then to have supper in a Chinese restaurant in Soho as a Christmas treat. Zoë's offer of a Christmas lunch was another event for him. But there were at least three weeks to be filled, and she passionately did not want him to be bored. He had always been remote, courteous, but earlier Christmases had clearly been dull for him: sitting at the table after roast chicken (a turkey impossible for three), a very small Christmas pudding and a mince pie, and then a box of crackers that never had anything interesting in them; listening to the Queen's speech on the wireless and the prospect of playing cards with her until tea . . . It wasn't as though his siblings helped at all. Teddy and Louise would pay duty visits; she knew they were that, although Teddy took more trouble than Louise to conceal it. They were awkward with Roland – didn't really try to make friends with him – and Lydia was away acting in a pantomime. Perhaps we should go and see her, Villy thought, but then she realised that of course they couldn't leave Miss Milliment for so long. Northampton and a show would take the whole day.

One of her periodic fits of rage came over her now. Why the hell couldn't Jessica take her share of caring for Miss Milliment, who, after all, had been her governess as well? And while she had gone through the humiliation and impoverishment of a divorce, Jessica and Raymond had inherited property and a great deal of money from Raymond's aunt. They had recently bought a villa on the Costa del Sol where they went for most of the winter and that let Jessica off doing anything for Villy at Christmas. But she was pretty good at evading any 'governess duty' at all, as she called it.

'I have come to the conclusion that I'm really not very good with old people,' she had said, on one of her rare visits, as though that settled the matter. 'And you're so marvellous with her – it's much better if she stays with you.'

'Shall we get a small tree this year?' she'd asked Roland, on the way back from the station.

'I don't mind,' he'd said politely.

All these years she had been choosing a small tree and decking it with the same old baubles and tiny candles (so much prettier than electric lights), arranging the presents under it, always making a small ceremony of it before lunch. And he hadn't minded! No more trees, she thought now, before eventually she slept.

THE FAKENHAMS AND
THE LESTRANGES

'I thought the best thing was simply to tell them where they're all sleeping to prevent arguments about it.'

Polly had arranged everything beautifully, Clary thought. Harriet was to sleep in the big night nursery with the twins, Eliza and Jane; Bertie was to sleep with Andrew. Spencer slept in Gerald's dressing room next to his parents. Surprisingly, no one objected to the arrangements. The Lestranges had arrived in time for a late tea in the kitchen, presided over by Nan – a piece of bread and butter before they could go on to jam sandwiches and cake. In spite of claiming car sickness, Bertie and Harriet were, they said, nearly starving. Sickness, however, proved a fascinating subject.

'I've never been sick. What's it like?' Andrew asked.

Harriet considered. 'Well, your mouth gets full of water and you have a sort of awful rumbling in your throat and then, whoosh! Up it all comes over everything.'

'But what does it look like?'

'A sort of mixture between scrambled egg and porridge. It smells horrible too.'

Eliza, who was the best at reading, said, 'They often say in newspapers that people choke and die in their own vomit.'

291

'Well, think how nasty it would be if it was someone else's.' Jane was very good at capping Eliza's remarks.

Nan, who seemed not to have noticed what they were talking about as she was busy feeding Spencer, came to life. 'I've told you, Miss, little girls don't use words like "nasty" or "beastly". You say "horrid".'

'People do at school, Nan.'

'You're not at school now.'

After tea they played Torchlight Ogres, which meant that they turned off every light they could reach. Nan kept to the kitchen and the parents to Polly's sitting room, which was strictly forbidden to the children anyway because a lot of secret things were going on in it. For what seemed like hours, they rushed about the house armed with torches supplied by Eliza.

The rules of the game were utterly mysterious to the onlooker, and sometimes to the younger players – Andrew, in particular, who resorted to weeping in a cupboard about the unfairness of it all.

'It may make them a bit sleepier than they would otherwise be,' Archie remarked. He was tired from the long drive and his bad leg ached. He stretched it out gratefully in front of the large wood fire. She'll be in Surrey with her family, he thought. He need not think about her. 'You have made this room nice, Poll.' It was warm, with lamps that cast a friendly light, the huge windows curtained in green velvet, one wall covered with books, and the rest in a sea-green jasper paper.

Gerald said he was going to brave the dark to get ice. 'We could all do with a stiff drink before their bedtime.'

Clary said, 'I'm doing bedtime, darling Gerald. You can confine yourself to a goodnight kiss.' She had been kneeling on the floor by the window and she and Polly were unpacking the cardboard boxes that contained the decorations.

But when Gerald returned from 'a positively polar expedition' with the ice and had mixed them a strong reviving concoction, they all sat by the fire to enjoy it. There ensued a long, comfortable silence, and Gerald thought how good it was to have even more children in the house, how charming Polly looked with the firelight flickering on her copper hair, and wondered whether the tree nursery he had planted with Simon would yield some sort of income, since hiring out the house had so far barely broken even . . .

Polly thought how lovely it was to have Clary and Archie, and how sad it was that their lives were so distant that she almost didn't know Clary, which was largely because she, Polly, could never get away: she could not leave the children with Nan any more and Gerald – whatever he said – could not cope alone with the house, the children and his plans for improving the grounds. She thought, as she often did at this time of year, of Christopher in his monastery, and hoped that he was happy with his life. She remembered the time with him in his caravan when he had had his beloved dog, and had also wanted to be in love with her. Luckily that had come to an end quite quickly, as he had never mentioned it again. She thought of her father and how careworn he had seemed when he came. Jemima had told her about the subsequent dinner with Edward and Diana: at least some progress had been made for a reconciliation . . .

Clary was thinking how lovely it was not to be the main person responsible for Christmas. She would help, of course she would, but she would only have to do as

she was told. Polly was amazing. She organised everything while looking as though she did nothing. She has
real glamour and it's such bad luck for darling Archie
that I don't have a scrap of that, she thought. She had
put her hair up at home that morning, but pins kept
dropping out, and the more she tried to push her hair
back, the more strands kept falling. Just as another pin
fell out, Archie leaned over and gently pulled the whole
lot down. 'That's how I like it,' he said, and she felt such
a surge of love for him that she blushed.

It was a little like the old Christmases at Home Place
– only no Mrs Tonbridge or Eileen to bear the domestic
brunt. We have to do that now for ourselves. Which is
probably very good for us but must be very hard on the
older generation, people like poor Aunt Villy and even
Zoë. It was one of those apparently small changes that
had come about together with the welfare state and a
Labour government. Having Mr Macmillan didn't bring
any of that back, although if you were rich, of course,
you still had the old advantages. She wondered whether
all the people who had been in domestic service were
having nicer lives out of all that. Both Archie and her
father had always been left-wing, although Dad had
never said very much about it; he was so awfully good
at seeing the other person's point of view that he often
agreed with the people who weren't on his side, and
Archie hardly ever talked to her about politics, although
he read the *Observer* and the *Manchester Guardian* every
week. Life was supposed to be getting better for women.
He had pointed out to her that there were going to be
life peers in the House of Lords. 'Baroness Clarissa
Lestrange took her seat last week, and her maiden speech
about children's education was warmly received . . .' But

no: she was going to be a playwright; she was going to
join what Archie called the Club, which only practising
artists could join . . .

Archie gratefully acknowledged his glass being refilled by Gerald. He was the perfect host, seemed to
anticipate everything. And he so clearly adored Polly.
He was also, Archie thought, secretly in love with the
hideous old pile he had inherited. He remembered Polly
talking about how she wanted to make a house entirely
beautiful – she could never have bargained for this but
she had made pockets of luxury and comfort. His and
Clary's room, for instance. It had been painted and
papered, had a moss-green carpet and rose-coloured
curtains that matched the roses climbing up the wide
trellis on the walls – a French paper, by the look of it.
Polly had explained that it was the bedroom they had
chosen to be the brides' dressing room, but meanwhile
it was the best guest room. 'I had to try and do it to suit
them,' she said. She had hung what she described as
furnishing pictures, blameless meticulous sea- and landscapes, and one of the less sinister family portraits, *Lady
Agatha Barstow*, wearing a blue taffeta evening dress,
with an agonisingly tiny waist. Her face – the china
complexion, the slightly protuberant blue eyes, the tiny
dark red mouth and the faintest indication of a double
chin – gazed upon the room utterly without expression.
'The agent people love it because she's got a title,' Polly
had said. 'And the room has a loo and a basin en suite,
which is more than we have.'

Polly had certainly done her best, he thought, but the
major part of the vast, sprawling house was unoccupied:
the upstairs passages led off to rows of bedrooms in
various states of disrepair. The place had been built to

entertain huge idle house parties attended by a battery of staff. Polly had told them that Nan was the only person who really knew her way around it.

A little while after Polly and Clary had gone to get the children to bed, Gerald said that he was going to see if more help was needed. Archie was left by the fire with his replenished drink, and she came into his mind yet again. A shit and a bastard was what he had been, and Clary's play had brought it all home to him. The play had impressed him: she had certainly dealt fairly with the three people involved – she had a real talent for dialogue – and she had kept the tension right to the end, which, Archie supposed, they were all living through now. It was all very well for him, he thought. He had never stopped loving Clary, but the girl had been left with nothing. The play certainly revived all these guilty feelings, and he repeated for the hundredth time that she was very young, she would get over it, most people began their love lives with an unhappy affair – look at him and Rachel, whom he had cared for for so long and so much. All in a peaceful past.

It was the future that was less certain – particularly for old Rupe. He had confided that the firm was losing money. He had never wanted to join the family business anyway, had done it because he wasn't earning enough teaching art and selling hardly any pictures, and he felt that Zoë deserved a better life. He had told Archie about the affair he had had when he was in France and how difficult it had been to adjust to the old – new – life. Much as Archie longed for someone in whom he could confide now, it was not possible to tell Rupe. He had married Rupert's daughter, was several years older than she, and to admit to any kind of infidelity was out of the question. It was awful, he thought, how everything seemed to depend upon money. And fear.

Fear made people greedy and therefore selfish; that small minority who honestly did not care for themselves in that way, who could sincerely say that money was unimportant to them, almost always had no dependants. When he and Rupert had been students they had thought like that; they had been admirably high-minded and scorned those who did not agree with them. Hardship and poverty were romantic, and when either occasionally touched them, they put it down to the cause of Art . . .

'They want you to say goodnight.' It was Clary. She looked hot and she had tied her hair back with a piece of string.

'Where are they?'

'Harriet is with Eliza and Jane. Bertie is with Andrew. You'll hear them if you just go upstairs. Polly's getting supper. Hot soup and smoked-salmon sandwiches. We're going to have it in here, then do the tree and the stockings. It's all lovely, don't you think?'

She had a smudge on her forehead, but below it, her eyes sparkled with pleasure: he could never resist their beautiful candour.

LOUISE AND TEDDY,
WITH EDWARD AND DIANA

'Do you think anyone has Christmas where they want to?'

She was in a bad mood, Teddy thought. He had come to pick her up to drive them both down to Hawkhurst. The flat reeked of burned feathers, and the shop below her ghastly flat was crammed with dead dressed turkeys. 'I'm used to it,' she said, when he remarked on the smell. She had kept him waiting and he'd sat in her small, bare sitting room.

There was a bookshelf and a small gas fire, but most of the elements in it were broken so it gave out uneasy blue flames and no perceptible heat. Come on, Louise, he begged silently. He didn't want to say anything that might make her crosser.

But when she finally emerged, she looked so marvellous that he felt better at once. She wore jeans, boots, and a navy blue fisherman's jersey, her shining blonde hair dressed in a French plait and small silver rings in her ears. 'Don't you agree?' she said. 'We all have to do duty visits at this jolly time of year.'

'Well, I'm just glad to get away from Southampton. And we've never been to Dad's new house: it might be fun.'

'Not with Diana in it.' She had lugged her heavy suitcase into the room. 'It's all yours. Sorry it's so heavy.'

'Why do you hate her so much?'

'I suppose because she hates me. And Dad's so tactless about it – he keeps calling us his two favourite women. She can't stand that. Are we going to have lunch first?'

'If we do, the traffic will be even worse.' He looked at his watch. 'It's nearly two now. But we will if you really want to.'

'I don't care. I can't afford to care too much about meals in my job.'

When he'd stowed her case and they were in the car, he said, 'I went to Mum's last night.'

'Oh, well done you. I went at the weekend. Poor Roland. It must be so dreary for him.'

'Pretty bad for all of them, I should think. Miss Milliment didn't seem to know who I was. That's hard on Mum.'

'I think she likes things to be hard.'

'You seem to have got rather cynical in your old age.'

There was a pause, and then she said, 'Sorry, Ted. I'm not really cynical – just a bit sad.' Silence. 'Sometimes it's not much fun being a woman.'

'You're in love with somebody?'

'I think so. Yes, I must be.'

'And he doesn't love you?'

'I don't know. I suppose he does, in a way.'

'But he's married, is that it? So you can't marry him.'

'I don't know if I'd want to marry him. But I can't anyway. He spends five evenings a week with me, and goes back to his wife at weekends. Oh, yes, and for long holidays in the south of France – weeks and weeks.

While I stew down in London.' She made an effort to laugh. 'I'm the icing rather than the cake.'

'I can see that's difficult.' It's quite difficult being a man, he thought, recalling Ellen and the frightful mess he'd made of that. She had got pregnant, after that one day on the Isle of Wight – had told him six weeks later. He'd been trying to see her only in the pub, had made no plans for time off with her although he could see that she was unhappy. He told himself that it was just as difficult for him, but really he knew it wasn't. He couldn't face marrying her, had begun to realise how little they had in common, so one evening when she had served him his pint and very quietly said she wanted to talk with him in private, he had agreed, and waited for her to emerge from the pub after closing time. He had thought that she was going to ask him what was wrong, why they weren't seeing each other, so her news was a bombshell.

'Are you sure?'

She had missed two periods and she felt sick in the mornings – threw up sometimes – so, yes.

'Couldn't you go back home to have it?'

She could not. Her family would throw her out; she'd land up in some home run by nuns who would force her to get it adopted. 'It's your baby, Teddy. I couldn't let that happen.' She was speaking quietly, but her eyes were bright with silent pleading.

'I have to tell you, I can't marry you, Ellen. My family wouldn't hear of it.' As he said that, he was sharply aware of what a coward that made him.

But she seemed to accept his rejection. 'That's what families are like,' she said, a single pear-shaped tear falling from one eye. There was a sad, resigned silence.

'I think the best thing would be for you not to have it.'

'That would be a wicked sin. It's what my friend Annie did and she may well burn in Hell for it.'

'She won't, you know. I'm sure she won't.' Desperately, he began improvising about religion, of which he knew very little. 'God doesn't punish people who repent. At least, my God doesn't. He's merciful, and – and— Well, there it is.'

'Is it?'

'Of course. Why don't you ask Annie what she did? I'll pay. It's the least I can do.'

And that, in the end, was what had happened. Annie did know someone. They wanted four hundred pounds for it so he had pawned his watch and his gold cufflinks, and just about scraped up enough to give Ellen. She was not in the pub for a week after the abortion, and when she returned to work, she was pale and seemed much older. 'I'd rather not see you any more,' she said. So he stopped going to the pub, but he didn't stop feeling bad about her.

'You've gone very quiet.'

'I was thinking. All the things you're supposed to do aren't much fun, and the other things simply seem to end in disaster.'

'What other things?'

'You know, going to bed with people, and drinking too much, staying up all night so you're no good for work the next day, smoking hash – all that lot – and sleeping around—'

'You said that before. Have you got anyone now?'

So then he told her about Ellen.

'Oh, poor old Ted. What awfully bad luck.'

He hadn't thought of it like that. It didn't seem right, but at the same time it was oddly consoling.

'You should lay off barmaids, darling.'

'And you should lay off married men.'

'Oh dear! It's so easy to give other people good advice, and so hard for them to follow it. I think you ought to marry someone,' she said.

They were well out of London now, through Sevenoaks, and there was far less traffic. There had been a long, comfortable silence between them, during which each had had kindly thoughts about the other.

'I think you should, too, Lou. Just because we chose the wrong person the first time doesn't mean it wouldn't be a good idea. Think of the future if you don't.'

'The future, as far as I'm concerned, is Christmas with Dad. I must say, I'm glad it's both of us.'

'So am I.'

∞ ∞ ∞

The house was difficult to find, and it was dark by the time they arrived. They were met by the Labrador, which seemed vociferously delighted to welcome them.

Her barking produced their father, who embraced them both. 'Well done! Was it an awful drive? Come and have some tea. Diana's in the drawing room. Down, Honey!' The Labrador instantly sat at his feet. He led the way with his arm round Louise. 'I must say you're looking wonderful, darling.'

'Ted's pretty wonderful, too,' she said.

'Of course he is.'

The room was delightfully warm, with a large log fire,

302

and Diana was lying on a sofa with a tea tray on a low table before her.

'Hello! You must be dying for tea. I'm afraid my greedy two have demolished all the chocolate cake, but there are still some crumpets left, although I'm afraid they'll be rather cold by now.'

'Crumpets will be fine,' Teddy said. 'We missed lunch because the traffic getting out of London was so thick.'

'You must have started very late, then. But I suppose you don't mind, do you, Louise? I mean, you must have to keep worrying about your figure in order to get into the clothes.'

'I don't worry about it too much.'

She and Teddy both started eating crumpets that were slippery with butter then Teddy dropped his on the yellow carpet. He picked it up, but it left a mark.

'Oh dear! Edward, darling, get some soda water and a cloth. Quickly!'

Teddy apologised, and Diana said it didn't matter at all, which was clearly untrue.

When Edward returned with the soda siphon and a cloth, she insisted on doing the squirting and cleaning herself, in spite of Teddy offering.

Louise said she would like to unpack, and Teddy offered to take up her luggage. Edward said he would conduct them upstairs.

'Where are they sleeping, darling?'

'Oh, Teddy's in the old night nursery and Louise has the maid's bedroom at the back.'

A look of embarrassment crossed her father's face. It's going to be just like France, she thought, loving him for minding, hating him for being so weak.

'Here we are,' he said, opening the door on a bleak little room that was icy cold. 'I'm afraid the heating doesn't get as far as this. I'll see if I can find you an electric fire. Teddy is next door.'

'Where's the bathroom, Dad?'

'At the end of the passage. I'll go and see if I can track down that heater.'

Teddy dumped her case on the little iron bedstead. 'Not exactly the Ritz, is it? I'll come back when I've unpacked.'

She hung her two dresses, stored her suitcase with the rest of her things, and decided to explore the bathroom. When she returned, it was to find a tall young man standing outside her door with an electric fire. 'Hello! I'm Jamie, your half-brother. Sorry about the fire. Susan pinched it, in spite of having a perfectly good radiator in her room. Shall I plug it in for you?'

He had a charming easy manner, although he didn't look a bit like Dad. 'It's bloody cold in here,' he said. 'There'll be drinks quite soon, so come down as soon as you're ready. I missed you in the south of France last summer. Susan and I turned up after you left. I must say that was a pity.' His admiration was open and she felt cheered by it. 'Sorry you've got such a dud room. I'd have given you mine if I'd known. Hope you'll get warmer soon. By the way, my sister Susan is absolute hell at the moment. Mum says it's just a phase, but it sure is a long one. She's fifteen, and she's been like it for nearly two years.'

But before Louise could ask what sort of hell, he'd gone.

She changed her jersey for a white silk shirt, brushed

her hair, put on some lipstick and went downstairs for the drink and the welcome log fire.

∞ ∞ ∞

That was the beginning of the three days she and Teddy spent in their father's house, where everyone ate and drank too much, exchanged presents, spent embarrassing interludes when Susan regaled them with her ghastly well-known-speeches-from-Shakespeare and, worse, speeches she had written for herself, the latter requiring much tedious explanation to set the scene. She was going through the unfortunate stage of adolescence where she bulged out of her clothes, had acne on a face that was pear-shaped with puppy fat, and adopted a voice for her acts that was a nauseating blend of martyr- dom and self-righteousness. They sat through these pieces because Diana explained that it was important for her to express herself, and Edward, though he was clearly both embarrassed and bored, said nothing. At one point Jamie suggested that they should play charades but no one seemed enthusiastic. By the evening of Boxing Day they all picked at pieces of cold turkey and mince pies with a certain relief that Christmas was nearly over although, of course, nobody said as much.

∞ ∞ ∞

'Phew!' Teddy said, when they were safely in the car. They had left immediately after breakfast on the grounds that Louise had to be in London by lunchtime.

'We needn't ever do it again.'

305

'What were your best moments?'

'Do you mean what were my best worst moments?'

'OK, them, and then your truly best ones – if you had any.'

Louise thought. 'Seeing my awful little room. Having to sit through Susan's dreaded displays—'

Teddy interrupted: 'They don't count. We know about them, and they went on all the time.'

'All right. They weren't moments anyway – they were hours. Having to seem pleased with Diana's present. A tin of talc, a tube of hand cream and a cake of soap – all done up in a gift box from Boots. And the real joke about that is that she gave Mrs Patterson exactly the same.'

'How on earth do you know that?'

'It was on the kitchen table when I went to get some more ice for Dad. He only said "my two favourite women" once, but you should have seen her face. Those awful unmerry meals! And every time she said, "Quite frankly", you knew some whopping lie was coming.'

'Yes, several times she said, "To be quite honest with you," to me and then something disparaging came out – usually about Dad. Poor Dad! He was far better off being unfaithful to Mum. Better for both of them, actually.'

'Who's the cynic now?'

'I'm not a cynic, I'm a realist. Our father is simply not given to fidelity. Few men are – look at your Joseph. And the funny thing is they mostly seem to think that other people ought to be. Dad told me to get married and settle down. He didn't, did he?'

There was a short silence, and then Louise said, 'I suppose if you were really in love, you wouldn't want anyone else.'

He took a quick look at her. 'Yes, I'm sure there are

people like that. I also think women want to be in love far more than men. I've come to the conclusion that I really don't know much about it. I agree with you about our bedrooms. Mine was larger but just as cold and nobody produced a heater. I slept in my clothes. And Diana gave me a completely horrible tie. So I'm with you about not going back if I can help it. One good thing. I thought I was going to dislike Jamie, for being sent to Eton and then going on to Cambridge. I thought he'd be snotty and superior, but he's actually very nice. He told me that Dad wanted him to go into the firm, but he's refusing. He wants to do some kind of medical research, you know, finding out how to eradicate disease. He's leaving today to stay with a friend who's set up an experiment. He didn't say anything, but I got the feeling that he's fed up with home. I must say, though, that I don't think he is Dad's son. He doesn't look in the least like him. Another of Madam's traps, perhaps.'

'Well, even if you think that, you shouldn't say it to anyone – ever. I'm serious, Ted, promise you won't.'

'I was only telling you. All right, I won't.'

She sensed he didn't like being told not to do things, and after a silence, she said, 'My date is at a party this evening. Would you like to come to it? There'll be lots of girls.'

'Really nice girls?' Teasing her.

'Awfully, awfully nice. You might find one to marry.'

'OK. I would like to.' He realised then how much he didn't want to go back to Southampton.

RACHEL AND SID,
WITH THE TONBRIDGES

'A little steamed fish, Miss Rachel, with some mashed potato and a purée of spinach?'

Rachel hesitated. Asking Sid what she would like to eat had proved unprofitable. She would simply ask for Brand's Essence, which came from the chemist in Battle, and would only take a few teaspoonfuls and then say it was too rich. The cancer had invaded her liver, and the nausea and the pain that the tumour near her spine was causing her made food of any kind an ordeal.

She insisted upon getting up every day, but for the last week she had agreed that there was no need to dress, and spent the daytime lying on the sofa that Rachel had imported from the drawing room, wearing her winter dressing gown over her pyjamas. The morning room, being small, was much easier to heat and she was always cold these days.

'I think we might try the fish,' she said. 'And I can have the same.'

'Miss Rachel, it is Christmas dinner we're talking about. I've got a nice roasting chicken for you and a little Christmas pudding made specially. The job you're doing, nursing and that, you need proper meals. You look really worn out. Even Eileen passed a remark about it at yesterday's dinner: "Madam looks really fagged," she said, and although, of course, I told her not to be so forward, it's the plain truth.' Here, she – fortunately – ran out of breath.

'All right, Mrs Tonbridge, I'll have whatever you give me.' It was true: she was so tired that she hadn't the strength to argue about anything. The last two nights had been ghastly. Sid had insisted upon them sleeping in separate rooms – 'I want you to have a proper night's sleep, my darling,' she had said – but this had simply meant that she had spent the nights with her door open and therefore still heard the heartrending sounds from Sid's room. The painkillers she had been given no longer made much difference. The nights were worse than the days, and she supposed this was because they contained no distraction. Neither of them had slept much and she had rung their local doctor and asked him to come. 'Please don't ring the bell, just come in and I'll see you in the study to the right of the front door.'

He came, as she asked, and shut the study door as requested.

'I wanted to see you alone, because my friend is in such pain most of the time, especially at night. There must be something that could be done to help her?'

'I should see her first, of course, but it sounds as though the time has come for morphine.' He gave her a penetrating look. 'You look pretty rough yourself. Have you thought any more about our local hospital? The nursing is good there and you could visit as much as you wanted.'

'She begged me not to put her in any hospital, and I promised I wouldn't.'

'Right. Well, perhaps I'd better see her.'

309

'She's still in bed. I'll take you up.'

There was no need for her to do this, as he knew the house, had attended her mother when she had had her last illness, but he let Rachel escort him. He had thought the National Health an idealistic and admirable idea, but he very much doubted Aneurin Bevan's belief that people would become healthy because of it and end up needing far less medical attention.

And he still clung to the old ways of a country GP, visiting seriously ill patients at home, generous with his time and resigned about the hours he was called out.

'Do you mind my being here, or do you want to see her alone?'

'That's for the patient to decide. I don't mind in the least.'

Sid was sitting up in bed sipping her tea and lemon. The pieces of dry toast that were meant to accompany it were untouched. She had clearly lost weight since he had last seen her: her naturally round face was bony and diminished and there were dark circles under her eyes. Almost all of her hair had gone – the few tufts that remained only accentuated her baldness. The effect had something of the pathos associated with clowns.

Rachel asked whether she minded her staying and she said no.

He went through the routine physical examination. She was running a temperature, he knew that by looking at her, and for the rest, he had discovered that the routine was vaguely comforting to the terminally ill – creating a glimmering hope of recovery that helped them through the last painful weeks. At the end he told her that he was going to give her some morphine for pain and a prescription that would control her sickness. 'But you must promise me that you will try to eat more – keep up your strength. I'll be back this evening to give you another shot.'

'She might want to stay in bed to have a good sleep,' he said to Rachel, on his way out. 'And it wouldn't be a bad thing if you were to follow suit.'

By the time she had arranged for Tonbridge to drive to Battle to get the prescription and gone upstairs, she found Sid asleep. She told Eileen to keep the fire in the morning room burning well, and then, because it was the nearest to Sid's room, she went to her own; her back ached, and she decided to lie on her bed for a while to rest it, and almost at once she, too, slept.

∞ ∞ ∞

'Well, all I can say is that I've never known a Christmas like this one.' Mrs Tonbridge was attacking her slab of puff pastry with angry vigour, cutting knobs of butter and dotting the rolled crust, folding it and rolling it again. Tonbridge did like his mince pies and she was famous for her pastry. Steaming two bits of fish and mashing potato hardly showed off her talent as a cook.

'The house is ever so quiet,' Eileen agreed. She was standing on a chair putting up the paper chains she had made, as Miss Rachel had said she didn't want them in the morning room. Outside, it was beginning to snow; large, reluctant flakes kept colliding with the kitchen windows and melting. 'It seems such a waste to have a white Christmas without the children.'

'You get on with peeling the potatoes, girl, and don't

comment on matters that don't concern you.' She was trussing the bacon hock they were to have for lunch. 'And I want celery, carrots and an onion from the larder.'

She treats me like a kitchenmaid, Eileen thought resentfully. She was in her late forties and could hardly be described as a girl. But she climbed down from the chair and did as she was told.

By elevenses, Mrs Tonbridge was in a better mood. She had rolled out her pastry, chopped parsley and made a sauce for the hock, and she now sat at the table with Eileen while they both drank a strong cup of tea and finished off the flapjacks. 'Tonbridge won't be back for his. I will say one thing for him, he's a slow shopper but he had quite a list. Your decorations look quite nice, though I say it myself.' She rolled her sleeves down over her fat white arms, and then vigorously polished her glasses on a corner of her apron.

'You'd best go up to Miss Rachel and see when she would like lunch served.'

∞ ∞ ∞

Rachel woke with a start to find Eileen standing in the doorway, speaking in what Rachel described to Sid as her doomed voice: 'I'm ever so sorry to disturb you, but Mrs Tonbridge would like to know when you want lunch.'

'What is the time? Oh – a quarter to twelve. I should think half past one, Eileen. Is the morning room nice and warm?'

Eileen said it was, and Rachel asked her to wait a minute while she found out whether Sid wanted to get up.

312

She was sitting up in bed and looked far better. 'I've had a wonderful sleep and the pain has almost gone. Of course I want to get up.'

∞ ∞ ∞

Lunch was much more animated than usual. Sid ate at least half of hers, and afterwards they did the crossword together. But some twenty minutes later, she said apologetically that she was afraid she was going to be sick. Rachel gave her the basin kept for this purpose and fetched a towel for her. 'It's my fault, darling. I forgot to give you the anti-sickness pill. I'm so sorry.' Seeing anyone being sick used to make her feel the same, but she had got used to it now, and could help clean up with scarcely a tremor. 'You're meant to have one half an hour before each meal. What a rotten nurse I am.'

'You're the best nurse for me in the world.'

'Why don't you lie down on the sofa and we could go on with *Emma*?' She had found that Sid liked being read to, and Austen was a good choice.

'Yes, I would like that.'

Rachel settled her down with a cushion for her head and a blanket wrapped round her permanently cold feet. 'We've reached the insufferable Mrs Elton's visit to Emma.'

But after she had read for a few minutes, she saw that Sid was restless, shifting about as though she could not get comfortable.

'Are you in pain?'

'It's my back. It's started again. It's not too bad.'

'Would you like some lemon tea?'

'Yes. But I'd like some of my old pills first. Now,' she

said irritably. Rachel fetched them, then went to the kitchen to see about the tea.

When she returned with it, Sid was sitting up. 'Sorry I snapped.'

'That's all right. Are they working?'

'They are a bit, yes. The tea will be too hot to drink. Anyway, I want to talk to you – seriously. Give me your hand.'

Her heart sank. She knew that Sid was going to talk about her death – which they hadn't done since before Christmas. Since then it had lain between them like a sword. They both knew it was there, but both felt in different ways that by refusing to acknowledge its presence they were somehow warding it off – Rachel because she could not bear to think beyond it, and Sid because she was desperately anxious about how Rachel would cope.

'My darling, you know that I'm going to die, and sooner rather than later. I want to talk about you, because the only thing I grieve about now is what will happen to you. I don't think you should stay on in this house alone. I think you should move to London. I've left you my house in case you want to live there. If not, you can sell it and choose somewhere else. I think you should find some work to do. You always want to help people, and perhaps you could find some charity – children, for instance, you've always loved them. Think of the Babies' Hotel.' She had run out of breath, and reached for her tea.

Tears were streaming down Rachel's face, and after a moment she said, 'I can't bear for you to die. I can't.'

'And I don't want to leave you, but we both have to bear it because it is going to happen. I can't go on much longer like this – it's becoming too difficult. I think I shall be quite glad when the time comes, except for you, my dearest Rachel. And I beg you to think about what I have said, about your life. We should be grateful for the marvellous years we've had together. Imagine if we had lived in Emma's time how impossible it would have been.' She was smiling now and stroking Rachel's hand.

Rachel wiped her face with her other hand and tried to smile back as she said, 'There were the Ladies of Llangollen. They brought it off.' They had visited the redoubtable lesbians' house, Plas Newydd, on one of their country walking tours.

'So they did. That was a lovely holiday, wasn't it? That amazing waterfall, and the aqueduct carrying that canal over the valley . . . Now, blow your nose and give me one of those anti-sickness pills and I'll try to eat some tea. What is the time?' It was only half past three, Rachel saw. There were hours to go before the doctor would come again, she thought, as she dried her face with one of the Duchy's elegant, but inadequate handkerchiefs.

She had left the pills in Sid's bedroom. And she waited a minute or two with the bottle in her hand, before returning to the morning room, while she tried to collect herself. She *must* stop crying: it would only distress Sid more. At least death had been mentioned – talked about – and it was Sid who had had the courage to do it. Nurses don't cry all over their patients: they nurse; they try to make things as easy as possible for them. If you love someone, she thought, you can do anything for them.

By the time she returned to the morning room, she felt comparatively calm.

Sid was lying back with her eyes shut, but she was

not asleep. Rachel propped her up, and gave her the pill. 'Would you like a little sleep now before tea, or do you want me to go on reading?'

'Think I'll try to sleep. You won't forget what I said, will you?'

'Certainly not.' She pulled the blanket round Sid's shoulders, then rang for Eileen to stoke up the fire and, when she had done so, followed her out of the room. 'We'll have tea at half past four and would like a few honey sandwiches with the crusts cut off.'

'Very good, Miss Rachel.' Ladies, she knew, never ate the crusts on their sandwiches; after all these years Miss Rachel should know that she would never send in sandwiches without the crusts off, but there you were. Miss Rachel was not herself. Who would be with this tragedy hanging over them?

For the next hour, Rachel read to herself and sewed. Every now and again she checked Sid. Her eyes were closed, but small tremors, contorting her face, looked like attacks of pain. Nearly at the end of the hour, Rachel was startled by a curious sound – a muted howl – and saw that Sid had crammed her knuckles into her mouth. She flew to her and knelt by her side. 'Is the pain very bad?'

'A bit.' She seemed to have no breath. Her forehead was burning hot. 'Thirsty.' She was barely audible.

Rachel held the glass for her to drink, then said she would fetch a compress for her forehead.

'Don't go. Please.'

So she rang the bell for Eileen to bring her two bowls of hot and iced water and napkins. Sid had another attack, cramming her knuckles into her mouth. As soon as Eileen had gone, she let out a subdued shriek of agony.

316

It was unbearable. It must be borne, Rachel told herself. Somehow these next hours must be got through. She hoped that bathing her forehead would distract Sid from the waves of pain. She told Sid that the hot and cold compresses would make her feel much better, discovering as she did so that her voice had a new, calm authority that she had not known she possessed. Tea arrived, and she helped Sid to sit up – to try to eat a honey sandwich. She did try, and failed, so she sent for the jar of honey and stirred two spoonfuls into the lemon tea. 'You have to drink this, darling. I shall expect you to drink all of it.'

And Sid, with her eyes trustfully on Rachel's face, did make a great effort to do so. The really agonising pains seemed to come in waves, rising to a peak when she could not help crying out, and then Rachel would squeeze her hand hard and tell her to scream if she wanted to. As the pain slowly diminished, Sid would try to apologise, but she had little breath now. A few scalding tears would trickle down her face, and Rachel would wipe them away as she uttered endearments. She felt that she had never loved Sid so much as she did now.

∞ ∞ ∞

When the doctor had administered the morphine, Sid asked whether it was a dose that would last all night. No, he said, but he would be back last thing to give her a shot for that. 'I have hired a nurse for you, Nurse Owen. Unfortunately, she cannot come until late tomorrow as she has to do Christmas lunch with her family. But she will come afterwards, and she will be able to give you the medicine you need. I shall pop in meanwhile, of course, to see how you are doing. You're running a bit of a temperature by the look of you, Miss Sidney. We must see if we can get that down.' He put a thermometer in her mouth; it read 102 degrees when he removed it. 'A couple of aspirin every four hours should do the trick there.'

Rachel walked to his car with him. 'The nurse will be living in?'

'Yes. She will do the night duty for you. You can't go on like this, my dear. Nobody can do a twenty-four-hour job with a patient as ill as this. In any case, I don't think it's going to go on much longer, which should be a comfort to you. A tumour on or near the spine can be one of the worst pains in the world.' He glanced down to see that her hands were tightly clenched together, rigid.

'I should like you to take one of those sleeping pills I prescribed for you. You need at least a couple of nights' proper sleep. I'll be back about eleven.'

Just as he was getting into his car, she clutched his sleeve. 'Dr Murphy, thank you so much for taking such trouble.'

'Not at all. Only wish I could do more. See you later. Go on in, before you become a snowman.'

The snow was falling steadily, and was settling now, decorating the trees, speckling the brick path to the front door. It was dark, and Rachel could only see her way because of the lights inside. A nurse in the house, she thought. What would that mean for their relationship? A return to secrecy – to the façade of simply being good friends? No, it could not. She would only care about what Sid felt: nobody else could matter at all.

She found Sid much calmer, cheerful even. She wanted to stay on the sofa so that she could doze if she felt like it.

318

'I'm so glad that a nurse is coming. It means you won't have to deal with any more bedpans. I've so hated you having to do that.'

They had been a very new addition to her nursing, as Sid, in spite of her increasing weakness, had insisted upon being helped to the lavatory.

'I didn't hate it.' She kissed Sid's forehead – not burning so much now. 'I'm going to give you the sickness pill because we're going to have an early supper and I really want you to eat it.'

'Would it be possible to have a small omelette?'

'Of course it would. You swallow these and I'll go and tell Mrs Tonbridge.'

Supper – compared to the rest of the day – was a success. Rachel made Sid eat her omelette with a spoon, as her hands were so shaky that she dropped most of it if she used a fork. During the meal they listened to the carol service broadcast from King's College, Cambridge.

After the programme, Rachel suggested Sid going up to bed while she was still feeling good, and Sid agreed at once. She had become much more compliant, calmer, completely trusting that Rachel knew best for her. The stairs took time because she had become so weak, but at least she seemed not to be struggling with severe pain. She gripped the banister with her right hand, and Rachel held her left arm, and with a couple of short rests they reached the top.

When Sid was safely in bed, her teeth brushed, clean pyjamas and her knitted woolly hat firmly on her head, she wanted to sit up and talk, so Rachel draped her in one of the Duchy's paisley shawls.

It was approaching late evening, and the doctor was due during the next hour. But it was not soon enough:

the pain came back, and soon Sid was shifting restlessly, cramming her hand into her mouth in an effort to muffle her cries. She had earlier complained of being cold; now she was burning, her mouth parched and cracked. Rachel fetched a bowl of cold water and wiped her face with a flannel in an attempt to cool her, and put water from her finger onto Sid's lips, which she seemed to like. Supposing, Rachel thought with panic, the snow was so bad that Dr Murphy couldn't get to them?

She tried everything she could think of: rocking her in her arms, bathing her forehead, talking quietly with endearments – the doctor would soon come and then the pain would go away . . .

It was nearly eleven when she heard the car, and ran downstairs to meet him. 'She is much worse, Doctor. Her fever is bad, and the morphine you gave her isn't even lasting four hours and I don't know what to do! Oh, it is good of you to come!'

'It's *very* good of me to come. I got stuck in our lane and had to dig myself out. But I'm here now and—'

There was a shriek – not at all muffled now – from Sid's room.

'We can't have that,' he said, and mounted the stairs at a surprising speed.

Sid had thrown off her bedclothes and was trying to clutch the small of her back.

'Miss Sidney, I'm sorry you're having such a rough time. I'm going to see to it with a stronger dose so that, with luck, you'll get a good night's sleep.' He was preparing his syringe as he spoke. 'You're very brave, Miss Sidney,' he soothed. 'I know that it's a devil of a pain. Now just hold still if you can.'

He was saying just the right things to her, Rachel

thought. Although she shook her head, a very faint smile came and went.

'Now I want you to drink a good glass of water,' he said. 'The fever has dehydrated you, and that always makes things worse. Hot or cold, I don't mind which. I'll pop in again tomorrow morning.'

As Rachel was seeing him out, she asked, 'Couldn't I give her an injection if she needs it in the night?'

'No, my dear, I'm afraid not. It's against the rules. In any case, I don't suppose you've given an injection of anything in your life, have you?'

She hadn't, of course.

'She should be out of pain quite soon, and then she'll sleep. The dose I started her on was minimal, this time it will be different. Goodnight to you.' And he went.

∞ ∞ ∞

She poured a glass of Malvern water and added a slice of lemon. By the time she reached Sid's bedroom, she found her calm. 'The pain is going,' she said. 'I can feel it go, further and further away, and soon it won't be there at all. Such bliss!' She drank the water and when it was finished, she said, 'This is our last night together, isn't it? Before the nurse, I mean.'

'Yes. She'll be here tomorrow evening.'

'Do you know what I would like most?'

She didn't.

'I would like to go to sleep in your arms, my darling. More than anything, I would like that.'

'I won't be a moment.' Minutes later Rachel climbed into the bed and took Sid in her arms. She seemed so fragile that she was afraid of hurting her. But Sid snuggled up to her, with her head on Rachel's shoulder and gave a sigh of contentment.

'Do you remember that rather tiresome sentimental song the children used to sing round the piano when Villy's father stayed?' Rachel said.

'I do. He hated it. "My True Love Has My Heart",' Sid said. 'You are my true love, and you have all my heart.' And later, when she was nearly asleep, she said, 'Hold my hand, keep me. Don't turn off the light.'

Rachel took the proffered hand and kissed it, before wrapping her fingers round the frail, hot bones. Another small sigh and her eyes were shut. She had thought that she would never sleep with Sid in her arms (how odd: always before it had been the other way round, her in Sid's arms), but her own exhaustion, and the tremendous relief that she was at last relaxed and free of pain induced a kind of serenity and peace, and almost at once she joined Sid in a deep sleep . . .

She woke suddenly because she was cold. They were both cold. She shifted to pull the blankets round them, and Sid's head fell on her breast. She was still holding Sid's hand, and when she gently released it, it, too, fell with an awful involuntary ease to her side. Rachel propped herself up on one elbow and, with the other hand, stroked Sid's head, her shoulders, her body. It was all cold and still. She was dead.

The shock was so great that for minutes she did nothing but stare at Sid's face, which was calm, smoothed of fear and pain. She looked suddenly far younger, more as she had been when they had first known each other.

It was ten past six: the doctor would not come until half past eight. They had two and a half hours alone together. Rachel lay down and once more took Sid's body in her arms. It was all for the best, she told herself; there had long ceased to be any chance of recovery. She must have died in her sleep; there had been no more pain; they had been together, had had one last evening. Sid had died without having to go into a hospital; she had escaped being nursed by a stranger. In many, many ways it could not have been better.

Although she made no sound, Rachel discovered that tears were pouring down her face, and she was rocking Sid's cold, unresponsive body, for a desperate moment trying to ward off her grief and panic at being left alone.

This would not do. She wiped Sid's face where her tears had fallen and then lay quietly beside her. As though by some magic, she was filled with love for this friend and lover who had given her so much. The feeling was intense and it came as a balm that soothed her heart.

HUGH, JEMIMA
AND FAMILY

'Mummy, I've been awake nearly all night and I really *need* to open my stocking.'

Jemima turned towards the door where Laura stood shivering in her red flannel nightdress.

'I told you, you have to wait until seven o'clock.' This was the old Home Place rule designed to give the grown-ups the chance of a decent night's sleep. It had been all very well, Jemima thought, as she yawned, and began sitting up, fine when the bedrooms were full of children who could complain to one another, but hard if you were the only child. 'All right,' she said. 'But you're to stay in bed until I come to fetch you. And don't wake Daddy. He's very tired and so am I.'

'You often say you're tired. I suppose it's your age, and you can't help it. All right, I promise to stay in bed until seven. There!'

When she had gone, Jemima glanced quickly at Hugh, who had not been woken, thank goodness. Poor darling, he seemed permanently tired these days, but asleep, all his worry lines were smoothed out. He had helped make up the stockings for Tom and Henry as well as Laura, had decanted the port, wrapped presents, wired the lights to go on the Christmas tree and prepared the turkey, while she had made brandy butter and cranberry sauce. Might as well turn the oven on now, she thought. She always cooked the bird for four or five hours at a very low temperature. She got out of bed very carefully, tucked the blankets up to her husband's neck, and put on her towelling peignoir – not very warm, but better than nothing.

There was complete silence from Laura's room, and also from the spare room in which Simon was sleeping. He had arrived last night – late, because the train from Norfolk had been held up due to the snow. Tom and Henry were very much awake in their large room on the top floor; they were playing some game that involved a number of challenging shouts followed by fits of laughter. Their voices were in the process of breaking and veered uneasily between a squeak and a baritone. They were always engaged upon vast projects: this holiday they were writing a book, which they called *A Thousand and One Things to Do When It Rains*, but so far they did not seem to have got much beyond designing and painting the cover, which was surprisingly beautiful. When Hugh had asked which of them had done it, they looked surprised and said they had done it together. They were good boys and she was deeply proud of them. Hugh had had a lot to do with their upbringing, and this made her especially glad that Simon had agreed to come for Christmas, too.

Once the turkey was in, she made some tea for herself and Hugh. It was going to be a long, ceremony-fraught day: breakfast followed by present-giving, then lunch, and a drive to Richmond Park where they were to meet Zoë and Rupert for a walk, then everyone back for tea until it was time to get Laura to bed.

It was half past six – just time for half an hour in bed with Hugh. They always gave their presents to each other then, when they were on their own. She had knitted him a black alpaca jersey and bought him a very pretty Russian snuffbox for his headache pills. He gave her a beautiful cashmere dressing gown and a cameo ring set in gold with a shell backing. 'You can have breakfast in your dressing gown, and if you're feeling really extravagant, you may wear the ring as well. I'm going to wear my jersey and use my pretty box all day.'

'Isn't it wonderful how we give each other things we really want? Think of all the poor wives opening boxes of black chiffon nightdresses that are too tight for them, while their husbands receive ties they wouldn't be seen dead in.'

'It's a hard life for some,' he agreed. Then, raising his voice, 'Here comes Miss Ghastly.'

Laura was wearing a Father Christmas costume, with a large white beard, not so securely hooked behind each ear.

'Oh, no, it's Father Christmas. Silly me. Merry Christmas, Father Christmas.'

Laura burst out laughing and her beard fell off. She sprang onto the bed. 'A clockwork mouse,' she said, 'and a pack of weeny little cards, and chocolate money and a tangerine – I had to eat the money because I was starving to death. I wouldn't have otherwise. How ghastly am I, Dad?' She stroked his face with sticky fingers. 'How ghastly am I?'

'Probably the ghastliest person I've met in my life.' He gave her a kiss. Her face was hot with excitement. She sighed contentedly. 'And you never know what ghastly thing I'll do next, do you?'

'Haven't the faintest idea. Now, sweetheart, I've got to get up.'

Jemima, who had been watching them with great affection, said it was time for breakfast.

'I want to have it wearing my beard.'

When she had finished undoing Laura's pigtails and combing out her silky honey-coloured hair, she said, 'You can go upstairs and tell the boys to come down for breakfast, too. But don't wake Simon. He's tired and said he would save up for lunch.'

JULIET AND NEVILLE

'I don't mind in the least. I can't think why you're bothering to talk to me at all.'

Everything she said was not what she meant, he thought. It made conversation very exhausting.

He had a bit of a hangover. It was true that he hadn't done anything about her for weeks – probably months – but he hadn't expected her to be so icy and dramatic about it. He tried again. 'My darling Juliet, you have to understand that most of my time is not my own. I work in a very competitive field—'

'And you're in love with someone else.'

'What on earth makes you say that?'

'I've heard people talking about you. Your new girl. You take her everywhere with you, even have her back to your flat.'

There was a longish silence, while they trudged through the snow in Richmond Park. 'You might like to know – you might care to know – that I'm not in the least in love with Serena.'

This much was true: he did not need to say that Serena was in love with him, that they had had the odd tumble in the sack because she had been so importunate. 'I am working with her a lot this season because the new magazine wants to feature her as their top model so of course we've gone about together.' He took her shoulders

328

and pulled her round to face him. 'You know perfectly well that you are the person I love. And it's not my fault that you're seventeen.' Beneath her absurd make-up, her eyes were full of tears and her lower lip was trembling. 'Even if you look like a cross between a panda and a clown, I still adore you.' He gave her a shower of hurried little kisses, ending with a kiss on her mouth. It was like watering a garden after a drought: her face lit up, positively sparkled with excitement and joy. She flung her arms round his neck. It had come right.

∞ ∞ ∞

'He's called a Belgian hare, but really he's a rabbit.'

Laura gazed at him, entranced. 'Can I stroke him?'

'He might not like it. He's awfully new, you see. Mummy gave him to me for Christmas. I wanted a parrot, but they were too expensive. Dad gave me a python. I'll show you him in a minute.'

'I'm not sure if I like snakes.'

Georgie gave her a severe look. 'But I'm sure I'd get to like one,' she said hurriedly.

Georgie opened the rabbit's cage. The rabbit remained still; his ears were flat on his back and he crouched, poised for nothing very much. Only his nose was quivering. Georgie stroked his thick chestnut fur.

'Couldn't we give him some food?'

Georgie put his hand into one of his deep pockets. 'Ow! I forgot Rivers was there. He's in a bad temper because I've had a lot to do settling the python, as well as Morris, of course.'

'Who's Morris?'

'This rabbit. His name is Morris – it's just come to me.

329

Rivers will have eaten all the best food.' Georgie pulled the rat out of his pocket, its jaws firmly clenched round a carrot. Laura admired the way he calmly detached the carrot and gave it to her. 'You can feed him if you'd like.'

'Oh, thank you, Georgie.'

But when she pushed the carrot up Morris's nose, he remained motionless, was not interested either in carrots, or anything very much. The Zoo Room, as Georgie called it, was really one of the icy cold ex-sculleries that were stuck onto the house like limpets. They were mostly unused, and Georgie had taken the largest to keep most of his animals and all their clobber. Tortoises were hibernating in an old wine crate. Rivers had a cage where he lived when Georgie was at school. Morris and the python had new cages hastily built yesterday after Georgie had been warned of the zoo's two new inmates.

At that moment the twins burst into the room, shouting about tea being ready.

Rivers, meanwhile, had climbed onto Georgie's neck, and remained there, nibbling his ear very delicately.

'He's apologising,' Georgie said.

∞ ∞ ∞

'It was all most agreeable,' Miss Milliment said, once she had been levered into Villy's car. 'There was only one thing that mystified me, that I didn't quite understand.' She was sitting in front beside Villy, with Roland silent in the back.

'What was that?'

'Well – I could not understand why neither Jessica nor dear Viola was there. It seemed so strange that they were not.'

330

'Perhaps I didn't tell you but Jessica is having a lovely hot holiday in the Bahamas.'

'How nice for her. Did Viola go with her?'

There was a pause, then Villy said, 'I think you will find Viola at home.'

Roland was still silent in the back.

To change the subject, Villy said, 'I hear you beat both the twins at Scrabble.'

'Oh, well. As we grow older, we know more words than the young. They were very good about it, I must say. Roland and I should have a match.'

And Roland, bless his heart, said, 'No one could beat you, Miss Milliment.' Villy glanced at Miss M and saw that she was smiling gently into her pale chins. The compliment had pleased her.

∞ ∞ ∞

They had all gone, except for Laura, who had pleaded to stay the night to help Georgie with his Zoo Room. She had wept, and implored and cajoled until, with Zoë's agreement, she was allowed to stay. 'But,' Hugh had said, 'you have got to do every single thing that Aunt Zoë and Uncle Rupert tell you to. If you don't they will report it to me, and then you will *never* be allowed to stay with them again. Is that understood?'

Yes, it was.

'*No* horribleness, *no* ghastliness.'

'And, darling, you will clean your teeth and let Aunt Zoë plait your hair and stay in bed till you are told to get up? Aunt Zoë's got a spare toothbrush.'

'I promise. I deadly promise.' The prospect of getting what she wanted was so dazzling that Laura would have promised anything. 'And I'm known for keeping my promises,' she added.

The other unexpected guest was Neville, but he had been so charming and helpful that Zoë did not at all mind his staying on. He seemed to have transformed Juliet from a sulky uncooperative teenager to an animated, charming young woman. Neville had made her take off her absurd make-up, and wear the green silk dress that had been Zoë's Christmas present to her, which she had refused, initially, even to try on. 'She looks like I did when I first met Rupe. And I was just as awful with my mother, even then.'

When she and Rupert were, thankfully, tucked up in bed, Zoë said, 'I think she has rather a crush on Neville.'

'Well, that can't do any harm. She's quite safe with him. Remember that wonderful sketch Joyce Grenfell did of the mother trying to persuade her daughter that getting engaged to a middle-aged Italian conjuror with two marriages behind him would not be the happiest situation in the world?'

She did.

'At least we don't have any of that. Look how helpful she's been today.'

'It was Neville who made her. When he said, "Juliet and I will clear up supper and the Christmas tea", she got up and started doing it at once.'

'Yes, well, as an older brother one would expect to engender some respect.'

'A half-brother.'

'Sweetie, what difference does that make?' He pulled her towards him. 'You've done a marvellous job today. Even Villy enjoyed it all. And Georgie is thrilled with his baby python. I won't have you worrying about Jules's future. She's so very pretty that there will be no shortage of suitors when the time comes. Then, like you, she will probably get snapped up by a lovely man like me.' He gave her his usual three goodnight kisses – on her forehead, her mouth and her throat. He went to sleep holding her hand.

But before sleep engulfed her, Zoë reflected that the immediate future – whether or not they were going to be moved to Southampton – had not been mentioned by either of them.

HUGH, JEMIMA
AND FAMILY

In spite of not having all the family together (no Edward, no Polly), Hugh felt it had been a very good Christmas. He was particularly pleased that Simon had turned up because Wills had announced that he was staying with a friend. He had recognised that Simon, when he stayed with Polly, seemed to be happy, and was glad that he had found a career that really interested him. He still felt sad that Simon had no interest in the firm, but there it was. When he marries, he thought, and has a family, he may well change his mind. Meanwhile, he had been the most charming asset: sweet with Laura, and very good with Jemima's boys. After all, it was early days – look at Rupert! When he had got home after the war, he had been quite happy to relinquish his precarious life as a painter and a teacher to become a director of Cazalets'. The trouble was that he was not really cut out to be a businessman. Putting him in charge of the Southampton wharf might turn out to be another disaster. Everybody liked him – staff and customers all found him most agreeable – but he was not an administrator. He forgot things, mislaid papers, which infuriated the accountants, and seemed to find it almost impossible to take decisions. He was not lazy, but he spent too much time talking to a customer simply because he liked them. And often not about business. He had come across Rupert having a lengthy and animated discussion about the French Impressionists; another time it had been about Sibelius, who'd died recently. It might be better to keep Teddy on where he was, but under McIver who knew the business backwards and could teach him. The wharf had been steadily losing money, and after his last, difficult meeting with the bank, they had been very clear that this could not go on. They had even recommended selling off Southampton, which he felt was out of the question.

'Darling, you're worrying. You really mustn't. This is your holiday.'

They were sitting amid the wreckage of breakfast. The twins and Simon had finished theirs. And Henry and Tom had been quite stern with Jemima. 'Mum! We would like to point out that when we ask you what's for breakfast, you say, "Boiled eggs." You don't say, "One boiled egg." That means at least two eggs per person. We might as well be at school – starving.'

So she had boiled them more eggs. After cereal, the eggs, and six pieces of toast and marmalade, they announced that Simon was going to take them ice skating, then back for lunch.

'It sounds like a threat,' Hugh said, as they thundered up the stairs.

'They're bottomless pits, those boys. But at least there's far more food available now. It was much worse in the war, and just after it when we had bread rationing.'

She was clearing the table when the telephone rang.

'I'll answer it,' Hugh said. 'It'll be about Laura. I'm not sure whether we're collecting her, or whether they are bringing her home.'

'I think they're bringing her because Georgie wants to go to the zoo.'

But it wasn't about Laura: it was Rachel.

'Hugh – is that Hugh?'

He said, yes, it was, and he had been going to ring her today to see if she had had a nice quiet Christmas with Sid. There was a pause, and then she said, 'I have to tell you that Sid died on Christmas Day.' Her voice, calm, but with an uncharacteristic flatness.

'Oh, darling! You should have rung me before!' But as soon as he'd said it, he realised how futile it was to upbraid her for something that didn't matter at all.

'I couldn't speak to anyone. Had to get a bit used to it first.' And although he couldn't hear it, Hugh knew she had begun to weep. 'I wanted to tell you first, because of Sybil, because you would know what it feels like. I just wanted you to know.'

'Rach, I'm coming down to you—' But she had rung off and he didn't know whether she had heard him say that.

When he told Jemima, she agreed at once. 'Oh, darling, you must go to her. Bring her back here, if you think it would help. Poor Rachel! She shouldn't be alone.' When he kissed her, she said, 'Do you want me to pack your bag?'

'I'll do it. But you ring Rupe and ask him if he's going to bring Laura back. And tell him why I've gone.'

As he packed enough for a night or two, the memory of Sybil's dying came back to him as freshly, as painfully, as if it were yesterday: her agony, until the doctor relieved it, and holding her hand when she became unconscious, then left him – became nothing at all. Tears pricked his eyes and he had to sit on the bed for a few moments, overcome.

Jemima met him in the hall. 'I've made you a turkey sandwich to eat in the car.'

'Sure you can manage the troops?'

'Quite sure. Call me if there's anything I can do.'

As she helped him into his overcoat, she said, 'Darling Hugh. You'll be a comfort to her. You're her favourite brother.'

'How do you know that?'

'I just do.'

She saw him into his car and waved him goodbye from the front door. The snow on the streets was already turning into grey slush. She remembered then the morning when the telegram had arrived telling her that Ken was dead, and how it had seemed as though the earth had opened up where she stood in her parents' narrow hall – nothing was solid, nothing safe except the baby inside her; she had then been too frightened for grief. It wasn't until she had received a letter from his wing commander containing a eulogy about Ken's courage, his popularity with his crew, his devotion to his duty, that mourning had enveloped her. For weeks she went for solitary walks, sat silent during the anxious meals her mother urged her to eat, and wept most of the nights alone in her single bed in her parents' spare room. Then the news that she was to have twins was broken to her on one of her monthly visits to the doctor, and the reality of her situation began to impinge. She would have to earn at least some of her living, and how was she to do that with two children to bring up? Her parents, who, she knew, had next to no money to spare, none the less paid for her to do a shorthand and typing course. She found a cheap flat in Maida Vale and got spasmodic work typing manuscripts for an agency. It was not well paid, but it meant she could work at home, and as the children grew old enough to go to school, she ventured upon an office job with a firm called Cazalets' and then ... Hugh. She was the luckiest person in the world, she thought, as she so frequently did, and she had everything she could possibly want; her only anxiety was Hugh's health. The disagreement between him and Edward was exhausting him, and he was working and worrying far more than he should. His headaches had become more frequent and he came home every night grey with fatigue. I might try talking to Edward, she thought. If I knew more about his side of it, I might find a way of getting them to talk reasonably to each other without being so angry.

She thought of poor Rachel; her losing Sid meant her losing everything; with her parents gone and with Sid gone, she was left with nobody to love and need her, and living alone at Home Place seemed a desolate future. She rang Rupert's house and got Zoë, who said that Rupert was on his way to drop Laura off before taking Georgie to the zoo.

She set about making the turkey sandwiches for lunch, wondering how to explain Hugh's absence to the children. He had been due to take the twins and Simon to *The Bridge on the River Kwai*, but Simon could perfectly well do that on his own while she dealt with Laura, who would almost certainly be tired from excitement and Georgie's company. The turkey sat before her looking like some architectural ruin; Hugh was not a brilliant carver, and had been hacking so much with the carving knife that it was now blunt. She had barely detached one of the immense haunches when the doorbell rang and Laura was back with Rupert.

'Mummy, Georgie's going to the zoo and I so awfully want to go with him.'

She said no.

'Uncle Rupert doesn't mind. He said I could.'

'I didn't, Laura. I said you had to ask your mother.'

'Well, I am asking you.' She was all set for a big scene.

'And I have said no, and I mean it.'

Laura gave her a belligerent glare and burst into tears. 'You've ruined my whole day. I hate you. Georgie was going to show me really poisonous snakes that you can't see anywhere else.'

'That's enough. Go up to your room. Thank Uncle Rupert for having you and then go. At once.'

'I won't thank him. He's not having me. I've never been so sad in all my life.'

But she went. And as Jemima walked to the gate with Rupert, she told him about Rachel, and Hugh's departure for Home Place. 'He's going to ring me this evening and will say if there's anything we can do.'

'I knew Sid wasn't at all well, but I'd no idea it was as bad as that. Do you think I should go down?'

'Better wait and see what Hugh says.' She'd let him know. She hoped Laura had not been too much of a trial.

'Good as gold,' he replied. 'They always behave better in other people's houses, don't they? Georgie had a whale of a time showing off to her.' He bent to kiss her. 'Must be off. There's a tyrant in my car.'

∞ ∞ ∞

Hugh rang her in the evening to say that he was going to stay two nights with Rachel to help her arrange the funeral, to provide general support, 'And to try and persuade her to stay with us for a little while afterwards. She's dead tired and in a state of shock. I don't think she should be on her own here. She doesn't want everybody to come to the funeral, just me and Rupert and Archie, the three of us whom Sid loved most.'

'What about Edward?'

He snorted. 'No. Ever since that disastrous evening, she hasn't seen him at all. And in spite of living so near, it turns out he had no idea that Sid was so ill, and Rachel feels it would distress her if he came. She's afraid that Diana might come with him, and she simply couldn't cope with that. She wants the funeral to be very quiet, and she wants Sid to be buried next to the Duchy. She sends you her love, Jem, and to Zoë and Clary. Will you tell them that? I'll ring you again tomorrow.' And after some endearments, he rang off. She could tell that he was exhausted from his quiet, tired voice.

∞ ∞ ∞

'The funeral is next Wednesday,' Archie said. 'And Rupe is going to drive me down.'

'Good,' Clary said. It was the day that they were auditioning for the young girl's part, and she desperately wanted to be there.

'It's all right about the children. I've fixed for them to go to Zoë.'

'They're meant to be at school.'

'Well, they'll just have to have a day off.'

'Oh, all right.'

'Sometimes, my darling, I wish you could be a bit more gracious when things are arranged for you.'

'Like what?'

'Like saying, "Thank you, kind Archie," and "Whatever would I do without you?" that sort of thing.'

'Would you do that, if it was the other way round?'

He thought for a moment. 'Possibly not. But it's not quite the same, is it?'

'It ought to be. Supposing I wanted to go on the Aldermaston march, which would take ages longer than a funeral, would I have to butter you up to be allowed to go?'

'I'd hate it. Days of awful food for me and the children.'

'So you'd rather have a hydrogen bomb.'

'Of course not. Oh, Clary, don't let's quarrel. I feel too depressed – haven't the heart for it. Think how lucky we are to have each other to talk to, or quarrel with, or bicker. Poor Rachel has no one.'

She ran to him so suddenly that she nearly knocked his jar of turps out of his hand. 'You're absolutely right. And I don't know what I'd do without you, and we are lucky.'

'Darling, you're not a painter so how come you've got paint in your hair?'

'I may not be a painter,' she said, running her rather sticky hands round his neck, 'but I have a close relationship with one.'

'It sounds thoroughly unhealthy to me.' He prised her arms off his shoulders. 'And it is advisable to dry your hands before you assault strange men.'

'They're perfectly clean – it's only soap. If you ask me, you're not very good at intimacy.'

341

'It's all my English blood. Anyway, you've cheered me up. I promised Harriet I'd take her to Bumpus to choose a book from the token Polly gave her.'

'Do ask whether she's written to thank her for it. I told them four letters each before any more treats.'

The visit to Polly had been a real break for her, but she realised that it had been nothing of the sort for Polly: more like unremitting hard work and responsibility. Gerald, for all his sweetness and warmth, had to be monitored: he clearly had no idea about money or how to manage it, and was constantly thinking up wild schemes to improve his monstrous house; he seemed quite unaware of the perils surrounding Nan's approaching senility.

While she made the batter for the toad-in-the-hole they were to have for supper, Clary reflected that lives were not easy things to live.

PART EIGHT

JANUARY–FEBRUARY 1958

BOMBSHELLS

'Darling, of course I know you're seventeen, but you are *not* twenty-five, and you sometimes behave like someone of twelve. You think you know everything, but you don't. I will not have you careering round the West End on a Saturday night with another girl of your age. If you want to see Audrey, you can have her to supper here.'

'Oh, thanks very much.'

Zoë, who had been collecting various pieces of laundry from the floor of her daughter's bedroom, replied sharply: 'Juliet, I will not have you speaking to me like that. And I would ask you not to be so rude at meals in front of Georgie. It's bad for him, and for you. You're too old for such puerile behaviour.'

'I see. I'm not old enough to do what I want, and only old enough to do what you want.' Juliet had been collecting dirty mugs and cups and putting them on a tray that her mother had brought for the purpose, and now she collapsed so angrily onto a chair by her dressing table that the tray fell off it, and dribs of cold coffee spilled over the carpet.

'Go and get a wet cloth from the bathroom.'

With a face of thunder, she went.

Was I like that at her age? Zoë wondered. Not as bad, surely. I'll have to get Rupert to read the Riot Act. But poor Mummy didn't have a Rupert: she had had to cope with me on her own. This made her feel that she should attempt to be more patient, try to find out whether Juliet was unhappy at school, whether she was upset about the possible move to Southampton, which she could see would be upsetting . . .

Juliet was back with the cloth and, without looking at her mother, started scrubbing furiously at the carpet.

'Darling, I feel that something's worrying you, and I wish you'd tell me what it is.'

'Why?'

'Well, I might be able to help.'

Juliet stopped scrubbing and sat back on her heels. She looked at her mother with, Zoë thought, a rather pathetic defiance.

'If I decide to tell you perhaps you'll stop treating me as a child. You'll take me seriously for a change.'

'I promise to take you seriously.'

'All right, then. If you must know, I'm in love.'

She wanted to laugh with relief. Laurence Olivier or James Mason? she wondered, but she must be serious – mustn't even smile. 'Oh, darling, that must be rather exciting for you. I can remember when I first fell in love – with Ivor Novello. All of us girls were mad about him.'

'It's not a silly schoolgirl's crush. I'm in love with a real person. And as soon as I'm old enough, we shall marry.'

'I should love to meet him. Is he Audrey's brother or one of your other school friends?'

'No, you know him. It's Neville. And he's deeply in love with me, too. Since last Christmas – a whole year.'

There was a silence, during which Zoë tried desperately to think how she should respond.

'Darling, it's a lovely idea, but you can't possibly marry him. He's your brother.'

'Only my half-brother.'

I'm afraid that doesn't make any difference.'

'Neville says it does. He says other people have married their sisters and it was quite all right. He says we shall go abroad to marry. It's only this country that's so stuffy. He didn't want me to talk to you about it because he knew you'd be against us. I expect he'll be cross with me for having told you, but I'm so sick of being treated like a child. I suppose you know that Romeo's Juliet was fourteen when he married her. Fourteen! And I'm miles older than she was.' There were tears in her eyes, and Zoë longed to take her in her arms, but she was afraid.

'Poor Jules. It's very rough being in love – especially the first time. I do sympathise.'

'I'm not going to be in love any more times.' She gave her mother a kindly, pitying glance. 'I expect you're a bit too old to really remember what being in love is like. In any case, my love is not like any other, and Neville agrees with me. I don't think anyone has felt as we do. You will keep it a wonderful secret, won't you? And I promise to tidy my room.' And, glad of her *congé*, Zoë escaped before Juliet could ask her not to tell Rupert, which, of course, she must. Rather shakily she went downstairs, feeling very angry with Neville.

347

VILLY AND
MISS MILLIMENT

'*Why* am I here?'

It was a question – a cry – that poor Miss Milliment repeated every two minutes, as she thrashed about in the high bed that looked too small for her. It was not a question that she could answer honestly. She could not say, 'I had to put you here because I could no longer look after you properly myself, because your dementia or senility or whatever it is goes on night and day and I can't manage that alone any more.' She was simply racked with guilt and pity every time the question was asked. It was a dreary place, this nursing home on Holland Park, converted out of one of the immense stucco mansions. The room had been sliced in two to accommodate more patients, which meant that the ceiling was far too high for the new dimensions. The large sash window had bars on the outside, and yellowing net curtains that gave the effect of fog. There was a commode, a small table on which Villy had put some books and Miss Milliment's wireless, and a rickety chest of drawers. It was hardly a place to be if one had any choice, but after much searching it had been the best she could find and the best she could afford.

She was crying now, small, mewling, heartbroken sounds.

Villy leaned forward from her chair to take her hand.

'*Why* am I here?'

'You haven't been very well lately, and we thought a little rest in a nursing home would be a good thing. When you're better, you'll be able to come home, darling.'

'I've been here for weeks and she doesn't come.'

She was sobbing now, and suddenly clutched Villy's arm. 'Will you do one thing for me? Ask her what I've done to displease her. After all the years together, she has suddenly turned me out! I don't know why she has done that! She doesn't love me. I don't think I shall be able to bear that. So will you at least tell her, ask her, beg her to come and rescue me? She is such a kind, good person, I'm sure she will listen to you. Oh, please do that!'

When she left the home and walked to the street where she had parked her car, Villy got into it and cried. Nothing she said to poor Miss Milliment made the slightest difference. She had not once recognised her – indeed, seemed to be getting more and more demented by the day. Her arrival in the home had clearly been the most awful shock to her, as bad, she now thought as the bombshell Edward had delivered when he'd told her he was leaving her. But what could she have done? She had tried to explain things, but she couldn't, of course, really be truthful. She could not say, 'I can't cope any more with you getting up in the night wanting breakfast or, worse, trying to cook in the kitchen, getting partly dressed and leaving the house.' Even after she'd secured the front door Miss Milliment had found the key to the French window leading onto the garden. Then she'd knocked over her electric fire so that it had burned the carpet, and would have been more serious if Villy hadn't woken in time. Villy had slept very lightly because of these anxieties, and often hardly at all.

The doctor to whom she had gone for help had been amiably vague: there was not really much that could be done for such cases. He had prescribed something to be taken at night, but he had implied that it might not make much difference, and it hadn't. The best thing would be for her to go into a home, he had said, and seemed to feel that this solved the matter.

After finding two places that seemed good but proved to have long waiting lists, several that were too expensive, and many that had appalled her, she had settled on Holland Park, and went every day to visit, hoping that in time this regularity would register and that Miss Milliment would recognise her again. This did not happen, and in spite of the matron saying that her patient was settling in nicely, Villy saw no signs of it.

And then there was Roland. She had been so grateful to Zoë and Rupert for inviting them all to lunch, had realised then that she was actually enjoying the large family gathering with its shared jokes and reminiscences, its traditional Christmas fare, and the general affection that everyone seemed to have for one another. She relished the almost mythical stories about long-dead ancestors, remembering the Duchy recalling that her mother gave her servants a bar of Wright's Coal Tar Soap and a handkerchief embroidered with their initials in chain stitch for Christmas, the Brig taking a police horse to ride in London to wherever he wanted to go, and so forth. It had been a lovely day, and she had realised when she went to bed that she had not missed or even thought about Edward at all. But there had been repercussions.

When she had asked Roland the next day whether he had enjoyed himself, expecting a simple, enthusiastic response, he had said, 'Of course I did. It made a super change. It was good fun.' Then he had added, 'Mum! Why don't we see more of the family? I hardly ever see my cousins, even if they don't have anything much to do with Dad. Last Christmas they had it at Home Place and we didn't go. We just had the usual boring time here.'

The usual boring time! And she had tried so hard to make it festive for him. He could have no idea how hard she had tried . . .

And suddenly she saw something different about her life with Roland. She realised that, yes, she did all she could on the domestic front, but the emotional deprivation, the lack of anything fun in the house, she had blamed on Edward's absence. Everything about that was, quite simply, his fault and nothing to do with her. And Roland was paying for it. He was loyal, patient, tender about Miss Milliment, but he came home to a house with two unhappy old women. Edward seemed to take no interest in him, and that, too, was her fault. She had been so bitter about his leaving, so hostile to his new life, that she had made any advance on Roland's side a treachery.

She felt so ashamed, so paralysed, by these insights that she did not know where to begin, but before she could, with apologies, with promises of change, he interrupted her.

'I was wondering, Mum, whether you would like me to do the visit to Miss Milliment today. I know it makes you awfully sad, and it isn't your fault. You've been marvellous to her, and I could easily go. I haven't got anything to do and you could have a nice rest.'

She looked at him – he was cleaning his nails rather dangerously with a penknife – and knew that the change must start now.

'Oh, darling, that would be angelic of you! I was wondering whether we might go out to dinner tonight and I thought perhaps that you should choose somewhere ritzy that you would like.'

He looked embarrassed. 'Well, as a matter of fact I had made a sort of plan to spend the early evening with Simpson.'

'That's fine by me. We could have our dinner afterwards. And I'm really grateful to you for going to see Miss Milliment. I do warn you, she may not know who the hell you are.'

'That's all right. Don't look so worried, Mum. You'll be all right this evening, then? You won't mind being alone?'

'Of course I shan't.'

'OK, then. I'll be off.'

He gave her a brief hug, and went. The house seemed very silent after the front door slammed. I've got to not mind being alone, she thought. Because that is what it is going to be like, with Roland at university and Miss M gone. So either I have got to learn to like it, or I must get a lodger. Or move somewhere smaller: this house will be too large once Roland is launched. She felt it right not to indulge in a wealth of apologies, since she could not be certain that they would not be laced with self-pity and the subterranean self-hatred that accompanied it.

And much later, in the night, when all kinds of random and undesirable thoughts occurred, it suddenly struck her that she must have had something to do with why Edward had left her.

HUGH, RACHEL
AND THE BANK

He had done all he could to comfort her, and she had been most touchingly grateful. For the first two nights she had talked about Sid, about the awful weeks before she had died. She had wept steadily, but at least she had someone to listen, to help her unburden some of her anguish. 'I know that you have been through all this with darling Sybil. You know how terrible it is to watch someone you love so much suffer so much, to recognise that the only way out for them is their death. I would so gladly have died for her.'

'Perhaps it's harder being the one who is left.' As he said this he realised that it had not been true for him, he had had the children to care for, but she, Rachel, had nothing. He took her hand. 'It will not always be as painful as now. Of course you will always love her and miss her, but it will get easier to bear with time. You have to trust me about that. We all love you, you know.'

Later, when they were about to go to bed, she said, 'I suppose I shall have to leave this house. It costs too much for me to be knocking about alone in it.'

No, *no*, NO! Hugh assured her. This was her home: she would never have to leave it unless she wanted to.

He and Rupert would pay their share, and the families would all come down in the holidays – just like the old times. He noticed a little glimmer cross her face – not actually a smile but some relief.

The following week there had been the funeral, with Rupert and Archie, and they had brought an enormous wreath made entirely of snowdrops, and Rachel had been pleased about that. He had announced that he would be staying the night, as he knew how bleak the house would be for her if they all left after the wake.

That evening, over the excellent fish pie that Mrs Tonbridge had made, he suggested, very gently, that perhaps Rachel might like to stay with them in London. 'Jemima asked me to ask you, because she would love to have you for a bit of a rest.' It was no-go. It was awfully kind of them to ask her, but she thought she would rather stay put. Too soon to ask, he thought. Aloud, he said, just let him know if she suddenly felt she needed a change.

He had to leave early the next morning because he had a meeting with the bank. He had been dreading this for some time now, and he felt particularly cross with Edward, who did not want to be there. He hadn't come to the funeral either, which Hugh felt was most unreasonable of him. Selfish and weak. He knew that Diana had been rude to Sid, but nobody had expected her to come. Edward could have cared enough to have made a discreet appearance

To his immense surprise, however, Edward did turn up at the bank. 'Thought I'd better see what's going on,' he said.

It turned out that he knew more about that than Hugh.

The bank had asked to see last year's accounts, and Edward had had them sent over.

∞ ∞ ∞

The meeting was at eleven. In the old days, their father would have been invited to lunch in the heavily panelled boardroom, with some other favoured customer. Light City gossip and excellent port, he remembered, when his father had taken him to be introduced to Brian Anderson, the old manager. Now, since the small private bank had been taken over by a much larger one, there was a new manager whom he had met only once, and who had seemed indifferent to the long connection the Cazalet family had previously enjoyed with it. He met them in the boardroom.

'Ian Mallinson,' he said, as he entered the room. He had a long, cadaverous face, and when he shook hands with them, his bony fingers were cold. He was accompanied by a secretary and a second man, both of whom were carrying sheaves of papers. He glanced at his watch as he sat down. 'I think we should start with what you have come to see us about,' he said.

Hugh glanced at Edward, who intimated that he should begin.

Hugh explained that although their London wharves were doing quite well, yielding a reasonable profit, they were still struggling with Southampton, where they were not able to buy as much hardwood as they would like, with the consequence that the sawmills were left without enough material to cut. The site, with its mills, had been bought at a very good price by his father, but they had not yet been able to operate at full capacity, and therefore were not yielding the profit expected. In short they were in debt and needed a further loan to get on their feet. For one year only.

'And how much money are you asking for?'

Hugh named the sum; his mouth was dry. Spoken baldly, it seemed enormous.

'And your collateral?'

'As I'm sure you know, the firm owns a very great deal of valuable property, both here in London and in Southampton.'

Mallinson told his secretary that he required one of her pieces of paper, which he perused in silence. 'Unfortunately, Mr Cazalet, it would seem that you have no free collateral left. It has already been pledged to earlier loans that have not yet been paid off. You are therefore not in a position to offer us any security at all for the money you now want. Coffee, please, Miss Chambers.'

While this was being arranged, he turned to Edward. 'Mr Edward Cazalet, isn't it? I should be interested to hear your views on the subject.'

'My view is, and has been for some time, that we should sell off some of the property – probably Southampton – pay off the loans and run a smaller company in London.' He did not look at Hugh as he said this, which, in any case, was only half of the truth: he was dead set on the firm going public, but it did not seem sensible to say that now.

Mallinson eyed him with some approval. 'That may certainly become a solution.'

The coffee arrived and was served by Miss Chambers. Mallinson indicated that he wanted a document from the other attendant, and smiled. 'Our accountants have been analysing your firm's tax papers, and although the

London side of your business has not made any losses, for some time the profits have been less each year. Not a very good outlook.'

If that's a smile, Hugh thought, I'm a crocodile.

'There are also dates for repayment of earlier loans, only one of which has been honoured. So I am sure you will understand, gentlemen, that no further loan can be contemplated.' He looked at his watch again. 'And now, if you will forgive me, I have another appointment. Miss Chambers will see you out.'

And that was that. They had both been staring at their untouched coffee, and now got up to follow Miss Chambers out of the boardroom and out of the bank.

Edward was the first to speak. 'I'm sorry, old boy, but I had to say what I think. Otherwise, in my view, we're heading for a first-class disaster.' He then suggested they go to a pub, and Hugh, who was clearly in a state of shock, agreed, providing it was a quiet one, out of the City where employees would shortly be flocking for their lunch break.

Half an hour later they were ensconced in a dim cavern that contained only one other customer, immersed in his racing paper. After Edward had got their drinks, he said, 'I do know how much you hate all this, but supposing we start by considering the pros and cons of getting rid of Southampton? Or, if you like, you state the cons and I'll do likewise with the pros.'

'I certainly want to say why I think we should hang onto it. First, our father bought the site at a very reasonable price. It must be worth far more now than he paid for it. Second, Cazalets' has the largest collection of hardwoods in the business. Third, the hardwoods – most of them – are shipped to Southampton. If we didn't have a sawmill there, we would have to go to all the trouble and expense of moving the logs to London. Fourth, that side of our business has been failing because we haven't had the right manager. Teddy hasn't enough experience. If we put Rupert in there—'

But here Edward felt obliged to interrupt him: 'My dear Hugh, you know as well as I do that Rupe would be hopeless as a manager – of anything. He has his talents – marvellous with people, the men love him and not a bad salesman – but actually running something? No. Simply being called Cazalet may once have been enough, but it isn't any more. He's far more use in London, and the only thing wrong with McIver, who has been with us for at least twenty-five years, is that he isn't called Cazalet. Can I have my turn now?'

'Go ahead.'

'Well, one of the reasons we're doing so badly is that we're crippled by the interest we're paying on existing loans. Did you realise that when we default on our repayments the interest is immediately increased? No? Well, it is. My view is that we have to sell some of our assets in order to get rid of the interest burden. We should get rid of our very expensive London office and rent somewhere far cheaper – in fact, we should try to cut our overheads in every direction . . .'

EDWARD AND DIANA

'But I don't think it made a blind bit of difference. Thanks, sweetie, I could certainly do with a stiff one.'

'Poor old boy. What did he say about your idea of selling out – going public, isn't it called?'

'We didn't even get that far. I was trying to get him to agree to selling off some of our property. He doesn't even want to do that. Although, once I've really gone through the figures with him, I think he'll have to agree to it.'

Honey padded up to him, and laid an ice-cold nose in his hand. He stroked her absently until she made it clear that she intended jumping onto his lap. 'No, Honey, *no*.' She got down at once and gazed at him with loving, reproachful eyes.

'Oh, well, I suppose you'll just have to have another go at him. Dinner now.' She had been going to tell him about an author friend of hers whose publishers had recently sold their firm to Americans, and after a luxurious breakfast at the Connaught Hotel, the two partners had left with six and a half million each, but this didn't seem to be the right moment.

JEMIMA AND HUGH

'I think he thinks that I'm simply full of nostalgia and sentiment, and while some of that must come into it, it's not all I'm fighting for.'

'Take off your tie, darling. I'm going to massage your neck.'

'I ought to ring Rachel – make sure she's all right.'

'Not now, Hugh darling. Just relax while I do your neck.' Her strong little fingers kneaded and probed, and he could feel the muscles easing and the hammering in his head becoming quieter – more distant.

'Bless you, Jem,' he said, when she had finished.

'The boys are at the cinema, and Laura has a friend staying the night, so we can have a nice quiet evening together.'

He said he would just go up and say goodnight to Laura, and she grilled the bacon that they were going to have with their kidneys, a dish that he particularly liked; none of the children would eat kidneys so they had them seldom.

'They're playing hospitals,' Hugh announced, when he joined her. 'Poor Jennifer is bandaged from head to foot. I don't think she's liking it very much. Laura, of course, is the doctor.'

Jemima said she would see to that.

She sees to everything, Hugh thought gratefully. He

yawned. Apart from being tired, he realised that he was extremely hungry. He had not been able to eat anything at the pub with Edward, and he had simply drunk one cup of coffee before setting off from Home Place. He would ring Rachel tomorrow morning. First thing, he added to himself, to make him feel less guilty.

But when Jemima came down, she said, 'I've just rung Rachel and said you were worried about her, and wanted to know whether she was managing alone. She said that Mrs Tonbridge and Eileen were angelic to her, and that Edward had rung and said he'd go and see her next weekend. I hope that's all right, darling.'

'It's more than all right. You are even more angelic than Mrs Tonbridge and Eileen combined.' He felt light-headed with relief.

CLARY AND HER PLAY

The small theatre was icy cold and smelt faintly of gas. Auditions were being conducted in the circle bar (the only bar, actually). The couple had been cast; the wife, a reliable actress who had done her time in rep and had played a couple of small parts at Stratford. For the man's part, the husband, Jake, the director, had eagerly courted Quentin Frome: 'Marvellous actor, bit of a prima donna, but women adore him. He'll fill the house for us, you'll see.' He had not yet put in an appearance. 'But he'll turn up today for the auditioning of Marigold. He can be quite difficult about the girls cast opposite him.'

He sounded stuck-up and rather unpleasant, Clary thought, and wondered whether her opinion would be sought. They were drinking fairly horrible coffee from plastic cups.

They waited an hour, then Jake said they'd better go ahead with the auditions. 'Can't keep those poor girls waiting all day.'

The scene, Jake explained to Clary, was to be the one where Marigold declares her love for Conrad, and he, who has clearly been deeply attracted to her, reciprocates. The first actress had a heavy cold and, although she claimed to have learned the scene, forgot her lines and subsided into a misery of defeat. The second girl, who had such tumultuous hair that you could hardly see

363

her face, was sporty about it all and struck quite the wrong note. Just as she was being dismissed, Quentin arrived. He came into the bar loud with apologies for being late, saw the girl about to leave and put his finger elaborately to his lips. Jake introduced him to Clary and he laid two fingers against her cheek before kissing her hand. 'Our genius playwright! Madam, you have left me bereft of all words! Only my blood speaks to you in my veins!' His melodious voice dropped an octave, as he continued, 'Seriously, though, you've written a damn good part – right up my street.'

Clary, concealing her distaste, muttered her thanks with a sinking heart. He was awful: swanky, pompous, a proper old ham to boot. While they were waiting for the third Marigold, she examined him closely. His hair, once red, had faded to an indecisive ginger grey. He had pale blue eyes, and a fleshy mouth. His nose was a beak – slightly too big for the rest of his face – and his complexion florid. His forehead could be described as noble if it didn't occur to one that it was so large because of his receding hairline. She couldn't remember feeling so catty about anyone in her life.

The third Marigold appeared. Quentin took one look at her and said, 'Sorry, dear. You're too tall. She would tower above me,' he explained to Jake, who nodded regretfully at the poor girl who stood trying to droop before them.

'I'm so sorry – Miss Miller, isn't it? Better luck next time.'

'How many more?'

'Just one, Quentin.'

And, to her delighted amazement, the stage manager returned with Lydia Cazalet. Lydia! Whom she had not

364

seen for years. She was wearing a duffel coat over her jeans, and her long golden hair was tied back in a ponytail. She winked at Clary, then concentrated on being introduced to Quentin, who livened up at the sight of her.

'I don't want any moves – just a read-through. Miss Cazalet, isn't it? Are you related?'

Clary said, 'Yes, as a matter of fact we're cousins, but I had no idea she was coming today.' She passionately wanted Lydia to be good, to get the job, but she was afraid that Jake would consider it nepotism.

'Well, I'm parking my bum on this bar stool, and I suggest, darling, that you sit in this chair beside and below me.'

'Right.' Lydia pulled out some pages from her jacket and composed herself. What followed confounded Clary.

They played the scene as for real. She became at once younger, vulnerable, out of her depth and painfully in love, and he – she could hardly believe the transformation – he became tender, haunted and protective of her. His voice, which had been so smug and self-important, dropped down to a gentleness and charm of which she would not have believed him capable: he became irresistible, and she was quite unable to resist him. He even looked different, Clary thought, but she was so excited by the whole thing that she could not think much at all.

She watched as they both sloughed off their characters: the change was instant – like turning off a pair of lights. Then Quentin said, 'Right, darling, you'll do. If His Majesty there agrees?'

'He agrees,' Jake said. He had been quite moved by the scene and was dabbing his eyes with a grey handkerchief.

Clary saw Quentin say something inaudible to Lydia, who replied, in a cool voice, 'Thanks, but I arranged to have lunch with my cousin.' Clary could see that he didn't like being turned down but then Lydia seized her arm and was saying goodbye to Jake, and in no time they were down the stairs to the foyer.

'Wait a sec while I get my bag.' But at that moment the stage manager appeared with it. On being asked, she said that there was quite a nice Italian place she could recommend for lunch round the corner.

When they were out of sight of the theatre, Lydia stopped to change arms with the suitcase, which was bulging and held together by a piece of rope.

'Let me carry it for a bit.'

'I'd be jolly grateful. I feel quite dizzy having got the job.' She seemed to sway a bit, and Clary put her arms round her.

'Lydia, are you all right? You're not all right.'

'I'm OK. I think I need some food. I thought there would be something to eat on the train this morning, but there wasn't.'

'When did you last eat?'

'I had a cheese sandwich some time yesterday, I think. But things have been rather fraught. I told them I'd have to go, but Billy didn't believe me, and we were rehearsing all day and then he came to my digs and made such a scene I couldn't even pack, until he finally left, which was about one in the morning. And then I had to get up very early to catch the first train, and it was quite a trek to the station, and I kept thinking he'd follow me or be at the station, but luckily he wasn't.' By now she was out of breath and they had arrived at Marco's restaurant, which was comfortingly warm. A waiter took their coats, settled them in a corner, and brought them a Tuscan bean soup and glasses of red wine. Lydia's white face became less white. 'You've written a bloody good play. Have you been writing plays for long?'

'I haven't. This is my first go. I feel incredibly lucky. You were so good in that scene. You really made it work just as I'd imagined. How did you know about it?'

'Well, I got so cheesed off working in rep and being paid the Equity minimum. I've done it for nearly four years now, and my then agent hadn't even come to see me in anything. So I got a new one, and he did come to see me in an Ibsen production. He sent me your play, but I didn't want to tell you in case you thought I was wrong for the part.' She took a large swig of wine. 'What are we having next?'

'Some pasta and then grilled sardines. This is my lunch.'

'Thank you. Oh, Clary, it's so lovely to see you again. I've been so out of touch. We hardly got any time off, and when I did, that fiend saw to it that I had no time to get away.'

'I take it Billy's the fiend.'

'Yes. I contracted an unfortunate alliance with him and it's taken me all this time to realise that I'd only be able to break with him by getting out. He's mad, you see. But let's forget him. Tell me about the family.'

So for the rest of the meal Clary gave her all the news she could think of. At the end of lunch, when she had paid the bill, something occurred to her: 'Where are you staying while you're in London?'

'I haven't thought. I'll have to find somewhere.'

'I wish I could have you, but I can't. The children are sharing our other bedroom.'

'Oh, I didn't mean to descend on you – honestly!' There was a pause, and then she said, 'I suppose I ought to stay with Mummy.'

There was another short silence. Then Clary said, 'Roland's away, and I told you about poor Miss Milliment. So I should think your mother is pretty lonely. You could try it for a week and if it's too depressing we'll find you somewhere else.' She looked questioningly at Lydia, while her case was brought to her. 'Is that all your luggage?'

'Yep. All my worldly goods. I had to leave a lot of books behind, and things I'd bought for my digs, but I don't mind that at all. Of course I must go to Mummy's. I've been awful about her. And I really would like to see Miss Milliment. I owe her a lot. She made me see the point of poetry.'

Clary said she would go with her to Aunt Villy's. They lugged the case to where they could catch a bus that would land them at the end of Villy's road. Lydia insisted upon carrying her case the rest of the way, but as they trudged along, she said, 'Oh, I do so hope she'll let me sleep before she asks me questions. I just want to go to bed and sleep for England.'

Clary said, 'Don't worry, I'll tell her. What did you think of Quentin?'

'I knew he was a very good actor. I expect he'll be tricky, though. He'll make a pass at me but I expect I'll be able to deal with that.'

Clary experienced a strange feeling – utterly foreign to her, but disturbing. All things being equal, which they hardly ever were, she might (laughingly, of course) have said that she actually had a pang of jealousy about Lydia's assurance that this rather glamorous actor would 'make a pass'. Theatre people were used to that kind of thing. But that kind of thing was not limited to actors: many people experienced it. It had just not happened to her. The only person who had really gone for her was Archie. And he had made a pass at someone else.

'It's my turn to have the case,' she said. 'I know you're exhausted.'

∞ ∞ ∞

Villy, who had been mending a set of ivory spillikins, was delighted to see her daughter. The look on her face gave Clary a fleeting memory of what she'd been like before Edward had left her, and she went home thinking how marvellous it was to have children, how nothing could change one's love for them, which was unconditional . . .

It was some time before she recognised that she had been struck and that it had begun that day. By then, though, she was past anything but the submission to a positively tidal wave of desire – lust, she angrily called it – but that made no difference. She went to as many of the rehearsals as family duties allowed, each day watching (and imagining) that it was she whom he was making love to, she whom he was giving up, and she who was trying to understand his infidelity. When he kissed Lydia as Marigold, she felt faint with desire. But when they broke for coffee or lunch, she hardly spoke to him: she did not want him when he was being himself – in fact, she almost disliked him then. During those weeks of shame, and her repression of shame, she was acutely sensitive to him – knew when he made the expected pass at Lydia, knew he was rejected – knew when he turned to Betty Parker (that didn't last long), and finally knew that he would turn to her. Of course it was out of the question: she was a happily married woman aged thirty-two with two lovely children . . .

He asked her to have lunch with him. No harm in that, surely. Perhaps spending that much time with him being his obnoxious real self would cure her, would enable her to separate the actor from the man.

It didn't, of course. The moment they were seated in the small expensive restaurant, where clearly he was known, he became the actor, courting her, in his low, seductive voice, telling her that he had noticed her from the first day but had been so much in awe of her 'amazing piece of work – for a first play something like genius,' that he had almost felt he would have to love her from a distance . . . Now a waiter brought them oysters and another waiter poured him a little wine, which he sampled and indicated would do – but, he continued, during the last week, whenever their eyes had met, he had sensed a current. Of what? Electricity? Something magical that was drawing them together. 'And sometimes, when you were watching me with such creative attention, I imagined that you felt the same.' He had been gazing into her eyes, and she felt mesmerised, unable to look away.

'You have the most beautiful speaking eyes that I have ever seen.' He picked up her hand and kissed it. 'Eat your oysters,' he said. 'Or we shall spoil our Dover sole.'

Eating steadied her. 'Do you have the same lunch every day?' she asked. She had noticed that there had been no menu and no ordering.

'When I come here, I do. Of course I presumed that you like fish.'

She nodded. 'But I'm not very hungry.'

'That is a very good sign.'

'Of what?'

He looked at her with so much affection that she felt faint. 'For me, love always makes me fiendishly hungry.' He had finished his oysters and now he laid two fingers caressingly against her cheek. 'Eat, my darling Clarissa, to keep up your strength.'

She remembered two things at once: Lydia saying he would be the new fiend, and his laying his fingers against her cheek when they had first met, and Clary felt herself blushing. His affection trapped her more than anything he said or did.

'You have the most enchanting blush,' he said. 'A heroine's blush.'

'What are the other kinds?' She was actually proud of this sophisticated response.

'Oh, you know, people talk about blushing to the roots of their hair, and looking as though they have just played fifteen games of squash – sweaty stuff, adding up to a general shortage of romance. But not you, sweet Clarissa – you are not like that, at all.'

The fish arrived.

He said they would have to eat quickly because of getting back to the theatre on time. In the taxi on their way back, he put an arm round her waist, turned her towards him and kissed her. A few seconds of panic, as one about to drown, assailed her, and then the extraordinary sense of freedom, as she sank blissfully into this new experience that assuaged her wildest dreams: she locked her hands behind his neck and kissed him back until the kisses became one.

It was he who parted them, who paid the driver and

said he would go back through the front of the theatre, and that she should go to the stage door. 'And you will be able to put your hair up again, and it will be our secret. I'll meet you at the same corner with a cab when we finish rehearsal, and we'll go to my hotel where there is a very nice quiet bar.' He said all this very fast, then left her collecting hairpins from the cab seat.

They were rehearsing the two final scenes of the play: when Conrad has to tell Marigold that they must part, and then his final scene with Martha, his wife.

They were playing on the stage now, and she sat, by herself, in the darkened stalls. She needed to be alone. Halfway through that interminable afternoon, she rang Archie to tell him she would be late, and could he give the children supper?

'How late?'

'I'm not sure. Have supper with the children. I'll probably get a sandwich here, with the cast.'

'OK. Time for a chat?'

''Fraid not. You are angelic to do the children.'

'Angels usually come in groups. See you soon.'

If one was behaving as she was now, telling lies about it seemed like nothing, she told herself. But she had to make herself watch those last scenes, and the short coda that followed them, where the kiss-and-make-friends scenario did not actually work, where the permanent damage done to all three became apparent. She had done this by placing each character on a chair downstage while a record player played what people who didn't know about them thought. It was Marigold's turn first. A flurry of voices: 'You'll get over it'; 'You've been working too hard'; 'Staying up till all hours, all you need is a little fresh country air – put the roses back in your cheeks';

'You'll have to learn about men, dear – they can be very trying'; 'She needs a nice, steady young man – none of this art nonsense. Somebody with a good job and prospects.' Marigold starts up from the chair and runs off the stage. Then Clary began to watch Martha – herself – but could not bear it and fled to one of the unused dressing rooms.

Here, she was confronted by a realisation: what the whole thing must have been like for Archie, something she believed she had thought about enough to understand it. But now, in the throes of her passion for Quentin, she realised she had dismissed it as something that could be dealt with by a little willpower. She remembered, with shame, that she had even been impatient with him, that in her own unhappiness she had belittled his.

She knew that Quentin's arrangement for them to go to the 'nice, quiet bar' at his hotel was only the prelude to being seduced. And she had been aching for it. She had not thought of Archie at all: she had simply longed for Quentin to make love to her, to be in love with her, to fuck her until she wept.

Archie must have felt something like this, but he had not succumbed to bedding Melanie. He had told her that, and Clary had believed him. But then, to her, it had seemed the very least he could do. Now she recognised that 'the very least' was a contemptuous and patronising response. It was why most people didn't want to do the least if they could help it. Sacrifices, if they are known to another person, need acknowledgement and support – gratitude, even. But self-pity breeds a ruthlessness that pre-empts any of that. And she had certainly been sorry for herself, had played the betrayed wife who would never have behaved as he had.

And here she was, behaving even worse, without a thought for the consequences. She must not do it.

But before she could begin to deal with renunciation, she had to look at the plot. She was already halfway into the trap, and how to get out of it without upsetting Quentin's ego was a serious problem. His vanity was involved: two women had turned him down, and it was clear he felt that, the third time, all was going his way. He would be angry, he might even leave the cast in a tantrum but, no, he wanted the part, he almost certainly would not go to such lengths. But because of the play, they would perforce have to go on seeing each other – awful thought. She realised then that she was – subconsciously, perhaps – trying to make a case for going ahead this evening, then writing him a letter saying that her husband had found out and was threatening both of them. Shame again. That would be the worst of both worlds and utterly despicable.

Perhaps she could simply tell Quentin the truth. That she loved Archie, had never been unfaithful to him, but that she had been momentarily swept away and flattered by his attention to her. But she was pretty sure that truth, if uncomfortable, was a foreign language to him; he would not understand a word of it; he would simply redouble his efforts to seduce her (horrible excitement at such a thought occurred and had to be quenched). So she passed the seemingly interminable afternoon.

∞ ∞ ∞

'What's the matter, darling? You're nervous, aren't you? Nothing escapes me. But you don't need to be, my little one.' And he laid two fingers against her cheek caressingly.

'I need to talk to you.'

'Drink some of your nice champagne first, then.' And he smiled indulgently.

She took a swig – for courage. 'I'm afraid you're going to be angry at what I've got to say.'

'I could never be angry with you.'

So then she told him. That her husband had found out about them; he was an exceedingly jealous man, and he was furious, was threatening to beat him up. He had made her promise to break things off – at once – or he would see to it that she would suffer as much as he. She watched his face darken, become wary.

'How the devil did he find out? You must have told him!' His eyes were hard, like marbles.

'No! Of course I didn't tell him. But he found a picture of you that I kept in my purse. He was suspicious anyway because of my coming to so many rehearsals – we'd had a row about my neglecting the children. I couldn't help it, Quentin, really I couldn't!' Her voice was trembling because she was frightened, really afraid that he would not believe her . . . She had seen how he had reacted to the idea of being beaten up, and when she mentioned that a second time, he flinched. 'The last time he did that, the wretched man had to go to hospital to be stitched up.'

'I can't think why you didn't tell me any of this before.' He was still angrily accusing, but she could see he was also frightened.

'It's all my fault!' she exclaimed. 'I know it is. But I wasn't used to a glamorous and famous man being attracted to me. It was all too much. You swept me off my feet, and of course I had no idea that he would find out.' Relief, the feeling that she was nearly off the hook, made it easy for her to burst into tears, making no effort to be discreet about the scene.

He looked uneasily round the bar – it was filling up now with drinkers – and handed her the purple silk handkerchief he had used in rehearsal with Marigold and eyed her with anxious distaste as she used it. 'I think you'd better be off,' he said, 'and don't you dare tell that husband of yours that I made a pass at you. Savvy?'

'Oh – I promise I won't.' Clary was shaking so much that getting to her feet was difficult, but she managed it. She took one last look at him: no longer the angry lover in any way, he had reverted to the cocky, spoiled child, only this time he had been thwarted, which made him even more unlikeable. 'I'm sorry,' she said again, then ran out of the bar and into the street.

∞ ∞ ∞

Three hours later, Archie sat alone at the kitchen table. She had told him everything he hadn't wanted to hear. Perhaps I'd have felt worse if she hadn't, he thought. She had kept saying that now she really understood what he had gone through in giving up Melanie, but this had not only forced him to go through what it had felt like again, it had engendered a shock of such raging jealousy that he had wanted to beat that shabby little actor within an inch of his life. The idea that she had even wanted to go to bed with anyone else was too much. He had never imagined her being such a person and found it unbearable: her penitence, her desperate efforts to equate their situation simply hammered it home. If she had really wanted this little worm, it must have diminished her feelings for him and this opened up an abyss of anxiety in which the difference in their ages became a stark fact. He had loved and married her, but had never been able to give her the fun and pleasure that her youth deserved. Perhaps he had never been the lover she should have had ...

Now he was exhausted by the violence of his emotions, had reached the point where all good memories are swallowed whole and disappear while bad ones recur and loom to be tasted again and again.

This would not do. He suddenly remembered Bertie, aged four, setting fire to a wastepaper basket because he had made some sausages out of Plasticine and wanted to cook them, and how he had arrived on the scene just too late to rescue his roll of special rag paper used for landscape painting but in time for him to chuck the basket into the kitchen sink and douse it. Of course he had been cross with Bertie, but in no time he was cuddling him, wiping his sooty tears and loving him just as much as ever. I love her like that, he thought, and felt an uncertain peace descend upon him. She's had a shock, poor darling, and I must help her over it.

PART NINE

AUTUMN 1958

EDWARD AND HUGH

They had, at last, agreed upon one thing, Edward reflected, as he settled back in his Bentley and let McNaughton take him home. They had stopped, as they always did, for the news-vendor at the Strand end of Waterloo Bridge, and exchanged the right coins for an *Evening Standard* thrust through the driver's window.

'Here you are, sir.'

'Thank you, McNaughton.' It was wonderful to know that from now on, in the journey, McNaughton would not speak again unless he was spoken to. Edward relished the silence. He could read his paper in peace, fall asleep if he was so inclined, or he could try to make more sense of the pickle they were in.

Tonight he had bad news for Diana, and he needed to think of the best way to break it to her. She was going through the change – something about which he knew nothing. He realised that Villy must have gone through it, too, but she had never mentioned it.

It wasn't something that people talked about much, if at all. Anyway, Diana was given to fits of crying, to starting unreasonable arguments, to blaming him for stupid little things, like losing the buttons that had come off his jackets or not managing to bag a brace of partridge at a Saturday shoot. In between these fits of gloom and aggression, she was full of apologies and generally abject, and he often found this worse.

But today he had had a shock. Two shocks, actually.

He seldom looked at his bank statements, but he had noticed rather a lot of red ink on the last two months' worth, and rung the bank about it. After some delay, he had worked his way up from the chief cashier to the manager. It was explained to him that he had been drawing out more money than his salary paid in. 'That is why I gave you instructions, years ago, to top up that account from my savings account.'

'Yes, Mr Cazalet, but there is no more left there either – hasn't been for at least six months. As a matter of fact I've just dictated a letter about the matter asking you to come and see me about it.'

There was a pause while Edward tried to digest this shock. 'I don't see what I can do about it.'

'I think we might be able to find a way round it. You could, for instance, take out a mortgage on your country house.'

'I don't want to do that!'

'Well, there may be other options, but we must certainly discuss them. The present situation cannot continue. Would three o'clock this afternoon suit you?'

The meeting had not cheered him at all. The options turned to asking the firm for a bonus – an unfortunately large one that he knew the company could not afford – but otherwise a mortgage on Park House seemed the only alternative.

Edward then broached his scheme for the firm going public; his brother had finally agreed that it might be the best thing to do.

Ian Mallinson shook his head. 'It takes about two years to effect such a change, and I'm afraid you have left it far too late for that. For that you need a business that is thriving with a good track record of profit, which I am sorry to say your firm no longer has.'

'We have large assets in terms of property. If we sold some of them off?'

'You would simply be left with an even less inviting proposition for potential shareholders.'

He ended by suggesting that Edward should go away and think about it and have further discussions with Mr Hugh.

That had been the second shock. Edward had spent all his capital on Diana: the house had been expensive and she had used a lot of money doing it up. Not to mention holidays, like the French one, where he had been expected to pay for everyone, including her relations. She had the idea that he was far richer than he was, and he, out of some sort of silly pride, had never disabused her of the notion. It wasn't really her fault, but he knew she would not enjoy the change. If they were to live on his salary, there would have to be many economies. Blast Hugh. If he hadn't been so obstinate, they might all be rich by now, the whole family, since all the shares were owned by them.

Thank God he wouldn't have to worry about Villy. Apart from a few shares, her alimony was tied up so safely that even if the firm was bankrupt they couldn't touch it. It was the first time he had said that word to himself, and it made him feel sick. What on earth would he do? What would any of them do?

Well, he would have to face Diana first of all. Warn

her that things were pretty bad – that the skiing holiday in Switzerland was out of the question for a start . . .

∞ ∞ ∞

'You're so late I was beginning to worry.'

'Traffic's never good on a Friday.' He said this as he did on most Fridays.

She kissed the side of his face, and then, taking him by the hand, led him into the drawing room. 'I'm afraid the Martinis may be a bit watery, as the ice will have melted by now.'

'Add a bit more gin, and perhaps a bit more ice.' Edward closed his eyes. The room, with its low lamps, yellow damask curtains and tactfully burning log fire, smelt strongly of freesias. Although she was a great gardener, Diana insisted upon buying flowers from the local shop, where she had an account.

'One doctored Martini. Poor old boy, you look as though you've had a bad day. Did you go to the bank?'

'I did. It's bad news, I'm afraid. They're really not going to stand for any more loans.'

'How disgraceful, when the family has been with them all these years! Well, we'll just have to tighten our belts, won't we, darling? You must admit that I'm a good housekeeper. There always seems to be enough money for us, doesn't there?'

This was it. This was when he was going to have to tell her that they had not been living on his salary but had been supplementing it with capital.

'. . . and today I discovered that it's all gone. In fact, I owe them thousands of pounds.'

There was a pregnant pause. Then Diana said slowly, 'You can't have had all that much in the first place.'

This appraisal, which felt much like a prelude to judgement, made him feel as though someone had dropped an ice cube down the back of his neck. For a moment it seemed that everything had been for nothing. With an attempt at bravado, he tried to laugh as he said, 'I'm afraid that if you married me for my money, you were barking up the wrong tree.'

There was another, rather awful, silence. Then she burst out, 'How can you say such a terrible thing? As if I would ever have done that! That I should ever have thought such a disgusting thing, let alone done it!'

'Diana, I was only joking – trying to joke. I spent the money on you! This house cost more than the one we sold in London. Then you wanted to furnish it and that cost a lot, but I wanted you to have what you wanted. Then the French holiday ended up being far more expensive than I thought it would. All those things added up. But I'd no idea we'd spent so much till today. Bit of a bombshell. It's all my fault, I know that, but if we work things out, we could live on my salary, and I could probably come to some arrangement with the bank about paying them back.'

'Do you mean we'll be so poor we can never have another holiday? What about Switzerland? I suppose that's off – and Susan was so looking forward to it.'

'Yes, I'm afraid it will be.' He held out his glass and she refilled both of them.

'Most of this is Hugh's fault, isn't it?'

'He was a bit slow about us selling up, but he's come round to it now. The rest of it is my fault alone. I'm awfully sorry, darling.'

'Well – what do we do now?'

'I think we should make a list of our expenses and then it will be clearer for us to see where we can cut down. What about dinner first?'

She drained her glass and stood up. 'We're having oysters and grouse, but I expect you'll say it's far too extravagant.'

He hauled himself out of his chair. He felt inordinately tired, had reached the anything-for-a-quiet-life stage. She had had a shock, of course she had, and needed reassurance. He put an arm round her waist and smiled at her. 'It's going to be all right, sweetie, you'll see. And the dinner sounds quite delicious.'

For some reason, he then remembered the reassuring things he had said to terribly wounded men – the few they managed to collect at night on and behind the wire – the comforting but necessary lies that no one believed but most wanted to hear. Men choking in mud, stinking of their own excrement, voiceless from crying out all day for water, for help, for an end to it all. They had taken it in turns to shoot the ones who had to be put out of their hopeless misery; the very few that remained were hauled, screaming, onto stretchers where they would at least die with their friends. He had been sick frequently after these missions . . . Edward swallowed the memory, rammed it back where it belonged in the black pit of his past – so long ago now that he'd thought he had finished with it for good.

The oysters calmed them both, and by the time they had demolished the grouse, plus an exceedingly good bottle of La Tâche, 'last one I'm afraid', he wanted nothing more than to go to bed with her, but he knew he must get it over with.

'Let's have brandy in the drawing room and see if we can make a start. Sit next to me and we'll do it together.'

But it proved to be far worse than he had thought. They began with wages: McNaughton, Mrs Atkinson, the cleaner, and a man who did odd jobs of maintenance. Then there were Susan's school fees, her uniform and holiday clothes, Jamie's allowance, plus other costs while he was at university, and the two family cars. When he got to Diana's housekeeping allowance, Edward found that she had run up large accounts with the butcher, the fishmonger and the grocer, not to mention the florist, and some shop in London where she had had the lampshades and the curtains made for the drawing room. Then there was a personal allowance for Diana, paid monthly into her own account, which proved to have nothing in it. On top of all this, he had paid for three foreign holidays, which had included her friends and relatives, all of which had cost far more than he had planned for. Wine bills, boxes of decent cigars, subscriptions to his clubs, a couple of new suits from his tailor – it went on and on. 'What about your clothes?' he asked.

'Well, obviously, I couldn't pay for my new fur coat out of my allowance. But you said you wanted me to have it. So, naturally, I assumed you would cover it.'

'I don't know how I'm going to do that. I owe the bank at least six thousand pounds that I shall have to pay back out of my salary, which, incidentally, is the only money we shall have to live on. We're going to have to scale down.'

'Well,' she said, making it sound like a great concession, 'we could cut Pearl to one day a week.'

'And what would that save?'

'Er – two pounds, two shillings.'

'And what about Mrs Atkinson? Do we really need her – just the two of us? She must cost a lot more than the cleaner.'

'You mean I should do all the cooking myself – not to mention the shopping and general housekeeping too? Besides, it would only save us just under two hundred a year, plus her keep.'

'Hugh and Rupert don't have cooks.'

'That's their own affair. Anyway, it's beside the point.'

'It isn't, Diana. It isn't.'

'I notice that all these cuts affect me the most. What about you?'

'Well, for a start, I shall have to resign from both my clubs. That will save us at least a thousand a year.'

That silenced her for several moments. Then she said, 'What about McNaughton? If we can't afford a cook, surely we can't afford a chauffeur.'

'So far, the firm has been paying, but I don't think they'll be able to go on doing it. I shall be driving myself in future.'

'But I need him here! He does the mowing, and chops wood for the fires, and all sorts of other odd jobs. We can't possibly do without him!'

He agreed that they couldn't. 'We'll have to stop all these accounts with tradesmen.'

'What difference will that make? We have to eat.'

'When you have an account, you always spend more because you aren't paying cash when you buy. We have to make a budget for housekeeping, and it will be your job to keep within it.'

There was a heavy silence while he nerved himself for the next difficult thing.

'And I'm afraid, darling, that you will have to cancel the fur coat. You haven't worn it, have you?'

She hadn't. The shop was sending it down next week. 'It will be like the war,' she said bitterly. 'Endless housework, living on cheap food, and never having any fun.'

'Diana! Darling! We had fun in the war, in spite of everything – you know we did.'

'You had enough money then for us to go to restaurants and the theatre. And we didn't have children. Now I'm tied here all day every day, and you come back so tired you don't want to do anything except eat and sleep.' She was crying now, but too angrily to sound pathetic.

'If you find this house too much for you, you can always sell it. It's in your name. We could easily find something smaller and easier to run. That's up to you.'

'Oh, thank you very much! After all the work I've put into making this a lovely comfortable home for you, you're perfectly prepared to ditch it!'

And so it went on. Second brandies, the air thick with blame, while the fire burned out; resentment, self-pity and exasperation. Diana could not understand how he could be so uncaring of her feelings – of the shock the whole thing was for her. He became increasingly angry with her for her thoughtless selfishness – could she not, for one minute, see how awful the whole business was for him? Did she care about him at all? Briefly, he thought of Villy, how kind and practical she would have been, but then, with her, he would not have had this extravagant lifestyle and house to cope with in the first place. And the future was possibly bleaker than Diana knew. He could not face telling her that. He shut the account book, and stood up. 'It's very late, darling, and we aren't getting anywhere now. Let's have a truce and call it a day.'

She had been sitting with her hand clenched round the empty brandy glass, which she now held out to him.

He took it from her. 'I think we've both had enough of that.' He took her other hand, pulled her to her feet and put her glass on the coffee tray. He knew what he had to say next to move things on. 'I love you. And all married couples have rows from time to time. I'm really sorry to have upset you so much, darling'

She smiled then – a watery smile but still a smile. 'As long as you love me, I can bear anything.' And she put her arms round his neck and gave him a kiss.

He wished he could say the same to her, but he knew that he couldn't.

RUPERT AND NEVILLE

'So, perhaps you would explain to me what on earth has been going on.'

After what Zoë had told him, Rupert had sent for Neville and had taken him up to the vast drawing room that ran the whole length of the house with a fireplace at each end. Even when lit, they only provided warmth in their immediate vicinity, and they were not lit now. The room was remarkably cold, its four beautiful windows letting in streams of icy air that only the most extravagant central heating could have vanquished, and they had long ceased to afford it. It was a room for summer – for large parties – and now it was November. Rupert had chosen it because he knew they would not be interrupted.

Rupert looked at Neville now, lounging on the worn velvet chesterfield. He was wearing his usual threadbare black corduroy trousers and a rather Byronic white shirt, with a dramatic collar and wide sleeves. He had slung his jacket over one shoulder. Now he felt in a pocket and produced a battered packet of cigarettes. 'Want one, Dad?'

Rupert refused, then changed his mind. He couldn't stop Neville smoking, and in view of the general discomfort he felt at having this showdown, a smoke would help. When their cigarettes were lit, he said, 'You haven't answered my question, Neville.'

'I don't know what you mean. Nothing's going on.'

'You know perfectly well what I mean. What is all this nonsense about you and Juliet?'

'Oh, that! Well, I've told her I love her, and I do.'

'And, according to her, you've told her you're going to marry her.'

'When she's old enough, yes, I probably shall.'

'You must know that's out of the question. She's your sister!'

'My half-sister. And Cleopatra was the result of six generations of incest.'

'Neville, this is no laughing matter.'

'Good Lord! I wouldn't dream of laughing at Cleopatra – I should think hardly anyone ever did that.'

'Juliet is just a schoolgirl—'

'Don't I know it!' Neville interrupted him. 'But she's seventeen – she's growing up. Please don't think I've done anything vulgar. I haven't "interfered with her", as they say in Victorian novels. I only kiss her, and she loves it. We both do.'

For some reason – relief at hearing it – this made Rupert angrier. 'You must see, Neville, that your behaviour is completely irresponsible, and you should be ashamed to have given the poor child such idiotic ideas. I sent for you to tell you that you are not to communicate with her in any way from now onwards. You are not to come here, or write to her, or try to telephone her—'

'She'll be extremely unhappy—'

'Yes. That ought to show you the damage you've already done. But she will get over it, and so will you. Although that shouldn't take you long from what I hear. Reports of your passing affairs with some of your models get around.'

For the first time Neville looked a bit shaken. 'Oh, them! They don't mean anything.'

'They certainly would to Juliet.'

'Dad! Please don't tell her about any of that. She'll think I've been lying to her.'

'Well, you have, haven't you?'

'Not exactly. I didn't want to upset her – that's all.'

'But not telling someone something is a kind of lying. And it's not her you don't want to upset – it's yourself.'

There was a long silence. Then Rupert said, 'I'll have a pact with you. If you will do as I say about Juliet, I'll do my best to see that she doesn't hear about your affairs.'

And, to Rupert's surprise (the pact on his side was on pretty rocky ground), Neville agreed to it. For one year anyway.

They both stood up at the same time: there was a mutual desire to finish this uncomfortable meeting.

'I'll be off,' Neville said. He had been hoping to be asked to stay to lunch, but now he just wanted to get away, and Rupert wanted him gone before he wavered.

'It's bloody cold in your grand room,' Neville said, as they left it. 'My teeth are chattering, but not because I feel cowed. I wouldn't want you to think that.'

Rupert replied that of course he didn't as he – rather thankfully – saw his son to the car. The morning ended with a kind of pallid courtesy.

∞ ∞ ∞

'He's gone?' Zoe was ironing and the kitchen felt remarkably cosy.

'Yep. God! It's cold up there. I need a strong alcoholic

393

drink.' He walked to the stove, rubbing his hands. 'I think there's some left in the cooking-drinks cupboard. Join me?'

'No, thanks. I'm longing to hear how it went, though. I hope he was very contrite, as he jolly well should be.'

'Not exactly. He has a hell of a nerve – I almost couldn't help admiring him for it.'

'Oh, Rupe! Don't tell me you could see his point of view! You're always doing that with people.'

'Well, they do have them, you know. Anyway, I read him the Riot Act – told him he was not to have anything more to do with Jules. In the end I blackmailed him with threatening to tell her about his various affairs. He didn't like that, agreed to keep away for at least a year. He said he "might" marry her when she was old enough.' He took another swig of his whisky. 'I suppose it means that there's something to be said for us moving to South-ampton for a bit.' He added, rather carefully, 'Help her get over it.'

'Is it settled, then? Is Hugh determined to send you? Please tell me, Rupert. I'd much rather know.'

'It's not settled or of course I would have told you. Hugh has decided to go down there himself twice a week to see if he can sort things out.'

'Well, that's something. He is head of the firm.'

'He might be able to deal with it. You know that I don't want to go. I'm absolutely no good at managing things and I've told him so. But I'm beginning to wonder whether any of us are.'

She walked over to him and smoothed the lock of hair that kept falling over his forehead. 'You need a haircut, darling. If you don't go soon, I'll do it for you.'

'It was fine when we had the Brig,' Rupert continued. 'Our father was really good at it. But the three of us – we just got catapulted into the business because he expected us to join in. Edward was good at selling, and Hugh got caught up in the tradition and did everything the Brig told him to, and as for me, it's true that I get on with the staff, but otherwise I think they only took me because I'm a Cazalet or out of sheer kindness. None of us – since the Brig – really understood the figures. We haven't moved with the times. We haven't got the capital or the structure to deal with expansion.'

Their conversation was unexpectedly interrupted by Georgie's sudden appearance.

'Why aren't you at school?'

'I said I had a sore throat. But, actually, I'm severely worried about Evelyn. He didn't eat yesterday's mouse and I left him another lovely one for breakfast and I had to come home and see if he'd eaten it, and he hadn't. So I'm afraid we'll have to take him to the vet. Mr Carmichael is the only one who understands snakes and he goes off at lunchtime on Mondays so could we go quickly now?'

'I'll take him,' Rupert said. 'But you shouldn't just bunk off like that, Georgie. Did you tell the school?'

'Of course not. They might have stopped me.'

'I'll ring them,' Zoë said. 'You get Evelyn.'

'I've got him.' Georgie removed his scarf, and revealed the python wound loosely round his neck.

'Mum! You won't forget to keep the bacon rinds for Rivers, will you?' he called, as they left. 'Dad, you will drive as fast as possible? It may be a matter of life and death.'

395

So Rupert increased his speed slightly and added to the sense of emergency by making very good ambulance noises that delighted Georgie.

∞ ∞ ∞

Mr Carmichael was very fond of Georgie and always made time for him. His waiting room was full of resentful cats in cages and overweight dogs, but Evelyn was called in the minute he had finished with an otter, which lay on his table out for the count.

'Thought you'd like to see him,' he said, stripping off his heavy leather gloves.

Georgie gazed at the otter, absolutely entranced. 'Can I stroke him?'

'While he's out, you can. But they're nervous creatures, and they have a devil of a bite if you frighten them. The keepers of the otterhounds used to pipe clay round the dogs' legs, because an otter will bite until he hears the bone snap. They thought the clay was the bone, you see.'

'He's got the most beautiful fur in the world. And his face! Those whiskers! Can you tame them?'

'Some people have tried. But don't think of having one, Georgie. Their digestion works through food in two hours so they cost a fortune in fish. And they need running water and space to swim. The wild is the place for them.' He motioned the young girl attending him to take the otter away, having lifted it carefully into its cage. 'Now, what is wrong with Evelyn?'

He unwound the python from Georgie's neck, and felt along its body. 'Hold his head, Georgie, while I have a feel . . . I think he must have a minor obstruction that's preventing him swallowing. Better leave him with me for a day or two. He'll be all right.'

'Can't I stay with him?'

'You cannot. But if you leave him here until the weekend, you can help me with the patients on Saturday afternoon, if your father agrees.' Rupert did agree and the nurse produced a cardboard box into which Evelyn was gently laid.

'I've been thinking,' Georgie said, on the way home. 'I could dig a pond at the end of the garden, and if I went round all the fish-and-chip shops, they'd be bound to have old fish they'd be throwing away that I could get for hardly any money . . .'

'No, Georgie, you are not going to have an otter. I'm not going to argue about it. You are *not* going to have an otter.'

'Oh, Dad, don't be so firm. You aren't usually firm about things . . .'

'Well, I am about this.'

There was a long silence. Then Georgie, rubbing tears out of his eyes, muttered, 'It would be a good thing to have a pond to keep my newts in, and if Carter would swap some of his tadpoles I could have frogs as well.'

'I see your point of view. I'll think about it.' And Georgie, who knew that the more his father thought about something, the less firm he got about it, felt that that was enough. He had wanted a pond for a very long time and, after all, having a pond didn't exclude having an otter.

HUGH AND OTHERS

His decision to visit Southampton twice a week turned out to be far more taxing than he had thought it would be. To begin with, it forced him to recognise that times had indeed changed. His father had bought the site just before the war. It had been cheap, as the company that had owned it had gone bankrupt. He had built the saw-mill, and it had thrived, until Southampton was badly bombed during the war, and a great many of the businesses round the mill had been razed to the ground. The docks were a sea of rubble, of broken glass, of burned-out buildings, of boarded-up shops and houses. Very little of the port remained intact, but the main hotel, the Polygon, had survived and so, miraculously, had the Cazalets' wharf and sawmill. They had taken the precaution of put-ting the most valuable hardwoods into the river, and so, apart from one or two minor fires, the wharf had been able to continue trading. It had fared better than London, in fact, where the business had been badly damaged by the Blitz. Then – timber being regarded as an essential commodity – the War Damage Commission had coughed up, and they were able to rebuild. So, over the years, everyone had been preoccupied with London and had not paid much attention to Southampton. Much had changed there. Rebuilding the docks had gone ahead, and the Cazalets' monopoly had dwindled. In particular, their arch rival, Penton and Ward, had started up after the war and taken a good deal of business off them. Added to that, it had proved disastrous putting Teddy in charge. He simply didn't have the experience, although he had inherited Edward's talent for selling.

When Hugh first started going down, he had found much more of a mess than he had expected. The order book was chaotic, morale was low, and orders constantly went astray. Several firms had written saying that in view of the delays in delivery and 'other matters' they were moving their custom. This appalled him. There seemed to be no loyalty, no sense of tradition left.

He discovered that there was a split between the sawmill and the office: an atmosphere of non-cooperation and blame prevailed. 'The manager just doesn't like me,' Teddy said. 'I'm no good at figures.'

A little later, he saw McIver, who admitted to him, 'With respect, he doesn't know what he's doing half the time. The men don't trust him, Mr Hugh, and that's a fact.'

He got back home to Jemima at half past eight.

'I don't think this is a good idea. Wouldn't it be better if you stayed down one night and did two days running?'

In the old days he would have stuck to his guns and argued, but that evening he felt he had no guns left and agreed. While she got him a whisky, a horrible fear assaulted him: that it was all no good, that he had made a mess of everything, let his father down, the whole family. He feared, too, that Edward had been right, that they should have sold out years ago. Now, when there was a serious crisis and a need for bold, energetic leadership, he felt drained of all ideas and energy to do anything.

'I'm making scallops and bacon for us. You just sit and have your drink in peace. You'll feel much better when you've got some food inside you.'

Like most women, he thought, Jemima was a firm believer in food as the answer to almost anything. As he sipped his drink, he had a sudden vivid memory of lying in the hospital in France, just after his hand had been amputated, and Edward appearing in the ward like magic – the only person in the world whom he wanted to be with. Edward had made a joke about how he'd got into the ward, and he'd wanted to laugh, but he'd cried instead. Edward had sat with him and mopped his brow with one of his wonderful silk handkerchiefs, and when he'd got up to go he'd actually kissed him, and told him to look after himself. 'You too,' he had muttered, and Edward had winked and said, 'You bet.'

Matron had arrived, and now stood implacably by. 'Look after him especially well, won't you?' Edward had said. 'Because he's my brother.' She had actually smiled and replied that of course she would, Major.

Then he had stood up and strode away down the ward, and Hugh had watched the doors gently swinging after he had gone. He remembered being afraid that he would never see him again.

Of course this feud must stop. He must tell Edward that he had been wrong, and the only way to put things right was for them to work together in perfect agreement. He had not been good about Edward's marriage, either. He had felt very much for poor Villy, but it had helped no one to take sides about it. Perhaps he could beg more time from the bank. Perhaps they should sell Southampton. That should produce enough money to keep the bank quiet about the rest of the loan.

These random thoughts circulated at increasing speed until he could feel one of his really bad heads coming on. He got out his pills and took two.

Jemima called him from the kitchen, and he hoisted himself up to walk through.

She knew at once about his head, helped him off with his jacket, loosened his tie and massaged his neck with her wonderful cool, searching fingers. As always on these occasions he took one of her hands and kissed it.

'Better?'

'Much better. Thank you, darling.'

So at supper he felt able to tell her some of his worries, and about his plan to talk to Edward about selling Southampton. When he came to admit that he hadn't been nice about Diana, she agreed. 'One way and another, we have none of us been nice about her. I should think she must feel fairly prickly about the family. It will take time for her to trust us. Supposing I ask her to lunch with me and go shopping afterwards. I have a feeling that she likes shopping . . .'

'But you hate it!'

'Well, it's not a very serious thing to hate. And I don't hate it all that much. Actually, I think I only say that to sound high-minded. Do you think I should have a go?'

'Yes. And now are you too high-minded to come to bed?'

'Well, I am, actually, but I'm prepared to make an exception just for you.'

As they went upstairs hand in hand, she said, 'Hugh! I've just thought. Wouldn't it be a good idea to have your accountant there when you and Edward have your talk? He'll know all the figures and that could be helpful.'

'It would. You're a genius. I can't think why I didn't think that myself.'

You wouldn't, my darling, she thought, and smiled. Because it's the kind of practical thing you never do think.

TEDDY AND SABRINA

'I was only ringing to say don't call me on Thursday because my boss is coming down and he doesn't approve of private calls in office time.'

'Was I meant to be calling you on Thursday?'

'No – not especially. I just thought you might.'

'Well, now, is that all you rang up to say?'

'Not really. I've got some good news for us.'

'Do tell, *do*.' Immediately she sounded less bored.

'Well, it looks as though I may be transferred to London. Anyway, I'm coming up on Friday night for the weekend.'

'Oh dear! What a grim pity. I've promised to go down to the Frankensteins for the weekend.'

'The Frankensteins' was the nickname she had given her parents.

'Surely you can get out of that.'

'I simply absolutely can't. I've overspent my allowance, and the only way I can get Daddy to produce more money is by being around for a bit. You can't imagine how ghastly they can be about money. And being a deb does cost a bomb. It was nearly the last Season and Mummy kept saying how lucky I was to do it, but if I'd known what it was going to be like I'd have refused. I had to keep taking taxis everywhere, always leaving at least one glove behind, and having to buy new ones –

you couldn't go to a deb lunch without them – then dances nearly every night with the same old boring chinless titled twits . . .'

'They can't all have been like that.'

'Of course they weren't – not *absolutely* all – but don't stop me, Teddy, when I'm trying to be amusing. Anyway, the worst part was pretending to enjoy myself with Lady Frankenstein yawning in her chair against a wall with a string of other old women keeping beady eyes out for earls or at least eldest sons of earls. And then in the taxi home wanting to know who I danced with, and I could never remember and took to making them up. The whole thing was a ghastly failure from the parentals' point of view, and now they're moaning about the expense.'

She had run out of breath at last. He imagined her with her long blonde hair that kept getting into her eyes, her long narrow nose – too big, people said, for real beauty – signed off by a wide, wandering mouth, also narrow, but relieved at each end by turning up at the corners. She was not pretty, he had decided, from the moment he had spotted her standing alone at the crowded party Louise had taken him to, but she was alone and he didn't know anyone, so he'd made his way across the room to talk to her.

She was wearing a sheath dress in some dusky pink material, and the first thing that struck him was her breasts: they seemed to him the most beautiful he had ever seen in his life. The discreet neckline meant, of course, that they were only partly visible, but they surged upwards, smooth and perfectly rounded each side of her fascinating cleavage.

'As you're here, you'd better tell me your name.'

'Teddy Cazalet.'

'I'm Sabrina Browne Fanshawe. Have you got any small-talk handy?'

'Do you mean, "Do you know many people here?" '

'That sort of thing. I've run out of it myself, and I never was much good at the other kind. Most of the people here have careers, so it's easy for them. They can just take it in turns to talk about themselves.'

'Well, I suppose,' Teddy said, trying hard (and, he thought, successfully) not to look too much at her breasts, 'I could talk about you, and you could talk about me.'

'As long as it's not about my breasts, I don't mind.'

Three things happened at once: he felt himself go painfully red in the face (it was like being caught out at school), he was staggered by her perception (incredible intelligence) and he knew he was going to fall in love with her. He was speechless.

'I'm starving, why don't we go out to dinner?'

This was a brilliant idea, except he had only a five-pound note on him. 'Must just tell my cousin. I came with her – but she won't mind.'

'I'll meet you where the coats are.'

He found Louise talking to an attractive man, older than her, wearing an overcoat.

'This is my brother, Teddy Cazalet, Joseph Waring.'

'I just want a word with my sister.'

'I'll wait outside, Louise, but don't be long or I shall boil to death.'

'I know you, Teddy. You've found some beautiful model, you want to take her out to dinner and you haven't any money. Here.' She fished in her purse and pulled out a ten-pound note. 'It's my emergency taxi money, but I'm OK with Joseph. Have a good time.'

'Bless you, Louise. I'll pay you back tomorrow.'

'Where would you like to go?' he asked Sabrina, when he got back to her. 'The Berkeley, or somewhere like that?'

'Nowhere like that. I'd like a small, dark place with intensely foreign food.'

So he took her to a Turkish restaurant he used to go to where they ordered a huge plate of mezze with a bottle of house wine (red). Their waiter lit a candle, then brought a plate of flat bread wrapped in a napkin, filled their glasses to the brim and said if they wanted anything they had only to call and he would be instantly with them. 'My name is Johnnie,' he added, as he melted away into the dimly lit background.

'I wasn't joking when I said I was starving. I've got so sick of cold chicken and cold salmon that I've practically stopped eating anything except Bendicks Bittermints, which are tremendously nourishing.'

'My grandmother told me that in Scotland the servants had a clause in their contracts that they wouldn't have to eat salmon more than three times a week.'

'Gosh! My grandmother's never told me anything except to talk more quietly and not touch anything. My family really are a dead loss. The only good thing about them is their horses.'

'Do they have a lot?'

She had split open a flat bread and was stuffing it with aubergine and tomato and two kinds of olive. 'A sort of sandwich,' she said. 'I adore sandwiches. My mother thinks they're common except for picnics. She is a truly wondrous snob. You know, most people have areas they're snobby about – of course they don't admit

it but they do – but she has it about absolutely everything. You aren't eating!'

'I'm going to copy you. What are you a snob about?'

She thought for a moment, licking her fingers carefully. 'Shoes,' she said at last. 'And novels. Really pretty
shoes that are also comfortable are always very
expensive.'

He would give her a pair for her birthday whenever
that might be. 'How expensive?'

'Oh, perhaps fifty pounds. But some cost a lot more
than that.'

He would not be giving her a pair for her birthday. A
worrying thought struck him. 'Are you frightfully rich?'

'My parents are quite rich. I wouldn't say frightfully. I
haven't got a bean. And what's more, I haven't been
brought up to earn any money. The Frankensteins think
the only career for a girl is marriage. You haven't asked
me about the novels yet.'

'I don't know anything about novels, so I wouldn't
know what to ask.'

'Well, I had one good teacher at the ghastly boarding
school I was sent to, and she got me interested. She told
me to read the best ones first, then go on to the rest. So I
did. I wanted to go to university, but Daddy wouldn't
hear of it. He said men didn't like brainy girls. As though
I had to be just what men would like. So here I am –
utterly useless. I failed to make a "good marriage" after
doing the Season and now none of us knows what on
earth to do with me.'

She said all this as though it was a bit of a joke, but
when she pushed her hair out of her eyes, he saw that
she didn't feel it was a joke at all.

'Time to talk about you.'

So he told her some things about himself. About being a Spitfire pilot and the war ending before he'd had a chance to fight; about his marriage with an American he'd met in a nightclub in Phoenix and how she had mercifully left him and filed for divorce. Then he told her about working in the family firm, about being sent to Southampton and not making a very good fist of it. He didn't mention any affairs.

That was the beginning of it. He made the mistake of telling her on that first evening that he had fallen in love with her, and she became querulous and distant. She did not utterly discard him, however, seemed to want his company, was soon treating him like an old friend (or a brother, he sometimes bitterly thought). All through that spring and summer he escaped to London at weekends to spend time with her. He listened and sympathised with her attempts to find a job, getting one, getting fired and trying something else. Her parents allowed her to live in their Berkeley Square flat when they were not using it, on condition that she did a cookery course with Cordon Bleu. But doing this, however half-heartedly, effectively ruled out keeping any other job. She did not seem to understand that her various employers would not take kindly either to unpunctuality or, worse, her failure to turn up at all. Her parents had been harsh or spoiling in all the wrong ways. She was an only child, and he suspected that they had not wanted children at all.

The curious thing about it, he thought, was that none of this stopped him loving her. Love, he was beginning to understand, was an unconditional state – you didn't need to judge the beloved, give them marks out of ten for good points and black marks for bad. You accepted the whole package, and with Sabrina he felt pity for her awful background. It was a bit like trying to tame a wild animal who had been ill-treated and could never forget it. It became a matter neither for lust nor sentiment. He would argue with her, disagree, sometimes lose his temper, finding that it was no good pretending to be patient and gentle when he felt nothing of the kind.

She would sometimes allow him to kiss her, to hold her in his arms if they were sitting on a sofa, or put one arm round her shoulders in a cinema – indeed, she sometimes seemed to long for these affections – but if for one second he overstepped the fine and, to him, initially invisible line, she would freeze, sulk or, worse, rant at him until she burst into tears. And how do you comfort someone in tears if you may not touch them?

Back to the telephone: he had an idea.

'Couldn't I come with you to meet the Frankensteins? You never know, they might have unexpected good taste and take to me.'

Almost before he finished saying the last bit, she started to reject the idea. 'Oh, no, Teddy! I couldn't stand Mummy being rude to you – I'd hit her.'

'I'm deeply touched that you would even think such a thing. But don't worry, I'm tough, I can take it. You've got two options. Either you ring them up and ask them or you just turn up with me as a surprise.'

'I'll think about it.'

'Sabrina, darling, Friday is in two days. Don't think, just do. And ring me back about which you've done.'

'Goodness! You are being masterful,' she said. 'I'm going to stop talking to you before you think of more awful things for me to do.' She rang off.

He spent the rest of the day trying to find out why an order placed by some builders in Portsmouth six weeks ago had not reached them. It turned out that the wood had been delivered to the wrong builders, a firm with a vaguely similar name. There wasn't a lorry free to collect it and redeliver the order to the right firm until late next week. McIver, who had imparted this information, stood stolidly by while Teddy raged at everyone's incompetence, then asked if he might see the order book. He looked at it for what seemed a long time, and then, as he handed it back to Teddy, said, 'It seems that the error was made in the office. If you'd care to look, Mr Teddy?'

He looked. It was entirely his fault. Without thinking, he had written the name of the wrong builders. It was true that Cazalets' dealt with both firms, but that was no excuse. He had been hopelessly careless and one minute's lack of concentration had caused this mess: a bad mark for the firm. Word would get around and the workforce would rightly sneer at his incompetence. And Uncle Hugh was coming on Thursday and would have to be told about it. He became conscious of McIver watching him, but refused to meet his eye.

'It's all my fault,' he said. 'The muddle is entirely my fault. I'll ring up Dawson's to apologise, and let them know we'll deliver as soon as possible. And I'll get in touch with Dorling Brothers and apologise to them, too.' He looked despairingly at the older man. 'I'm so sorry, McIver. You should be doing my job and I should be your assistant. But is there anything else I can do about it now?'

There was a distinct thawing of the atmosphere while McIver rubbed his chin consideringly. 'Well, Mr Ted, I might be able to persuade the transport people to change their schedule and do the redelivering today. Then we could at least show Mr Hugh that we've done our best.'

The 'we' and 'our' were very comforting to Teddy; he almost loved McIver for it.

'And perhaps when you ring Dorling's you might be able to sell to them. They like hardwoods, and we've been cutting a nice piece of padauk.'

'I'll certainly try. I'm most grateful for your support.'

They parted on good terms, McIver remarking as he left that it was a wicked world, a view that he invariably expressed when he was feeling sanguine about it.

When he had gone, Teddy resolved not to smoke, not to think about Sabrina until he had made the horrible telephone calls, the second of which he couldn't make anyway until he'd heard from McIver. Meanwhile, he would go through the order book to see whether he could rustle up some more business. He struck lucky with Dorling's, who wanted teak for a fitted kitchen they were making for a client. He asked them to submit the order in writing, addressed to him personally; he had begun to realise that many written orders had gone straight to the manager of the sawmill, which had meant he hadn't been keeping track of them. And behind that lay the sinister implication that that was exactly what the manager had intended.

However, Sabrina rang back just before the office was closing to say that she'd told the Frankensteins about him, and they had been asked to arrive in time for dinner on Friday. His spirits rose: life was not too bad, after all. He would have the whole weekend with Sabrina, and the prospect of meeting her parents instilled in him nothing more than the mild excitement that curiosity engendered. It was true that he had inflated the hint

Uncle Hugh had given him of there being serious changes at work: the possibility of Uncle Rupe coming down to run things had developed into the likelihood of himself being moved back to London, but he was an optimist and always tended to think that what Teddy wanted Teddy would get.

THE BROTHERS
AND MR TWINE

There was a long silence after Mr Twine had finished speaking. Then Edward said, 'What I can't understand is how the bank can do this to us without warning.'

Mr Twine coughed nervously. He had been dreading this confrontation. The Cazalets were old clients. 'I think if you consult your file you will find that they have, in fact, issued more than one warning expressing their dissatisfaction.' The bank had actually been writing such letters for the past three years with no replies except for one brief missive, signed by Hugh, to the effect that the matter would be seriously considered.

Hugh now said: 'I know that when I went to see them for some more money, they were distinctly sticky about it, but not a word was said about foreclosing on previous loans.'

Mr Twine selected three sheets of paper from the large pile and handed them to Hugh, who sat at his desk flanked by Edward and Rupert. He had known this old office when the Old Man was chairman and it hadn't changed at all. Panelled in koko, his favourite hardwood, its walls were hung with faded framed photographs of men standing by colossal logs or enormous old trees, heavily captioned with names, provenance and dates.

There were two very large photographs showing the London wharves after the Blitz that had destroyed them. A scarlet and peacock Turkey rug covered most of the floor. Hugh's desk, in addition to pictures of his family, was still encrusted with the old blotter, the Dictaphone and an ancient typewriter. All that had changed was the man now sitting in his father's chair. 'Well, I'm damned! I don't remember any of these letters.'

That, Mr Twine thought, was probably because you never read them.

Edward, who asked to see the letters, now said, 'But if we sold off Southampton surely there would be enough money to pay off the bank, and then we could concentrate on London. Or, better still, perhaps we should bite the bullet and go for turning the whole business into a public company. I've been urging that option for years.'

Mr Twine coughed again, a sign, Rupert recognised, that he had something to say and was not going to enjoy saying it.

'I'm afraid, Mr Edward, that it's too late for that. The value of the Southampton business has become so much less, due to the last years' track record of loss, so now you would not get sufficient capital from its sale. And it's too late planning to go public. That would take at least two years, and in any case the bank does not consider that the business is any longer yours to sell.'

There was a short silence. Then Hugh said, 'Does that mean we're going to be bankrupt?'

'I'm afraid it does.'

'And that means that we, personally, are bankrupt. They'll take everything – our houses—'

'No, Mr Hugh. If you will remember, I advised you to put your private properties in your wives' names. As you most sensibly agreed to that, you will keep your houses. And, also, the directors' pensions. Mr Hank and I saw to that when you became a limited company. '

'What about Home Place?' Hugh then asked.

'That will have to go, I'm afraid. Your father bought it in the firm's name.'

'What about Rachel? It's her home! I won't have her turned out of it!'

Twine coughed again. 'According to Mr Hank, with whom Miss Sidney made her will, her house in London, together with its contents, were all left to Miss Rachel, so she will not be homeless.' His mouth, unused to smiling, made a heroic effort now.

'She may have a house, but she has no income other than her shares in Cazalets'. She will be literally penniless! We have to do something about that.' Hugh looked defiantly at the others; their faces showed varying degrees of concern and hopelessness. 'It's awful, but I'm out of my depth,' he concluded mournfully.

'I think we've had enough for one morning,' Edward said. 'One more question: what is the time scale for all of this?'

Mr Twine, who had been returning papers to his file, looked up. 'I cannot give you precise dates. The assessors will probably take at least two months to produce their report to the bank. In the meantime, you should continue trading and say nothing to anyone about the impending bankruptcy. Nobody at all. Particularly not to any of your employees.'

'So that they will be thrown out of a job at a moment's notice without the chance to look for a new one,' Rupert said, with deep bitterness.

'Anyway, it will get around,' Edward observed.

415

'Even if it does, do not tell anyone that you know anything. I will be in touch with you as soon as I have any more to communicate.' Twine got thankfully to his feet, shook hands with each of them and made his escape.

∞ ∞ ∞

The trouble, he thought, as he boarded his bus, was that none of them were businessmen. He felt sorry for them in a way, but had lost respect. He would not personally have put any of them in charge of a sweet shop. He opened his paper and decided to take the afternoon off and go to the motor show. He was rather keen on the new bubble cars that sounded both cheap and practical; 'bus suppositories', the French called them, an insult probably generated by sheer envy of the Germans being better at car manufacture than they were.

Yes, he'd get a sandwich and a pint at one of the Earl's Court pubs, and then he'd have a good look round the motor show before catching an earlier train back to Crouch End.

∞ ∞ ∞

After Mr Twine had left there was a heavy silence in the room. Nobody moved. It was rather, Rupert thought, as though the injection of reality had paralysed them – as though they had become a still in an action film. Noises from the street below impinged: a paper boy crying for people to buy the latest edition of the *Evening Standard*, a squeal of brakes and some shouting. He heard the brief crescendo of an aeroplane, before they all finally stirred and became animate. Hugh reached for his pills and swallowed two with the dregs of his coffee. Edward flipped open the laurel-wood box, always kept full of cigarettes, and lit one. He offered the box to Rupert, who shook his head, then changed his mind.

Hugh said, 'If only we knew what they will sell Home Place for, we would know what money to raise.'

'We're in no position to raise any money at all,' Edward replied glumly. 'Speaking for myself, I'm broke. I've got debts, and nothing but my salary to live on and try to repay them.'

'Edward! Do you mean you've saved nothing?'

'I did have a nest-egg, but it's all gone now.'

'I'm afraid I haven't got anything saved either,' Rupert said. 'What with moving from the flat into a house, and the children getting steadily more expensive, I really haven't been able to. I'm sorry, Hugh, but I can't help you there. About buying Home Place, I mean. You and I pay our bit towards its upkeep as it is.' The fact that Edward had refused to help with that still riled him. 'Anyway, as Twine said, Rachel has the house in London.'

Edward looked at his watch. 'I must leave you. It's business not as usual. A Danish bloke wants to buy teak for hi-fi speakers.' He stubbed out his cigarette and got to his feet. 'I should go home, old boy. You can't do anything when your head's giving you gyp.'

Hugh scowled at him, but he pretended not to notice.

Christ! Edward thought, as he collected his hat and overcoat from his office. What the hell am I going to do? The thought of facing Diana with even worse news made him feel cold at the back of his neck. He again thought of Villy then. She would have been easy to tell: she would have grasped the essentials at once, would have supported him and also been intelligent about how to cut

417

down expenses . . . If only she had enjoyed going to bed
with him . . .

∞ ∞ ∞

Rupert left Hugh's office to settle some dispute down at
the wharf: the drivers were acting up again. They had
been grumbling ever since last Christmas when four of
the lorries had simultaneously broken down. They had a
point, he knew, because nearly the whole fleet was long
past decent service. Most of them had gone through the
war, been patched up, had new or reconditioned engines
fitted, but apart from the expense of maintenance, there
was all the nuisance involved with them so frequently
being late with deliveries, or failing to deliver at all.
Edward had persuaded Hugh to agree to buy four new
lorries so they now had, Rupert hoped, four satisfied
drivers although, these days, that would not prevent
them striking to back up the others.

At least he didn't look like having to move to Southampton, and Zoë would be pleased about that. But
looming on his horizon, hardly acknowledged by his
brothers, was the likelihood of his being without a job, of
them all not only ceasing to be employers, but un-
employed.

This set up a conflict. On the one hand it let him off
doing something he had never really wanted to do. He
wasn't, never would be, a businessman. He had been
persuaded, notably by Hugh, that it was what he ought
to do, had seen the argument that theirs was a family
business, and with a wife and two children to look after,
it had become the soft option. But he had never stopped
minding that he had given up even trying to be a painter,

feeling that thereby he had betrayed himself. After all, Archie had continued to paint, and was beginning to make a bit of a name for himself as a portraitist. And he had a wife and two children to care for, too. It could be done: he simply had not had the courage to do it before. The thought excited him now – it would give him freedom; it was the road less travelled. He and Archie might band together to teach, take some cheap place in Italy or France where their families could enjoy a holiday while they worked. He longed to skip the problems of the wharf and go and find Archie to talk to him about all this. On the other hand, he would be plunging Zoë into poverty; they might not be able to afford the house, and then there were school fees, Georgie's zoo, and Juliet going through a most difficult stage – Zoë had been talking about sending her abroad to learn cooking and French to get her over Neville. They wouldn't be able to afford that now anyway.

Then he thought of all the men who would have to be laid off, and his heart sank. 'I must be sympathetic but firm,' he told himself, as he drove to East London. But somehow these two pieces of advice didn't seem to go together very well at all.

∞ ∞ ∞

Hugh, left to himself in his office with a raging headache, resisted the desire to go home. He rang his secretary, told her he was going to lie down for a bit, and, no, he didn't want any lunch. He arranged himself on the stiff little horsehair day-bed he had always kept for this purpose and tried to sleep but his anxiety about Rachel kept him awake. If he mortgaged his house, would that provide enough money to invest for an income? He simply didn't know. If all three of them took out mortgages, surely that would be enough. If Rachel kept the little house in Abbey Road, and perhaps took in a lodger, that would help, too. But he knew that Edward would not agree to a mortgage, and he didn't like the idea of persuading Rupert to do that either.

The whole mess was his fault, he thought miserably. If he'd listened to Edward and the advice given them by that banker chap of Louise's they would not be in this pickle. If they'd gone public they would have walked away with millions. And then, when the same chap had offered to sound out the most successful of their rivals, he had refused to consider it. He'd been, in fact, a bloody fool. And as a result, he and Edward – both now in their sixties – would have to look for jobs. So would Rupert, of course, but he was so used to thinking of him as his little brother that he forgot he was fifty-five. None of their ages augured well for new starts. And, worst of all, there was Rachel. She had no income at all, and it was all his fault.

RACHEL

It had taken her months to brave Sid's house, shut up now for nearly a year – since last November, to be precise. She had asked Villy, who lived nearby, whether, if sent the keys, she would go and see that it was all right. Villy had reported back: nobody had broken in, but she had closed the shutters on the ground-floor windows, made sure that the water was turned off, but left the telephone, electricity and gas for Rachel to decide about when she came. She returned the keys and said that if she wanted any help she would be glad to supply it and, in any case, Rachel was always welcome for lunch or supper.

When she finally opened the front door and stood in the tiny hall, the dank stillness enveloped her. It was dark in the house and she hastened to open the shutters. The sitting room was covered with dust and the rug sent up little eddies of it wherever she trod. She could have written her name on the top of the Erard upright, and the sheet music that lay beside it was not only grey with dust but also limp with damp. She went to the far end of the room, where French windows opened onto the steps down to the garden, which was now a yellowing jungle, thick with fallen leaves that almost obscured the few emaciated Michaelmas daisies that had survived. She steeled herself to go upstairs – she knew that this would be the worst – and went first to Sid's bedroom, which she had shared with her. The wardrobe had Sid's clothes hanging there still: her winter coat, her Aran jersey, a tweed skirt and her best dress – a silk crêpe affair that she hated and never wore.

The chest of drawers was full of her underwear and night clothes – and when she opened the top drawer, Sid's aroma rose to meet her: the dear familiar scent of China tea and pepper was overwhelming. For minutes she stood inhaling the precious essence, then saw an opened box nestled among the garments. It was half full of painkillers, much stronger ones than she had seen Sid take. All part of her trying not to worry me. Rachel looked wildly round the room to stop herself crying. On the table by the window stood a small vase of dead chrysanthemums, with the silver-backed brush and comb that had belonged to Sid's mother. She had cleaned them regularly, although she never used them; the silver was tarnished now.

She went down to the basement, with its dark kitchen and bars on the windows, and there were the dishes from their last breakfast, washed up and lying on the draining board. Everything in the kitchen was dirty, covered with a thick layer of dust, and smelt overwhelmingly of damp.

Rachel realised that she was extremely cold – unable not only to do anything but even to think of what she should do. Make some coffee or tea. She remembered that the water was turned off, but there might be some left in the electric kettle. She shook it, and there was. Coffee would be best since there was no milk. The kettle took a long time to boil, since it badly needed descaling.

She wiped a mug with a drying-up cloth, and also

wiped the seat of a kitchen chair. Every now and then a bus rumbled down the road outside, but otherwise there was an oppressive silence.

She sat at the table with her hands clasped round the mug. 'I can't live here,' she said aloud. 'I can't.'

WARNING THE FAMILY

'Well, at least it means we shan't have to move.' She was undressing, getting ready for bed, which she always did extremely slowly; she seemed impervious to the cold, and wandered round the room in her petticoat. Rupert lay in bed, watching her.

'We'll be pretty hard up. We might not even be able to keep this house.'

'Oh, Rupe! We will! I can easily do without a cleaner.' She picked up her hairbrush and sat on the bed beside him to have her hair brushed.

'I just feel I ought to warn you. I'll need to get some sort of teaching. But even so—'

'Archie manages it. The point is, my darling, that you will be able to paint at last, which is what you've always wanted. And when you've got enough pictures painted perhaps you and Archie could have a show together.'

'Perhaps we could.' And, more likely, perhaps we couldn't, he thought. She was so pretty, and she still had her rather imperious optimism.

'Well, I think it's exciting.' She took the brush from him and began peeling off her pale green petticoat. Most of her underclothes were green as she had decided years ago that they not only matched her eyes but set off her charmingly white skin. She did not have the

424

same vanity now but some of the earlier rules had stuck. 'A painter's wife,' she finished, stepping out of her knickers.

'Come here, I'll do your bra.' He unhooked it and cupped her breasts in his hands. 'You're not to start dressing again. Join me just as you are.'

∞ ∞ ∞

Edward went to sleep on the drive home: the shock of the morning meeting was still with him. He was sixty-one and, in a matter of months, he would be out of a job. He had no other source of income, he was in debt to his bank and he hadn't the faintest idea what he could do to earn his living (and Diana's). All the painful retrenchments he had discussed with her might have worked if money was coming in, but it wasn't; you can't cut down if you've nothing to cut down from. Susan would have to leave her expensive school; he would have to stop Jamie's allowance and the boy would have to start earning his living. He could resign from both his clubs, and there were a few things he could sell – his Purdey guns, for instance: a very fine pair inherited from his father; they would be worth a bob or two. At this point he began to feel sick: everything seemed so black, just a long tunnel with no light at the end of it. When the same hopeless horror came back to him in the car, he had taken the only way out – sleep. I'm not even afraid of tackling Diana about it all any more – she'll simply have to lump it, he thought, as he drifted off.

∞ ∞ ∞

'Darling, do stop blaming yourself. If you tell me once more that everything is your fault I shall scream. You're much too keen on blame. It never does anyone the slightest good.' She was glad to see that this shocked him.

'But it is. It is my fault for being so pig-headed and not listening to anyone – especially Edward.'

'All right. Supposing it is. The question is, what are we going to do now? I think it's rather exciting. I know quite a lot about not having much money. We'll manage.' She stretched out her hand to his good one and shook it firmly. She was wearing her round horn-rimmed glasses, and looked, he thought, like an angry little owl. It made him smile.

'Let's talk properly about it tomorrow.' She'd started her period that morning – the flat iron dropping down her stomach – and had a splitting headache, and it was nearly midnight.

When they were in bed, and he had started up again about what was to become of Rachel, she asked about Sid's house. 'What is it like? Have you ever seen it?'

'Only once. It's a detached early-Victorian villa. The kind that rich men bought to install a mistress in. A pretty little house, but it looked run down when I went there. If it really has been empty for a year, I should think it will need quite a lot doing to it. In any case, she'll have to sell it to get some income.'

'No more now,' she said quickly. 'We're going to sleep, but if you want a change of worry, worry about me. I've got a horrible headache and my monthly tum.'

That worked. He turned to her at once, took her in his arms, murmuring endearments, comforting her with his love and concern, repeating his private words for her until she felt small and young again.

The next morning it was agreed that he and she, with Laura, should propose themselves for the weekend at Home Place, when Hugh would break the news to Rachel about having to sell the house.

∞ ∞ ∞

She realised, as the day wore on, that not only did she not want to live in Sid's house, she did not want to spend a single night there. Quite apart from the extreme discomfort of the place, the idea of getting into the bed they had both slept in frightened her: she felt that she would sink under a weight of grief she would be unable to bear. She rang Home Place and arranged for Tonbridge to meet her train, then set about packing a suitcase with Sid's most private possessions. In the desk she found that Sid had kept every single one of her letters, tied in a bundle with a piece of blue ribbon. There was also another bundle, of heartless self-absorbed postcards from Sid's awful sister Evie, who had emigrated to America several years before in pursuit of some music conductor or other. 'Having a wonderful time'; 'Another 4-star hotel! This is the life!' She never asked Sid anything about herself and never gave an address.

She would throw away that bundle. There was also a little photograph album that contained sepia pictures of Sid's parents and her attenuated childhood. She would keep that because Sid had treasured it. She packed Sid's jersey, which she could wear, and one or two other things – some ties, and a favourite woolly scarf that had been attacked by moths but that she had refused to discard. It was enough for one day. Downstairs, she remembered a framed picture of Sid playing a violin sonata with Myra Hess and managed to cram it into the top of the suitcase. Home. She just wanted to go home.

∞ ∞ ∞

'There's nothing to do in a car.'

'You can look out of the window.'

'I've tried, Mummy, but it goes too fast for me to see anything properly.'

'Well, have a little nap.'

'Oh, all right.'

Jemima looked to see if Laura was lying down and she was. The car was passing Lamberhurst. Hugh said, under his breath, 'To think Edward does this journey five days a week! I couldn't.'

'You don't have to, darling. Just the trek to Ladbroke Grove.'

After a short silence, Laura said, 'Mummy! Going away for the weekend is quite grown-up, isn't it? Children don't mostly go away for weekends.'

'No, they don't.'

'That's what Miss Pendleton said at school. I could see it displeased her.'

Hugh said, 'Well, now you're going on such a grown-up venture, you must be grown-up. No Miss Ghastly for you this weekend.'

'All right. But, Dad, I shut my eyes just now and it didn't make me sleep at all.'

'And promise to be especially nice to Aunt Rachel.'

'I promised last night. I can't keep promising about the same thing – it just makes it weaker.'

'How about you sing us a song?'

Laura loved singing and set about one man mowing a meadow immediately. The meadow was followed by the interminable green bottles and then a medley of Christmas carols, until they reached Home Place.

∞ ∞ ∞

'It will do Miss Rachel a world of good to have some company,' Eileen said, when they arrived. 'You're in your usual room, madam, and I've put Miss Laura in the dressing room next door. Miss Rachel's in the morning room. The fire went out while she was having her rest . . .'

'I'll go and help her,' Hugh said.

When he had gone, Laura took Eileen's hand and said, 'I want to have tea with you and Mrs Tonbridge. In the kitchen. Now?'

Eileen looked gratified. 'What does your mother say about that?'

Jemima said it would be lovely, if they didn't mind. 'And, really, it's not just tea, it should be her supper.'

'I shall drink tea at it. I shall drink a lot of tea with my supper.'

Eileen bore her off wreathed in indulgent smiles. 'I could give her her bath, Mrs Hugh, if you cared for me to do it.'

Her usual room. It was not Hugh's old room – the one in which Wills had been born and, later, where Sybil had died – but a room that had been Edward's when he

429

had been married to Villy. Like all the bedrooms it still had the wallpaper the Duchy had chosen for it when the house was bought – a trellis entwined with honeysuckle and a few rather improbable butterflies. The floor was covered with coconut matting – coffee-coloured but interwoven with black and scarlet stripes. The paintwork, once white, had aged to a musky cream that reminded her of the twins' cricket flannels. The bed was flanked by four posts topped with brass balls, and boasted a rather splendid patchwork quilt that had taken Villy two winters to make. The large mahogany wardrobe emitted a blast of mothball so strong that she decided not to hang her dress in it. The dressing table had its pretty Georgian mirror set at a rakish angle, plus a pincushion. 'Darling Mummy', it said, in shaky letters of alternate red and blue. She always looked forward to seeing it. In fact, Jemima loved the whole room, the way that things that were needed had gradually accumulated with no thought of design, no anxiety about colours clashing or periods of furniture rubbing together, no need to change anything unless it wore out, nothing new except the webs that spiders spun every year.

By now she had unpacked and went next door to inspect Laura's room, where a large stuffed tiger was tucked up in her bed.

She should go down. She tried for one last time to imagine what it must be like to be Rachel – and failed.

The morning room was not warm exactly, but noticeably warmer than the rest of the house. The only lighting, apart from the fire, came from an ancient standard lamp whose parchment shade was so discoloured by smoke that it cast a mere foggy glow.

Hugh had been talking as she entered the room but he

stopped when he saw her. Rachel sat bolt upright in a chair beside the fire. Jemima went at once to kiss her. 'It's lovely to see you.'

'It's so good of you to come.' Her face was very cold. 'I'm afraid I made rather a mess of the fire, but Hugh has revived it.'

'I have other uses as well. Rachel and I have been drinking whisky, but you'd rather have gin, wouldn't you, darling? You sit next to Rachel and get warm.' She sat. Her sister-in-law's face had become gaunt: she had dark circles under her eyes, almost the colour of the heavy dark blue jersey she was wearing. She had cut her hair very short, which might have made her look younger, but didn't.

'I've been trying to explain to Rachel what's happening about the firm. I'm afraid it's all rather difficult to take in.'

Jemima said, 'I don't think what is happening, or going to happen, is complicated. It's more what we all do about it afterwards.' She turned to Rachel, and said, 'Cazalets' owes the bank a great deal of money, and since they cannot repay it, the bank are calling in receivers before declaring the firm bankrupt. That means the end of the firm. There's a chance that whoever takes it over may keep on some of the people who work in it now, and that includes your brothers, but it's only a chance, and in any case we won't know about that for some time.' Her quiet, practical voice made everything clear.

'Does that mean the whole family is bankrupt?'

'No, it seems not. The extremely clever family lawyer advised us to put our houses in the wives' names.' Here she stopped because she didn't know whether Hugh had yet broken the news to Rachel about Home Place. They exchanged glances. He handed her her drink and sat in the third chair.

'Hugh, darling, I wonder if you would get me my cigarettes. On the table by the Torture Couch.' This hard little day-bed had been the Duchy's only concession to comfort; she had always urged Rachel to rest upon it. 'Torture Couch' had been Sid's name for it. Hugh collected her smoking gear, a packet of Passing Clouds, an ashtray and her silver lighter.

'Thank you, darling. Well, at least it's good news about the houses. I know you all love this house as much as I do—'

Jemima interrupted: 'We thought you might want to live in the house that Sid left you.'

'Oh, no! I couldn't bear to do that! No, I shall sell it. I went up to London to see it, and I knew almost at once that it was not for me. She told me to sell up if I wanted to. No. I would far rather stay here. This is my home.' She took a sip of her whisky, and at that moment Eileen poked her head round the door to say that Miss Laura was ready for her bedtime story.

'Oh dear! I haven't even said hello to her.'

'Tomorrow,' Jemima replied, as she got up to go.

She gave Hugh a bracing look as she left the room. It was up to him now.

'Rachel,' he began, 'it's more difficult than that. Like us, you held a great many shares in the firm.'

'Oh, yes! Far more than I needed, really, because the Duchy left me all hers. It has enabled me to buy a television set for the servants, which they simply adore, and I'm paying for Mrs Tonbridge to have her poor bunions done by a really good man in London—'

'Have you saved any of it, darling?'

'I suppose I have. Yes, of course I have – several thousand pounds, I should think.'

'Because, you see, from the moment we're declared bankrupt, all our shares will be worthless. There will be no more money coming in. You will have no income.'

He could see that this news shocked her.

There was a pause, during which she drank some more whisky.

'Well,' she said at last, 'it simply means that I must learn how to economise. The Duchy taught me a great deal about that – especially in the war. I'm sure I can live on the income from selling the Abbey Road house. You mustn't worry about me – you have far more important people to worry about.'

She looks her most grief-stricken when she tries to smile, he thought. 'My dear, I'm afraid I have even more bad news. But I have to tell you. This house will no longer be ours. The Brig bought it after the first war, in the name of the firm. Cazalets' owns the freehold, which means that we don't. And even supposing the bank was prepared to sell it to us, we simply haven't got enough money to pay for it. I know that this is worse for you than for any of us, and I promise I'll sort something out for you—'

But here he was interrupted as she gave one small cry of anguish – then clapped her hand over her mouth to silence herself.

'I didn't know. I had no idea.'

He went to her, knelt before her and took both of her hands in his. The agony in her eyes became blurred by tears. 'Bit of a shock,' she said; she was scarcely audible.

'Oh, darling, of course it is, and you do not deserve it. You of all people.'

'Oh, no. Think if it was any of you with children and everything. And I do deserve it. I've never done a hand's turn in my life.' She fumbled for the handkerchief that she kept – as the Duchy had – tucked into her wristwatch band.

'That is completely untrue. You looked after our parents wonderfully, you ran your charity, the Babies' Hotel, you made this house a place where the whole family loved to come.'

∞ ∞ ∞

At dinner – parsnip soup and shepherd's pie, with salsify and spinach, then a damson tart – there was a tacit agreement not to talk about the situation; instead they fell back on less painful subjects. Jemima remarked that President de Gaulle's – she thought rather peevish – question as to how one could govern a country that produced two hundred and sixty-five cheeses was both silly and irrelevant.

'I'm sure he simply said that to make people think he had a sense of humour,' Hugh retorted, and Rachel wondered aloud how they could need so many cheeses. Anyway, '*Vive la différence*' was a much better remark.

'Think how awful it must be,' Jemima said, 'to have people, newspaper people especially, hanging about waiting for you to produce some pearl of wisdom.'

'I agree with that,' Hugh said. 'Dropping cultured pearls before real swine.' At least Rachel's listening, he thought, but she's hardly eaten a thing.

'Where did you get that phrase from?'

He thought for a moment. 'From Rupe, when he was teaching at that boarding school.'

And then they fell back on Laura stories. Jemima told the first. 'She came to me one day and asked why Hugh had said he was going to a board meeting. Why? To meet the other board members. She burst out laughing. "But, Dad, if you're bored, meeting a whole lot of other bored people, won't make it any better. You'll simply be more bored than ever." She got quite sulky when Hugh tried to explain to her.' Rachel smiled and murmured that children could be quite killing sometimes.

They had their coffee in the morning room, where it was decided that both Sid's house and Home Place must be valued immediately. Jemima offered to arrange the one in London, and Hugh said he would go to the estate agents in Battle – he knew one of them slightly as they had played golf together at Rye.

'I don't want the servants to know,' Rachel said quietly.

They were all very tired by now, and longing not to have to talk about any of it any more. Hugh and Jemima each gave Rachel a hug, which she received with patient courtesy. She had gone beyond their reach.

TEDDY AND SABRINA

'I'm afraid you're not enjoying yourself.'

'Not exactly enjoying, but it is quite interesting.'

They had been left alone, at last, in 'the library', a room whose walls were lined with leather-bound sets of books that showed no signs of ever having been read, with leather armchairs and an immense desk on which were stacked copies of *Horse and Hound* and *Vogue*.

Everything in the mock-Georgian house was like that. The Frankensteins had said that early bed was necessary: they were going hunting in the morning. At dinner he had been subject to cross-examination by Sabrina's mother whom he had discovered was called Pearl. Her father was Reggie. 'Do you hunt, Mr Cazalet?' When he said that he didn't ride, Pearl seemed astonished. 'Did your family not keep horses?'

He said that his grandfather had, and one of his aunts had ridden, but the rest of the family hadn't been interested. 'My father preferred shooting.'

'Ah, yes, shooting,' Reggie had said, with some relief. 'Might do a bit of that tomorrow.'

Pearl persevered. What did his father do for a living? And what did he do? She supposed that he had met Sabrina during the Season? No? 'We met at a party, Mummy, and as it was during the Season we met then.'

'I fail to see, m'dear, that it matters *how* they met. They met.'

They had finished their dressed crab and were being served roast partridge; he was extremely hungry and didn't let the questioning interfere with the delicious food. His examiner didn't do so well, he noticed. She was very small and bony, and wore half a dozen gold bracelets, some with charms attached, that slid noisily up and down her left arm whenever she raised her fork to eat. But when she got it near her mouth, she thought of something else to ask him and the fork remained suspended in the air, and often the food dripped off it. Sabrina looked from the parent who was speaking to the person replying as though she was at a tennis match. She hardly spoke a word during the meal, which ended with chocolate mousse, followed by angels on horseback. The moment everything had been consumed, Pearl got to her feet and motioned Sabrina to follow her. Teddy got to his feet, too, but she cried, 'No, no, Mr Cazalet, you may not join the ladies yet!'

Teddy was about to retort that he had been taught to stand whenever ladies got up to leave a room, but then he saw that Reggie had not moved, was engaged upon pouring port, and decided to say nothing. He did not wish to embarrass his host.

As it turned out, this proved to be quite a difficult thing to do. Reggie handed him a glass, and belched loudly. 'Well, that's better out than in. Now. Let's see if you know what this is.'

'It's port. Isn't it?'

'Of course it's port. Try it.'

Teddy sipped. It made him think of very dark red velvet and was intoxicatingly good. He said as much, but

Reggie retorted, 'Ah! But that's not good enough, young man. Whose port?'

'Cockburn?' he hazarded.

'Not bad. You're right there. But what year?'

Teddy thought furiously. ''Twenty-nine?'

'Got you! It's 'twenty-seven. Although, I'll grant you, 'twenty-nine's not a bad choice.' He took a huge swig. 'My opinion of you has gone up,' he said, and at once began an attack of hiccups.

Teddy offered water, but he waved it away. 'Never touch the stuff.' He leaned over, so close to Teddy that he could see the riot of hairs in his nostrils.

'Give me a good thump on the back.' Teddy did. 'Harder!' He did it again. 'That's better.' He emptied his glass. 'The port is with you.' It wasn't, but Teddy did an imaginary circle of the table and the decanter ended up two inches from where it had started.

'You pour out.' He had the kind of very bushy eyebrows that were designed either for insensate rage or overwhelming benevolence. 'I'm coming to think quite well of you. Cockburn, and then only two years off. Drink up, boy.' He took another large swig, which meant that he got a bit further away, which was good, because his breath was hideous. There had been three wines at dinner and Teddy began to feel that he was very nearly drunk. He suggested that perhaps they should join the others, but Reggie hadn't finished with him.

'I suppose you've come down here because you want to marry my daughter.'

'Yes, I have. I do.'

'Thought so. I'm never wrong. Well, young feller, you'll have a job pulling that off. I'm a broad-minded sort of chap, and provided you've got a good job, with good prospects, and can afford to keep her in the circumstances to which she's accustomed I might be open to some agreement. No – I'm by no means the nigger in the woodpile. It's the missus. It's Pearl. She's set her heart on Sabrina marrying up. She keeps asking young Lord Ilchester down for weekends, but he's so wet you could shoot snipe off him, and Sabrina hasn't taken to him at all.'

'That's because she's in love with me.'

Reggie, who had poured himself a glass unashamedly full to the brim, waved this assertion aside. 'She's threatened to cut her allowance – sanctions, you see. She won't manage long without it.' He now drank the contents of his glass at one go.

'She's trying to get a job,' Teddy said. 'She's done one or two.'

'Hasn't kept them, though, has she?'

'I don't think she's found the right one yet.'

'She's not made for work, boy. And she's too young to be married without our consent.' He reached for the decanter again, and poured its remains rather sloppily into his glass. 'And that's not all,' he said thickly. 'A little bird's told me that all is not tickety-boo with your family's firm. I notice you haven't mentioned that.'

'I haven't, because it's news to me. Who told you?'

Reggie laid one finger against the side of his nose. 'Ah! That would be telling.' He took another gulp. 'If I want to find anything out, I can usually find the right person to tell me. Usually.' He finished his drink. 'Always. I'm very 'fluenshall man – the Shitty, politics, you name it.' But Teddy didn't have a chance to do that because, with another immense belch, Reggie collapsed, his head and arms spread upon the table.

Teddy looked at him with dismay. He shook Reggie's

439

shoulder tentatively, but the only response was a steady, stertorous snore. After a minute or two, he left the room and escaped to the library, where he discovered Mrs F, as he privately called her, embroidering a piece of canvas that had two Christmas trees and a gnome on it. Sabrina was biting her nails.

'Mummy, I've told you, I can't bear him—' They both stopped when they saw him.

'I'm afraid he's passed out. Gone to sleep,' Teddy added, to make it sound better.

'Sabrina, ring the bell for George.'

When George arrived he was told to get another servant and put the master to bed. 'I simply cannot imagine why you let him drink so much.'

'*You* can't stop him so I don't see why you should blame Teddy.'

Teddy, who was feeling slightly dizzy, made for a chair and collapsed into it. He felt grateful to Sabrina for standing up for him.

Pearl had got to her feet: she said she was going to bed and that Sabrina should go up, too, as she would be called at six. Then she left the room.

'I expect you can see now why I wasn't keen on you meeting the Frankensteins. They really are simply the end, aren't they? No wonder Daddy drinks so much. I would if I was married to Pearl.'

'I'm afraid she doesn't like me.'

'Well, she wouldn't, would she? You haven't got a title and you're not in line for one.'

She looked so sad when she said this that Teddy got up to put an arm round her. 'As long as you like me, I don't care what she thinks.'

'I do like you, awfully.' She put her face up to him so that he could kiss her a little.

'Darling, why don't you skip hunting tomorrow and stay here with me?'

'I can't do that! It's all been arranged. Mummy would be absolutely furious!' She was silent for a moment while she extricated herself from his arms. 'Anyway, I love hunting – and riding generally. It's the only thing I like about being here. I'll be back about four thirty – we'll go for a lovely walk in the park.'

'What park?' Teddy asked petulantly. A stupid question because it really didn't matter – the point was that she was abandoning him. And the worst thing about it was that she didn't seem to realise it or, even worse, seemed not to care. He wanted to be in bed, by himself, in the comforting dark, no more challenges to deal with. 'I'm going to bed. And I think you should, too, if you're getting up at six.'

∞ ∞ ∞

His bed had been turned down, his pyjamas laid out elaborately as if to remind him of what shape he was, and in the adjoining bathroom his toothbrush was already decorated with paste. The bedside table had a small lamp and a carafe of water topped with a tumbler. His mouth felt like hot fitted carpet, so he drank two glasses, got into bed and turned off the light.

In the dark, he struggled for a while with images from the evening, like stills from a film, flickering across his brain: preposterous Reggie, with all his contacts and money, who had seemed to let his vulgarity off its leash the moment the women had left the dining room, blustering, hectoring, patronising. In spite of all that, he had felt sorry for the old man, whose ghastly wife had dragged him down to such depths of gentility that, refusing to sink, he was ill-equipped to swim. What he had said about the family firm surfaced and disturbed him. Surely Uncle Hugh would have said something about it last Thursday, but he had only repeated that Teddy might very soon be needed in London. On the other hand, he did not think that Reggie had been bluffing. Then there was Sabrina, who had shown most clearly that she was both spoiled and selfish. It was strange that she could be so rude to her mother and also be so terrified of her. One might become mildly bored with one's parents as one got older – a flash of his mother sitting in her gloomy little house came to him, with the customary shot of guilt that he didn't make enough effort to see her – but, then, since he had moved to the country, he hardly saw his father at all, which he missed. He had loved to go shooting with Dad, to play squash and tennis with him, to have festive meals at the Thames Yacht Club; none of that had happened for a long time now, largely, of course, because of his being moved to bloody Southampton. He would make a point of seeing Dad and telling him that he wasn't up to managing there: selling was his strong point, administration was not. This resolution cheered him – but then he thought of the day and, worse, the evening ahead.

∞ ∞ ∞

He woke late – after nine – with a raging thirst and a headache, the signs of a hangover. He ran himself a very hot bath, rummaged in the bathroom cupboard and found some Alka Seltzer. The bath, followed by a cold shower, made him feel much better, but it also came to him that, of course, he was going to have to put up with another evening: it was only Saturday. He had to stick it out, if only for Sabrina's sake . . . During those hours: a hearty breakfast, a walk in the park – it was a bright shiny day and there had been a frost, a few disconsolate deer picking at the crunchy grass, and loudly complaining crows – coming back for his solitary lunch, game pie and Stilton, nothing to drink, thank you, and an impressive array of Saturday newspapers that he skimmed in the library.

He thought about Sabrina lustfully – he had never seen her wonderful breasts naked – her silky hair, strands of which kept falling over her face, her long white neck, her tiny waist, elegant knees and pretty ankles; and then, protectively, of the way she swung from a childish cockiness when she landed a job to bewilderment when she lost it. She did not understand advice – seemed to regard it as something critical that people said to her – but she was far from stupid. She read voraciously and kept a notebook, which she had once let him look at. It was full of essays and criticism: 'A comparison of the strengths and weaknesses of Trollope and Dickens'; 'The Brontë sisters: a reappraisal of Anne – too long demoted to third place'; 'The genius of Evelyn Waugh – virtuoso of inference through pure dialogue', and so on. She'd snatched it away at this point and said sadly, 'It's all about novels. It wouldn't interest you.'

He remembered yet again how much he had loved her then. How angry he had felt that her wretched parents had prevented her going to university, which was the only thing she had wanted; he found now that he was even forgiving her for leaving him to ride with her parents. She had said that her father might cut her off, and that she needed money to 'pay things'. He wondered for a moment whether she would elope with him, then realised that this was out of the question if things were going wrong with the firm and that, therefore, he might lose his job. To take his mind off this, he resorted to the newspapers, and read about Donald Campbell breaking his own speed record on water by achieving 248.62 miles per hour . . .

And then they were back, cold, rosy (in the case of Mrs F's nose unfortunately so) and, after a good deal of stamping about in the hall, they streamed into the library where an enormous tea appeared like magic. Crumpets, boiled eggs, scones, hot chocolate, several cakes, coffee éclairs and, of course, tea. Perhaps this meal was intended to replace dinner, Teddy thought with some hope, but that was dashed when Pearl announced that she had asked Lord Ilchester to dine. Sabrina rolled her eyes at him, and Reggie didn't seem pleased either, but this, of course, made no difference, and Teddy resigned himself to a different sort of awful evening.

∞ ∞ ∞

Ilchester was tall, with not very much blond hair, rather bulbous pale blue eyes and a falsetto laugh, which erupted after almost anything he said. He asked Teddy why he had not been hunting, and before he could answer, Mrs F replied that Mr Cazalet did not ride. 'Oh, I say, hard luck! What do you do in winter, then? I must say I'd be totally lost without something to do.' He laughed at such an idea.

'Teddy works, Ticky,' Sabrina said, with emphasis. 'He has a job – he earns his living.'

But her mother cut in sharply: 'Of course, some people have to do that. It takes all sorts to make a world.'

Reggie, who had been refilling glasses, stood up for him, too: 'He prefers shooting, and I bet he's a damn good shot.'

'Really? I'd no idea you'd brought your guns with you, Mr Cazalet.'

At that moment dinner was announced.

While they ate potted shrimps, roast pheasant and a cold lemon soufflé, it was Mrs F who dominated the conversation: she praised her daughter's horsemanship, said how exhausting it must be to manage the Ilchester estates – 'Two thousand acres, isn't it, Ticky?' – to which he replied that it was nearly three, actually, and laughed at the idea, and she proceeded to commiserate with him about the difficulty of getting landsmen and tenant farmers. 'By Jove! It's certainly that! Servants of any kind! I had a devil of a job to find a person to look after my aunt Agatha – she lives at Ilchester Court. I had to interview three women before I found someone suitable. Frightful problem! Quite difficult to please an aunt, don't you know.'

By now Teddy was wishing he possessed the wit of Oscar Wilde, but he couldn't think of any ripostes that would fit. 'Some aunts are tall, some aunts are small; it is surely a matter for an aunt to decide for herself,' cruised through his head. Better just eat and be careful not to drink too much . . .

Fortunately for him, Mrs F was determined to thwart Reggie in any attempt at a serious port-drinking session. 'Reggie, darling, I've arranged for the gentlemen to join us in the drawing room for port and coffee. We don't see Ticky very often and don't want to waste him.' She smiled at Ticky, who laughed (brayed, really, Teddy thought).

Nobody else smiled. Reggie's face showed a conflict of emotion. He had been looking forward to a men's drinking session but, on the other hand, it was clear that he had nothing at all to say to Ilchester. He shrugged the rich red-velvet shoulders of his smoking jacket and made some show of getting to his feet.

The library drum table was laid out with coffee and three tiny glasses of port; no sign of a bottle. Teddy saw Reggie shoot his wife a look of pure hatred, but he said nothing, busied himself offering gigantic cigars to Ilchester, who refused, choosing a herbal cigarette from a gold case. It smelt awful – rather like poor-quality hash.

'Do, everybody, help yourselves to coffee.' And Pearl took up her needlework. The coffee cups were tiny, like the port glasses – a doll's set, Teddy thought – and while Pearl was bent over her awful cushion cover, he managed to slip Reggie his port – the eyebrows went ultra-benevolent then. Emboldened by a third glass – he had swiped Ilchester's while he was lighting another herbal cigarette – he embarked upon a cross-examination of Ilchester about his politics. What did he think about all these cheap homes the government were planning to build?

Clearly taken aback, Ilchester said, 'First I've heard about it. Are they really? Where's the money to come from? Out of our pockets, you can be sure of that.'

'My friend – he's a junior minister in the government – takes a poor view of it all. What's your view? I don't see the House of Lords likely to welcome it.'

'I don't suppose they will much care for it, no. My chaps are all in tied cottages, you see, so the problem doesn't arise. 'Fraid I don't know much about that sort of thing.'

The rest of the evening was predictably awful. Ilchester went early, which should have been a relief but it allowed Reggie to take sweet revenge on his wife. 'Where are you going, Reggie?'

'None of your business, but as a matter of fact I'm off to my study. Goodnight, all.' His eyebrows were in angry mode. She wasn't going to stop him drinking – not she.

His behaviour clearly upset Mrs F. Shortly afterwards, she packed up her sewing and left them, telling Sabrina that she should go to bed after the early start that morning.

'She's gone to hunt him down. They'll have a ghastly row.'

'Oh, darling, do you mind?'

'Not much. Only I don't want Daddy to be in a bad temper tomorrow because I still haven't asked him for the money I need. But if he goes shooting with you, he'll probably get into a better temper.'

This was going to be difficult. 'I haven't had a chance to tell you, but I'm leaving tomorrow after breakfast. Of course you can come with me, darling.'

There was a silence. 'Why?' she said. 'You never said you were going to do that! And you know I can't!'

'Why can't you come back with me?'

'Teddy, I've told you. I can't go back to London until Daddy has given me some money. Anyway, why are you going?'

He decided to tell her: 'Your mother's been so offensive to me that I have to go.'

'What did she say?'

'She said, "If you think you can worm your way into this house in order to form some liaison with my daughter, you are very much mistaken."'

'When on earth did she manage to say that?'

'She came to my room before dinner, knocked on the door, said it, and went. Satisfied?'

She burst into tears. 'It's not my fault they're so awful!' she sobbed. 'It's not my fault that they won't let me do the only thing I might be good at – that they've brought me up to be useless, only good for marriage and breeding!'

Teddy took her in his arms (she always let him do that when she cried), and he did his best to soothe her. 'As soon as you're old enough we'll get married, and if you still want to go to university, you shall.'

This prospect pleased her; when he pushed her hair out of her eyes and kissed her, she did not resist.

'I think your father quite likes me. I told him I wanted to marry you, and he said that as long as I was earning enough to keep you in the manner to which you're accustomed, he might consider it. But,' he added quickly, 'it might take me some time to do that.'

'Oh, you mustn't bother about it. I can cook eggs, and we could go to very cheap restaurants and we could do without a car and just take taxis.'

He let her chatter herself into some optimism about the future while revealing her frighteningly shaky grasp of reality and any of the practices it required.

He decided to leave before breakfast. It would mean that he need not see either of the Frankensteins again and go through the farce of thanking them for a lovely weekend.

∞ ∞ ∞

He was so anxious to escape undetected that he rose at six thirty. He left a note under Sabrina's door and slipped out of the house. It was almost dark when he left and extremely cold – the massive trees that lined the drive, still darker than the sky, dripped rain portentously on the roof of his car and a few reckless rabbits ran wildly across his headlights.

He had to stop for petrol, and it was then that he wondered where he was going – where he ought to go. He had been going to spend the evening with Sabrina in the Frankensteins' flat, but that was out of the question now. All the same, he couldn't face returning to his dismal flat in Southampton; he decided instead to go to Louise and tell her his troubles. She might know more than he about what was happening to Cazalets'. Anyway, she would cheer him up.

∞ ∞ ∞

She took a long time to answer the doorbell, and he was just about to give up when she opened the door. 'Oh, Ted! How lovely! I hadn't got up because I hate dreary Sundays on my own.' She was wearing men's pyjamas of grey silk, and her blonde hair was in a thick plait hanging down her back. They climbed the three flights of stairs to the top floor, which contained a kitchen and a violently painted dining room, walls of a deep Suffolk pink and scarlet woodwork. 'Matthew Smith came to supper and loved it,' she said, when he whistled.

'Some décor!'

They settled at the small kitchen table and she made some very good coffee. 'Joseph is taking me to Paris again next weekend, so I'm in a very good mood. How was your weekend with the Frankensteins?'

'Very Frankensteinian. I came back this morning because I couldn't stand it any longer.'

'Oh, do tell. It sounded pretty grim when you first told me about them.'

So he described some of what it had been like. 'She was not simply a snob, as Sabrina had warned me, she was a poisonous bitch.'

'And what about Sabrina? You haven't said anything about her.' There was a pause while he thought what to say, but she interrupted, 'Have you been to bed with her, Ted?'

He felt himself going red. 'No. No, I haven't. The bitch of a mother has put the fear of God into Sabrina about sex. She has to be a virgin until marriage. She's a lapsed Catholic, but she's kept the awful parts. You know, hellfire and all that. It's awful, but I've learned that I can't do anything about it.'

'Do you love her?'

'Of course I do!'

'Because sometimes one thinks one loves somebody because one can't have them.'

'Is that how you are with Joseph?'

She looked away from him then. 'That's sharp of you. Yes, I expect it is. I didn't think I wanted to marry anyone after making such a mess with Michael, but I seem to be changing about that. I can't do anything about it. Joseph will never leave his wife. They both have affairs and keep up the happy family life – have it both ways, in fact. That's why I asked you whether you loved Sabrina.'

'I told her father that I wanted to marry her when she was old enough, and he didn't seem entirely against that. Said his wife would be, of course. And said I would have to be earning enough to keep his daughter in the manner to which she's accustomed. Which I'm certainly not doing now. He also said that there were rumours that Cazalets' is in trouble. Do you know anything about that?'

'Well, according to Joseph, it is. He tried to advise Dad and Uncle Hugh, but they wouldn't listen, or Uncle Hugh wouldn't. Now he says it's too late. The firm will go bankrupt.'

'Oh, Lord! I'll be out of a job, then.'

'It looks like it. I'm sorry, Teddy.'

There was a silence while he absorbed the shock. 'It makes me bloody angry,' he said at last. 'They haven't told me anything – even when I tried to ask. The most Uncle Hugh said was that I might be moved to London. I've been expected to manage a wharf and sawmill, which I was afraid I wasn't up to, but I have tried and I've got better at it. But they've never taken me into their confidence. It's like flying a Spitfire and not being able to vote.' A thought struck him then: 'They'll be out of a job! All those men – mostly with families to support. It's a disaster!'

'I'm going to make us some lunch. Scrambled eggs and smoked salmon do you?'

'Lovely.'

While she cooked, she told him that of course he would get another job; that in all probability a rival firm would take over and would want him to continue.

'But I couldn't possibly do that! Dad and Uncle Hugh would regard that as treachery. They would insist on the family sticking together.'

'Ted, what nonsense. The family will have nothing to stick to. And Dad and Uncle Hugh will be worse off than you. Who's going to give them a decent job after this? How is Dad going to keep Diana in mink dressing gowns and feather-boa-encrusted tops?' (They'd always joked about Diana's requirements.)

'Not to mention the little tiara she'd set her heart on for Christmas. And Rupe! What will he do? He's got a mortgage and two children. It's much worse than I thought.'

'Eat your nice lunch. It's not so awful being poor. I often am.'

'I'm sure your Joseph would get you a nicer flat.'

'He's tried to, but I don't want one. I may be a mistress, but I won't be a tart. I get a certain number of free clothes, and if I don't like them, I flog them and buy things I do like. Stella says I'm wicked, but with integrity.'

During lunch he asked if he could stay the night so that he could confront the bosses in the morning, and she replied that he could, but he'd have to stay on the top floor when Joseph arrived. 'He comes straight up from the country after an early dinner and we go to bed for a bit and then he goes home.'

'When do you have dinner? Couldn't I take you out? If you'll lend me the money.'

'I don't usually have dinner on Sundays. And, no, you

can't take me out because I never know when he's coming.'

After lunch, she fetched a Li-lo, which he blew up while she got him blankets and a pillow. 'Afraid there aren't any sheets. Stella and I have only got two pairs each. I'll leave a note for Stella to warn her you're here. I could give you a key and you could go out to eat, or to the cinema in Baker Street. I'm going to have a long, hot bath now. Have you got any money?'

'I'm always borrowing money off you,' he said sheepishly, as he shook his head.

'But you always pay me back, darling Ted. Will a fiver do?'

'Marvellous. Oh! Have you by any chance got a novel by Jane Austen?'

'I don't know. All the books I have are on that shelf. Why do you want one?'

'Sabrina likes them, and I thought it would be good if I had a go.' A fiver wasn't really enough for the cinema and supper, and he thought he could read while he ate. He found a battered paperback, *Pride and Prejudice*. 'I'll read it however boring it is,' he said to himself.

As he left the flat, the smell of turkeys pervaded the bottom flight of stairs, and their singed feathers were everywhere.

I might easily end up living somewhere worse than this, he thought, and his respect for Louise increased. It was still early for dinner, so he went to a pub in Marylebone High Street, got himself half a pint of beer and began to tackle the book. It turned out not to be boring at all.

RUPERT AND ARCHIE

'It's happened.'

'You were afraid it might.'

'I was sure it would. Just a question of when.'

They were in Archie's studio, which was unusually warm because he had a sitter that afternoon who wanted to be painted in evening dress.

Rupert was unwrapping the two baguettes he had bought. He handed one to Archie.

'God! You have to have a jaw like an alligator to bite through all this.' Small ribbons of tired lettuce began escaping from his initial effort. 'There's some ham somewhere if you keep at it.'

'Have you had any ideas about what you want to do?' Archie asked this question carefully: he didn't want to harass his old friend.

'As a matter of fact, I've had an enormous idea, but I'm not sure what you will think about it.' He put his baguette down on the nearest surface – a table covered with dried paint. 'Will you just hear me out before you say anything?'

'Go ahead.'

'I had a long talk with Zoë last night, and she's all for it. Of course I don't know how Clary will feel about it.'

'It?'

'You said you wouldn't interrupt.'

'Sorry.'

'You see, I don't want to hurt your feelings – but we have a house that is far too big for us and we shan't be able to afford it. And I imagine it's getting to be a pretty tight squeeze for you in your flat. So, we thought, how would it be if you moved in with us and you and I ran painting courses? You could have the whole top floor to yourselves and we'll share the rest of the house with you. The children can go to Georgie's school, and the girls can sort out the domestic arrangements. You could either sell your flat or, better still, rent it, so if things didn't work out you wouldn't have burned your bridges. That's what I – we – thought. So will you at least think about it?'

He was already thinking about it. It was true that his flat was too small; the children had to share a bedroom and that was making friction. They couldn't afford to move somewhere larger: although Clary's play was getting a tour of the provinces, a return to London was far from certain, and therefore it was not yet producing a serious income. The children adored Georgie and his zoo, and Clary and Zoë were undoubtedly fond of each other. It would be wonderful to have a students' class with Rupe; they had always enjoyed painting together, talking about it and having the occasional argument. On the other hand, sharing a house was known to be tricky – particularly for the women. He found himself hoping that Clary would think it a good idea. He said as much to Rupert, who looked relieved that his scheme had passed the first post. 'We could use the enormous drawing room on the first floor as a teaching studio.'

Then Archie's sitter arrived, and Rupert had to go.

∞ ∞ ∞

When Archie got home, Clary was washing up last night's supper and the morning's breakfast. Strands of her hair had escaped the elastic band that was supposed to hold it back. Sounds of Elvis Presley streamed down from above. 'It's one thing they agree about,' Clary said. 'I'm afraid I'm a bit behind.' She nearly always said that because she nearly always was. 'And all they want for Christmas is a dog and a cat. That would be all we need. Oh, Archie! I haven't got them to bed, and I haven't done the potatoes or the cabbage, and we've run out of eggs because I forgot. Sorry I'm such a rotten wife.'

'I've brought a bottle of wine,' he said, as he stooped to kiss her hot face. 'I'll settle the horrors, and then we'll have a lovely drink. I've got some interesting news for you.'

'Oh, do tell!'

'No. Not till we have some peace and quiet.'

∞ ∞ ∞

'Gosh!' she said when he did tell her. 'What did you say?'

'I said, of course, that I must consult you.'

'And here you are consulting me.' This clearly pleased her. 'They've got a washing-machine,' she said. 'Would we have any private time?'

'Of course we would. Rupe said we could have the whole of the top floor to ourselves.' He told her about the idea of him and Rupert running student courses. 'And we could let the flat so if it didn't work we could always come back.'

'We'd have to pay them rent,' she said.

'Of course. But we'd have the rent money plus what I earn.'

'What we both earn.'

'What we both earn, darling.'

She held out her glass for more wine. 'You won't fall in love with Zoë, will you?'

'As long as you promise me not to fall in love with your dad.'

She blushed. In spite of how good he had been about the 'affair' with Quentin, she still felt ashamed. She looked at him now across the table; he could see her eyes filling with tears. 'I'll never fall in love with anyone excepting you.'

'I'm delighted to hear it. Do you want to sleep on this idea, and tell me in the morning what you think?'

'I want to sleep,' she said.

When they were up from the table, he untied her very dirty apron.

'It's funny,' she said, 'how this apron always seems to have tomato sauce on it – even when I'm not using it. It's like toast crumbs in bed when you're ill and only having soup.'

So they went up, and he said, 'Well, I could in truth say, "Here is Mrs Lestrange. She looks much better without any clothes."'

457

RACHEL

Ever since they had come for the weekend to tell her, she had existed in a kind of frozen panic. She had never imagined that Home Place would be wrested from her. Her father had bought it in 1928 because the Duchy had so much hated London. That had been in the days when she had run the Babies' Hotel, when she had travelled by train three days a week with him to work and back on the four thirty to Battle.

That had been when she'd met Sid, through Myra Hess, as Sid's sister had been her secretary, and brought her down for a weekend when Myra and the Duchy had played duets. It had been the beginning of her and Sid falling in love, although at the time she had not known that. Then there had been the war, and the Babies' Hotel was evacuated well before the Blitz had razed the original establishment in the East End to the ground. It had been a time when more and more of the family had moved into the house, when Sybil had had one twin and lost the other. A time when Sid had declared her love and she had thought she reciprocated . . . How little she had known then about love!

In spite of the war it had been a happy time; she loved her brothers and their wives, and adored the children, and the house had welcomed them all. It had been easier then, because only one brother, Rupert, had been the right age for combat. There had not been the constant agony that they had endured about Hugh and Edward although there were losses enough: Sybil dying, Hugh's anguish, the destruction of the London sawmill and wharf, her growing fears for Sid who had driven an ambulance all over London, it seemed, but certainly where the Blitz was worst. The Duchy's three heroes – Toscanini, Mr Churchill and Gregory Peck – had sustained her serenity and teasing her about them was a merciful way of lightening the atmosphere. The Brig had given her the latest gramophone, the one with the enormous horn and wooden needles that could be reused if you pared them with a knife. The Duchy had immediately asked the young Jewish girls, training to be nurses, whom Myra had somehow got out of Germany to come for evenings of Toscanini, Beethoven symphonies and piano concerti. They would have tea and Marie biscuits for refreshment. They made good nurses, Matron had said, but the Duchy felt that they must be homesick. Rachel had tried asking one girl – Helga – if she missed her home and how she had got here. 'A man came one morning very early to our apartment and spoke to my mother when I was in bed. She came and made me put on two sets of clothes, vests, shirts, sweaters and my winter coat. Then she put her arms round me and said it wasn't safe for me there any more, and that a kind friend was going to put me on a train, that I was to say nothing and do everything he told me. I am lucky to be here,' she'd finished, as her tears fell. Rachel had hugged her and tried to find comforting things to say, but she could not think of any. There had been rumours of terrible and widespread ill-treatment of Jews but, to her, being torn from your family and not knowing when you might see

459

them again was horrible enough. The remembrance of that time pricked her already painful conscience. What she had to bear now was nothing to what those poor girls and, no doubt, countless others had gone through.

For the first few days Rachel had been so stunned at the thought of abandoning the house where she had lived for so long, where her mother and then her dearest Sid had died, that she had not begun to consider what was to become of her. She was naturally frugal, for years had spent her money on other people, and she had never given money a thought. But now she might have to. She had no idea what Sid's house (if she sold it) would bring her. She had no idea what was in her bank account. She had not even a very clear idea of what it cost to run Home Place, since Hugh paid all the expenses from the fund provided in equal shares by him, Rupert and herself. Now she might have to take paid work. When Sid had told her to find some work to fill her life, she had naturally thought of a charity she could support. But what could she do that anyone would pay her for? She could type with one finger – nobody would be interested in that. She could not cook, she could not drive; she had absolutely no qualifications, and this made her feel really frightened . . .

Just then, Hugh rang from London, which was a welcome relief. But her relief didn't last long. He had rung to say that the receivers had given them a month to get out of Home Place. He hated saying it, but she had to know. In fact, he'd managed to get them to agree to the 2nd of January, because he'd thought it would be good if they could have one last family Christmas there, but he wanted to know whether that was something she would like, or whether she felt it would be too much for her. If they came for about a week, it would enable him to discuss her future, which he particularly didn't want her to worry about. She did not hesitate. Of course she would love them to come for Christmas – all of them.

The moment he rang off, she remembered that she had meant to ask Hugh what would happen to Eileen and the Tonbridges. This had been worrying her ever since the bombshell had fallen. They were too old to get new jobs and as Eileen slept in the house, and the Tonbridges had the cottage above the stables, she was afraid that they would be not allowed to stay there. After their years of service to the family, she felt responsible for them. Eileen had a younger sister, a retired lady's maid, who lived in a flat in Hastings, and they occasionally had holidays together. But the Tonbridges! She wanted to buy them a cottage and she had already pledged to pay for Mrs Tonbridge's operation. She must find out how much money she had in her account.

She rang her bank, and found that she had nearly fifteen thousand pounds. Greatly cheered – it seemed an enormous amount – she rang Villy and asked if, sent a key, she would be kind enough to get a house agent round to value the Abbey Road house. As she lived so near, she might know which agent to go to, but not if it was too much trouble. Villy sounded so low, so unhappy, and at the same time so grateful to be asked that Rachel changed her mind, and ventured to wonder whether Villy could put her up for a night. 'Of course! Oh, Rachel, I'd simply love to see you!'

And so, dreading more bitter recriminations about Edward and 'That Woman', she went.

Villy looked awful. She wore cyclamen lipstick that made her complexion seem sallow and the dark circles under her swollen eyes look worse. They kissed warmly, and Villy led the way into the sitting room, which had a fireplace and drinks on a table in front of it.

'Something's the matter?' Rachel said, accepting a large drink.

'Yes. Miss Milliment has died.'

'Oh dear! I'm so sorry.'

'It's much worse than that. She died in a nursing home – I had to put her there because it got too dangerous to leave her on her own in this house, even for half an hour. She was demented, you see, hardly knowing me in the end. But she loathed it in the home, and she blamed me – my cruelty, my being uncaring for putting her there. Every time I visited, she cried and railed at me for my wickedness. The last time I saw her she recognised me and said, "Viola, you have betrayed me. I have loved you all my life, and I was wrong. You have never loved me. I do not know how to bear it. I cannot bear it." She was sobbing, and when I tried to hold her in my arms, she tore herself away. "Don't touch me – you devil. No love – no love at all. Go away, don't ever come back!"'

Tears were streaming down Villy's face, and Rachel knelt before her and held her shaking shoulders. 'She was demented, darling. You said that. And you were angelic to her. You gave her a home and looked after her. Of course she didn't mean all those horrible things she said. Of course you loved her and somewhere inside her she knew that. Oh, darling Villy, how awful for you!' And then, somehow, the thought flashed across her mind: supposing Sid had been demented, had said such things to her? Poor Villy, to be rejected for the second time in her life! And she was not bitter – she was only sad. How much easier that made it to try to comfort her.

But where was the comfort? Miss Milliment was dead; there could be no reconciling conversation – and, in any case, if someone was out of their mind, it was almost impossible to get them back into it. However, she tried to make Villy feel better, and in some part succeeded.

'Oh, Rachel! You're such a tower of strength! Enough about me. Tell me your news.' She had taken a paper handkerchief out of a box lying beside her chair and Rachel noticed that the wastepaper basket was already full of them. Villy offered her a cigarette, and she took it, in spite of only liking her Passing Clouds. 'You've decided to sell Sid's house.'

'Yes. As you know, I went back, and I discovered that I could not bear to live there. It was too full of sad things – the beginning of Sid being so ill and the time when we weren't talking about it. I don't know – I found that I just wanted to escape from it.'

'I do understand, darling. You want to stay in Home Place where you have always been happiest—'

'It seems that I cannot do that. I suppose you haven't heard what is happening with Cazalets'?'

A trace of the old bitterness: 'I have absolutely no idea,' she said coldly.

So Rachel told her. And Villy, always practical and intelligent, seemed to understand at once. 'Are they all losing their houses?'

'No. Luckily some lawyer or accountant advised my brothers to put their houses in their wives' names. But Home Place was bought by the Brig in the firm's name. I have to get out in the New Year.' Her voice was trembling as she tried to smile.

'Well, darling, I really do see how awful that is for you, but if you sell Abbey Road you'll be able to buy a little house in Sussex, and with all your shares you'll be able to live comfortably.'

'There won't be any shares. The firm is bankrupt. I shan't have an income from it – I'll have to get a job of some sort. But who is going to employ a woman of nearly sixty, who can't drive, or cook, or type?' She was silent for a moment, trying to quell the panic she always felt when she thought about it – which was almost always now.

Villy reached out and took her hand. 'Well, we must see how much you can get for the house. And you know you can always stay here as long as you want.'

The 'stay' hit her: she would still have nowhere to live, which was entirely different. But she said thank you, it was really kind.

They sat for a while with a second gin, which Rachel did not want, and while compassionate for each other, their own plight seemed worse now to each of them. Villy was grieving about Miss Milliment and lonely: Lydia had left some weeks ago to tour in Clary's play, so she was alone again, struggling to think how she might make Christmas less boring for Roland. And I'm sixty-two, she thought, too old for anything interesting to happen.

Rachel felt – although, of course, she was glad of it – that at least Villy had her own house and the income to live in it. And she had Roland, which must be lovely. She had lost the person she loved most in the world (and Sid had been only fifty when she died), whereas Villy's anger and resentment about Edward leaving her seemed the result of pride, rather than love.

But these thoughts were entirely concealed. They ate

macaroni cheese and stewed pears by the fire, and were kind to each other, as they smoked a last cigarette.

∞ ∞ ∞

The next morning they went to Sid's house, and Villy, appalled by its abandoned state, tactfully suggested that she should ask her daily, Mrs Jordan, to clean it before showing it to an agent. Meanwhile, she also thought that it might be a good idea for Rachel to clear the house of things that she wanted and that then they could decide what to do with the residue.

'The rest of Sid's clothes,' Rachel said. 'I'd be awfully grateful if you would stay with me while I do that. There's one old suitcase upstairs and I'll take it back to Home Place.'

So that happened. Villy asked her to stay another night, but Rachel said she had arranged to be met at Battle and so must catch the four thirty at Charing Cross. Villy said that she would deal with the house-cleaning and appoint an agent.

She could not have been kinder, Rachel thought, as she settled into her train. The main reason she wanted to get back was because she had the enormous Christmas party to deal with, and she felt very sad that Villy would be excluded from it.

Villy, emboldened by Rachel's courage, spent an awful evening clearing out Miss Milliment's clothes and few possessions: her lock-knit knickers, her woollen vests, washed until they were stiff and prickly, her battered egg-stained cardigans, her two smart outfits – bottle-green silk jersey and her fearful banana jacket and skirt.

She packed her mac, which had not kept out rain for decades, and her pathetically jaunty hats adorned with pheasant's feathers or artificial poppies, her sensible stockings that never stayed up, and her lace-up shoes, some with holes in their soles. Her possessions consisted of her wristwatch, an album full of photographs – there was a bearded tyrant who was clearly her father, her brothers, in sailor suits, in Oxford bags and V-necked pullovers, in army uniform; and then, by itself on a page, a tiny faded picture of a very small man with a fine head of hair and an anxious expression . . . She had no idea who he could have been. Then there were her books – poetry collections: Tennyson, Keats, Wordsworth, Walter Savage Landor, Blake and Housman. 'Eleanor Milliment' was written in each of them. Her prayer book contained notes of all the children she had taught, their birthdays and subsequent marriages, and sometimes their deaths, all written in a tiny black-ink hand.

It was dark by the time she finished, tired, dispirited, but also relieved; she would keep the books, and the album, but the rest had to go. The house was silent, so quiet that, from Miss Milliment's room, she heard a log fall from the fireplace in the sitting room. She missed Lydia very much: her theatre gossip, her excitement about the success of Clary's play. She had bought two chops for herself and Rachel, in case she had agreed to stay; she shut the door of Miss Milliment's room, with its chilly stale air, and went to the kitchen to grill her chop, which she decided to eat with bread and butter, and turned on the wireless for company. They were talking about Britain's first motorway, just opened by Mr Macmillan – an eight-mile bypass of Lancaster, 'a token of what was to come'. And the Queen, in Bristol, made the first trunk call, to Edinburgh where the Lord Provost was waiting to speak to her. The weather was expected to get colder, with periods of light rain and frost in some areas. There was just enough gin left for one small drink and she improved it with some dry Martini.

The news was followed by a concert of Mahler and Shostakovich; she did not care much for either of them, but it was better than silence.

PART TEN

NOVEMBER–DECEMBER 1958

PART TEN
NOVEMBER-DECEMBER 1992

EDWARD

On Monday morning the news about Cazalets' was out.

'I've asked for them to come to my office at eleven o'clock,' Hugh said to Edward. 'I was hoping you'd do the wharf in the afternoon. You're much better with the men than I am. Remember that strike you stopped when you went and talked to them? The powers that be have given us five weeks from now and I have negotiated three months' salary for senior staff. In the case of the staff at the wharf, I think you could tell them that there is a fair chance of some of them at least being taken on by whoever buys that set-up.' There was a pause, and then he said, 'I had young Teddy in here at nine o'clock. He seemed to know that things were on the blink and was angry that he had not been told. I've sent him off to Southampton with a note for McIver. I've told our accountant to come for this meeting in case there are questions about finance that we can't answer.'

'Right.'

The poor old boy looked dreadful – as though he'd been up all night. Which was almost true. His weekend with Diana had been a nightmare. It had taken until Saturday for her to understand that he had no money in the bank, and had only his salary – which he was also about to lose – to live on. In the end he had taken her by the shoulders and literally shaken her, yelling, 'I've got no money left! None!' The penny had finally dropped then. She had shrugged his hands off her shoulders – not difficult since he at once felt ashamed of assaulting her – and said coldly, 'Well, you'll have to get another job, won't you? And pretty damn quick.'

'Of course I've got to. But it won't be so easy at my age. I'm afraid we're going to have to sell this house and find somewhere more modest.'

'You seem to forget that this is my house, and I have no intention of selling it.'

A bombshell. Something awful that he had never expected, and the implication chilled him to the bone. 'Diana! You can't mean that. We're a partnership – married! If you refuse to sell this house, I shall become bankrupt.'

There was a silence. She had walked away from him to the French windows that looked onto the garden. Then, in a much softer, despairing voice, she said, 'I simply cannot understand how you have got into this awful mess so suddenly. It frightens me. It feels as though nothing is safe any more.'

He wanted to say, 'We have each other,' but the words died in his throat. That did not feel safe any more. Nevertheless, it was up to him. 'Darling,' he said carefully, 'I know this is an awful time for you. I know how much you love this house. I am determined to get another job. But I have debts to pay off – an overdraft at the bank, which is entirely my fault. I don't see how I can do that and pay for the upkeep of your house. I have wanted to give you everything, you see, and I've overreached myself.'

And, at that moment, the telephone rang, and Diana answered it.

'For you,' she said. 'A woman for you.' Her voice was dangerously calm.

'It's Rachel,' he said to Diana, who indicated that she knew. She helped herself to a cigarette and settled down to listen to the telephone conversation. This, he could sense at once, was going to be deeply embarrassing. Rachel always talked louder on the telephone than she did at any other time; she dropped her gentle drawl and became quite military.

'It's about Christmas! This house belongs to the firm, so I shall have to leave it in the New Year. So we've decided to have one last family Christmas, and I was wondering whether you and Diana would like to join us.' He glanced at Diana: it was clear that she had heard every word.

'That's extraordinarily sweet of you, darling. Could I think about it and let you know?'

'Well, yes, but could you not be too long about it? I have another idea I should like to put to you.'

'Of course. I'll ring you tomorrow morning.' The moment he had rung off, he realised that he had said nothing sympathetic about her having to leave Home Place. It must be horrible for her, and the least they could do would be to rally round.

'Poor Rachel,' he said. 'She's having to give up Home Place, which really has been her home for most of her life. So, you see, we're not the only ones.'

'But she has another house in London, doesn't she? The one that her little lesbian friend left her.'

'Yes, she has. But Hugh says she doesn't want to live in it.'

'Well, there you are. We are the only ones.'

473

'Oh, come on, Diana. I'll make us a Sunday special – it's nearly lunchtime so I'm calling a truce.'

'Oh, all right.' She rang the bell, and a flustered Mrs Atkinson answered it, wiping her hands on her apron.

'Mr Cazalet would like the juice of two oranges squeezed and some ice. Oh, and two cocktail glasses.'

But when he'd made the drink, he found that he didn't want it. He felt vaguely rotten, with a distant pain that he couldn't locate.

Lunch was worse. It was roast guinea fowl with Calvados, a purée of Jerusalem artichokes and creamed spinach. He tried a mouthful and gave up.

'What's the matter, darling?'

'Don't know. I just feel rotten. I'll take a couple of Alka Seltzers and lie down for a bit.'

'Want me to come?'

'No, no. You have your nice lunch. I'll have a kip.'

Diana explained that Mr Cazalet was not feeling well, and Mrs Atkinson rushed upstairs with a hot-water bottle and woke him up giving it to him. But he did sleep heavily until about six in the evening when Diana brought him a cup of tea and a ginger biscuit. 'Poor old boy,' she said. 'I've brought you a ginger biscuit because you liked them last time you had a tummy upset.' She was behaving as though there had never been a quarrel of any kind and he was grateful. He fell asleep again, and woke at two in the morning to find a cup of cold consommé by his bed and a note from her: 'Sleeping next door. Didn't want to wake you. Alarm set for seven. Love D.' His pain was gone, thank God, and he settled himself for more sleep. But sleep evaded him, and he began at once to worry. He started to tot up the possessions he could sell that would bring in a fair amount of cash. The Brig's guns, his Asprey watch, his gold and sapphire cufflinks, the Bentley, and finally his Gagliano violin. If he could find the right place to sell them, there should be enough money to tide him over. He began to think about what on earth he could do when he stopped being a timber merchant. His strong points, he thought weakly, were getting on well with practically anybody, and selling – he was certainly good at that.

The meeting in Hugh's office had been exactly as awful as they had expected. The office boy had been deputed to get the requisite number of chairs, but he hadn't and several of the men had had to stand. Edward had sat beside Hugh behind his desk. They had all filed into the room on time and sat or stood with resolutely expressionless faces.

'I'm afraid I have very bad news,' Hugh began. He went on to say that it was with great sorrow he had to tell them that Cazalets' was forced to go into receivership, which meant that six weeks from today everyone would be out of a job. He explained briefly why this was so. The bank would not honour any further loans and was calling in the money already loaned. Everybody would get one extra month's salary when the six weeks were up, and those who had been with the firm for more than ten years would get three months'. He could not begin to describe how he and his brothers had tried to avert this disaster, but they had failed. Here his voice nearly broke, and Edward saw that two of the secretaries were in tears. Hugh finished by saying what a wonderful team they had been, and that everyone could be sure of getting an excellent reference. Now, they might have questions and he would do his best to answer them.

There was an uneasy silence. Then Crowther, from

Accounts, asked whether Cazalets' would be bought by another timber firm. Hugh replied that he had no knowledge of this, but that of course it was possible. Miss Corley, the senior secretary, rose to her feet to say that she spoke for everyone in the room when she said what a pleasure it had been working for Mr Hugh, Mr Edward and Mr Rupert. There was a wave of weak clapping – not from all – and Rupert observed that his new secretary, Doris, did not join in. He had spent most of the meeting looking out of the window at the motionless plane trees, and wondering if he could paint the vista: the elegance of the bare branches against the weary grey sky . . . a sombre picture.

People were shaking hands with his brothers, then turning to him. He wondered whether he was the only person in the room who felt a certain relief that all this was coming to an end. Life would be tougher from now on, but exciting. Archie and Clary were putting their flat on the rental market immediately, and planning to move in before Christmas.

For Christmas they were all going down to Home Place – the last Christmas there. Poor Rach! But she did have Sid's house in London. Unable to face a gloomy lunch with his brothers, he decided to give Archie a ring to see when he could meet him at the studio flat to make a list of what he and Clary needed to take to Mortlake.

'If I'm doing the wharf today, I'll just grab a sandwich.' He looked at Hugh, who had been rubbing the side of his head with his good hand – a sure sign that it was aching badly. 'Why don't you pack it in for the day, old boy?'

'Out of the question. I have a great many letters to write, and I'll have to go down to Southampton tomorrow. I feel pretty bad about McIver and must see him.'

Alone, Hugh took a couple of painkillers, washed down with an old, rather dusty glass of water, and lay back in his chair to give them a chance to work. He still felt awful. As though he had been put in charge of a whole small world and let down every single person in it. Fragments of this anxiety kept coming to the fore, confronting him with his hopeless inadequacy. It was true that, unlike Edward, he had been careful with his finances, had taken out the right insurances and always saved. But Rachel! He did not have enough money to give her a steady allowance. For one wild moment he had thought of buying Home Place, his family living there with her. But even if he did that, there would not be enough money to keep it up. The new roof had taken every penny in the pot contributed to by himself, Rachel and Rupert. He was sixty-two and, apart from serving in the Army during the First World War, he only had experience in timber. It just might get him a job of a humbler sort in another timber firm, but at the moment he had neither the heart nor the will to continue speculating.

After a while, when his headache had temporarily subsided, he got out his cheque book and wrote a cheque to Rachel for fifty pounds towards Christmas at Home Place.

Then he put in a call to Polly, and told her the bad news. He asked – almost begged – her to join the family at Christmas. She said she would have to discuss it with Gerald, but she thought it would be all right. 'And Simon, of course,' he said.

'Of course. One thing. I might have to bring Nan

because she can't stay here on her own. She'll help with the children – she loves that. Poor Dad! What an awful time you must be having. I'm coming! Got to go, Dad. I'll ring you this evening.'

Cheered by this, he rang for Miss Corley, who arrived with a plate of egg sandwiches and a pot of coffee. 'I realised you didn't go out to lunch. I cancelled your appointment with Colonel Marsh and made a list of the people you're most likely to want to write to.' Her pale grey watery eyes were rimmed with red, but she was all set to be businesslike now.

He thanked her for the sandwiches and began to eat them while he looked at the list. 'We can send the same letter to a good many of these.'

'Perhaps you'd rather have your luncheon in peace.'

'No, thank you, Miss Corley. I'd rather get on with it.'

He realised, almost at once, that he felt better with something to do. He started by dictating the more general letter, and ticked the names that were to receive it. The more personal ones would be more difficult. The *Timber Trades Journal* rang to speak to Mr Cazalet, and the telephonist put them through. They had, of course, heard the sad news about Cazalets' and wondered whether Mr Cazalet would like to make a statement.

Hugh, who hated this sort of thing, said that naturally everyone connected with the firm was most concerned, and that when the business was sold, he very much hoped that many of his excellent staff would be re-employed. He had no further comment.

He put back the receiver to realise that tears were coursing down Miss Corley's peach-powdered cheeks.

'Oh, Mr Hugh! So many years I've worked for you. I could never work for anyone else now! Never ever! I feel as though my life is coming to an end.' Here she began sniffing and blowing her nose. 'I'm ever so sorry – I had a good cry in the ladies', but there was a queue so I couldn't stay. I'm ever so sorry, please disregard me – I hope I've always given satisfaction?'

'Always, Miss Corley. I couldn't have had a better secretary and helpmeet. I shall give you a reference that makes all that clear.'

She gave a great gasp, but managed not to succumb to a second outburst. Instead she blew her nose again and spoke far more quietly: 'I don't need one. I've got too old to cope with those young girls in the office. Always chattering about their love life, and most of them can't spell for toffee. In my day, work was work, and play was play.'

She didn't look as though she had had much of the latter, Hugh thought. He was feeling dreadfully sorry for her.

'I suppose,' she went on, tentative now, even shy, 'that when you start your new occupation, you will need someone, and then perhaps you would bear me in mind?'

'Of course,' he replied. 'I most certainly shall. And now I think the best thing would be for you to type all the formal letters while I make rough drafts of the others.'

When she had gone he reflected upon the ways in which she had irritated him for years: her exaggeratedly quiet speech and movements when he had one of his heads coming – this was entirely unreasonable of him, he knew; the way in which she always picked up his telephone and made it clear to the caller that it would be difficult to talk to Mr Cazalet as he was extremely busy, even when he wasn't. And the maddening nursery voice she had put on to his children on the rare occasions that they had come to the office. But in so many ways she had been the perfect secretary: never forgot anything, was always tactful at reminding him when deadlines fell due; her impeccable letters, her punctuality, her general reliability. He could not recall her ever being off sick . . . She must have been on holiday when he had employed Jemima. That had been a piece of extraordinary luck. It made him smile to remember it now. A need to go home to her came over him; to have tea with her and pretend to help Laura with her homework . . . He had invented a cunning ploy to make her do her arithmetic by getting her to ask him a question: 'What are three nines?' And he would say, 'Seventy-four.' And then she would laugh at him and get the right answer. He longed now to be home for that. But it was only half past three, and he always worked until five . . . He pulled a piece of headed paper onto his blotter and began to write.

RACHEL AND EDWARD

'Edward! How absolutely lovely! There's a fire in the morning room, although it isn't going very well. Would you like a drink?' He kissed her, and her body underneath the thick cardigan and shawl felt like a bird's.

'I'd love some whisky, if you have it.'

'Oh, yes! I've been getting in the drink for Christmas.' She rang the bell, and Eileen, who had heard the car, arrived.

'Hello, Eileen. How are you?'

'Keeping nicely, Mr Edward.'

They all loved Edward, Rachel thought. She ordered the whisky and asked him to stoke the fire. A flurry of little frowns came and went on her face – 'her monkey face', her brothers had called it – when she had something difficult to say.

'I'm sorry I couldn't talk more on the telephone, and you said you had something to tell me, so I thought I'd pop in this evening. So, fire away, darling.'

'Well. As you know, this is going to be the last family Christmas here, and I wanted everyone to come. Villy has been most kind helping me with the sale of Sid's house, and it occurred to me that she might like to come down to Home Place and bring Roland for Christmas. I haven't asked her yet, because I wanted to know how

481

you and Diana would feel about it. That's what I wanted to ask you.'

Here, Eileen brought the drinks and Rachel asked him to pour them. 'A very small one for me.'

'Will Mr Edward be staying for dinner?'

'I'm afraid not,' he said. 'Say when.'

'Oh, stop there. That's the most enormous whisky.' She offered him a Passing Cloud.

'No, thanks. I'll stick with my gaspers. We wouldn't be able to stay with you,' he began carefully. 'Susan has a friend from school staying with us. Her parents are in India. Perhaps we might come to lunch or something. Anyway, if you're having all the rest of the family, you really won't have room, will you?'

'Most of the children are bringing sleeping-bags but, yes, even then we shall be a tight fit. But what do you think of my asking Villy? With Miss Milliment gone – oh, yes, didn't you know? – I think she will be rather on her own.'

'I don't know – Diana—'

But she interrupted him: 'I don't want to know about Diana. I want to know about you – how you would feel.'

He felt cornered. He *was* cornered. He knew he would feel guilty seeing Villy again after such a long time. He would feel guilty about Roland, whom he hardly ever saw since she had done her level best to make it awkward for him to spend much time with him; those dutiful lunches during school terms – the same questions asked, the same replies given – smoked salmon being the highlight for Roland, his formal gratitude for a ten-shilling note being the – rather dimmer – highlight for him.

'We couldn't stay anyway,' he repeated. 'Diana – well, she's naturally upset about the firm going bust, and we may have to sell our house if I don't land another job pretty fast. It's frankly not the best time for her to have to face Villy. And, of course, we don't know how Villy will react.'

'I think I'll ask her. And of course I'll let you know.' She could sense that he wanted to go. Poor Ed. He had never liked facing up to difficult situations, and now he seemed to have to cope with so many at once.

They both stood up, and he put his arms round her to give her a hug, and kissed her cold face. 'Thank you for the drink, darling. I'll let you know about my end.'

'It's been lovely to see you.' She could not bring herself to send love to Diana, simply could not like her after her behaviour towards Sid.

She saw him out into the freezing cold, waited to hear his car start, then went back to the shabby little morning room. These days she always felt stabbed by loneliness when people left.

THE CHILDREN

Georgie: 'I could easily take practically all my zoo to Home Place. Laura will help me. We could go by train with crates. Except for Rivers, of course. He travels with me. You know, Mum, I can't help thinking that it would be better if Laura's family came to live with us. Harriet claims not to like pythons. *Claims!*' he repeated, with scorn at such an unlikely dislike.

∞ ∞ ∞

Eliza: 'The main reason why we don't like staying with people is the milk.'

Jane: 'It always tastes different from our milk. It's nasty. So, if we have to go, could we ask for orange squash?'

Andrew: 'Well, I want to go. I love exploring new places and it'll be good practice as I'm going to be an explorer when I grow up. I shall discover the East Pole and be extremely famous. Milk is just girly-whirly stuff.'

'Mum, he's so stupid! How can you bear him?'

∞ ∞ ∞

Harriet: 'Mum! How will he know we've changed our address?'

'Father Christmas always knows that sort of thing.'

'OK, but *how*?'

'Well, as a matter of fact, we tell him. And don't ask me how or the magic might not work.'

Clary had spent the whole afternoon making a Christmas cake. She now took it out of the oven for the fourth time and plunged a skewer into it. At last, it came out clean. She tipped the cake out of its tin and put it on a rack to cool. Thank goodness she wouldn't have to make more Christmas stuff: Zoë and Jemima were contributing too.

She had already made the marzipan, about which her household was divided. Archie loved it, but Bertie said even the word made him feel sick. Harriet, her fears about Father Christmas allayed, took the lofty attitude, saying that Bertie was simply too young to understand about marzipan. Both children were excited: about Christmas at Home Place, about going to live with Georgie, and having their own bedrooms for the first time in their lives, and about the thrilling uncertainty of what they would get in the way of presents, and the prospect of there being about eleven other children for the holiday.

Laura was in the same state, but she was also agitated about the presents she would be giving. She had embroidered a white handkerchief with a rather crooked J for her mother, but the linen had become grey and blood-spotted from her exertions, and she decided that Hugh must stand guard at the bathroom door while she washed it. She had saved up all her pocket money to buy presents, seven and sixpence, and she had made a list of the recipients. Against her parents on the list she had simply written 'Ha Ha!' 'It means that you and Mummy simply can't find out about your presents.' Against Georgie she had written 'rabbit, parrot, Komodo Dragon (if small enough), tortoise, two goldfish, and small snake'. Due to her large handwriting, this had left almost no room for possibilities for anyone else on the list. Hugh suggested that she give Georgie just one of the things she'd written down – but there was a very good pet shop in Camden Town, she'd retorted. 'I want to give him everything that's on the list. I love him, you see.'

'I think you'll find there is a marked shortage of dragons,' Jemima said comfortingly, as she saw them off.

∞ ∞ ∞

It was a difficult morning. Laura felt so rich, that she could not understand why she could not buy everything she wanted. She wanted to give Henry and Tom pen-knives and was aghast to discover that this would use up five shillings of her bounty. 'That only leaves half a crown for Georgie!'

'Never mind. The penknives are a brilliant idea. If the worst comes to the worst, I can help you with Georgie.' He was touched by her unbridled generosity. It reminded him of Polly buying a little writing desk for Clary.

'I'm afraid we're clean out of dragons,' the man serving in the pet shop said to Laura. He winked at Hugh, and she noticed.

'Rather a rude man,' she remarked – intentionally audible – to her father.

'I'm sure he didn't mean to be.'

'That's what I don't like. People being what they don't mean to be. They should be what they are.'

She was getting tired, Hugh knew. All the buses they had taken, the searching they had done in Selfridges, and now having to scale down her plans for Georgie. 'He hasn't got a single goldfish,' he prompted.

Laura thought this was a good idea. She chose two. 'One would be cruel. He'd die of boredom. And I want a proper tank for them – not a silly bowl. A tank with sand at the bottom, and green weed growing out of it.' She chose the fish after agonising uncertainty: one nearly all black and a gold one with black marks on it.

'They look more rare than the plain golds, don't you think?'

Eventually, with fish caught and ensconced in a polythene bag in the tank, and smaller bags with sand and the weed, and a very small bag for food, they had finished. Laura had used up all her money, and Hugh had helped with the equipment. 'Dad, you're so kind. You try to be secret about it, but it shows.' She pulled his good arm so that he bent down for her to kiss him, and they went in search of a taxi.

∞ ∞ ∞

> 'My mother is the best,
> She never gets a rest,
> She says I am a pest,
> But I know she loves me best.

'There! That's my poem for Mum for Christmas. It just came to me.'

Harriet, who was feeling anxious anyway, had been knitting a scarf for their mother for ages – mostly because she could only do it in secret, but also because she was a slow knitter. Now she was afraid that she'd forgotten how to cast off – and she felt decidedly jealous of Bertie writing a poem, which had only taken him a minute, and boasting about it. 'It's not a good poem,' she said. 'It's not even true. Mum loves me just as much as she loves you. There's no "best" about it.'

Bertie looked disconcerted. 'I'll copy it out in my most grown-up writing and she'll love it – you'll see.'

'And what are you going to give the others?' She knew he'd spent all his money on Dinky cars for himself. 'Or are you going to write silly poems for everyone?'

'Of course not. You can only write poems if they come to you. It's more like laying an egg. I shall ask Mum to bring her Magic Hat.'

Clary, one wet weekend when they had both been bored after a freezing walk in Regent's Park, had had a brainwave. She had a cloche hat that Rupert had said had belonged to her mother. She had never worn it as it was too old-fashioned – beige felt with a little emerald and diamond arrow placed at one side – not real jewels, but still extremely precious. For years she had kept it wrapped in tissue paper. That day, she had emptied all the packets of beads she had got for them to string, piled them in the hat, and then, in front of them, lifted it so all the beads fell out. Bertie and Harriet were deeply impressed. 'We could make necklaces for everyone!' they cried.

'Although I should think that Archie would look pretty silly in a necklace,' Bertie remarked, as they were each laying out beads on a tea tray. They always called him Archie after he had said he didn't mind.

'We can't both give necklaces to the same person,' Harriet said now. She loved the laying out of the beads, sorting them by putting good colours together, and they were friends again as Bertie had thrown his jacket over Harriet's knitting, and she had stood sturdily in front of him when Clary came into the room while he hid his poem.

'Shouldn't we keep the hat, Mummy, in case we run out of beads?'

'No. I'm afraid it will only produce one load a day, and it will only do it for me. It needs a nice rest now.' She left them making a list of the lucky receivers of bead necklaces.

∞ ∞ ∞

'She still doesn't know?'

'She doesn't. And it's fun for her not knowing. Don't you remember?'

'Honestly, Mum, it was such ages ago I've forgotten.'

Henry and Tom had emerged from their bedroom at noon, hot, sleepy and famished. As Henry started cutting wedges of bread to make toast, Jemima said, rather hopelessly, 'Boys! It's only an hour till lunchtime. If you start making toast now you won't want any lunch.'

'Mum! Have you ever known us not want lunch? It's just that if we don't have a snack now, we might die of hunger before it.'

'Well, you've cut that bread too thick for the toaster.'

'We'll have plain bread then. We're not fussy.'

Jemima, realising that she'd rather lost the thread about Laura believing in Father Christmas and her warning the boys not to give the secret away, returned to it.

'Of course we won't breathe a word. But it does seem a bit childish to me.'

'Well, you're grown-up. But she is still a child. Hugh's

out with her now, doing her shopping for Christmas.' She finished pinching the top and edge of her pie together and put it into the oven. 'One of you could lay the table.'

'We'll both lay it,' one of the twins said, as though this would be twice as kind. The bread had all but disappeared, except for crumbs on the floor.

RACHEL

'I think the best plan would be for Tonbridge to pour the drinks because you know what everyone likes.'

Some of what I like, thought Mrs Tonbridge, but she thought it fondly: it was Christmas, after all.

'And, Tonbridge, large drinks, please.'

They were in the drawing room where Rachel had lit the fire. Steam was rising from the two large sofas: Eileen had washed the covers but it was difficult to get heavy pieces of linen to dry in the current weather, and they had shrunk again, with the result that they could not be thoroughly zipped or hooked up. By the time the drinks had been poured, the room, which had also been steadily filling with smoke, became impossible: it was choking coughs all round.

'We'll have to move to the morning room.'

Rachel led the way, followed by Eileen, who had kindly helped Mrs Tonbridge off the sofa, and Tonbridge brought up the rear with the tray of drinks.

'We haven't lit that fire all autumn, Miss Rachel, and they usually smoke a bit at first.'

'It's that new sweep. He was in and out of here like a dose of salts and eating my rock cakes in the kitchen.'

Eileen tittered, but Mrs Tonbridge quelled her with one of her Looks. Rachel asked Tonbridge to fill everyone's glass, which he did. Port and lemon for the wife, gin and lime for Eileen, and a whisky and ginger ale for himself. Miss Rachel had refused – still nursed a nearly full glass of sherry.

She offered cigarettes, and everyone accepted. But only Tonbridge smoked his.

It could be put off no longer. Rachel told them about the collapse of the firm, about the house belonging to it, about the fact that they would all have to get out – in about three weeks' time. 'Don't worry too much about the time to get out being so short. I'm renting a cottage in Battle where you may all stay until you have decided what you want to do next. You may want to retire, or you may want to go on working. Whoever buys this house will possibly want you to work for them.'

There was a very long silence.

Tonbridge cleared his throat. 'If it isn't out of place, madam, may I ask where you are intending to reside?'

'I don't know, Tonbridge. I know that I shall have very little money. London, possibly. I'm selling Miss Sidney's house there, which will bring me some capital, but I've no idea how much. I shall have to get some kind of job.'

This seemed to shock them more than anything else she had said.

'You'll need a driver.'

'Tonbridge, I doubt if I shall be able to afford a car.'

'Well, you can't cook your own food. Starve to death you would, Miss Rachel, left to yourself. I can't see you making beds with your back and all, madam,' Mrs Tonbridge added, in case Rachel thought she was being cheeky. They all looked at her quite crossly, and she suddenly wanted to cry.

'Of course we can talk about this again – as much as

you want. But meanwhile I do want to say that I would like this Christmas to be the best the family have ever had. And I know I can count on you to help me.'

The room became brimful of reliability.

'Do you have the numbers, madam?'

'Roughly speaking I think we may be eleven children and eight or nine grown-ups. The children will bring sleeping-bags, and the Fakenhams will also be bringing their nanny as she's too old to be left alone. I thought that perhaps you and I should do some housekeeping to make lists of what will be needed.'

'Yes, m'm. I'll just fetch my book.'

Eileen went with her. 'It's lovely that Lady Polly is coming with her family. We've had sirs before but never a lord.'

As he got to his feet, Tonbridge unexpectedly remarked that it was a long lane that had no turning. Recognising that this was meant to make her feel better, Rachel thanked him and asked him to remove the drinks tray. Well, at least I've told them – not very well, I'm afraid – but it's done. Although it wasn't good news, which it could have been if she knew how much money Sid's house might fetch.

Although it was the expensive time, she rang Villy.

'We've spruced the house up a lot and I got the agent round to see it. He thinks that it might sell at about eight thousand. He says it needs a lot doing to it, but that St John's Wood is going up in the world and that he would put it on the market for eight thousand nine hundred and fifty. I had to sign a form on your behalf to get things going, and you'll get a copy in the post, which you must sign and send back to him.'

Rachel said she must pay for the cost of the sprucing.

'But thank you so much for all the trouble. Oh! Villy! I've been wondering whether you and Roly would like to join us for Christmas. It's the last family one here and I – we – should so much like you to be there for it.'

There was a short silence before Villy said, 'Will Edward be there? And his wife?'

'He won't be staying here, but he might come over for a meal.'

'With her?'

'He said he'd let me know, but I somehow think not. It would be nice for Roly, don't you think?'

And Villy, after a pause, said, yes, it would. 'You are an absolute angel,' she added.

Then Mrs Tonbridge came back with her book. 'It'll mean two turkeys, m'm,' she said. 'And we usually get them from York's farm. I'll have a word with him when he brings the milk tomorrow.'

'Do sit down, Mrs Tonbridge.'

She lowered herself heavily into a chair with obvious relief. 'I've postponed my operation until after the New Year,' she said. 'I've been making enquiries, and you can't work for a week after it.'

'That is most helpful of you. I don't know what we would do without you.'

'You'd have a funny old Christmas without me. I'd have to laugh.' She liked to think that ladies were no good at most things – barring arranging flowers and ordering meals. 'We'll need three pounds of sausage-meat, two pounds of chestnuts, and I'll order two extra loaves for stale bread. I've made four puddings and six dozen mince pies. I'll need brandy for the butter, and we shall need twelve packets for everyday use. Potatoes and sprouts we have in the garden. And onions, but not much else. Six dozen eggs and four pints of cream. And what other meals had you in mind, Miss Rachel? We can get two meals at least off the turkeys,' she added encouragingly.

'Fish, do you think? And toad-in-the-hole. The children love sausages. Irish stew, then, and the toad. And perhaps you could do a nice macaroni cheese for a lunch.'

She was still on wartime food, Mrs Tonbridge thought.

'I was thinking, madam, that perhaps we should have some game for Christmas Eve. I could get three brace of pheasant and stew them with apple and cream.'

'Won't that be a bit rich for the children?'

'I wasn't thinking of the children for that, m'm. I was thinking I could do stuffed pancakes for them. They'll have it earlier in the hall. You won't want yours till near nine, by the time the children are settled in bed. And I thought my trifle after the pheasant. I'll need to order two more pints of cream for that. And Mrs Senior always liked the sponge cakes to be soaked in Grand Marny as well as the sherry.'

Rachel, remembering her battles with this fiendishly rich and alcoholic pudding, said, 'Oh, Mrs Tonbridge, I was thinking of your delicious port wine jellies with macaroons after the game. Perhaps you could do the trifle for Boxing Day.'

'I could, m'm, as you wish. There's not much body to jelly. It's what I call light.'

'Yes, but I think everybody will be very tired after all the packing up and travelling so the jelly would be just right.'

'Very good, Miss Rachel. The cake has only to be iced. I'll order the fish by the telephone so that I can be sure of what I want. I'll send the menus in to you when I've made them up. Will that be all?'

It was.

'I'll send Eileen to see to that fire for you now. And Tonbridge will do the drawing-room fire. If it goes on smoking, I'll give Ted Lockhart a piece of my mind.'

Alone again, Rachel decided to wrap her presents. The way in which the servants had all seemed to throw themselves into the immediate present touched her. It was probably the only way to live, she thought, since looking ahead seemed only to paralyse her. She would get Tonbridge to drive her into Battle and visit a house agent about a cottage for all four of them.

JOSEPH AND STELLA

'Louise is out, is she?'

'That's why I answered the door.'

'Sorry to interrupt you, only I'm quite glad to see you.'

'If you want to talk to me you'll have to come up. I'm in the middle of cooking.' She wore an apron, and her face was red behind her round, heavy spectacles.

He followed her up to the top floor where dozens of chocolate truffles lay on a tray on the kitchen table waiting to be rolled in cocoa powder. She took a tray out of the oven that contained large brown sizzling splodges on it. 'Let me just do this batch and then I'll pay attention to you.'

He watched while she carefully loosened a splodge from the tray, then wound it round the stem of a wooden spoon.

'A brandy snap,' he said, with some respect.

'I make brandy snaps for my pa and chocolate truffles for my ma and aunt.' She wound five more snaps, then poured more mixture onto the tray and put it back in the oven.

'I'm most impressed,' he said.

'I suppose you want to talk about Louise.'

'Well, yes, I do. She's been very difficult of late, cross and snappy, and when I ask her what's wrong she won't answer.'

'Perhaps she thinks you ought to know without her telling you.'

'Well, I don't.'

'Oh, Joseph! She's in love with you and naturally that means she wishes she could spend Christmas with you. And last year you took her shopping for presents, kept asking her whether each was a good choice, and then it turned out that they were all presents for your wife!'

'I admit that was a bit of a mistake.'

'You didn't give her anything!'

'I took her to Paris for a weekend. That was her Christmas present.'

'You know perfectly well that that's not true. You take her to Paris, or wherever, when you have business there.'

He didn't reply. Stella turned back to the oven. 'You're never going to marry her, are you?'

'I am married. I've never said I would marry her.'

'And that lets you off the hook, doesn't it? I bet you've never told her that you can't or won't marry her.'

He did not like women in a 'no-nonsense' mood, and he was tired of her bets. But she went on: 'Louise is thirty-five. When she's about forty, chances are that you'll drop her for someone younger, and what happens to her then?'

Stella thought about these things because – let's face it – she was plain, heavy glasses, breasts not bad, but bum far too large: no one was going to be crazy about her. She'd probably marry the first man who asked her, if anyone ever did. Feeling sorry for herself made things easier. More gently, Joseph said, 'Do you think that all women want to be married, then?'

'I think that most women want children and, clearly, marriage is an obvious route to that end.' She had finished rolling the second batch of snaps, and now pulled off her apron and sat at the kitchen table opposite him.

He said, 'She has been married and had a child whom she abandoned.'

'She didn't know about love until Hugo—'

'Who's Hugo?' he interrupted sharply.

'Sorry, I thought she would have told you. Hugo was someone she fell in love with during the war. He was killed. He wrote her a letter before he died, but they never let her have it. Her husband and her mother-in-law. Between them, they nearly broke her heart.'

He offered her a cigarette and lit one for both of them. 'I didn't know,' he said.

'I assumed you did. Please don't tell her I told you.'

'I won't,' he reassured her gently. Having a secret with her softened things between them.

'What I've been trying to say is, please don't entirely break her heart.'

'So – what do you think I should do?'

'I think you should leave her.'

There was a pause. Then she added, 'Of course, I see that that would be hard on her, but not as hard as spinning it out until she becomes a cast-off mistress.'

'And what about me?' he asked, with some bitterness. 'What do you think I would feel? Having to lie to her about not wanting her, when I do?'

'I think you will have a hard time. You could lie to her, of course, tell her that there's someone else, or your wife has found out. But it might be better to tell her the truth. The truth would be cleaner.' Her calm clear-headedness both impressed and frightened him.

'Only don't tell her before Christmas,' she said.

'They're having a big family do and she wouldn't be able to cope.'

He got up to go. 'By the way, I have got her a present this time.' He pulled a small square box out of his pocket. 'Do you think she'll like this?'

It was a necklace of large green stones set at intervals in a delicate gold chain. 'It's eighteenth-century paste,' he said; 'I know she likes that sort of thing. There's a card in the box. I wondered whether you could possibly wrap it up for me.'

'I possibly could,' she said. He could be the most charming man.

HUGH'S FAMILY

'Sorry we're late, darling.'

'We've had a wonderful, lovely morning. I got three presents, Mummy, but I need to put Georgie's in the sink if we're going to have lunch immediately.'

Henry and Tom had heard them come in, and now clattered down the stairs and into the dining room, where the table was raggedly laid.

'What *is* for lunch?' one of them asked.

'Steak and kidney pudding,' Jemima replied, as she lifted the napkin-topped bowl from the saucepan.

'Goody goody gumdrops! One of our best things.'

'It's not gumdrops for me at all. I loathe kidney. Loathe it,' Laura repeated, with relish.

Hugh proceeded to cut wedges from the bowl using a spoon to add the gravy. Jemima was frying thin strips of cabbage.

'Mum! You know we don't need green food. It isn't proper food for a start, and we don't actually like it.'

'I loathe it.'

'That's enough! All of you. Mummy's made you a lovely lunch and all you do is criticise her. Come to that, I loathe all three of you, but here I am, having lunch with you without complaining.'

'But you don't loathe the boys as much as me, do you?'

'Of course not. You're easily the most loathsome. This cabbage is delicious, Jem. What have you done to it?'

'Fried it with butter and a spot of Marmite.'

When he was with the family, Hugh could put all his business troubles out of his mind; shopping with Laura had been physically exhausting, but he had loved the whole morning, and to come home to his family for lunch was a rare treat.

Laura picked out her kidneys and presented them to the twins, who also had second helpings.

'What's for pudding?' they asked, as the last morsels of the first course disappeared.

'Treacle tart.'

This was approved of by all. Immediately it had been eaten, the twins leaped from the table saying that they were going skating at the rink in Queensway. Laura said at once that she wanted to go, too, but Hugh pointed out to her that she must plant her aquarium. 'Oh, yes, I have to. I'm sorry I can't come with you.'

'We're sorry, too,' they replied, but it was only politeness: having Laura simply meant that they could have no fun at all, as she kept falling down, trying to learn her edges and do her figures-of-eight, crying and wanting sweets to cheer her up.

Hugh helped Jemima with the washing-up while Laura waited impatiently to get on with her planting.

'I meant for those wicked boys to do the washing-up,' Jemima said. 'I'll do the fish tank with Laura, and you put your feet up for a bit, darling. The bed's warm – I put on the blanket just before you came back.'

∞ ∞ ∞

She thinks of everything, Hugh thought gratefully, as he divested himself of jacket, tie, shoes and trousers. He had been afraid that all his miserable anxieties would loom, when he was alone, the chief one being what to do about Rachel. But the moment that thought occurred to him he remembered the Brig's study – untouched since his death. It might contain some valuable objects that could be sold to build up some capital for her. When probate had been declared on the Brig's estate, they had not taken more than a cursory look at the study, and although he knew that Edward had quietly removed the famous stamp collection there might still be other things. He fell – quite suddenly – into a dreamless sleep.

∞ ∞ ∞

Jemima had a very different afternoon. She found, as she had so often found before, that it was perfectly possible to look after a lively and demanding child while continuing to worry about grown-up problems. Hugh would need to get something to do, but what? It was becoming more difficult to get any sort of job when you were over sixty. And, besides, his health was not good although he would never admit it. He had never worked for anybody else in his life – he had gone out to France in the Great War as an officer, and come back to be a director, and ultimately chairman, of the firm. A firm that had now gone bust.

'Well, I do think you should ring Georgie.'

'I want him to have a surprise.'

'So you have said several times.'

'Because I seriously do want it to be one.'

'You're not thinking of the poor goldfish at all. How would you like to be stuffed back in a polythene bag for a very long journey, taken out again for a few days and then stuffed back again for the journey to Georgie's home?'

There was a long, thick silence while Laura battled with her nature. Virtue won. 'It's only because I don't actually know whether goldfish get car sick.'

Jemima offered to do the telephoning.

'Only don't tell anyone what it is. Then at least it can be a surprise here and I can see him being surprised.'

It turned out that Archie was taking a load of stuff from their flat over to Rupert and Zoë; he would pick Laura up and bring her back.

Jemima helped her take half the water out of the fish tank and then balanced it carefully between Laura's knees as she sat in the front of the car.

She saw them off quite thankfully; it would give her time to finish the packing. But as soon as they were gone, there were the twins back from skating, raging for tea.

'You can have hot buttered toast and finish the ginger cake, but don't, I implore you, eat anything else.'

'She implores us.' Henry turned to Tom.

'It's just hysteria. All right, Mum, we'll only have what you say. What's for supper?'

'Cold ham, salad and baked potatoes. I've scrubbed them so you can put them in the oven for me now, before your tea.'

She went upstairs with some relief. There should be time to do practically everyone's packing in peace. Hugh was still fast asleep.

TEDDY

'I quite see that you have to go, but why can't I come with you?'

'I've told you, darling, it's only family, and, anyway, there are so many of us there wouldn't be room.'

'I took you to see my family.'

'That was different. And it wasn't exactly a howling success, was it?'

'How long will you be away?'

'I don't know. Four or five days, I should think.'

He pushed her hair away from her face. 'Darling, do stop being difficult about it. You've got your family to go to. Don't spoil our last evening together.'

'What do you mean "our last evening"?'

'Tomorrow is Christmas Eve. I have to be down for that.'

'Oh,' she said, in a very small voice. 'I thought you meant for good.'

No, she didn't. He had come to know all her tricks by now, and he didn't like them. It wasn't what she was feeling, it was what she wanted him to think she was feeling. It flashed through his mind that perhaps he would prefer it to be for good, but that was mad: he was in love with her, wasn't he?

'I'll take you out for dinner.'

ARRIVALS

'That's all the flowers for the bedrooms – mostly berries, but the sprig of wintersweet in each vase will provide enough scent. If you take them up, I'll start on the bedrooms.'

But the bedrooms were proving tricky. There were not enough of them for a start, but the children liked sharing. The snag was that she had forgotten how many children were now grown-up. She started to make a list.

Polly, who had not been here since her marriage, should have Hugh's old room. And presumably Spencer would be with them in the old cot that had been kept for babies. Zoë and Rupert could have their usual room – the one with peacocks on the wallpaper. Hugh and Jemima could have Edward's old room. Archie and Clary could have the Duchy's room. Juliet and Louise could share the small room they'd had last year. The day nursery, which was large, could just about take Teddy, Simon, Henry and Tom. That would use up all the camp beds. Harriet, Bertie, Andrew and Polly's twins could share the night nursery and she could put Polly's nanny in the Brig's old dressing room. That left Georgie and Laura. She'd had a surprising postcard that morning: 'Plese arnt Rachel I want to sleep with Georgie, because I unnerstan him and I love him very MUCH. And I love Rivers. Love from Laura.'

She had left out Villy! And Roland. Well, he could go in with the other boys, but Villy must have a nice room. She had better have mine, she thought, and I will sleep in Sid's. She had not been able to do this since Sid's death, but now it was simply something that had to be faced, like so much else.

At five o'clock the house had been quiet, still, encased in the frost that had arrived with the dark. She had wandered restlessly through the rooms, drawing curtains, putting logs on the fires. But after a few minutes she'd heard a car and, wrapping a shawl round her, she went out to meet the first arrivals. It was Polly and her family. The three children scrambled out. 'Eliza and Jane were both sick in the car, but I wasn't,' the boy declared. 'I was definitely not sick at all.'

Polly hugged her aunt. 'Oh, Aunt Rach, it's lovely to be here. This is Gerald,' and Gerald unexpectedly kissed her.

'It is,' he said shyly. 'Eliza, Jane, Andrew, come and say hello to your great-aunt.'

'Hello, Aunt Rachel,' they murmured.

Gerald took Spencer from Nan, and helped her out of the car. She looked like a tiny bird in her nest of warm, sensible clothes. Eileen appeared and offered to help.

'Come in, children.'

After that there was a steady stream of family arrivals. Laura rushed up and, in a kind of shouted whisper, asked whether her postcard had arrived. Rachel said, yes, it had, but she must talk to Georgie and his parents first, whereupon Laura gave her a very black look. Rupert and Zoë set about unpacking sleeping-bags, and Georgie brought in Rivers's belongings and allowed Laura to give him some of his supper.

Then Clary, Archie and their two arrived. 'It's like coming home,' Archie said, as he hugged her.

Juliet, who had just extricated her case from the pile in the boot, said, 'Where am I sleeping, Aunt Rachel?' No greeting, and she had developed a new drawly voice, as though addressing everyone from a pinnacle of indifference.

'Hello, Juliet. You're in the same room as before and you're sharing it with Louise.' She was wearing a thick sweater embroidered with white sheep and one black one. She looked stunning – and sulky.

'Come on, Jules! Help me with the car!' Rupert called, but she took no notice, simply stalked into the house.

Minutes later, Teddy, Simon and Louise arrived, packed rather tightly into Teddy's small car. They all seemed pleased to see Rachel.

∞ ∞ ∞

Clary felt touched to have been given the Duchy's bedroom. It looked as it always had – white walls, white muslin-covered dressing table, the two Brabazon watercolours of Venice and two sepia photographs of the Duchy's parents in their late eighties, sitting on a bench in their garden at Stanmore. The blue linen curtains were ragged, and the patchwork quilt that had always covered the bed since Rachel had made it – of blue and white silks – now had gaping holes where some of the blues had rotted. Clary looked at it all, and tears pricked her eyes. It seemed an honour to be there; eddies of grief for the Duchy came and went. It would be awful for her if she was still here, with her whole world crashing round her, she thought.

Villy and Roland arrived: Tonbridge had fetched them off the train at Battle. Villy was clutching a large tin, and Roland carried a sleeping-bag and two cases.

'You're having my old room, darling. I'm so glad you've come. Hello, Roland, I haven't seen you for ages. You're sleeping in the day nursery with the other boys.'

He looked bewildered. 'I'm afraid I don't know where that is.'

'I'll show him. Are we sharing?' Villy asked.

'No, no. You're in my room. I'm in Sid's.' It was awful, she thought, that Roland didn't know his brothers or cousins. He was much taller than his mother, and did not look like Edward at all. He was of an age when he was practically always in the way, with a great anxiety to get out of it.

She went down to see that the drinks were in the drawing room and met Andrew on the stairs.

'I've explored the house,' he said. 'It didn't take me long. Not much good for hide-and-seek, I shouldn't think. Everybody would be found in a minute.'

'Perhaps you'd go and tell the girls that supper will be in the hall any minute now.'

'Oh, good! I will.' And he sped happily back upstairs.

Supper in the hall, beneath the glass dome that largely lighted it, was for Bertie and Harriet, Jane and Eliza, Georgie, Laura and Andrew, and consisted of scrambled eggs on fried bread with one rasher of bacon per child followed by jam sandwiches and a Victoria sponge. Eliza and Jane got their orange squash, which meant that everyone else wanted it too, so it ran out. The meal was presided over by Nan, who kept order with miraculous ease. Georgie asked people to save their bacon rind for Rivers. When Andrew picked the top half off a sandwich, Nan was after him at once. 'That's no way to behave, your lordship – just for that you'll get no sandwich at all. Hand me your plate. You'll wait to have your cake with the others.'

'Why does she call you "lordship"?' Laura asked.

'She only does it when she's cross. I am a lord, actually.'

'He's got a horrible name,' Eliza said, and Jane added, 'He's Lord Holt. He wanted to be Lisle like us, but Daddy said he couldn't be. He has to stay Lord Holt until Daddy dies when he will be Lord Fakenham, like Daddy is now. Me and Jane are called "Lady",' she finished smugly.

'That's enough of that. You're no better than the next person, any of you. We're all the same,' Nan finished sternly, although she thought nothing of the sort.

∞ ∞ ∞

In the drawing room the fire blazed, giving such a convincing impression of warmth that nearly everyone felt they must be, and this was aided by the strong Martinis that the older set were drinking. There was a divide here that required tact. Roland, as Villy now saw, seemed very shy and his large Adam's apple slid up and down his throat like mercury in a thermometer. Rachel had tried with him – asking what he was most interested in, and he had said something that clearly floored her. Villy watched him anxiously until Archie came up to give her a hug, and said, 'Don't worry about him, he'll be fine,' and filled her glass from the jug he was taking round.

The Christmas tree, potted by McAlpine, stood gaunt and majestic in the bay window, its decorations stacked in tatty old cardboard boxes round it.

The children were all in bed, but audibly not asleep. Rachel clapped her hands, and everyone became silent. 'I just want to say two things. One, wouldn't it be a good idea not to discuss our – difficulties, until after Christmas? Let's just enjoy it.' There was a murmur of agreement. 'Second, this room must be out of bounds until Christmas morning – for the children, I mean.'

'Well,' Archie said briskly, 'Rupe and I have always done the tree, and since we're both rotten at the lights system, it would be good to have Roland: he knows all about electrical things, don't you?'

'I could certainly install the lights on the tree,' Roland said, then blushed, so that his acne stood out even more fiercely, like little pilot lights in a sunset sky.

Rupert said that that would be a great help, and Villy glowed.

Clary slipped out of the room to see if she could help Eileen.

The kitchen was an inferno. Even Mrs Tonbridge's sallow complexion was suffused to a more classic red, and kirby-grips clattered – like dwarfs' ninepins – onto the stove. Eileen was draining beet spinach; only Nan sat quietly, knitting a shawl. She and Mrs Tonbridge approved of one another, and Nan had had a good day, as far as her memory went, and she was reminiscing about her long service with the Fakenham family, while Mrs Tonbridge was able to contribute a few things about Polly's early life. Eileen was so entranced by this that Mrs Tonbridge had to keep shouting at her to get on with the vegetables, while she removed a large dish of stewed pheasants from the oven. 'And you're to take them pies one at a time into the dining room.' Clary, who had turned up to help, said she would carry one. She was still wearing the clothes she had arrived in – jeans and a fisherman's sweater.

'In my day, they all changed for dinner. Even if his lordship dined alone, it was always in his dinner jacket.'

'Times have changed, Miss Smallcott,' Mrs Tonbridge offered uneasily. Changing like that in this household had only been for celebrations, and had meant a four-course dinner, although since the war they had made do with two.

Clary and Eileen now returned to take the vegetables. 'Come back for the sauce, Eileen.' Mrs Tonbridge had been stirring it in its saucepan. Her vigour made the kirby-grips even more precarious.

∞ ∞ ∞

'Everybody help themselves,' Rachel said. Even so, it took a long time. We shall have to have two rooms for Christmas lunch, she thought, as she looked round the room with pleasure. And another leaf in the hall table. How her parents would have liked this!

'I hardly eat pheasant,' Juliet said to Teddy, when he exclaimed over her tiny helping. 'And I never eat potatoes.' But when the sauce came round she poured a selfish amount onto her plate.

Gerald was enjoying everything immensely. Originally, he had not wanted to come, but he had known that Polly was really keen, and it was a joy for him to please her about anything. He looked at her now, talking to Archie Lestrange, who'd married her best friend, and whom, she had told him, she had had a crush on when she was very young. 'He was so kind to us – treating us as grown-ups when we weren't quite. We both loved him because he listened to us seriously, and he was a very good tease. And nearly as funny as Uncle Rupert,' she'd added.

They were a good-looking lot, but no one was a patch on Poll. Her copper hair was not as burnished as once it had been, and she was no longer the slip of a girl he had married, but maturity became her, and whatever she was doing, feeding babies, cleaning the house, looking after dear old Nan, her beauty was always apparent. She caught his eye across the table and blew him a kiss. Her clothes became glamorous because she was wearing them: tonight it was a long woollen skirt with a scarlet silk shirt. He was grateful for her mere presence. He was very good at gratitude.

∞ ∞ ∞

'Perhaps, Miss Smallcott, you'd care to partake of some supper in my sitting room. I've fed Tonbridge, because of his ulcer, so it will be just the two of us.'

They repaired to her room where Tonbridge had made a nice fire. There was a small fish pie for them, and the supper was such a success that by the end of it (with a nice strong cup of tea), they had progressed to Christian names, Mabel and Edith. Mabel had been able to say that ordinarily she would not dream of working in her carpet slippers, but she was due an operation and could not possibly do her present work in her shoes. Edith had told her then of her memory lapses which her ladyship had said did not matter in the least, and were simply due to age. 'Not that I've ever told her my age. I don't tell anyone my age.' She did not add that this was chiefly because, most of the time, she had no idea what it was. The evening ended because Edith said she must go and listen for Spencer. She wondered whether Eileen would show her up to her ladyship's room as its whereabouts had slipped her mind. Eileen, who had had a lonely dinner at the kitchen table, and had now been washing up for a good hour, escorted her. Spencer had woken up, and Lord Fakenham was walking up and down with him in his arms. 'If you'll take him, Nan, I'll get his mother.'

Nan took the baby, who gave her a token smile of recognition, and then got down to the serious business of yelling for food.

Polly's appearance excited him to operatic strength, but as she sank gratefully into an armchair and took him, his cries ceased in midstream as he found what he wanted.

'Nan, dear, you go to bed. It's long past your bedtime.' And as she hesitated, Polly said, 'Gerald will take you there. It's the fourth door on your left.'

'And show Nan where the bathroom is,' she called after them as they left the room.

Alone with her baby, she could indulge in a passionate adoration that she imagined she concealed from everyone. His eyes, that had turned from slate-blue to brown like his father, were fixed trustfully on hers, his copper-gold hair was damp from his exertions, and she gently smoothed his curls from his forehead. 'You are the most perfect, beautiful baby in the world,' she told him. 'I love you – passionately.'

She knew that she was taking far too long to wean him, but she clung to this special intimacy: this was her last baby, so it was an intimacy she would never have again.

∞ ∞ ∞

'The thing is,' Harriet said, 'we're more likely to get snow if we all want it. Couldn't we just say, "Let there be snow" – like God – and there will be?' You had to hold your own against the twins, since there were two of them and they always agreed with each other.

Eliza and Jane both had their hair in pigtails and they were all snug in their sleeping-bags. The space they'd made for Laura was unoccupied, and they found out that she was sleeping with Georgie. This, they thought, was very unfair, and they all agreed that Laura was spoiled. 'She's too young for us, anyway,' Eliza had said. 'I mean, I often read in bed, and she can't read without a grown-up helping her. Andrew is awful, too. I think all very young children are pests. I shan't have babies when I get married. I shall wait for them to be at least seven before I have them.'

Harriet was aghast. 'Eliza, you can't just go about with a seven-year-old baby inside you. You'd explode – like a balloon.' She could not suppress a slightly hysterical giggle at the thought.

'Goodness, Harriet, of course I couldn't. I'd have it at the normal time and then lend it to people until it was old enough.'

There was a silence while Harriet digested the snub. 'Are we staying awake for Father Christmas?' she asked rather timidly.

She saw the twins exchange a look. 'I think it would be best if we all went to sleep,' Jane said, adding kindly, 'and please don't worry about birth and all that. I can quite see that as you don't live in the country you couldn't know much about that sort of thing. Do you want to go on reading, Lizzie?'

'Not specially.' She shut her book with a snap; she'd

515

only been pretending to read it. They were all tired – being sick on the journey had meant the twins had had a rather small supper, and Nan had made them have baths.

The light was turned off by Eliza, who said, 'I'm going to undo my plait: Nan made it far too tight.'

'Me too. You're lucky to have such lovely thick hair, Harriet – ours is far too mingy.'

Harriet lay in the dark, savouring this compliment. Nobody had ever said anything like that to her before. She decided to remember it all her life.

∞ ∞ ∞

Roland, having successfully installed the Christmas lights, packed up his tool case and said he would go to bed. He found Teddy, Tom, Henry and Simon in the nursery trying to play records on a pretty ancient machine. One of them was also struggling with a wireless that emitted constant crackles and small bursts of jazz. 'We've not to make too much noise,' one of them was saying.

'Roland will know what to do,' Simon said. He was dealing with the gramophone.

It was marvellous to feel so useful and informed, Roland thought.

Louise and Juliet had soon got bored by all this, and had gone to bed, where they were exchanging important confidences – Louise about Joseph, and Juliet about the new love of her life. They were most honourable about dividing the time spent on discussing Joseph and Tarquin, while at the same time going through the elaborate process of cleaning and nourishing their skins for the rigours of the night. 'Tarquin's at a drama school, on a scholarship, so he must be frightfully good. My best friend at the school I used to be at took me to the end-of-term play they were doing, and he played a very old man in it, and I thought he must actually be very old, but when we met and he was taking off his make-up, he wasn't – at all. He's twenty – the perfect age for me. So we fell in love. He says I ought to be an actress, which I'd far rather do than go to France. He said that being a model was just mucking about. Oh! I'm sorry I said that because it's what you do – I didn't mean that you muck about because you're at the top, aren't you?' She had dropped her drawl now they were alone, and her faint blush made her look even more beautiful.

'Oh, no. I don't mind you saying that in the least. I think I do muck about. Ought to find something more interesting to do.'

∞ ∞ ∞

In the drawing room, they had finished filling the golf stockings, and had laid all the other presents under the tree. Gerald had returned to say that Polly was putting Spencer back to bed, and that he had told her to go too. 'But are we missing anyone?' Rachel said.

'We're missing Lydia because she has to do panto with her rep company.' This was Villy. 'I rang her before leaving and she sent her love to everyone.'

'Wills wanted to spend the time with his girlfriend's family. Fair enough,' Hugh said, but he looked sad.

'Well,' Rupert said. 'I think I can beat you all with Neville's excuse.' He took a piece of paper out of his jacket pocket and read out a message: 'Sorry can't be with you. Am working in Cuba where I shall probably get married.'

'Good Lord!'

'The "probably" is a typical Neville touch. I didn't want to produce it at dinner, because I wasn't sure how Juliet would react. She's had a bit of a crush on him.'

'She's over it now,' Zoë said quickly. 'She's found an actor to be in love with.'

'Right.' This was Archie. 'Let's do the stockings and call it a day.'

So, some time later, they filed upstairs with the creaking stockings, which Gerald, Archie and Hugh deposited in each of the bedrooms.

∞ ∞ ∞

Clary could well remember pretending to be asleep, listening out all the while for the stocking to be laid carefully on her bed. Louise and Polly would be fast asleep, but she – especially in the war years when Dad was missing – always just opened her eyes a slit so that she could see who it was. The drawing room had been out of bounds then; this evening she had been examining it with a grown-up eye. The lovely curtains that Aunt Rachel had insisted on – dark green chintz with creamy white roses – were now in tatters; you had to draw them very carefully not to split them more. The sofas and upholstered chairs were also worn and shiny on the arms. The lampshades had darkened with time so that they were almost the colour of coffee, and the immense carpet that had covered the room was now full of dangerous if familiar rents.

Her play was hopefully coming back to London some time in the New Year. She had not earned very much money from it so far, but an agent had written to her saying he would be happy to represent her. Archie had said that would be a good thing and meant she would not have to worry about money. So she was to see him in the New Year. What did worry her was the alarming fact that she did not have a notion of what to write next. She had started trying to compose a new play several times, but all the scraps that she had managed to put onto paper remained scraps – incoherent and pointless. She was looking forward to living with Rupert and Zoë and kept deciding that she would postpone trying to write again until they had settled in. Saying goodbye to Home Place was the immediate thing. She and Archie were the luckiest members of the family: Hugh and Edward and Rachel were the hardest hit, and Rachel faced the bleakest future. When she thought of Rachel, she began to imagine awful things. Supposing Archie died as Sid had, and she did not have Bertie and Harriet, and she had no qualifications for any decent kind of work, but had lost all her money and needed to make some . . .

'What are you crying about?'

She told him.

'My darling, you must be deliriously happy if you have to invent things to cry about. I am extremely well, and so are the children. And you are now a playwright. I do agree that we have to worry about the others, but now, as Rachel said, we're here to enjoy Christmas. I'm going to put my lovely healthy arms round you and you're going to go to sleep at once.'

∞ ∞ ∞

Rivers, although he had been dozing round Georgie's neck, was immediately awake when Hugh came in with

519

the stockings. He had learned to lie low when people who weren't Georgie turned up, and scurried under the blanket until they had gone. He had no intention of spending the night in his cold cage, and as Hugh did not put on a light, he would not know that he wasn't in it now. Awake, he felt like a snack and luckily discovered half a digestive biscuit under the pillow near to Georgie's hair. He nibbled this very quietly, so as not to wake his friend.

∞ ∞ ∞

Rachel undressed quickly. She was cold to the bone: her hands had gone that horrid mauve colour and her feet were blocks of ice. She had kept telling herself how well everything was going, how funny Laura could be, that adorable baby of Polly's – she had always loved babies, each one seeming more charming than the last – how wonderful Mrs Tonbridge had been with so many people to feed, how kind and supportive her brothers and darling Archie were being, how welcoming and nice they had been to Villy, how clever Roland had been with the lights for the tree, how thoughtful Zoë and Jemima, Clary and Polly were with their determination to help, how they all seemed to get on together ... This made her think of Edward, from whom she had not heard, and she could not help praying that Diana would decide not to come to Boxing Day lunch with him. It would be so much easier for Villy.

Now, she lay in the dark with two hot-water bottles – and tears were streaming down her face. She allowed herself a brief sob before telling herself to pull herself together. Tonight would be the anniversary of Sid's death.

∞ ∞ ∞

'I don't suppose he meant it, darling. You know Neville – he's always enjoyed teasing people.'

'It isn't that I mind him getting married. I mind his not telling us properly. He really is a master of the flippant message. Still, it might have been difficult for Jules if he was here.'

'Jules has fallen for someone else. She thinks I don't know, and it's best to keep it like that.'

'Who has she fallen for?'

'A student at an acting school. But you don't know, either.'

'All right.' He had got into bed. 'Be quick, darling, it's so cold.' She always took ages. He had taken to reading to stop himself getting impatient, and he now dived into his paperback volume of Chekhov's short stories.

∞ ∞ ∞

Jemima was undressed in a matter of seconds; Hugh always took longer. Tonight he seemed to be taking longer than usual: he had gone down the passage to the bathroom and, after nearly ten minutes, had not returned. She got out of bed and went to find him.

He was sitting on the bathroom stool, and turned to her when she came in. He looked shaky. 'Got a bit stuck,' he said, in a slurred voice. 'Dropped my toothbrush and when I bent down to pick it up, it was too far away. Felt

521

dizzy – couldn't reach . . . Not drunk,' he said, looking at her with frightened eyes.

She put her arms round him. 'You're just tired. Never mind about the toothbrush. Come with me.' She spoke calmly, but she did not feel calm at all.

∞ ∞ ∞

Snow fell in the night, large flakes as big as feathers, and after a while it began to settle. The bare trees became heavy with it; it thickened on the ground so that it became like the icing on a cake, then a satisfactory three inches of dazzling crunch. Spiders' webs sparkled with icicles; the sky was the colour of dirty pearls and the air smelt of snow.

Simon, who had decided to clean out and lay the fires, had to brush the snow off the logs before he wheeled the barrow into the house. The only other person up was Eileen, who was amazed and grateful that he was doing this chore for her. She showed him where the newspapers and kindling were to be found, and offered him a cup of tea. It meant that she could also have one, which she badly needed – it was perishing. They drank their tea standing in the kitchen, then he raked out the kitchen stove and she counted the cutlery for laying the two tables in the dining room and hall.

Simon loved doing fires. He had felt rather out of it last night, with Teddy constantly steering the conversation round to girlfriends and, in particular, his own. 'Haven't you got one?' he had asked, and Simon had said, no, he hadn't. He felt himself blushing then because he thought of the gardener's boy who worked on a neighbouring estate and with whom he had quite unexpectedly but deeply fallen in love. He had met Roy at a nursery garden centre some months back, and to begin with they had talked about trees. Roy was collecting a lorry load of fruit trees while Simon was picking up stuff for the avenue. He came from Glasgow, but his father was Italian, had been a prisoner of war and had met Roy's mother then. After the war, Roy's father had not wanted to return to Italy, and the family of the farm he had worked on as a prisoner offered him a job. He found and wooed Maggie, their young cook, and Roy had been the result. He was wonderfully good-looking – with abundant curly black hair, melting brown eyes, and a smooth olive skin that never seemed to change. They had agreed to go to the cinema together on their day off. They sat side by side in the dark, and Simon kept looking at Roy and his lovely profile. And then, after about an hour of this, Roy had put out his hand and rested it upon Simon's erection.

He had given a little grunt of triumph and then he'd leaned over and kissed Simon's mouth. Simon had been unable to contain himself and was flooded with shame. Roy had responded by taking his hand and leading him out of the cinema to his lorry. The back had a tarpaulin that covered it. Roy let down the tailboard and sprang into the lorry. He held out a hand to Simon and hefted him up. It was dark in the back, and for some reason this had made them whisper.

'You not done this before?'

No, he hadn't.

Roy undid one of the lashings of the tarp, which let in a little light. Simon could see that the lorry had been swept clean and that a sleeping-bag lay in one corner. For a second he wondered whether Roy had planned everything, but this only excited him more. Roy was speedily stripping himself bare, until he stood before Simon, naked. He was smiling – a teasing, inviting smile. Then, with a swift, elegant movement, he knelt in front of him and began taking off his clothes. 'Good,' he said, when Simon was also naked. 'You have a nice body.'

'Nothing like yours.'

'No, no. Mine is the best. But you have good cock. Let me . . .'

There ensued the most amazing time of Simon's life. After a furious, sometimes painful, sometimes ecstatic session Roy drew away from him. 'I need a fag. Half-time,' he added, as he found his packet and lit up. He offered one to Simon, who didn't smoke, except now he felt he wanted to do everything that Roy did.

'I love you,' he said, as they lay together on the sleeping-bag; the cigarette made him cough, and he gave it up. 'I love you,' he repeated, willing Roy to say it too. But he didn't. He stubbed out his cigarette.

'We have a good time together. We don't need more. We have good sex – it'll get even better for you. And now, as they say in pubs, one for the road.'

There had been more times, and then Roy had said he was off to Scotland for Christmas and, more importantly, New Year. And here he was, in the house where he had been born, back to say goodbye to it. And more in love with Roy than ever. In his dreams he imagined Roy returning to tell him that he was in love, too. They would live together and perhaps run a nursery garden. A bliss-ful dream, for Simon still found it impossible that such a degree of physical intimacy could exist without love.

∞ ∞ ∞

'I don't think books should count as presents.' Georgie and Laura had raced unwrapping their stockings and were eating their tangerines. 'I think anything except them could be a present. Except sand or earth,' she added, after thinking about it. She had privately loved her stocking. 'You couldn't have had a live animal in a stocking. It would have died in the night. And you've got things that are useful for your zoo. It's a pity you didn't get a book on how to look after your goldfish,' she added pointedly. She felt that Georgie had not been quite grateful enough for her splendid present.

'I know perfectly well how to do that. The bowls for the rabbits and mice are useful.'

'And your penknife, and your torch. And that notebook that says "Reports on my Collection". I think that's a lovely present.'

'Do be careful, Laura. You're beginning to sound like a grown-up.'

'Am I? I didn't mean to. Honestly, Georgie, nothing was further from my mind.' She was secretly delighted at the idea.

Rivers, who did not care for tangerines, scampered inside his owner's pyjama jacket to keep warm.

Laura had got out of bed to see if there was snow and, passing Rivers's unoccupied cage, suddenly saw something. 'Oh, look! A lovely little stocking specially for Rivers!'

'Give it to me.' Georgie was clearly delighted.

It was in fact one of Laura's socks, and she sat on Georgie's bed while he opened it. It contained a little bag of Good Boy Choc Drops, a partially stripped drumstick, a really beautiful little brush and comb for his fur, a tiny tin that had mixed biscuits in it, and an envelope full of scraps of ham. 'A very thoughtful stocking,' Georgie said. He was almost laughing with pleasure. 'Look, Rivers!'

Rivers, who had smelt the ham and the chicken, emerged, his whiskers twitching.

'I'm going to give him the chicken first, and it means we can eat our chocolate money. He loves chicken, and he's never really cared for chocolate.'

That was how the three of them were occupied when Zoë and Jemima came to get them up.

∞ ∞ ∞

'Now, this is what's going to happen,' Polly said. 'You get dressed and have breakfast. Then Daddy is going to take you for a walk—'

Andrew interrupted. 'I don't like to be taken. I like to do my walks by myself.'

'Well, today, you'll have Daddy. He's never been here before, so you can show him round.'

'He doesn't know anywhere here,' Eliza said.

'Well, I can explore him round. Oh, I do hope I get a dog for Christmas. It will be my dog and nothing to do with you.' He and Bertie had swapped a good many of their stocking presents, and resented the girls' invasion of their room.

Polly, who had arrived with an armful of clothes, was laying them out on Andrew's bed. 'And after your walk it will be presents in the drawing room. Then it will be lunch – Christmas lunch. And after lunch there will be a competition for the best snowman.'

Clary arrived then, wearing Archie's dressing gown as she had forgotten to pack her own. 'You are to wear exactly what I have laid out for you,' Polly warned Andrew, 'or I shall send for Nan.'

This threat proved most effective, and Andrew did as he was told.

∞ ∞ ∞

'I shall skip breakfast,' Louise said, when they woke up.

'Me too.' Juliet was actually ravenous, but she knew this was childish, and she was no longer a child. After a moment, she said, 'I suppose we could both have black coffee. People on diets are always drinking it.'

'Yeah, we could. You wouldn't be an angel and fetch us some?'

'Of course I will.' Juliet slipped on the very old peach-coloured kimono that had belonged to her mother and sped away.

Alone, Louise decided to open the present Joseph had left for her. She had been saving it up for Christmas Day, but she wanted to open it when she was by herself. It was a small box wrapped in gold paper with a little label that said 'L. from J.' The tag had 'Happy Christmas' printed in red with a sprig of holly. He wouldn't have wrapped it himself. Inside the paper there was a dark red leather box, and inside that, gracefully coiled on its velvet, lay an eighteenth-century paste necklace of a delicious watery green. Each piece of glass was backed with gold, and small golden links joined them together. It was extremely beautiful. She lifted it out of its box and put it round her neck. It was a necklace for wearing at parties, and she had to push away her longing for something she could always wear – like a ring. It wasn't. But it was her first

Christmas present from him. He must have touched it. She undid the clasp, and put some stones into her mouth. If he was with her they would kiss.

∞ ∞ ∞

Rachel got up in time to go to the eight o'clock service, and as she trudged down the lane towards the church, she saw Villy ahead of her. In church they knelt side by side and went up for Communion together. Afterwards, Rachel said that she had picked a few hellebores for Sid. They would not last, but that was all there was. At least the Duchy's grave still had a vase of berries next to it. Rachel planted the flowers in the thick snow, and swept away the drifts that had stuck to Sid's gravestone. She shut her eyes and said a prayer, but Villy could not hear it. As she got up – she had been kneeling – Rachel brushed the snow from her skirt and took Villy's arm. It was very good to be with someone without having to speak. As they walked back up the lane together, the snow began again – large graceful flakes that quickly covered their previous tracks.

'The children will love this,' Rachel said.

∞ ∞ ∞

'It's all very well on Christmas cards,' Mrs Tonbridge grumbled. She was frying eight eggs in a huge shallow pan for the dining-room breakfast. The rest of them had had cornflakes or porridge and bread and butter and marmalade. 'But to my mind it's otherwise nothing but a nuisance.'

'It's ever so pretty,' Eileen offered.

'You get that warmed dish out of the oven, Eileen. The snow has nothing to do with you.' She slid the eggs onto the proffered dish and set about separating them with her spatula. She could feel her feet ache already, but she would soon be able to take the weight off them with a nice strong cup of tea, as the turkeys, stuffed, were already in the slow oven. She wondered whether Edith would be wanting breakfast in the kitchen, but Eileen reported that she was presiding over the hall breakfast. Spencer was in his high chair having Farex spooned into him by Nan, an expert's job, since he was fascinated by everyone else at the table. And when he didn't feel up to a spoonful, he would turn his head away at the last moment, plunge his hands into the bowl and slap the tray with his palms, which sent the stuff everywhere. Another time, he would run his sticky, laden fingers through his hair. He was no longer hungry, he did not particularly like Farex and, in any case, if it was there, he wanted to feed himself, like all the others were doing. In the end, after some sharpish demands, Nan mopped him up and gave him a rusk.

∞ ∞ ∞

Roland got up at his usual time, but the others were all dead asleep. They had started a game of poker late at night and had asked him if he wanted to join in, but he had been tired and it wasn't a card game that he knew. He was starting to enjoy the visit and wondered why Mum hadn't brought him here before. The food was terrific, and all the older men had been very nice to him. The only slightly sad thing was that at home he would have had a stocking, but on the other hand it was good to be considered too old for that kind of thing. He dressed in his flannel trousers and the thick navy blue jersey that Mum had knitted for him, then slid down the banisters to the hall for breakfast.

∞ ∞ ∞

'Let's have a spot of Christmas love,' Archie said. So they did, and just managed to finish before Bertie rushed into the room, saying that Andrew had been beastly to him. 'He wanted my torch for exploring, and when I said it was too important for him, he simply grabbed it. He really is horrible. I don't like him.'

'We'll get it back. And you know you've done that sort of thing to Harriet, so now you know what it feels like.' But as she said this, Clary had put her arms round him to give him a hug. 'Happy Christmas, darling.' And immediately he felt much better. Clary said she must go and see to Harriet, and he and Archie must get each other up.

∞ ∞ ∞

Jemima had slept badly; she had got Hugh back to bed where he almost immediately fell asleep, but she'd lain in the dark worrying about him. Had he had a stroke? If so, it must have been very minor, but he might have another – more serious – one. Should she get a doctor? Could one get a doctor on Christmas Day? And Hugh would be furious with her if she did. This fear prevailed: he would be angry because everyone would know, and he loathed being what he called mollycoddled. It would effectively spoil not only his Christmas, but the whole family's too.

So she was immensely relieved when he woke up,

rolled over to kiss her, and was his gentle smiling self, asking how the Monster was doing.

'She hasn't turned up yet. I think you have rather a rival in Georgie.'

'Well, I'm not prepared to consort with a white rat to get her affection.'

At this moment, the door burst open and Laura took a flying leap onto the bed, landing on his chest.

'Oh, Dad! Happy Christmas! I've brought your presents for you both so you can open them now.'

'How was your stocking?' Hugh asked, while she struggled to get the presents out of her dressing-gown pockets.

'I got a book, but otherwise it was lovely. And Rivers got a stocking all to himself so Georgie was pleased.'

'What was your book?' Jemima asked. She wanted to know whether Laura had even looked at it.

'It was called *The Lion, the Witch and the Wardrobe*. Honestly, Mummy, what on earth good is that for me? I don't even want to be one.'

'It might come in handy if you wanted to fly on a broomstick.'

Laura rolled her eyes. 'Now, Dad, sit up and have your present.' She moved and sat cross-legged on the far end of the bed, to watch how pleased he would be.

It was a tiny diary of pink leather. 'It's for you to write all your business things in. It will fit in your pocket and it even has a pencil here for writing things down. The pencil will often need sharpening, but I can lend you my sharpener whenever you want. You do like it, don't you, Dad?' She was beaming with anxious generosity.

'It's just what I wanted. Couldn't be better.' He gave her a hug, but she wriggled away from him to present

Jemima with her limp little package. The handkerchief, washed and ironed.

'I'm afraid there is a bit of blood left on it, as I pricked myself, and it wouldn't all come out when I washed it.'

'Darling, you did all the embroidering by yourself? It's really beautiful.'

'It is, isn't it? I put a J on it, so you'll know it doesn't belong to Dad or Tom or Henry.'

Jemima smoothed the crumpled lace edging with her fingers. 'Oh, no! I shall never do that. Thank you, darling, for such a thoughtful present.'

After a pause, Laura said, 'And what about me?'

'I'm afraid you've got to wait until the present opening before lunch.'

'Oh, Mummy! It's so many hours away! Couldn't you give me just a little clue of what it is?'

'Yes,' said Hugh, promptly. 'It's long and thin and very good for riding on to go out and do wicked things.'

'A broomstick? Oh, no, Dad, it can't be that. I don't want to go out and do wicked things!'

'Of course you don't. Dad's teasing you. Now, let's get dressed, sweetheart, and start the day.'

∞ ∞ ∞

The day – that day – proceeded much as Polly had told her children it would. For the lunch, a sofa table was placed at one end of the dining room for the children and Nan, who kept wishing people many happy returns of the day. The glamour, the excitement, the secret disappointments about unsuccessful presents would follow tradition. Simon had offered to take the children for the walk: he wanted to go back to the wood with its stream and the place where he and Christopher had made their secret camp. Only the few burned bricks remained, and he thought of Christopher in his monastery, wondered what sort of Christmas he was having.

Harriet found a small clump of snowdrops in the wood; there was less snow among the trees. The return to the house was delayed by a snowball fight. Georgie found a dead robin on the way home, which distressed him, and he decided to make a huge Christmas lunch for the birds.

'It's not important,' Andrew said. 'On grown-up expeditions whole people get frozen to death.' Nothing he said was very popular.

'What will you give them for lunch?' Laura enquired.

'Stuff off people's plates and I shall ask Mrs Tonbridge for things. You can help me if you like.'

And Laura, who had just finished crying because a snowball had hit her in the face, cheered up like anything.

∞ ∞ ∞

Eventually, when the drawing room had become a sea of paper almost obliterating the careful clumps of people's booty, the children were sent off to wash their hands before lunch; a really stupid rule, someone said, and most of them agreed.

Jemima asked Villy whether she would carve the turkeys; she was famous for her carving. 'Won't Hugh want to do it?'

'He'll want to, but he's so tired that I'd rather he didn't.' Villy gave her a quick look and said that of course she would.

Harriet gave Rachel the bunch of wilting snowdrops she'd picked in the woods (she had hidden them next to her chest when they were snowballing). 'I thought you might like them for your dead person,' she said, and Rachel, deeply touched, said that she would.

'She always used to carve for Christmas,' Jemima said to Hugh, 'so wouldn't it be nice for her to be asked to do it today?' And Hugh said she was a kind, thoughtful creature and of course.

Rupert and Archie fetched the turkeys – they were too much for Eileen, who followed with dishes of vegetables. Zoë and Jemima dished out Brussels sprouts, mashed potato and gravy onto each plate of turkey and stuffing, and Clary took them to the children's table, where Spencer, who had illicitly consumed more tissue paper than was good for him and been colourfully sick, now sat depressed, but lordly, watching Nan mix an egg into mashed potato for his lunch.

Everyone had dressed up, many of them sporting presents that they had been given, but Louise and Juliet outdid them all: Louise in a low-cut dress of olive-green velvet with her paste necklace, her hair piled up at the back of her head; Juliet in a pale yellow satin frock that she had persuaded Zoë to buy her for Christmas, with strings of *faux* pearls wound four times round her neck.

They were really in evening dress, but had assumed that since lunch was the main celebration, this was the time to dress up. Villy had put on the dress that Louise had helped her find for the occasion: a black velvet affair with a long skirt and a black sequined bolero. She had not had anything new for years, and found it really exciting. With it she wore the garnet necklace that Edward had given her when she had had Roly. After all,

Edward – if he came – would be here tomorrow, with or without Diana. This did not cause her the resentment and misery she had once felt: she told herself that she was merely curious to see the woman who had succeeded in marrying Edward, and made a martyr out of her. But, of course, she had made her own martyrdom . . . She remembered now Miss Milliment saying that martyrs did not make very good company and found herself blushing. She must have been intolerable. Responses, Miss Milliment had suggested, were the thing. It was possible to have power over them, and she realised she was beginning to find that out.

Hugh had given Jemima a canary-coloured twin set, a collar of pearls and a fur hat. 'There,' he had said. 'If you don't like them you will have to sing that A. P. Herbert song, "Take back your mink, take back your pearls, What made you think that I was one of those girls?"'

And Jemima, delighted that he seemed so much better, retorted, 'I wouldn't dream of it. I *am* one of those girls.' And wore everything at lunch.

All Rachel's presents had been designed to keep her warm. A splendid cardigan, two scarves, a sheepskin hat and slippers, mittens and a quilted bed-jacket (far too grand for her, she thought). She wore the cardigan over her best blue woollen dress for lunch and was far too hot in no time.

When everyone was full of Christmas pudding the children were raring to start on the snowmen. Teddy and Simon were leaders of the two teams, and took turns to pick their henchmen. Both pairs of twins were split up, and the last person to be chosen was Andrew. 'I was thinking of not playing,' he said, but nobody took any notice.

The point was, the captains said, they could not just be any old snowmen, they had to be special, have a profession, that sort of thing. People were full of suggestions. A burglar, a pirate, a wicked sultan, a clown, an explorer. 'Who's going to judge us?' Henry asked. It was to be Rupert, Archie and Gerald. 'Nobody from my family!' Laura wailed. 'It isn't strickerly fair!'

'Yes, it is,' Simon said firmly. 'Now, each snowman can have up to three props but no more.'

'Better hurry up, teams. It'll be dark by half past four.'

So everybody worked hard, and the result was one pirate snowman with a black patch over one eye and a red cotton bandana on his head, and an explorer wearing goggles and smoking a pipe. After the judges' deliberation (they all said it was a really difficult decision), the pirate won, rather controversially.

∞ ∞ ∞

Hugh and Rivers spent a peaceful afternoon in their beds.

After tea everyone played with their presents. Archie and Clary had given Harriet a large jigsaw puzzle of the picture *When Did You Last See Your Father?* She loved jigsaws and this was not only huge, the pieces were made of proper wood.

Roland made a wireless for Tom and Henry, who were deeply impressed.

Louise and Juliet spent the afternoon watching Mrs Tonbridge's television: after lunch, she had gone back to her cottage where she could soak her feet in hot water.

Poker was resumed from the previous night and raged until supper.

The grown-ups collapsed with books they had been given, and also listened to the record that Roland had bought his mother: Horowitz playing Rachmaninoff's third piano concerto. 'Marvellous tune, that opening,' Rupert said. 'Nearly as long as the Schubert posthumous sonata.'

The four wives cleared up the drawing room, and Simon brought in more logs before joining the poker gang; Laura and Georgie went to their bedroom to feed Rivers, who was crossly glad to see them. 'You wouldn't have liked it, making snowmen,' Georgie said, and Rivers, after nibbling his ear rather sharply, settled for a game in which he rushed round the room and Georgie was supposed to try and catch him – a game Rivers invariably won and that restored his good temper. Laura looked on, but she was so thrilled by the grown-up watch her parents had given her that she couldn't stop looking at it. 'Ask me what's the time,' she kept saying to Georgie, until he was sick of it and escaped with Rivers.

Word had got about that Uncle Rupert could be very funny. 'We'll make him be it,' Harriet had said.

'What sort of funny?' Eliza and Jane asked.

'Oh, dogs being sick, sea lions being fed – we throw him old socks – and pigeons landing on a branch that isn't strong enough for them, various things like that.'

'Let's make him be it, then.' And they marched to the drawing room.

At first he said it was out of the question, but they were good at pestering and wore him down. He said he would do only two things, and they settled for the dog being sick and the sea lions. Clary and Polly exchanged glances: they had pestered him in their day and still enjoyed the acts.

After that, the mothers decreed bed. 'There's not a lot

of hot water, so you'll have to share baths. Youngest first.' The children all stood, looking mutinous, and as tall as possible.

'Laura, Georgie, Harriet, Bertie and Andrew first.' Zoë and Jemima were dealing with them.

'What about supper?' Andrew asked, when he had run out of other objections.

'You can each have an apple in bed. You've had quite enough to eat today.'

Eventually all the younger set were bathed, had been read a story by their fathers, and the grown-ups could collapse in the drawing room. Edward rang to say that he couldn't manage lunch tomorrow but would love to come for a drink at noon. Rachel, who took the call, looked anxiously at Villy when she returned with this news, but Villy smiled at her calmly. 'Is Diana coming?' she asked, but Rachel said he hadn't told her.

'He seemed in a hurry,' she added.

The rest of the evening passed peacefully. Gerald said he had brought some champagne, which he had thoughtfully buried in the snow, and wouldn't this be a good time to have it? It would. Supper, Rachel said, was going to be bits and pieces, as she felt that Mrs Tonbridge had done enough for one day.

Clary offered to go and help with it and found Mrs T, as she called her, sitting in her housekeeper's room with her feet up, watching television and eating Black Magic chocolates. So when Clary said that they would just have sandwiches in the drawing room and that she didn't have to do any more, she realised how tired she was, and when Miss Clary carried the trays for her, she made herself a turkey sandwich, boiled water for her hotty, put all her presents into a basket then walked over to the cottage and plodded upstairs to the attic. She was going to eat her sandwich in bed and start one of the Barbara Cartlands that Miss Rachel had given her for Christmas. What could be more luxurious than that?

Simon, Henry and Tom came down from the poker room for provisions. 'How many sandwiches each?' Henry asked, and Jemima answered three. 'Do you mean three of those triangles, or three whole rounds?'

Hugh said they could have four triangles and after that they must make do with mince pies, and because it was Hugh, they agreed. When Jemima said they were taking too many sandwiches, Tom replied that they needed enough for five, as Louise and Juliet were joining in the poker game. 'Don't stay up all night,' Jemima said rather hopelessly: she knew that they would stay up just as long as they wanted to.

On their own, unencumbered by the young, people said what a lovely day it had been and how beautifully Rachel had arranged everything. They were clinging to the present, but some of them were finding it increasingly difficult to ward off bleak and anxious thoughts of the future. They were leaving the house that had been their home for so long. A few more days and it would be over. Nothing would be the same again.

∞ ∞ ∞

Polly found it quite a relief when she had to go and put Spencer to bed. She found him with Nan in her bedroom and there was Nan choking back tears. 'I don't know where I am, my lady. Nothing to eat all day and a strange woman in my kitchen. I don't think this is my home at all, you know, because my bed is facing the wrong way and I couldn't do my crochet for the baby.'

Polly made Nan sit on the bed and explained that they would all be going home in a few days. Nan always cried when she forgot how to crochet, which was happening more and more often now.

'When Spencer is settled, I'll get you some Horlicks, and when you're ready for bed we'll do the crochet together. Look, Nan. Isn't he sweet?'

Nan's face had softened and she wiped her face with a Harrington square.

'You had lunch, you know, with all of us in the dining room, and you gave Spencer a little bone to chew and he loved it. You're so good with him, Nan. I don't know what I should do without you.'

A spot of appreciation did the trick, and Polly could see her remembering.

∞ ∞ ∞

In bed at last with Gerald – she had not gone back to the drawing room because it had taken her ages to get the Horlicks and then show Nan how to do her crochet – she said how good the family were being about their misfortune. 'You have a wonderful family,' he replied. 'I really admire them. Particularly your aunt. Hugh was telling me what dire straits she's in.'

'I know. And nobody has enough money to help her.'

'I was wondering if you'd like her to come and live with us.'

'Oh, my darling, how good and kind you are! Oh,

Gerald!' She turned to him and he felt her warm tears on his face.

'I'm pretty dull, though. You get that with people who mean well. It's a real danger.'

She kissed him.

'You see?' he said, when she had finished. 'You've been kissing me for years now, and I've not turned into a prince, just stayed a plain old frog.'

'My own most interesting frog,' she said. 'Mind my breasts – they're a bit sore.'

∞ ∞ ∞

Of course, she'll be hunting tomorrow, and won't have another thought in her head, Teddy realised. His parting from Sabrina had not been happy, and he was almost relieved to be without her for a few days. The poker game had broken up with Roland winning. They had only been playing with matchsticks, but these were to be converted to cash when they finished the final game. Teddy had enjoyed the male camaraderie of it. Perhaps he could get a pilot's licence and then an interesting job, even in Africa. Rather a thrilling idea.

∞ ∞ ∞

'He'll be in bed now, but in the dressing room. He doesn't share a room with her any more. He said that she'd asked him to go to bed with her twice during the last four years, and both times she got pregnant. He'll have given her very expensive presents, though, and I expect she'll have given him the same, and his sister will stay and it will be a nice family Christmas. With-

541

out me.' Louise had returned the necklace to its box and put the box under her pillow. Juliet was already asleep.

∞ ∞ ∞

Simon thought of his love – whooping it up in Glasgow, going to pubs, getting stoned, probably nipping into bed with someone if he fancied them. That hurt: he didn't want to think about *that*. Better leave it that he – he was two years older, after all – had seriously fallen in love with somebody who was only just learning about love. He would be back in exactly seven days. Meanwhile, it felt good to be in the old house – especially if it was for the last time. The other, absolutely marvellous thing was that Aunt Rachel had given him the Duchy's piano as his Christmas present. At first he'd thought that she wanted him to play her something – he had played when the family sang carols: 'The Twelve Days of Christmas', 'I Saw Three Ships', and 'The Holly and the Ivy'. Later, Laura had come up to him and asked what the holly bear was like. 'I just thought I ought to know, in case he came suddenly out of a wood, or something.' He'd explained about there not being a holly bear – to her great relief. 'I only wondered.'

'You said just the right things,' Aunt Rachel had told him later.

And now it became clear that she was actually giving him this lovely old piano: a Blüthner drawing-room grand. It was old, but that meant it had the Schwander action, made in France before the factory had closed during the First World War. The felts needed pricking, but otherwise it was perfect. He tried to express his thanks, but it was so much the most amazing present he had ever had in his life that he became lost for words and ended up hugging her, screwing up his eyes to forestall tears. 'I'm very glad,' she said, 'that it means so much to you. Your grandmother would have been so pleased.'

∞ ∞ ∞

Rachel went to bed in a far more peaceful state of mind than she'd experienced the night before. They were a very close-knit family, and she was so grateful for that. It was true that they had not accepted Zoë at first, but gradually, during those long war years, she had become enfolded and welcomed, and the Duchy had always stood up for her. Perhaps, in time, Diana will become like that, she thought. Rachel was always optimistic about potential goodness.

Tomorrow, early, she would take dear little Harriet's bunch of snowdrops to Sid's grave. The thought that she might be forced to live many miles away in the future pierced her yet again, but she pushed the pain deeper into her heart.

∞ ∞ ∞

Villy lay in the dark thinking how much better it was to be back with the family, and how Roland was enjoying his siblings and cousins. He seemed happy and she had noticed that his wretched acne – the bane of his life – was definitely better. The doctor she had taken him to had said that it would clear up in its own good time. She had no idea what he felt about meeting his father in the company of his new wife, but there was nothing she could do about it now, except to be calm and absolutely unemotional. Which she was determined to be.

∞ ∞ ∞

'Dearest Hugh, I will not have you worrying about Rachel. I would love her to stay with us as long as she'd like.'

'That would be marvellous, but we simply haven't got room, have we?'

'Yes, we have. I've thought it through. Laura goes into your dressing room, the boys go into Laura's room, and Rachel can have the boys' room. You would have to dress and undress in front of me but I'm sure we could get over our embarrassment in time.'

'I'm afraid it might be followed by a frenzy of lust. Darling Jem, it would be a load off my mind. I'm sure we could find her some little job to do – working for a charity, perhaps – so she wouldn't be in your hair all day. Do you mean all this, darling? Have you *really* thought about it?'

'Yes,' she replied patiently. 'I've really thought about it. Rachel has always been so very kind to me and the boys. She's treated us as family from the first time we came here, and now I want to treat her as family back. Let's go to sleep.'

'Not quite yet.'

∞ ∞ ∞

Roland, who had had a smashing day, waited till the others were settled and lights were out before he smeared his face with camomile lotion. Mum had said it would help, and the spots certainly didn't seem quite so noticeable. She had been wonderful. She had given him a cheque before Christmas so that he could buy the tools and equipment needed for an experiment he was doing with his friend. Others had given him book tokens, a squash racquet, and a very superior torch – and other things that he was too sleepy to remember. And tomorrow Dad was coming for a drink with That Woman, as Mum used to call her. He hated his father; he sometimes said this to himself to keep the hatred going. He'd ruined Mum's life, and on the few occasions when they were together, they had nothing to say. The fatuous questions! 'How are you getting on at school?'; 'Looking forward to the holidays?'; 'Made some good friends, have you?' God! It made him sick. It was only for something to say – to get through the once-a-term hotel lunch he was taken out to. On one occasion he had brought Louise, the older sister he hardly knew, and she'd livened things up a bit, but she'd only come the once. Well, he was due to go up to Cambridge: he'd won a scholarship to Trinity next autumn, and he'd planned to get some sort of job before that to help Mum with the fees. The scholarship would only go so far, was not designed to cover everything, and his blasted father had indicated that he was unable to help. I really do hate him, Roland thought before he fell asleep. He's not a proper father at all.

∞ ∞ ∞

'I think, after all, that I will come with you tomorrow. I don't feel it's fair for you to face them all on your own.'

'Splendid.' He spoke as heartily as he could manage.

Far from being an escape, the drink at Home Place was going to be an ordeal. He had sold his guns and his cufflinks and this had provided him with some money to buy Christmas presents. Diana had done the rest. She had a small income of her own, derived from her Army widow's pension, and the rent from a flat she'd inherited from her parents. She had jazzed up Christmas quite a bit on it, buying a large tree, and on Christmas Eve they had had a cocktail party for about twenty neighbours, who had drunk them clean out of vodka and gin. Edward hardly knew any of the guests, and spent most of what seemed a very long time going round and filling everyone's glasses. He used to love parties and meeting people, but somehow he hadn't the heart for it any more. The fact was that he'd got himself into a hell of a mess, and didn't see how to get out of it. He had let it be known at his club that he was in the market for almost anything, but although several friends there had said they would bear him in mind, nothing had so far materialised. Early days, he said to himself, but his membership ran out in March and he would be unable to renew it.

Diana seemed to have put the future firmly out of her mind; she had been more upset when Jamie had said that he was going to spend the holiday with his grandparents and older brothers in Scotland. Comforting her about that had gone down very well – almost too well from his point of view as she had gone all out to seduce him in bed after the cocktail party. In the end, he'd managed to make enough love to satisfy her, and she'd whispered to him that, with their mutual love, nothing else mattered.

So when, on Boxing Day morning, she said she was coming with him, he wasn't surprised but warned her that Home Place was freezing compared to their house, 'So wrap up, darling.' He was terrified that she would choose some revealing attire but, no, she put on a navy blue jersey dress with a polo collar, and a pair of sapphire and diamond earrings he had given her long before their marriage. This, with an old squirrel-fur jacket, completed her outfit.

'How do I look?'

'Perfect, as always.'

∞ ∞ ∞

Hugh met them at the front door, and Diana presented her cheek to be kissed. 'Such a long time since we met. Happy Christmas!'

Hugh touched his brother on the shoulder in greeting, then waited while Diana got out of her jacket.

Most of the family were already assembled in the drawing room, Villy on a sofa with Roland standing behind her. Rachel was sitting in an armchair near the fire, but got up to kiss Edward and then to greet Diana when they came in. Rupert and Teddy were serving drinks; Clary was on her knees helping Harriet transfer her half-done jigsaw to a large tray, 'Then you can do it anywhere, but not here,' she was saying. Simon was stoking the fire, and Gerald had been talking to Rachel. When Polly came in bearing a tray with canapés he introduced her proudly to Diana: 'This is my wife, Polly.'

'Yes,' Harriet said crossly. 'And they've got a boy called Lord Holt. He's not very nice, actually.'

Clary said, 'Shut up, Harriet! That's not at all a kind thing to say.'

'I only mean he's very unpopular with us. There may

be people in the world who would love him, but I doubt it.'

'I love him,' Gerald said.

'That's different. Fathers have to love their sons.'

'Not necessarily.'

Everybody looked at Roland then, who blushed scarlet but continued to stare pointedly at Edward. Villy put a hand on his elbow as though to check him, but he – gently – shook her off.

Edward and Diana, drinks in hand, now advanced towards Villy. Edward introduced them while everybody tried to take no notice. Diana saw a small, rather faded woman, unexpectedly well dressed, whose heavy dark eyebrows contrasted dramatically with her nearly white hair. It was pulled back severely from her face and secured with a large black bow.

'Hello, Villy, my dear. You do look well. This is Diana.'

Villy saw a tall woman wearing a dress that was a size too small for her, and a great deal of make-up. She had large, rather ugly hands encrusted with rings. 'How do you do? I believe we met once before – during the war.'

'Oh, yes! Ages ago. I'd almost forgotten. And is this your son? He looks almost the age of my – our – Jamie.'

This was intended to wound, Villy knew, and the most irritating response was to show the opposite. So she smiled. 'We all had babies in those days,' she said. 'I suppose it was to make up for all the poor young men who were getting killed. Don't you think?'

'Hello, Roland, old boy.' Edward was getting unnerved by Roland's stony stare.

'Before you ask me some fatuous question about school, I'd like to tell you now that it was a beastly place. For the first year a gang of older boys used to bully me,

548

tie me in a bath, turn on the cold tap and leave. And I never knew whether they'd come back before I drowned. One of their little escapades – just for the record,' he ended bitterly.

'How dreadful!' Diana exclaimed. 'I don't think they did that sort of thing at Eton. Jamie went to Eton, like his brothers.'

Archie quickly came to the rescue: 'You need a top-up, Diana, and you, too, Edward. Roland, get your mother a drink.'

Roland took his mother's glass from her trembling hands (the bath story was news to her) and collided with Archie at the drinks table. 'No more of that,' Archie said to him sternly. 'You'll upset your mother. It's only a drink, and they'll be gone before lunch, so show a little more of the white flag. You could try feeling a bit sorry for your father, you know,' he added gently.

'Could I?' The idea seemed incredible.

Gerald had diplomatically enticed Diana to the far side of the room to show her the snowmen and talk about gardens.

Louise and Juliet, who had decided to try the drinks on offer, eyed Diana with mild contempt. 'I met her once before they were wed, at Dad's club. I never for one moment thought he'd marry her.'

'She doesn't know the first thing about make-up,' Juliet said. 'Her face is like a dog biscuit, and look at that awful lipstick!'

'Older women tend to overdo the make-up. It's some-thing to watch out for when you get older,' Louise informed her. But Juliet felt she was unlikely to get as old as that and, anyway, she knew.

Sounds from outside indicated that the children were

getting fretful and hungry; then Nan appeared in the doorway, clearly distressed.

'Oh, your lordship, his lordship's playing up something awful. He's broken some of the twins' toys and they went for him and that palaver upset everyone.'

Polly stopped talking to Clary and went over to comfort her. 'Gerald, I think you'd better deal with Andrew.'

And Gerald, who had found in Diana's remarks the all-too-usual blend of competitive showing off, was grateful for an excuse to go.

He left her triumphant: her garden was not only larger, but contained plants that he had either failed to grow or had never even heard of. She was on her third cocktail by now, and was taking in the shabbiness of the room; it really looked as though nothing had been done to it for years. She glanced about for Edward, and saw him talking to Villy (again!), standing next to two very pretty girls: Louise, whom he kept maddeningly describing as his second favourite woman, and a younger girl of startling beauty, who reminded her of Vivien Leigh.

She worked her way towards them, but her heel got caught in a rent in the carpet, and if Rupert hadn't been close enough to seize her arm, she would have fallen over. Rachel rose from her chair to apologise.

'Don't bother. I'm sure it was my fault.' She was seething with humiliation. As Diana reached them, she heard Villy saying, 'Do you remember that Christmas when Edward put the wrong stockings on Teddy and Lydia's beds? The outcry!'

'Until you rushed in and put it right.' Edward was smiling. 'Always quick off the mark, your mother was.'

'Edward, I'm afraid it's time to go. Susan will be frantic for her lunch.'

'Right you are.' He picked up Louise's hand and kissed it, then Juliet's too. He saw Villy watching him, and smiled affectionately. 'Goodbye, ol' boy,' he said to Roland, who made no response. Diana stopped at the open door of the drawing room, as Hugh and Jemima saw them out. 'It's been so nice to see you all.'

In the car, she exclaimed, 'Phew! Glad that's over! It's a pity Roland was so rude to you. And that disgusting story about his school. Quite out of place, I thought. I suppose he's spoilt.'

'Poor chap, I haven't been much of a father to him.'

'I've never stopped you seeing him.'

Yes, she had, he thought. She had more than once suggested that it might be kinder to leave Roland to his mother, and at the beginning, after he had left Villy and before she'd consented to a divorce, Villy had said that Roland was not to meet Diana, and he, at the time, had been in anything-for-a-quiet-life mode, and had simply gone along with whatever either Villy or Diana wanted . . .

'Edward! Wake up! I'm talking to you! I said, what did you think of Villy?'

'What do you mean what did I think of her?'

'Oh – you know. Did she look much older? Does she still care about you? That sort of thing.'

He thought for a moment, and spoke very deliberately: 'No, she didn't look older – younger, I'd say. She looked better than she's done for years. And, no, I don't think she is still carrying a torch for me.'

'What were you laughing about, you and Villy and the girls?'

'We were reminiscing about earlier Christmases, actually.'

He was thinking of them again now: so many since the twenties, when the house had been spanking new, painted and papered, the Duchy machining curtains from morning till night. Hardly anything had been changed since then. Even the claw marks that Bruce, the Brig's Labrador, had made on the doors were still there. And this was the last of them and, now, the last of the house for him: he would never see Home Place again.

'I suppose Rachel is selling the house. It's far too big for her alone.'

'It is being sold, but since it belongs to the firm, Rachel will get nothing out of it.'

'Oh. Poor her.' Her indifference maddened him – a new and horrible feeling.

'Could we please stop talking about my family? I know you don't like them much, but I do. I'm very much attached to every single one of them.'

'Even Villy? You're still attached to *her*?'

'For God's sake, Diana, will you stop? Of course I have affectionate feelings for Villy. She's had four of my children. I was glad to see her this morning. And apart from being glad, of course I feel guilty about what I've done to her and Roland. So do me the kindness and shut up.'

And Diana was so surprised – shocked – by his outburst that she remained silent for the rest of the drive.

∞ ∞ ∞

Lunch was followed by an extremely cold game of Ogres, where the old outdoor kennel was the prison in which the captured were put to wait for someone to rescue them. The trouble was that the youngest always got captured first and the adults got tired of rescuing them. Jemima, who had been worried about Laura, went out to find her sobbing in the kennel. 'Oh, Mummy, let me out. I hate this game and want to not play it.'

Jemima took her back to the house. She was blue with cold. 'There's even snow in my wellingtons.'

'I'm going to pop you into a hot bath and then you can have tea in your dressing gown. Special treat.'

'I can stay up while all the others are having theirs.' The idea pleased her enormously.

Much later, when the children had had their high tea, and had finally been coaxed to bed, it was discovered that they all wanted Uncle Rupert to continue his story about a bear and a tiger who start by fighting but become friends and decide to steal a small aeroplane and fly to England. Tonight he described how they came down in the gardens of Buckingham Palace where the Queen was very kind to them and offered them tea and sausage rolls – the tiger ate twenty-four – and Mars Bars – the bear ate sixteen but then he felt a bit sick . . .

'No more tonight,' Rupert said firmly. 'And you all go to your beds at once or there won't be any more adventures tomorrow.' So they went.

∞ ∞ ∞

'Although, you know,' Georgie said to Laura, 'the whole thing is most improbable. Bears and tigers wouldn't get on at all, in real life. They would avoid each other.'

'It's not meant to be real life. It's a story. Stories are better than real life. In my opinion.'

'I prefer real life.'

553

There was a coldness in the room, until Laura said, 'I've had an idea. I bet you Rivers would simply love a Mars Bar.'

'Yes! I think he might. Good idea, Laura. Just a small bit, though – we don't want him feeling sick . . .'

∞ ∞ ∞

'All done,' said Rupert, rather smugly. 'I could do with a strong drink.'

Rachel, who had been toying with a dry sherry that she did not really want, straightened herself in her chair. 'Listen, all of you. I want to be practical this evening. This house is full of family furniture. I shall not need very much of it, so I want you all to choose what you would like to have. Please stick a label on it with a name and address so that the carriers can deliver everything correctly. I expect you know that I've given the Duchy's piano to Simon as he's the musical one, and Gerald has kindly said that he can house it. I have sorted out some linen and kitchen things that I shall need, otherwise it's a free-for-all. I'm telling you now because you may need time to make your choices. I should like to keep some of your pictures, Rupert, and the drawing you made of the Duchy playing the piano, Archie. In fact, I've already put labels on those. And, finally, don't any of you thank me, because I don't want to burst into tears. The labels are on the desk.' She took a swig of her sherry – too much – and it made her choke.

It was Hugh who patted her on the back, and Clary who said, 'You are the most thoughtful person in the world.'

Then Juliet said, 'Do I count, Aunt Rachel? And if I do, could I have the beautiful little silver teapot?'

'You do, and you may.'

∞ ∞ ∞

A new poker game was ongoing, and as soon as supper was over, Louise, Teddy, Simon, Roland, Henry and Tom and Juliet went off to the boys' room to resume it.

Until now everybody had refrained from talking about Edward's visit, with the dreaded Diana. But now, because they were not talking about what was going to happen to them any more, they fell upon the gossip. Archie said he thought that Edward had looked awful, grey and as if he'd shrunk.

Zoë said she didn't think Edward loved Diana, but was frightened of her, whereupon Rupert observed, unsurprisingly, that one had to look at the other person's point of view. Clary told Villy that she thought she had been wonderful, so calm and dignified. Villy apologised that Roland had been so hostile, and Hugh said that he rather admired him for it and, anyway, Edward had earned it. Rachel pointed out that he had married Diana, and this had to be accepted. 'Let's face it,' Jemima countered, 'she doesn't like women very much. They seem to bring out the worst in her.'

Whereupon Polly bitchily observed that all that meant was that the worst of her was usually out. Gerald said that he didn't think Diana was actually very happy.

'I bet she's not!' Hugh exclaimed. 'She thought she was marrying a rich man, and there he is, out of a job, and he told me he'd spent everything he'd saved on her.

He's even sold his guns and some cufflinks to buy them Christmas presents.'

'Oh, poor Uncle Edward! No wonder he looked so awful!'

Clary's eyes filled with tears and Archie put his arm round her. 'She cries for England,' he said.

Zoë began to say how stupid Diana had looked, bulging out of that dress . . . but Rupert intervened: 'I think we've all been unpleasant enough for one evening, and I, for one, am longing to be in bed with my vituperative wife.'

∞ ∞ ∞

That was Boxing Day over. Rachel was glad. It had been a long day for her, starting at seven when she had gone up to the churchyard with the snowdrops. She had been appalled at how much she didn't like Diana. And she'd had no idea that Edward was so poor. If only he'd told me when he came for a drink, I could have given him something. But she knew she couldn't have given him much. There were the servants to think of. As she was unable to give them large retiring presents, she must find them somewhere to live. And there was Mrs Tonbridge's operation. I shall be gone in a few weeks now, Rachel admitted to herself. I shan't be able to look after Sid's grave. That seemed like yet another parting from her. But that is what I have to do, somehow. And find some work that will pay me money. I'm glad I told everyone to choose things. I've got that bit over at least.

It was a small congratulation, but it would have to do.

∞ ∞ ∞

The next two days – the last two days – were occupied by the family making their choices. The linen, for instance: the wives all wanted some. A great deal of it was threadbare, very fine linen, marked in Indian ink that registered its date of birth, so to speak. In the end, it was divided between Zoë and Clary, as Jemima said she didn't really need it. Polly, after consultation with Gerald, asked if they might have the hall table, four of the single beds and two chests of drawers. None of the others wanted these things. Teddy said he would like the Brig's desk. He had nowhere to put it yet, but he suddenly very much wanted something of his grandfather's. Georgie wanted the cabinet that contained the Brig's collection of beetles. (This had been Rupert's suggestion, and had deflected Georgie from wanting to unscrew the mangers in the horseboxes in case he ever got a horse.) Louise chose a very pretty set of Wedgwood coffee cups while Rachel urged Simon to take all the sheet music to go with the piano. Clary asked Mrs Tonbridge's advice on kitchen equipment for the new flat at Mortlake: she had a small *batterie de cuisine* at home, but most of it was in a poor state.

Hugh, Rupert and Archie were all invited to share the silver – when Archie protested that he was not really family, Rupert and Hugh said he certainly was. Laura, unsupervised, rushed to the nursery with a sticky label, which she attached to the battered old rocking-horse. 'I shall paint his face better and the spots on his back and ride him to do wicked deeds at night.' Polly's twins asked for the dressing-up box, which was stuffed with feather boas and beaded dresses, while Tom and Henry wanted all the tennis and squash racquets. Bertie mysteriously found a top hat in a cupboard that he said he'd need in case he was a magician when grown-up.

'What can I have?' Andrew wailed. 'This house is full of things I simply don't want.'

Rachel came to the rescue with *The Times Atlas* and a pair of binoculars. 'Essential for an explorer,' she said.

Bertie was easy. The only thing he longed for, apart from the top hat, was a very large stuffed pike in a glass case from the Brig's study.

By the end of the second day everyone had chosen, excepting Villy, Roland and Harriet.

Rachel suggested that Villy have the set of garden tools that had been the Duchy's. 'I should love to think of you using them.' Harriet finally admitted to wanting a patchwork quilt sewn in cotton of many different blues, some rather faded now from the sun. 'Why didn't you say so, darling?'

'I thought it might be too precious for me. That you would want to keep it.'

'No, I'd love you to have it. Here is a label for you. Put your name and address there. I'm glad you like it. This quilt was made by your great-grandmother during the war.'

'Oh! So it's very, very old!' This seemed to add to its charms, so Rachel agreed on its advanced antiquity.

And so the only person left who had chosen nothing was Roland.

'Surely there's something you would like,' Villy said. Roland said there was, but it would be inconvenient for Aunt Rachel if he took it. 'It's that marvellous old telephone in the study. I've never come across one like that before, only seen them in films.'

Rachel, on being asked, said that she certainly wouldn't want to keep it, but that she might need it until she left.

'Oh, good! And do you want the Remington type-writer, by any chance?' Rachel, who could only type with one finger, didn't. 'And there's a very early camera I'm rather keen on. Or is that too much?'

'No, Roland, it's helpful, thank you. Put your labels on everything.'

∞ ∞ ∞

When word got round that Roland was getting several things, some of the others wanted more too. 'We can't just leave all those poor old bears and monkeys and golliwogs to be got rid of, Mummy. I could look after them,' Harriet offered coaxingly.

'It seems a bit silly to leave all the board games, Mum,' Polly's twins said. 'Aunt Rachel is really too old to want to play them.'

'You've got lots of games at home.'

'Not all of these. And then supposing four people want to play a game that's meant for two? They'd have to wait for hours.'

Georgie said, 'I wonder if I could have those stuffed pheasants as well. The Lady Amhurst is quite rare and the Golden Pheasant is too. I could have them in the museum part of my zoo, with the beetles.'

Parents apologised profusely to Rachel for this surge of acquisitiveness, but Rachel said she found it priceless. In fact, she thought of more things they might like.

The Choosing Game, as the children got to call it, proved a blessing. It kept everybody active with things to do. 'Oh dear!' the children kept saying. 'The last two days!' But Georgie was longing to get home because his best Christmas present would already be there, while

Bertie and Harriet were excited by their impending move, and Laura was pretty sure that the present held back for her in London would be either a bicycle or a cat, both of which she really needed.

No, it was the older ones who were stricken: too reliant on an effortful reminiscence, effortful because each memory too easily provoked grief and anxiety.

Rachel told stories of the Brig, which were safe to laugh at: 'Do you remember the way in which he would ask you if you had heard the story about the elephant he was given in India, and you said – rather bravely – that you had, and he would simply say, never mind, he would tell you again?'

'And when rabbit's fur came out of the well tap, he said we must not bother our pretty little heads about that.' (This was Villy.)

'And the terrifying way he would drive on the right-hand side of the road, and when the police stopped him, he said he had always ridden on that side and was too old to change now.'

There was a respectful silence after stories about the Brig seemed to have run out, and everyone reverted to private thoughts. Hugh was remembering Sybil – her giving birth to Simon; her terrible cancer, and how good Edward had been to him after her death. He had thought he would never get over it, but his darling Jemima had given him a whole new life. Villy thought of the good times she had had in this house, the days when Edward had seemed happy and devoted . . .

All over now. She had been shocked at the sight of him on Boxing Day. In some way, Diana's brash uneasiness had confirmed the good realities of her own marriage to Edward. It had been happy; she knew now that sex had been the only problem. It had eventually occurred to her that pretending to like it was not good enough. It was a bit like what Miss Milliment had said about martyrs being dull to love; her distaste for sex must have communicated itself to Edward, who probably thought that 'nice' women were generally like her so went elsewhere for satisfaction. He had clearly married Diana for sex: she looked the sort of woman who might actually like that kind of thing. Villy wished – not for the first time – that Miss Milliment had not died, particularly had not died mistrusting her . . .

Clary looked round her. Anxiety, unhappiness, was like a fog in the room, slowly enveloping everybody. 'I want to say something. I think it would be far better if we all expressed what we're feeling. I know, Aunt Rachel, that you said not to talk about it during Christmas, but Christmas is over, and this is our last night here, and we're all fearfully sad about that. But most of us are even more worried about what's going to happen to us next. I think we ought to talk about that. And as I've introduced the subject, I think I'd better begin.'

In the short silence that followed, a log fell from the grate onto the hearth, and Rupert got up to retrieve it. Nobody took the slightest heed of this: everyone's attention was on Clary.

'This house,' she began bravely. 'I shall always love and remember it because this was my first home. And it was where I really got to know Polly. And you, Zoë, who I was determined to dislike because of my mother's death and you marrying Dad. And you, darling Archie, most of all. All through the awful time when Dad was lost and I remained the only person who believed he was alive

561

and would come back, you were here. You became my family, too. But the house stayed the same through that time. If I shut my eyes, I could still tell you the detail of any room, and outside, the orchard and the fields and the wood with the stream running through it. I could walk blindfold and still tell you where we were. What I'm trying to say is that this is the same for all of us. This house is inside us and we shall never forget it. I think we're lucky to have somewhere so dear to remember in our hearts.'

A murmur of approval spread throughout the room. But that had been the easy part and Clary took a deep breath and began again: 'The other thing we're not talking about is what is going to happen to us when Cazalets' has gone. I know you may think it's all very well for Archie and Dad and Zoë and me, because we've decided to live together so Dad and Archie can start some art classes together. Archie and I are going to let our flat rather than sell it so that if the Mortlake idea doesn't work we've at least got somewhere to live. Also, I hope I'll be earning some money from writing. So, in a way, I feel we're the luckiest people here. Gerald and Polly have their own problems, but luckily they're not affected by Cazalets' demise. But Uncle Hugh, you and Aunt Rachel are, and I suppose poor Uncle Edward too, but he's not here.' She looked expectantly at Hugh, who cleared his throat.

'I don't think any of you should worry about me. I have some money saved that should tide me over until I get some sort of job. Jemima has a small inheritance from her parents that should see the twins through university, and she owns our house. So you needn't worry about me,' he repeated, almost irritably this time.

All eyes then turned upon Rachel. She shrank from their gaze, but could not escape it. She had been sitting with her hands clenched round a small white handkerchief. She was incapable of lying, of dissembling at all, but she dreaded the prospect of exposing her real terror at the future now facing her.

'As you all know, I'm selling Sid's house so I shall have some money, but I'm told it will not be enough to live on. So I shall have to try and get a job, although goodness knows who would ever want to employ me. But I shall find something, I'm sure.' Rachel looked up at her family before continuing: 'I've had four incredibly kind invitations from you, Hugh, from you, Rupert and Zoë, from you, Villy, and from Gerald and Polly to come and stay.' Her voice cracked at this point, her knuckles turning white as she clenched the handkerchief. 'I'm just so grateful to all of you, but I know how busy your lives are. An elderly spinster aunt is hardly a brilliant addition to any household.' She tried to smile – quite unsuccessfully, as her eyes were now full of tears – as she muttered, barely audible now, 'I really am not needed any more.'

Hugh went to her, then knelt by her chair and put his arms round her. 'You are loved and needed by all of us,' he said. 'You're talking a lot of sad nonsense. Of course it's worse for you, you've lived in this house for forty years—'

'Forty-one.'

'Forty-one, then. It's been your home all this time. Miserable to leave it.'

'I would need you awfully, Aunt Rach,' Polly said. 'With four children and all the wedding stuff we're struggling with, not to mention our rather large house, I could keep you occupied from morning till night.'

'She'd wear you out if you weren't careful,' Gerald added jokingly.

The others all made practical cases for her staying with them, too, excepting Villy, who wanted Rachel desperately to come and fill her silent little house with her company. So she simply said, 'You know I'd love you to come – any time,' and left it at that.

All this somehow made it all right for Rachel to cry now, which she did until Hugh gave her his handkerchief. 'That silly little thing you have in your hands wouldn't even mop up the tears of a mouse.'

And then Gerald suggested that he open a valedictory bottle of champagne – which he did to good effect – and even Rachel drank her small share, relieved that the evening was over at last.

∞ ∞ ∞

'Jolly good, my little playwright, the way you made them talk,' Archie said, when they were in their bedroom.

Down the passageway upstairs, Hugh discovered that he could not reach his shoelaces. Rather, he could reach them but he couldn't seem to grasp them – even in normal circumstances no easy matter if you had only one hand. It made him feel dizzy trying, and in the end he called Jemima. 'I don't know what's the matter, but I don't seem able to get my shoes off.'

Jemima took one look at him, and her heart sank. He looked exactly as he had in the bathroom. 'You're just tired, darling,' she said. 'I'm going to undress you – I love doing it.' She got him out of his clothes and into his pyjama top without his having to get up from the stool he had been sitting on. She eased on the bottoms, then said, 'Hold on to me, darling, while I pull them up. Then I'm going to lead you to bed.'

He sank upon his pillows with a sigh of contentment and held out his arms for her. She kissed his forehead and said, 'Now you're going straight to sleep.'

He did, almost at once, but for a long time Jemima lay awake full of fears for him. She must call the doctor and get him to London without fail as soon as possible.

∞ ∞ ∞

'It really is hard for Rach,' Rupert said, as he ripped off his clothes, leaving them in a trail from the window to the bed. 'Do be quick, darling, I want us to have one last comforting roll in the hay before we leave.'

∞ ∞ ∞

Polly said, 'It would be pretty difficult. I think we'd have to get her home first so she could see all the things she might do there. We're going to have to pay for more help as Nan gets worse anyway. She won't be able to look after Spencer or lend a hand with the cooking for much longer.'

'It crossed my mind that perhaps the Tonbridges would come.'

'Gosh! That's an idea. But Mrs T may be wanting to retire. Her feet are awful these days. Rachel says she's arranged an operation for her bunions.'

'Well, of course it would be after her convalescence. But she's devoted to Rachel, and if she was with us, I think there's a fair chance that Rachel would come, too.'

'What about Tonbridge?'

'He can be in charge of all the cars for the weddings. He could even drive that ghastly white Daimler we have to have.'

'Gerald, I think you are very, very clever.'

∞ ∞ ∞

Tomorrow, Rachel thought, I'll move back into my own room. She was so exhausted with emotion that she slept the moment she put out the light.

∞ ∞ ∞

Mrs Tonbridge padded across the courtyard – the thaw had made it very slushy – and when she reached the cottage she announced to Tonbridge (who was ominously reading a newspaper) that she was off to bed. She knew if she stayed down for a cup of tea, he would read her bits from the paper about the state of the world and the politicians who seemed to make a mess of everything. Half of what he read she simply didn't understand and the rest bored her. If she retired, as Miss Rachel seemed to think she would want to do, she'd have to endure those readings morning, noon and night . . .

She had made a vast kedgeree for their farewell breakfast. It would only need to be heated. There was the old boy coming upstairs to bed. She rolled over onto her side and shut her eyes.

∞ ∞ ∞

The plan was for everyone to leave after breakfast, but the packing took a long time. Teddy, Louise and Simon were the first off as they were the least encumbered. Even so, it had taken time finding the others to say goodbye. Polly was in the girls' room supervising the packing of everyone's presents into one suitcase, a process that nobody liked. The twins wanted to include all the board games, and Andrew complained that this left no room for him. Polly said that they couldn't pack the board games, only their Christmas presents. Andrew, triumphant and still in a rage with the foul twins, tipped up the suitcase and then kicked it, whereupon, draughts, Peggity pegs, Monopoly cards and dice were spilled all over the floor. Eliza burst into tears. 'Say goodbye to everyone, and then pick everything up. I'm very cross with you, Andrew.' Polly felt weary already. She had packed all Spencer's things, then found that Nan had unpacked them again but could not remember where she had put them. Gerald had dealt with that.

Jemima had asked Rachel to engage Hugh in conversation about how the house was to be finally cleared. 'He's awfully tired, and I don't want him struggling with suitcases.' Laura was at her worst. She cried because she couldn't take the rocking-horse back with her; she cried because she wanted to live with Georgie. And finally she refused to wear the clothes that her mother had put out for her. 'If you try to make me wear that silly red skirt and stupid pretending Scotch jersey, my arms and legs will go all heavy and slippery, like seaweed,' she'd sobbed. And Jemima was so desperate to get Hugh to London that she weakly allowed Laura to choose her own wardrobe for the day, which included a gold-paper crown she had got from a cracker.

They were the next to go. Laura hugged everybody – the Tonbridges, Eileen, Aunt Rachel and Georgie. She even tried to hug Rivers, but he didn't like the idea. 'I'm driving,' Jemima said firmly to Hugh. 'It will stop me bursting into tears.'

Georgie shook hands politely with everyone. He had witnessed Laura's display with distaste, although he had admitted to Zoë that she was better than most girls.

Rupert gave Rachel a long hug. 'It's been so lovely. You can't imagine the pleasure and happiness you've given us all. Don't forget that we all want you, darling Rach.' Zoë also hugged her – not something she usually did – and Rachel stood at the white gate by the drive and waved them goodbye.

It was Villy and Roland next.

'I've had a super time. Best Christmas of all. Thank you so much for having me.' Rachel kissed him and his face went bright red, but she noticed that his acne was better.

She and Villy embraced warmly, and Villy said how welcome she would always be at Clifton Hill.

The house was emptying; fewer footsteps up and down the stairs, less opening and banging shut of the front door. Archie was loading their car, and Clary kept bringing extra things that hadn't been packed. Bertie said, 'I hope you'll come and stay with us one day. We're moving to an enormous house so there's sure to be room.'

Harriet clung to her. 'Do stay here, Aunt Rachel, because this is the best place.' They took a long time to go.

Polly and Gerald, meanwhile, had finished putting luggage in their Daimler; Polly had to lead Nan to the car and put Spencer in her arms. He fell at once into a stertorous sleep. The twins were herded in, and finally

Andrew, who refused to kiss Rachel because he said he hadn't had a nice enough time. 'The food was very good, though,' he added grudgingly.

'Please come and stay with us,' Gerald said. 'We should so much love to have you.'

And Rachel heard herself saying that she would like that very much. A final hug from Polly, and they were gone. She watched their car slowly disappear down the drive, and out of sight. Then she shut the small white gate, walked past the two melting snowmen, and back into the silent house. Eileen had lit the fire in the morning room, and soon appeared bringing her a cup of Bovril. It was all done: the last Christmas was over. The first Christmas without Sid, she thought, and found that she was able to be calmly sad about it; there was less of a weight on her heart. Harriet had whispered to her that she had found a very small primrose out in the hedge behind the monkey puzzle tree. She hadn't picked it yet, but she thought it might go with the snowdrops. She would pick it after lunch and take it up to Sid. She loved all the children, but Harriet and Laura had touched her most, and, of course, she adored Spencer as she had adored all of them when they were babies. Andrew made her laugh in much the same way that Neville had used to do. And she felt very warmed by all the adults' love for her. If only, she thought, I could be really needed again.

∞ ∞ ∞

The rest of the day slowly passed. She had lunch on a tray – fricassee of turkey and a mince pie – then put on several of the warm things she had been given for

569

Christmas, and her galoshes, and found the single brave primrose. It was still thawing outside – little streams of water were running down the sides of the lane – the sky was a clear blue, and the trees were dripping in the churchyard. Again, she scraped the snow from Sid's grave; the snowdrops had remained intact, and she put the primrose beside them. Usually she would say a short prayer for Sid; this time she talked to her.

'I am going to do what you said, my darling. I am going somehow to make a life without you, as you told me I should. I shall never, never forget you. You will always be my only love. You were so brave about dying, and it's time for me to have a little courage about living. I'm going to start by staying with Polly. I shall write to her tonight.'

She caressed the stone that had Sid's name on it, knowing that this was another farewell.

But I shall always have her in my heart, she thought, on the walk home. My dearest Sid.

When she was in the middle of her letter to Polly, the telephone rang.

∞ ∞ ∞

'Oh, Rachel! Hugh's had a heart attack. He's in hospital and I so want to be with him, but the boys have gone to stay with friends and there's Laura. I wondered whether you could possibly—'

'Of course. I'll take the first train tomorrow morning. Or, better still, get Tonbridge to drive me up to town. Is there anything you want me to bring?'

And Jemima said no, only to bring herself. She

sounded as though she was crying. 'He's at the heart hospital, and they're being very good. Oh, Rachel, thank you so much. It will make all the difference having you. Laura loves you, and I didn't want to send her away – she's distressed enough anyway because she was there when it happened. I must ring off now because the hospital might want to contact me. But thank you again, Rachel. I can't think of anyone better to help. We're in such safe hands.' And she rang off.

All the while Rachel was telling the servants that Mr Hugh had had a heart attack and she needed to go to London early next morning – would Tonbridge drive her, and would Eileen help her pack a case this evening? – she felt completely in command. She had obtained leave for the Tonbridges to stay in their cottage until the end of the month, and suggested that they took Eileen in, to help with cleaning the house. After that, and after Mrs Tonbridge had had her operation, she had found two possible cottages to rent in Battle. She had the three months' rent ready on whichever they might choose. But, of course, she would be in touch with them as soon as she found out the situation with Mr Hugh.

Mrs Tonbridge was speechless with emotion. Rachel had never seen her near tears before, and Eileen asked whether this meant that Miss Rachel would not be coming back to the house. For the first time she realised that she probably wouldn't. However, she said nothing, just asked for a plain omelette for her supper. Then she would pack and have an early night; she wanted to leave as soon after eight as possible.

Of course it will be my last night here, she thought. Better to have it like this, without my moaning and grieving and making the worst of it. I have Hugh to worry about now, and Jemima – and poor little Laura come to that.

All the same, after her supper, and packing with Eileen, and saying goodnight to her, she got into her dressing gown and walked slowly through all the rooms upstairs. There was the Brig's dressing room, where he had slept because his snoring was of a volume that even the loyal Duchy could not endure. The room where Sybil had had Wills and lost his twin, where Sybil had died, her own room where Clary, so lonely, had come to sleep on her bedroom floor. Then she summoned the courage to enter the Duchy's room where she had peacefully gone, and the room where her darling Sid had spent her last weeks.

She had always been the recipient of confidences – even this Christmas there had been one that shocked and disturbed her. She had found Louise weeping on the attic stairs. 'Oh, Aunt Rach, I don't know how to bear it, but I know now that I must.' It turned out that she had been having an affair with a married man who, she had now realised, would never leave his wife.

So she must leave him – get over it, somehow. Her misery was so intense that Rachel had stopped feeling shocked and simply gone to comfort her. Louise was doing the right thing, she said; the unhappiness would eventually go away, and she would find someone more worthy to love her.

∞ ∞ ∞

Sid's room was still full of her things. Rachel took the little woolly hat she used to wear when her hair was

572

falling out, and the long silk scarf that had been her last present. Tomorrow she would tell Eileen to clear everything else and give it to a charity. From the nursery she took a box of dominoes, and *The Brown Fairy Book*, her favourite when she had been a child; she had coloured all the black and white Henry Ford illustrations; all the princesses had long golden hair and the dragons were bright green. She would be able to read it to Laura now, and also teach her to play dominoes.

Then she went to bed, in her own room, which Villy had left immaculate. She knew she was tired, as her back was hurting, but she felt infinitely warm from all the love she'd received. And now – better still – she was going to be needed.